THE REAL DEAL

ALSO BY JOHNNY WORTHEN

THE REAL DEAL

A TONY FLANER MYSTERY
BOOK 6

JOHNNY WORTHEN

ROUGH
EDGES
PRESS

The Real Deal
Paperback Edition
Copyright © 2023 Johnny Worthen

Rough Edges Press
An Imprint of Wolfpack Publishing
9850 S. Maryland Parkway, Suite A-5 #323
Las Vegas, Nevada 89183

roughedgespress.com

Paperback ISBN 978-1-68549-329-5
eBook ISBN 978-1-68549-328-8
LCCN: 2023946618

For my father

THE REAL DEAL

1

WITH THIS INTAKE OF BREATH, I am breathing in.

With this...what? Outtake of breath? Okay. Outtake. With this outtake of—

Shit. Already breathing in again.

With this intake of breath—yeah. In.

With this outtake of breath, I breathe out.

Intake, like on a jet engine. A very quiet, nose-shaped jet engine intake. Like if Mardi Gras floats could fly at supersonic speeds, but the sound is very slow and deliberate. No. Not at all like a jet engine. A terrible analogy. Maybe more like a burping bottle of ranch dressing, but after the burp—the wheeze of air rushing back in as you assess the damage done to your shoes.

Oops. Out. Okay. Now in again.

In breath. Breathing in.

Outtake. There it goes. Outtake. Yeah, okay. But where does it go? Does it mix with my intake, or drop like unused footage to the floor of the editing booth to be swept off or stashed away hoping for a DVD extra blooper reel?

Now I'd stopped breathing. I was holding my breath imagining some middle-aged green-clad woman in cat-eye glasses staring into an editing viewfinder and forgot to breathe. I didn't know that was something one could forget. This is what thinking about things gets you.

I gasped.

Maybe her name was Gertrude.

Forgot again. Man, that was a deep rabbit hole.

I dared open my eyes.

The man sitting at the front also had his eyes open. He was staring at me. Allie to my right also stole a glance or rather, a glare. I guess my gasp was loud. Louder than the subtle breaths of other students to "Zen Calm for Beginners" all around me.

I looked at Dara Sutter, whose face was contorted in aggressive concentration like she was holding back an explosive bowel movement or biting her tongue in the face of an armed heckler. Standard Flox, another one of my comic friends, shifted in the chair he'd been smart enough to take. I'd taken a cushion on the floor. I watched him run his tongue under his lip and across his teeth, imagining spinach-flavored plaque. Perry Whitehouse, who'd tried this stuff before and was clinically—if not epically—insane at times, was the very picture of calm and stillness, sitting cross-legged next to Garrett and Critter. Garrett looked around the room bored, meeting my eyes for a moment before slamming them shut. Critter kept his eyes locked on me and stared. He had plastic eyes, so it was a cheat. He didn't need to blink. He was a hand puppet and so immune to the peer pressure of spiritual awareness. He looked at me coldly, judging me not only for my lack of concentration but also for dragging him here with the others. I blame Allie for that, but she blames me. So…yeah. It was probably my fault.

I closed my eyes and shifted on my cushion. Before we'd started, we'd mentally scanned our bodies and noticed it. That's the big word. Notice. And breathe. Notice and breathe. Breathe and notice. During the scan, we were supposed to feel all our muscles and such—our bones, nerve endings, endocrine cells—and come to love the feeling of our tushes on a two-inch fart-soaked pillow we'd be suffering on for the duration of the morning. If I forgot about the used status of the pad, I could accept it as a nice soft cushion, welcoming and Zen-like. Contentment. I would perceive it as a throne from which I would find enlightenment before lunch, but after what…ninety minutes?—Shit. Only fifteen. After fifteen tedious minutes, it had devolved into something less grand, and my hopes of hanging out with the saints no longer seemed like a good idea. Not if I had to sit here every week.

My breathing was all over the place. I returned to my third eye, the place on my forehead where bullets go, above the brow—I think that's where it is. From that third eye—or acne scar or freckle—I perched in calm and peace and melanin, and I noticed I was noticing things. Was that success? Breathing was good, but noticing it was good too? I comprehended I was breathing badly—erratically, self-consciously, like I'd just learned how, like I'd been taught by an asthmatic mud-skipper with a three-pack-a-day habit, a COVID-cough and a MAGA tattoo.

I noticed Allie's elbow in my rib and noticed too that I'd been laughing at the image of a wheezing tattooed fish frog.

Outtake. That's stupid. Out go. That's good. Intake and outgo. I'd need to tell everyone about this insight. I've broken through.

Another laugh. Another elbow. A round of "Sssssshhhhhes."

That wasn't fair. Yes, we were supposed to be engaged in silent meditation. But think about it. Technically speaking, the laugh happened in the past and if everyone was actually doing the meditation right, wouldn't they all be in the now now? It showed their utter lack of spiritual awareness and non-commitment to the exercise. Jerks. They should thank me for showing them the error of their ways. I am the sandpaper that scuffs their psyches into perfection.

Ouch. Allie had honed her pointy elbows. Maybe with psychic sandpaper.

In breath. News flash: I'm breathing in.

Out. My breath is going out. The outgo. Must remember to tell someone that. This earth-shaking discernment might even make the instructor forgive me for all my earlier cracks about lotus eaters and loving big Bodhi, I cannot lie. They were good jokes. A couple people had even laughed. One really loud and long. That was me. I was making a statement; I'm funny and if Allie thinks she can change me so easily—by dragging me to a secular Buddhist meditation class, she has another thing coming. And what the hell is a secular Buddhist? Is that like a vegetarian carnivore? A chaste whore? A gainfully employed fiction writer?

The instructor, I saw, was struggling to keep a calm face. His eyes weren't shut but squinting at me. He was a thin middle-aged fellow with curly gray hair—not thinning, I noticed, and he had a bushy comb mustache that would attract walruses and *Myth-Busters* groupies. He was a nice man, but he was no guru on a hill. He was not the real deal.

In breath. Out breath.

I closed my eyes. He probably did the same. Can't confirm or deny.

In a smooth, low baritone voice, rising from the silence like a breeze, past a whisper, and into our hearing, the instructor said, "If a thought enters your mind—"

"Share it with the rest of us?" I offered.

I wondered if all Buddhists had such mean stares.

"No. Mr. Flaner."

"Call me Tony."

"Please don't talk. We're meditating."

"You were talking."

"I'm leading the session."

"I'm backup."

"Shut up, Tony." Allie's voice had an edge to it that promised to deliver the fabled one-hand slap if I didn't play along.

Garrett watched nervously. Critter grinned. He always did like a dust-up. Dara stared darts, Standard worked his bottom row chasing a sesame seed between his teeth, and Perry was still as stone.

Later we'd have tea. I closed my eyes and wondered what kind of tea it will be. Jasmine? Peppermint? Earl Gray? Make it so.

"If a thought enters your mind, smile at it, and then let it go, like dropping a leaf into a clear stream and having it flow away. Then return to your breathing."

I wondered how long a clear steam would stay clear with everyone dumping their mulch in it.

I recognized a thought. Another one. The first one. Then the second one, the one that sussed out the first. The third followed suit, noticing the second, which was another. Oh, and again. I was in a feedback loop, chucking lawn debris into the stream of consciousness as fast as my mental rake could muster.

"Breathe."

It was Allie.

I gasped.

I got shushed.

This was for me. Allie had said so. My friends had all agreed. They said I have a problem with being chill, which really pissed me off. I struggle with impostor syndrome and other ailments, they said, like temper issues and impulse control.

"The hell I do!"

I got shushed.

"When a thought comes into our minds," the instructor said with a definite point, his gaze firmly fixed on me—I peeked—"we acknowledge it and let it go. We do not act on it."

"But—"

"We do not speak it aloud."

"Oh."

"We let it pass away, and we return to our breathing. Focus on the breathing. Only the breathing."

I could feel Allie's frustration. She really liked meditation. Really liked all this interior searching stuff. I do too, I guess, but most of my searching is external. I find out things about myself by doing things. Experiments. Like how would I feel if I chased a package or Oreos with a pitcher of martinis? Unlike this touchy feeling stuff, I have a concrete answer to that. I'd feel terrible. I'd feel like throwing up. I'd know that the bathroom was a step farther down the hall than I could manage. I'd have learned a valuable life lesson.

"Let the thought go and empty your mind."

What a complete waste of bandwidth. My mind could multitask. I can drive and listen to music, talk on the phone while texting another friend, and still, almost, see the stop sign. Lots of power in my brain. Shutting it down when my senses were active, i.e., when I wasn't asleep—seemed like a wasted opportunity. Think of the all the thinks I could think if...Seuss? Green eggs. The Lorax. Timber companies. Rainforest. Poison dart frogs. Zombies. Brains.

"Let it go."

Look at Elsa up in the front.

Right. Back on track. Where was I? Bandwidth.

I realized the bandwidth thing was a thought that had led to other thoughts, and let it join the choked stream of discarded leaves of my mountain mind. I considered how the water overflowed the banks for the clog, drowning moles along the shoreline who'd later be eaten by aquatic bugs with lisps. Ah, the circle of life. Not sure where I got the lisps.

Ten more minutes to go.

Arghhh. That at least was internal.

"Shhhh."

Maybe not.

Self-improvement is my middle name when it's not self-destruction, self-critic, self-sabotage or self-denial. The last is very rare. I try not to deny myself anything, which shows how far down the list the self-improvement moniker is. Allie thinks I can improve my self-improvement. I fell into a particularly dark rut during a recent pandemic and political implosion whose aftershocks continue to rattle my coccyx to this day. Love that word. Coccyx. Sounds like a sci-fi porn franchise with tentacles and beady eyes.

Finding peace, I'm told, is about finding it in yourself not outside yourself. So if some dick is being a dick, you should rise above it and not dick-punch said dick, no matter how cathartic it might be. To do so, is wrong, so said the officer.

That was my temper. He was a heckler and I wasn't even on stage. He was going after Dara, who can handle any heckler better than I can without resorting to dick-punching. But she was rattled. After Chris Rock's Oscar attack, and Chapelle's Hollywood Bowl stabber, comics were a little wary. She stuttered on stage, stunned by his Christian fascist's venomous, ignorant, sexist, racist, cruel, crude dickhead rant about how she could better apply her mouth. Why the hell did he come to a comedy club in the first place? Some people. Comics have learned to tolerate stuff like that. It was nothing new, but this was loud and threatening and surprising. And everyone is a little raw. And I was in a weird place so I took offense. While Dara readied a barrage of ego-slaying retorts, I mashed the moron's shriveled sack with righteous knuckles in a smooth flowing arc—like I was pitching a softball, low and outside. Steeerike! I might not have got him square in the nuts, but I definitely got his attention.

Hurts just thinking about it.

In the end I got a stern warning. The guy had a few warrants out for his arrest all related to an ugly divorce in Colorado Springs. Beyond that, despite punching the dick's dick in front of a bar full of patrons, no one saw it. Maybe they were distracted by the loud cheering that erupted after I did it. I heard several talk to the cops about wanting to press hate crime charges against the evacuated Nazi. Barry, the bar owner, doubled security and banned Mr. Mashed Manhood from his premises for ninety-nine years. He put it in writing, stapled it by the phone. This was all at The Comedy Cellar downtown Salt Lake City, Utah.

Right after Dara's abbreviated set, Garrett and Critter took the stage only to draw an attack from a young Black woman screaming "cultural appropriation" from the third row like it was a Texan battle cry. "Check your White privilege," she ranted. The appropriation concerned his act which she dubiously claimed was a rip off a Black plantation slave's fireside story. I never knew plantation slaves had a history of ventriloquist acts, but I'm not on social media a lot. The privilege was of course because Garrett is Caucasian. Interesting how she skipped over Critter's mixed ancestry. Seemed hypocritical. The same temper as before reared up in me, but I'd already done one A&B that day so I ground my teeth wondering if I was sexist or Twitterphobic for not confronting this woman. She wasn't as threatening as the Nazi, so there was that, and her racism was anti-white racism, which I'm told doesn't count. While my teeth turned to mulch, security escorted the woman out, leaving everyone again to wonder why would such a person go to a comedy club in the first place.

Since I restrained from direct action, the second rage was ignored by all but Allie who watched me with concerned scared eyes until I'd calmed down. The first incident, however, was of course noticed. Seen, heard, sympathetically felt.

The incident brought out lively discussions of ethics, cheap shots, knights in shining tee shirts, and assault versus battery. Finally, Critter suggested that I might be a little short-tempered. Hearing that, I damn near punched his stupid felt face before I remembered he was a puppet.

Operation enlighten Tony was born, a feel-good intervention-like catastrophe that led everyone I thought knew better into this smelly County Rec. aerobics room to be told "shhhh."

Allie started by buying me a book on patience, but after reading the first sentence of the back blurb I gave up. Not a big deal until you confess to doing that at a bar table full of friends mid-intervention. Enter peer pressure, the magic tonic when self-discipline and significant other disappointment aren't enough to get you to make an effort.

Long story short, I agreed to make an effort to calm the inner me. Find peace and chill.

Om.

Volt.

Ampere.

"Shut the fuck up, Tony." The language fitted Dara but it was Allie. I love Allie. She's my gal. This wasn't good. Had I gone too far? Could I recover? Could I survive these last—holy hell on a plate of lettuce!—nine and half minutes more of downtime?

My phone rang.

I jumped. The room jumped.

In light of my newly girlfriend-ordered hobby, I'd replaced my ringtone with an Om, the mantra word. I found a very clear recording of just that one sound performed by a Finnish death metal band called 'Satan Stabs Your Eyes.' Volume set to ten. I hadn't missed a call since I'd done that.

"I gotta take this," I said, getting up, drawing looks of both hate and relief. Balance is divine.

Outside in the lobby of the county recreation building, I turned off the chime and said, "Ahoy-hoy?" for something new.

"Is this Mr. Flaner?"

"Ahoy-hoy.

"Mr. Flaner, we need your help to save our mom. She's been taken by a cult."

"Oy."

2

ON THE WAY TO SELF-IMPROVEMENT, I made the very obvious mindful moves to: A, not silence my phone even after being told to; B, turn up the volume to kidney-shaking levels and hope for divine intervention to strike; C, rejoice when God heard me; D, answer the call directly instead of sending it message in order to E, flee the rec center, in this case to Denny's down in Murray for some pancakes.

Murray is a suburb of Salt Lake City, which is weird since Murray is like right in the middle of the Salt Lake Valley. If you wanted to nuke Salt Lake City—and who doesn't?—targeting Murray and edging a smidge west toward Taylorsville would pretty much wipe out what little sentient life there is here and leave piles of smoldering rubble, though judging from how Murray has slid down the gentrification scale in recent years, Murray residents might not notice the difference until their skin fell off.

I was already going to get it from Allie for being such a pill at the meditation. She should have known. I'd agreed to go, but I didn't promise to embrace the holistic lifestyle of mindful serenity without putting up a fight. That wouldn't be me. And I must be true to myself, right? So everyone should have expected some passive aggressiveness and biting sarcasm. Some whining too. These are the hallmarks of someone who's really got their shit together, doncha' think? Hey, at least I didn't dick-punch anyone today.

I could say now that it was an important call. I've been summoned to rescue someone's mother from cultists. See? I'm a goddamn hero. My friends would totally understand, not just my flight to America's Diner, but my quips and jokes. They're comedians too. How they held it together during all that quiet, was beyond me. Maybe they wanted to be there? Nah. They'd been drugged or something. I should look into that.

I should tell you too that I'm a detective. You probably already know that. Most people do by now. But some folks wander in late. So if you did, welcome, and here's the skinny: among other things, I'm a detective. It's kind of my job. If I have a job, that'd be it. Good? Nice. Now you're all caught up.

The voice on the other end of the line, a woman's, didn't want to talk over the phone, which was perfect for me because I didn't want to talk in the hall of the rec center with a quiet meditation class behind one door, and the Big Bopper sweating to the oldies behind another. And even *Chantilly Lace* couldn't soak up all the funk from an over-chlorinated swimming pool. Besides, Denny's had that one Grand Slam breakfast I like. The one with all the food.

Even so, I felt bad about leaving my friends to that torture. Especially since we'd all agreed that we would try to be better people, "philosophical-ly." That was the deal. Garrett had suggested "professionally" to rib Critter. Dara, on a new diet, said "physically" and Perry, with a huge bump in his streaming royalties, said "financially." Standard, looking up late to the fateful conversation, said, "ironically," and won the night. He has his moments. Allie said "philosophically," for my sake, with that a cute mean squint she wears sometimes. So philosophically was it.

I want to be a better person. Really. Knowing Allie alone has made me change. And lately, I'd let myself down by letting her down. You see, I'd been down. I'd been anxious and cranky. Lots of stuff found its way under my skin, like stop lights that only allowed two cars a turn, a freezing spring rain that ruined my hiking plans, every single human being existing in my field of vision. Patience, compassion and understanding are some of my greatest gifts, and by great gifts I mean they'd make great gifts for me since I don't have them. My friends were trying to do that, I think. I felt really bad about leaving, or I would have, if I weren't so excited to get the hell out of there. And I had a case. Cultists!

It was a mid-April afternoon, a Saturday. The traffic was bad because there was road work, which didn't surprise me. Tearing up roads is the state's official pastime and greatest jobs program. 'Inferior roads for a better economy' might as well be the rallying cry for the graft which is our construction services. Seriously, did you know some places lay down roads and then drive on them for, like, years before having to tear them up again? I read about it. Living in Utah where maybe, one week per year you can park on your own street, it's a far stretch to imagine.

Anyway, instead of pounding my steering wheel while weaving around orange traffic cones and abandoned dump trucks, I tapped my fingers along with a song I hadn't heard in years and used to hate, but somehow was okay now. The galaxy really does make love to the universe…eh, no it doesn't. Oh my god. Could there be crappier lyrics? Still it's a catchy tune and somehow I let it go. I was decidedly in a good mood. Maybe mediation works. Nah. It was the weather. Full-on sleet cloudburst, but it wasn't snow.

In a psychically sick attempt at rationalization, justification, and damage control, I did at that moment, notice I was feeling better than I had been. As I understood it, and God knows Allie has tried to explain it to me, this was a 'mindfulness moment.' Or as that instructor with the mustache all down his face might say, 'you thought about your thoughts.' He got paid to do that. Anyway, for a brief moment, there in the car, pulling off the freeway in weather that would send a Seattle duck to Bermuda, I forgot for a moment all the crap that was bothering me, known and unknown. I forgot how I'd messed up, how I had things left undone, how I was on a timer to a lonely grave. Thinking about how I wasn't thinking about these things, naturally made me think of them and before I found the parking lot, my mood, if not wholly sour, had a stiff splash of bitters in it.

Denny's is an institution, an ancient roadside diner become national chain and surviving the switch. Most don't make it. Death by corporate raiders, plummeting quality in food and service, a new trend and flashy competition. But Denny's survived, maintaining reasonable—dare I say, cheap—prices while dancing on the grave of The Big Boy and pissing side-ways on struggling free-pie day IHOP. Denny's is a survivor known far and wide for consistently mediocre food served lovingly hot within sight of an exit ramp. For locals, it's an all-night refuge for those all-nighters. Coffee and pancakes at oh-my-god thirty in the morning. A non-judgmental waitress offering you limited cheer but infinite refills of burned Folgers giving you time and space to retreat, rethink, and recover from whatever poor decisions brought you there. All this in a comfortable black vinyl booth smelling faintly of bleach and strongly of maple syrup. Denny's reminds me of college, of late night comedy shows after we shut the place down, and desert towns between here and there. A wave of recollected feelings, old joy and present worry, wafted over me and I felt a hangover coming on that wasn't there before.

Why just walking into a dive like that should elicit such strong feelings in me then I had to attribute to my new state of higher consciousness. Thinking this, I became distracted and forgot why I was there. A waitress had led me to a table before my eyes fell on a corner booth surging with alert people looking past me because I wasn't looking for them.

"Oh," I said to the waitress. "I think I'm there."

We both looked at the booth, at the five pairs of staring eyes, who slowly, each in turn, found me and took in my sweatpants and coffee-stained "Moab is for Adventure" tee shirt. The waitress handed me a menu and left me there in the glow of strangers' eyes.

"Looking for a detective?" I asked.

"You're Tony Flaner?" said one of them.

"Sure am."

"Were you sleeping?" said another.

"Sorta."

I waited to be invited to sit. While I did, I took in the group. Like I said, there were five of them. Three of them looked to be siblings, a woman and two men, with two significant others, a man and a woman.

I waited.

They waited and shifted and didn't know what to say.

I did not look *that* bad. I'd showered that morning. My teeth were clean, unlike some meditating friends. My sweats were clean, my shirt clean before the coffee spill. I'd shaved in recent memory and I had an inner glow that bespoke confidence and falling Jenga towers. That is to say, I'd looked worse. I was about to say something that would adequately express my feelings, when promises to improve my spiritual self came back to me.

"And who do I have the pleasure of addressing?" I said, calming the inner vitriolic sarcastic monster.

"Whom," said one of the women.

I growled. Audibly. The woman on the end pulled back. Look. A seat. I sat down.

"And whom are you?" I said to the shrinking woman. She was by far the youngest person at the table, dare I say younger than me. I put her at thirty. She had short brown hair, plain makeup. Fingers I think. She was not a sibling.

"I'm Lara," she said. "I'm married to Josh." She pointed to the sibling named Josh. He was maybe twenty years her elder, still had most of his hair, though it was graying. Conservatively cut. Polo shirt without the alligator or pony near his heart.

"Hello, Lara. Hello Josh," I said with a nod to each. Lara pulled a little farther away setting off a ripple of hip shifts until I had enough cushion for both cheeks.

"And you are?" I said to the oldest man, also not a sibling.

"I'm Hannah's husband."

"Does Hannah let you tell people your name?" I said this in a very soothing way to compound the snark.

It was not wasted because Hannah's husband stole a glance at the oldest woman at the table, the sibling called Hannah, I presumed. She offered him a curt nod as permission and he said, "Mark. My name is Mark."

"I have a great friend called Mark," I said, breaking ice like a champ. "He's so cool. True blue. He speaks French and—"

"We're not here to talk about you," said Hannah.

"Oh?"

She shook her head.

"Oh," said I.

I hate to stereotype people just for the way the look and act and are, but Hannah was that special breed of entitled White woman who (whom?) used to go the appellation of Draper Wife back in the day, this in reference to a certain upscale white neighborhood in Salt Lake County where husbands worked their multi-level marketing schemes while their wives made life hard on the grocery clerks. This breed slipped out of the state—or maybe they were in other places the whole time, I don't know—but at some point someone called them 'Karen,' which is a shame because Karen is a very nice name. I'm fond of it myself, but alas, like Adolf and Atilla, Karen may be forever stained by a few bad apples who need to talk for managers.

Karen, I mean Hannah, had the severe short haircut known to her kind, thick in the back with a rising angle coming off her neck to expose dark roots like her soul. Her bangs were long and cupped her face like open hands holding her in a constant pose of shouting. She also had the regulation over-sized sunglasses. I put her a decade below her husband, around fifty. She wore a fuzzy pink sweater that fit the season, not too warm, not too cold.

"I'm Samuel." The last sibling spoke. He was the youngest man, maybe forty-five. Fit and trim, unlike the other two men who had the girth of sedentary husbands. He had the same square features as the other siblings: strong jaw, Grecian nose, light-brown eyes. Bushier than normal eyebrows, except Hannah, who'd plucked hers into long arcs that reminded me of wings. Maybe seagull wings. Jonathan Livingston Seagull's I presumed, since it's to theme, but it couldn't be. Not on Hannah.

"You order?" I asked. I knew they hadn't. No plates on the table. Only waters and Diet Cokes. Menus in their laps. Dead giveaway. See? I am a detective.

I caught the waitress' eye, and she came over with her pad.

Around the table we went, starting opposite me. Each said something along the lines of "nothing for me," "another Diet Coke and put ice in it this time," and "Did you pass health inspection this year?" Okay, the last one was only implied, but I heard it. When the waitress came to me, I saw disappointment and disgust in her eyes. Hard to get a living wage on tips, harder still when no one orders anything.

"I'll have the grand Grand Slam with an extra side of grand bacon and sausage. Patties. Not links. I'm trying new things. Eggs, over medium. A pot of coffee—leave it on the table. Looks like we'll have room. Plenty of cream." I'd like to say that it was more than I could ever eat, that I was making a statement about taking up valuable booth space on a Saturday at a breakfast place. Denny's at night was one kind of animal. During the day, people needed to make a living. Breakfasts on Saturday were their bread-and-butter, or maybe buttermilk pancakes and dairy-like butter squares. I'd like to say that, and it's true, at least the Denny's part, but I knew I'd be able to put away all the food I'd ordered. I'd done it before. Several times before. It's not as much food as you think. Really. Don't judge.

"Before we get started," I said. "Let me first thank you for breakfast." I wanted to get the bill out of the way. They didn't look skint, but chintzy was not out of the question. Words are cool.

"Fine," said Hannah. "It's clear you just got up." She glanced at her teeny tiny wristwatch, a face nearly the size of a dime. Her sunglasses must have been prescription to see the numbers. I saw that it was after one in the afternoon. My watch could be read by satellite.

The coffee came. The table shrunk back as if I were imbibing the blood of an elder god, which, any coffee drinker will tell you, is actually the case. I should note here a strange quirk about Utah society. Mormons. There are a lot of them here. The state was founded by them and they stuck around, stuck together and stuck up the legislature like a band of robbers. I know a lot of Mormons, some cooler than others, some less cool. Some partially practicing—cafeteria Mormons, so to speak. Some are wholly engaged. Those people don't tend to hang around me. One of the reasons for this is I drink coffee. Coffee is a no-no for the hardcore Mormon. These people were Mormons. If Lara's CTR ring hadn't given it away, the garments under the short sleeves of all the men would have provided enough evidence for a full-on CSI investigation, complete with DNA testing and stool smear. They do that, right? I actually don't watch it.

Oh, for the uninitiated, a CTR ring is a ring with CTR on it. It's usually in the shape of a shield. It was invented by some LDS ladies in the '70s and given to children to help them navigate temptation, like which ice cream to take. CTR means "Choose The Right." So keep the ice cream you want on the chooser's left side, and you can to keep your Cherry Garcia all to yourself. It's like a WWJD—"What would Jesus Do?" thing, just easier to abbreviate and homegrown among the Saints. It's one of the few bits of iconography the Mormons have. They don't have crosses or logos. Garments are protective holy underwear that ward against evil and other icky things— bullets, think some, fashion, think most. And no, I'm not making this up. Devout LDS followers wear garments, and some wear the ring. These are encouraged, but like most faiths, the bite in the doctrine and central identity comes from exclusions.

Coffee is one of the banned things in the famous "Word of Wisdom" scripture. Hot beverages are bad, unless it's cocoa. I don't understand that. Caffeine is fine as long as it's not in coffee. Which is why there's more Diet Coke-flavored caffeine flowing through Utah veins than plasma and platelets. Alcohol is bad, and there might be good reasons for that, but church history isn't one of them. Brigham Young had a brewery and a distillery. I guess God changed his mind, or maybe it's just how we judge "strong drink" today. In any event, hardcore members of the Church of Jesus Christ of Latter-day Saints, known far and wide and for as long as they've been around as "Mormons," don't drink coffee. If they do, they are forbidden from doing their secret handshakes during their secret rites in their secret temples. Maybe they get a write-up by their bishop too, I don't know. But I do know that some of them will immediately judge down anyone who does drink the forbidden java brew. At least these people did me.

"Someone mentioned a cult?" I said, taking a long savoring sip.

3

"OUR MOTHER," said Hannah.

"Is in the clutches of a cult," added Josh.

"She's old," offered Samuel.

The non-siblings looked on and nodded agreeably. Emphatically even.

I won't lie, my first impulse was to blow these people off, high calorie-free breakfast offering and all. I wouldn't be rude. I would nod like Lara and Mark and pretend to listen, make believe I cared, lead them on to buy time as I consumed carbs, all the while mentally dismissing them as people I don't want to know because they were different.

My professionalism was not yet in gear. My mind was full of remembered Denny's exhaustions. This was a place of rest, contemplation and recovery. I was filled with muscle memory of cramming for exams, hangover prevention, and travel blankness. The slow road back from highway hypnosis. Ruts of thinking that made new information unwanted. Add to this my half-state of calm obliviousness had yet to play out from the morning.

I took a deep cleansing breath to a count of four through my nose, held for four, and coughed. It cleansed me in an unexpected way. I think I got spittle on Hannah's sweater. She did not look pleased.

"Sorry," I said. "I'm…"

They waited for me to finish.

"Sure you won't have something to eat?" I said. Samuel picked up a menu, which encouraged me. The others sipped iceless Diet Cokes and shook their heads.

I steepled my fingers against my chin and said with just the hint of an Austrian accent, "Tell me about your mother."

"Our mother has been sucked into a cult," said Hannah. "We need you to get her out."

"Which cult?" I said. "There are so many."

Josh said, "The group is called The COTTEO, The Church of the Third Eye Open. The leader is—"

"A brainwashing snake," put in Hannah.

"Go on," I said.

"What else is there to say?" said Hannah with just the right bob of her hair to match her impatience. "We're hiring you to get her back."

Plates started arriving. There was plenty of room on the table, so I spread them out. It was like eating alone.

"I'll have a grilled cheese sandwich," said Samuel. "No pickle."

I could only wonder in horror at what kind of upbringing Samuel had had where he had to suffer pickles in his grilled cheese sandwich. These people had suffered trauma. Maybe it was my portion to help them.

"Okay," I said. "But seriously, you've got to tell me a little more here."

"How far back?" asked Josh.

"Start at the very beginning? It's a very good place to start."

"He's teasing us," said Lara.

"I'm not supposed to tell him?"

"You are," I said.

Lara was the quick one. She looked sheepish, awkward, unhappy to be there, but clearly cleverer than her adopted family. Maybe she was just more on edge because she was next to me and I smelled like Patchouli, but she had a different vibe than the rest of them. Samuel also had a different vibe, different than hers but different also from Josh and Hannah's, the older siblings, who were intense and serious. Mark was straight up beat down.

Hannah took control. She even took off her sunglasses to grace me with an intense stare. "We are the Joneses," she began. "We are a good family. We can trace our ancestry to the first pioneers. Respectable. Established."

"Conservative," I added.

"Or course," she said and took another look at me, guessing my politics by my beverage and hair length. I needed a trim. I poured another cup. "That's nothing to be ashamed of."

She was unflappable, so unflapped, she went on. "Our father was a good man. Tobias Jones. He was an icon of the community for many years. A devout member of the bishopric, like his father."

"What? You're Mormons?"

Hannah recoiled. I'd flapped her. It could have been my snark getting through, but I think it was the name. According to recent powers that be, saying "Mormons" is bad. The preferred nomenclature is now "Members of the Church of Jesus Christ of Latter-Day Saints" As you can imagine, since this just rolls off the tongue, it has been slow to catch on. It hasn't caught me yet. Just look at the last chapter.

Hannah folded her wings and focused. "Daddy was a good man. Devout and hardworking. He left our mother with a substantial sum when he died."

"How'd he make his money?"

"Honestly."

I doubted that. "More detail is always appreciated."

"He was a builder. Had a construction company."

"Roads," said Mark.

"Oh god," I murmured.

Flapped again.

"Sorry. So, uh...how did he die?" Curious detectives want to know.

"Heart attack," said Josh.

"How long ago?"

"Seems like just yesterday," said Hannah, a tear manufactured in her eye.

"It's been five years," said Lara.

"It was hard on us," continued Hannah, "but it seems to have been worse on Mother."

"That can happen," I said.

"She went nuts."

"That's pretty strong."

"She changed her name," said Samuel.

"To what?"

"Rigsdale."

"What was it before?"

"Jones."

"Oh, she changed her last name. What's her first name?"

"Sylvia."

"So she went from Sylvia Jones to Sylvia Rigsdale after your father died?"

They nodded.

"Why Rigsdale? Was that her maiden name?"

They nodded their heads more, scandal on their faces.

"What's that expression you're wearing?" asked Lara. Yep, she was the quick one.

"It's disappointment and confusion," I said sagely. "Disappointment, that this is so mundane. You mentioned cult and one would expect any name change would be to something like "Rainbow Girl," or "Shiva-khan." Rigsdale, unless it originates from the sixty-sixth chapter of the *Necronomicon*, is pretty blah. The confusion is why anyone would think it's a big deal for a widow to change back to her maiden name."

"It's disrespectful to us," said Hannah.

"And the memory of Dad," added Josh.

The waitress appeared and put a plate in front of Samuel. A grilled cheese sandwich, with fries and a pickle on the side.

"Oh right," I said. "Pickles often come with sandwiches. A deli thing."

"What are you saying?" said Hannah.

Samuel pushed the pickle off the plate into a napkin with his fork. I met his eye and shrugged. He shrugged back.

"Did she change her name before or after she joined the cult?"

"Before."

"How long before?"

"Before Dad was cold in the ground," said Hannah.

"Two years ago," said Samuel.

I reminded myself that time is plastic, like that explained this. I asked, "Have you talked to your mother about all this?" I knew they had. Or at least Hannah had. I couldn't see her not speaking her mind to anyone at any time over anything.

"Yes. She dismissed us."

"Did you press?" Again I knew the answer.

"She told us to mind our own business."

"Us or you?"

Hannah sharpened her glare. "Us."

"We did an intervention last month," said Josh.

I slurped some eggs, chewed some bacon, gnawed a bit of sausage, doctored my coffee with two single serving cream cups and took a sip. They watched in rapt attention, or that's how I wanted to see it. "Did something happen to precipitate the intervention at that moment?"

"It was time," said Hannah. "Her behavior was unacceptable."

"Uh-huh..."

"She talked about moving out of state."

"Uh-huh..."

"Our father's memory—"

Samuel broke in, "She'd told us that we were cut out of the will."

"Ah."

"She's leaving everything to COTTEO."

More butter on pancakes. A splash of boysenberry syrup on the side to mix with the maple. Cut with edge of eggy fork. Scoop. Eat. Enjoy.

"Are you're all trust fund babies?"

"Babies?" said Hannah, offended.

"No offense. I mean, is there some trust or something that your father left you that's paying you?"

"No," said Hannah.

"But we are all, or were, expecting inheritance. It's what Dad wanted."

"Did he say that?"

"Yes."

"Did he say it in a legally binding form of any kind? Like in a will or a trust?"

"No."

"Did he ever actually say that he intended his money to go to you or did you assume that since he loved you?"

"He…" began Josh. "I'm sure that's what he wanted."

"How much are we talking here?"

"Seven million, give or take."

There was a time when seven million dollars would have shocked me, when I would have wondered how anyone could have so much money, but times have changed. As the haves take ever more from the have-nots, millions just isn't enough to get excited over. Wealth is measured in billions and poverty in thousands of dollars in debt. I was jaded by oligarchical scales. I focused my mind and said to myself, seven million is something.

"Yes it is," said Josh.

I smiled wisely as if I'd intended to say that out loud the whole time.

Looking over the clan I was reminded that Utah still had a middle class. Guessing, I would put Samuel as lower middle-class, Hannah and Mark as upper since he had last year's Apple Watch, scratched but working, begging for an upgrade; she had a ring that would choke a camel trying to pass through the eye of a needle. Josh and Lara were probably middle middle-class. Like me.

"She's moving to Oregon," said Hannah, putting an emphasis on the name that made it sound like an epithet.

"She stopped going to church," said Josh.

"Makes sense," said I. "I don't know many cults that like people to attend other…services."

"Exactly," said Josh. "She's turned her back on all of us."

"She's our mother," Hannah said.

I tried to parse the line, wondering if the emphasis was on *our* or *mother*, not sure if it mattered.

"I know how this looks," said Samuel.

"How does it look?"

"Like we're a bunch of greedy brats," said Lara. This earned her a hard look from Hannah, and a sidelong one from Josh, her husband.

"But that's not true?"

"No," she said.

"No," agreed Samuel.

"How is it then?"

"The money's something," said Samuel. "Who couldn't use a few bucks?"

"Or a few million." It was an unkind thing to say. I knew it even before I said it, while I was saying it and of course after I said it. Not like that stopped me from saying it though.

"She's unrecognizable to us," said Samuel. "She's undergone such a drastic change it's chilling."

"Total personality switch," said Hannah. "Drugs might be involved."

"Oh no," I said. "Does she drink coffee?" It was just the kind of low-hanging sarcasm Buddha was known for.

"Mr. Flaner," said Lara. "This is serious. We love Sylvia. They as her children, me as her friend."

"And me," said Mark sensing his moment to join the conversation.

It passed.

"This cult she joined is suspicious," said Samuel. "The leader is suspicious. Mom was in a vulnerable state after Dad's passing. This...conman, got to her. Filled her head with happy hippie crap and is taking her money."

"He might even be sleeping with her," said Hannah.

"Who's the leader?"

"A man named Smith."

"You're kidding?"

"No, why?" said Hannah.

"No reason. What's his first name?"

"John."

"John Smith?"

"Yes."

"Eh...okay."

"It sounds fishy doesn't it?" said Lara. "An alias."

"That's what I thought," said Josh.

"Do you know if it's an alias?"

"That's what you're supposed to find out." Josh was now more animated. It was like he was drawing energy from his wife.

"Is that all you want?"

"No. Of course not," said Hannah. "We want you to bring our mother back to us. She's getting old and she should be with her family now, not in some commune with chicken poop and chanting."

"How old is she?"

That stumped them for a while. Hannah finally did some math on her fingers. "A spry seventy-three."

Like 'millions' being 'rich,' 'seventies' used to be 'old.' Times have changed. Seventies is the new sixties if not fifties. Spry isn't applied to some people until they're in their nineties. I didn't say that. Something about their earnestness was sinking into me and pity had a toe-hold. The food had calmed me. Within my circulatory system processed sugar competed happily with creamed caffeine to make me feel alive and useful in a transcendent frenetic peace only chemical stimulants can offer.

"How is the cult suspicious?" I asked.

"It's a cult," said Hannah as if that's all it took.

I looked around the table for more.

"John Smith is doing some Netflix thing," said Josh. "A show. He's a showman."

"And?"

"And what kind of spiritual leader does television?" said Samuel.

I bit my tongue on several famous and unfortunately rather near examples and said instead, "I suppose it depends on what kind of Netflix thing it is."

"No it doesn't," said Hannah. "How can someone who claims to be all spiritual chase fame and money? It's antithetical to the calling."

I was about to react badly, instinctively finding the opposite position to anything she said, just like the saints of old. But I hesitated. I finished my breakfast meat and chewed on what she'd just said alongside the last of my sausage. Allie had put me on a philosophical diet of higher thinking and mindfulness. My reference to Buddha before was not arbitrary. He's been a part of my life for a few weeks now. The nature of enlightenment, happiness, suffering, lotus positions and leg cramps were more common in my house than Netflix and chill. We still chilled, but with candles and incense; chanting, not so much anymore. Don't ask me to explain. Just look up the police report if you must know.

Anyway, what Hannah said about fame and money being antithetical to the spiritual quest sounded true. It sounded true because of the mediation I'd done at home, because of the hours of YouTube videos Allie had made me watch, the articles, books and scriptures she'd quoted to me when my eyes suddenly hurt too much to read them myself. Probably because of the YouTube. I gotta say that Allie, for all her wonderfulness, shares one of my terrible faults at times—obsessiveness. For once, I'd been the one to try to slow down. This was because—and mindfulness had helped show me the truth of this—I didn't want to change so much.

"Okay," I said. "I'm interested."

I GOT A FEW MORE DETAILS, their contact numbers, Sylvia's address. They got the bad news of how much I charge. I got a retainer. They got the check. I went to the bathroom. They left while I was gone.

I had a full tummy and an empty bladder. I decided to take a calming moment and reflect. I'm supposed to do this often. It's supposed to be good for me.

The Joneses were not a bad lot. I had a prejudice against the type, I know that. Jealousy-based, surely. But their lives were their lives and they functioned within them as best they could. Lines had been drawn for them, barriers and openings. Some might say 'privilege' if outside the circle, others within it would say it's just how it is. I had to take personality out of it. Hannah was abrasive, but I didn't know her history. I didn't know what things had made her that way, what challenges had shaped her being. I should be compassionate and loving and not notice that she stiffed the waitress a tip. Bitch.

Allie would be proud of me for trying to be compassionate, for taking this moment to contemplate and express understanding. At least she would be proud after being pissed at me leaving her at the rec center without a car. Eeek. Should have thought of that.

I glanced at my watch. The mediation session had ended an hour ago. I looked at my phone. I had a plethora of texts. Eighteen to be precise. I signaled for another cup of coffee and wondered about the ethics of my contemplation space being alone at the biggest table at a Denny's during a weekend lunch rush.

Then Allie slid next to me.

"Hi," I said.

"Dork," she said.

Perry slid in beside her. Dara hip-checked me over and took that side. Garrett and Critter and then Standard arrayed on either side until I was boxed in good and tight at the innermost corner of the booth.

"You're buying," said Dara and signaled for menus.

The waitress perked up seeing patrons at the table, and fetched a stack of laminated menus.

"We are pretty mad at you," said Perry.

Everyone smiled serenely while they nodded.

"You don't look particularly mad," I said. "Dara usually stabs people when she's mad."

"Don't tell tales out of school, heretic."

"Heretic?"

"You want worse?" Dara had a way with words, the blue kinds. The words that take an R rated movie and move it to NC-17 faster than you can look that up on Google. She wasn't unleashing them on me. She was chill, relatively speaking.

"Seems to me that you have no reason to be mad at me for anything," I said. "Allie, does. Not you jerks."

"Whoa with the hostility," said Critter. His head slowly shaking no as his big googly plastic eyes stared softly into my soul.

"I figured you had a good reason," said Allie.

"A case."

"Seriously?"

"The bacon is thin enough to read through," I said. "Go for the sausage."

"Dammit, Tony."

"It's a kidnapping," I said.

"Who was taken?"

"Other way around."

"Oh, that is serious," said Perry.

Allie said, "You've been hired to snatch someone?"

"That's kind of the gist of it."

"I didn't think you did illegal work," said Standard.

"'Doesn't do illegal work?'" said Garrett. "Tony? Dude, where have you been? Tony's broken into more places than a Nixon's Plumbers."

"Nice reference, but dated," said Perry.

"I'll work on it," said Garrett. "Critter could probably have come up with something better."

"No doubt."

Critter, if I haven't mentioned, is a hand puppet occupying Garrett's left arm. He's part of Garrett's comedy act and part of his psyche. It is easy to forget they are, at the core, the same person, but they are. There is a Zen lesson there, I bet.

Standard thought for a second. "Oh yeah. Okay. Tony is a criminal."

"Whoa," I protested. "That's harsh."

"You better unpack this gist a bit," said Allie. "Before you go committing a felony for hire."

"Oh that's good," said Perry. "Gist the facts, ma'am."

"Thank you."

We all, except Allie, call ourselves comedians. With the exception of Perry, we all only do open mic and the rare occasional show when we toggle together enough material to get our names on the marquee outside of The Comedy Cellar. I say except for Perry, because he is actually making it in comedy. We all have day jobs to make ends meet. I'm a slacker detective by day for example, but Perry is a manic comedian by day and night. He's getting gigs and working on a streaming special. He has an agent. We all secretly hate him for his success, but it's hard to be mad at him because he's so funny and so mentally unstable. He's nuts. Certifiable and medicated. Sometimes in-patient for paranoid delusions, but damn can he bring down a house. Anyway, when he compliments a joke, we notice.

"Okay," I said. "Order up, and I'll fill you in."

The waitress took everyone's orders, filled coffee cups with scorch and water glasses without tepid tap water. My breakfast plates and Samuel's pickle were removed. I told the gang about the job, the Joneses, Sylvia Rigsdale, COTTEO and the mysterious John Smith while they listened with surprising, even alarming, patience. This was not the group I knew. When the first plates of pancakes arrived, I paused.

Allie was the first to speak. "I don't see the kidnapping."

"Oh. I forgot," I said. "Right before I went to the bathroom, right before they disappeared without tipping"—that got a few non-peaceful looks—" Hannah said to me, 'as long as the family has plausible deniability, nothing is off the table.'"

"That doesn't sound like a kidnapping," said Allie.

"It does a little," said Perry, "but more likely a murder."

"What?"

Dara nodded. "That's what I heard."

"Who am I supposed to kill?"

"The mother?" said Garrett. "Before she can give the money away."

"I didn't get that," said I.

"Then the guru."

"What about the kidnapping idea? I could kidnap the mother, deprogram her in a cabin up the canyon."

"I'm not seeing that," said Allie.

"It's what you do with cult victims."

"That's what you do with them?"

"Yes. That's what you do to cult victims and drunk sailors."

"I guess I never heard the second verse of that ditty."

"Well...you should pay more attention. And it's a shanty."

She smirked.

"It's all suspect," said Critter. "What made you take the case? I don't see a crime here."

Critter is always good at cutting through the crap. He's a sharp puppet.

"It fit," I said. "Enlightenment and all."

"Self-improvement," corrected Allie through a mouth of pancakes. "Just be a better person."

"Dick-punch one guy..."

They ate for a moment. I thought.

"Aren't we on a quest for truth?" I said. "Isn't that what this is all about? Looking for the real deal?"

"Actually it's about rage issues," said Allie.

"No it's not. Sometimes Nazis need a dick-punch."

"I just want to be comfortable in my own skin," said Garrett.

"I just want to meet some normal people," said Standard.

"In a fucking meditation class with bells and incense?" said Dara.

"Why were you there?" said Standard in a rare moment of standing up to the diminutive Dara.

"To support Tony, my dick-puncher in shining armor."

"I'm there for truth," said Garrett.

"I'm there to support Tony," said Allie.

"Oh, it's all for me, huh? You're so perfect you don't need a bit of meditation and philosophizing?"

"Not like you do."

Allie and I get along most times. Conflicts are usually resolved by the following rubric: Allie is right and I need to see that. It's an effective and proven rule. This time however, I felt the need to call bullshit.

"Bullshit," I said.

"Oh?"

"You've got issues too. Maybe they're not as amusing as mine, but you've got them."

"I'm not saying I don't," she said and stabbed at her eggs. The table went quiet, sensing that awkward moment of a public couple fight. After she bit some eggs, chewed and sipped her coffee, shifted her pencil-straight auburn hair off her shoulder, focused on a dozen things in some middle distance with her beautiful light-brown eyes, she turned them on me. "Like what?" she demanded to know.

I suddenly felt alone, exposed and in danger. I had said it without actually having a list ready. Not having a list ready spoke in my favor, since if I'd had a list of grievances ready to go it'd show that they'd been smoldering in my mind a while. Of course, at that moment, it was the opposite. I had to flummox around for an answer or look like an ass and affirm, erroneously I was sure, that Allie had no flaws.

I was saved however. Perry spoke.

"I went seeking truth."

"Is that capitalized truth?" said Critter.

"What's the difference?"

"One is like truth of the universe, the other is like true to you."

"What's the difference?"

Critter tilted his head thirty degrees and hung his mouth open in a powerful confusion pose. Sensing the lifeline, I said, "Go on, Perry. Very interesting."

"One can't go looking for truth in events without stumbling into truth in other places."

Allie still had an eye on me, but it was softening.

"Like what?" I pressed.

"Well, like who's really in charge," said Perry. "A lot of groups say the only way to connect with the real leaders of everything is through meditation. Some call it prayer, others call it 'psychic connective procedure,' PCP."

An obvious joke hung in the air, but none of us grabbed such easy low-hanging fruit. That's what happens sometimes with comedians edging for new angles. When a softball comes, it's too shocking to react to.

"Like the drug?" said Allie. Oh, right. She wasn't a comedian.

"I'd never thought of that," said Perry.

"Seriously?" Several of us asked.

"Really."

"Dude," said I, "maybe you need a few classes on critical thinking instead of mind expansion."

"I've never tried PCP," said Standard.

"No one asked you, Stan," said Garrett. I was the only person who called Standard Standard except maybe his dead mother at séances. I don't do it for love or for his mother; I do it because it bothers him. However, I've been doing it so long that I think it's no longer the tease it used to be. I'd like to think that I made him a stronger man and not that I was a shitty friend. I was shitty at the beginning. He bugged me, but now he is my friend and we get along fine. He doesn't correct me when I call him Standard now, though he does correct others who follow my example. There's something beautiful and beaten down there. I probably need to look into that in my spare time.

"Go on, Perry," I said, focusing my entire Allie-threatened attention to my friend.

"PCP is what the Community calls it."

"The sitcom?" said Allie. "Don't remember that episode."

"No. The Community. Headed by The Messenger."

We all waited and stared. Critter would have blinked dumbly with the rest of us if he could have.

"Come on," said Perry. "You guys have heard about the Community."

"What about our blank faces and confused stares leads you to that impression?"

"He's famous."

"So's washing and Dara hasn't heard of it."

"The fuck?" Dara would have punched me if I'd have been sitting closer to her. She punched Standard instead, which was bad because the joke was intended to name Standard as the no washing person as a tease, but after the flash of guilt I floated for his name, I blindly struck out at someone else so I wouldn't hurt him. Dara did that instead.

"Nice one," said Garrett and got punched too.

"The hell?"

Perry had his phone out and was Googling. I smiled at Allie who gave me a suspicious look. "You sure look pretty today," I said. "New eyebrows?"

She squinted but let escape a grin. I was safe.

"Oh," said Perry.

"Oh what?"

"The Messenger is going to ICOHEP next week. Didn't you say the group you were looking into was called the Coven?"

"No. I said, COTTEO."

"ACOG?"

"No. COTTEO."

"BORA?"

"COTTEO."

"Green Tomorrow?"

"COTTEO."

"Homecoming?"

"COTTEO."

"The Community?"

"That's yours," I said. "I'd like to buy a vowel. COTTEO."

"Oh yeah." Perry's face twisted up as he squinted at his screen. "Was it Peoplists?"

"Off his meds?" whispered Critter.

"Don't judge," said Allie and I fought back an urge to renew the quarrel having lit upon a possible attack vector with that line.

Instead I said, calmly, placidly, with love, compassion, and infinite, if strained, patience, "COTTEO."

"COTTEO?"

"COTTEO."

"COTTEO," he said.

"Yahtzee."

"They'll be there too." He smiled large.

"Where?"

"ICOHEP," he said earnestly.

"ICOHEP."

"It's an acronym," he said, like that made everything clear. When we stared, waiting, he repeated, "ICOHEP."

"Perry, dude, friend. Crazy-person," said Critter. "What the everliving auras are you talking about? You've spouted more alphabet soup than a botulism outbreak at a Senate Hearing."

"ICOHEP."

"Dara's prone to violence you know," he said with a knowing and warning nod. Garrett and Standard joined in the nodding.

"ICOHEP stands for the 'Interfaith Congress of Holistic Enlightened People.'"

"Progress," said Allie.

"Is there more to this?" I asked.

"Don't tell me you haven't heard of the ICOHEP?"

Dara, struck like a rabid snake, lunging across Garrett and Allie, upending a plate of white toast. Perry shrank back.

"It's on all the bulletin boards. All over the dark web."

Dara squirmed closer.

"On your own spud," I said. "Read the room or die."

"It's in Oregon," he said. "It's a thing. It's ICOHEP—Interfaith Congress of Holistic Enlightened People. Put on by Ted Tessner."

That slowed Dara's attack. There was a name we all knew.

"Ted Tessner of the mushroom-growing Ted Tessner?" I asked.

"Yes."

"Ted? I know Ted," said Allie, lighting up. "I trained his dog Psilly. Great guy."

"Silly"

"Psilly," she corrected him. "With a P."

"Like in Psilocybin?" I said.

Her shining light of excitement changed hue to the light of understanding. "That never occurred to me," she said. "Makes sense though, huh?"

"Huh," I said and got a punch in my arm.

Perry passed me his phone. He used a model I'd never seen, from a manufacturer I'd never heard of, using an operating system I thought only existed in fiction. The Tor browser I recognized however. A web page was up on it. I scrolled.

"Tony," said Allie. "You told me to tell you when you went too far on a tangent. This is one of those."

"What were we talking about?" I said.

"About truth."

"About killing an old lady," said Dara through a mouthful of Perry's toast.

"No," I said. "We were talking about cults and saving people from them. John Smith will be at the ICOHEP conclave. Since it's in Oregon, I'm betting Sylvia will be there too. I might as well go."

"You just want to take some magic mushrooms," said Garrett.

"When the stars align," I said, sagely, "who am I to question fate?"

5

I LEAPED at the idea of going to Oregon to investigate. I had negotiated a generous expense account and the subject of a trip to the Northwest was even mentioned by Josh who had furnished me Sylvia's last known address —an Airbnb in a place called Creswell Oregon. Though I hadn't decided what my first move would be—I'd not had time to wash my hands between their gang and mine—but it made sense to go. It was where she was last known to be and I needed to get a look at the cult leader, the aforementioned John Smith. ICOHEP, or "the conclave of cults" as we quickly renamed it to Perry's chagrin, would give me the perfect cover. I would be a humble seeker testing the waters of higher thought. Perfect. Plus it would get me the hell away from all these people trying to change me. I know they meant well, especially Allie, but come on? Is enlightenment a group project? Looking over the offerings of ICOHEP, I had to concede that maybe, in some cases, the answer was yes, but I wasn't feeling it. I had the familiar push and pull of my life however. Push–get away from these do-gooders; pull—I was getting paid to see green landscapes.

I was therefore disappointed when the gang unanimously voluntold me that they would help me in Oregon. Knowing that any resistance from me would only make it worse, "Neat-o," was what I said.

"We do need a vacation," Allie said.

"It's been a hard couple of years," said Standard, including himself in Allie's 'we,' doing nothing for my new tender feelings for him.

"I was planning on going anyway," said Perry. "The Messenger doesn't do many public appearances. I'd be a fool to miss it."

"A fool," I repeated.

"There's a group called the Coven," said Critter, reading off Garrett's phone. "Weird."

"I've heard about Green Tomorrow," said Allie. "Surprised to see them there, but I guess environmentalism could have a spiritual side."

"Side."

"Isn't The Abundant Church of God led by that shit-smear Bartalemuw Benson?"

"Shit-smear." See? I was communicating.

I nodded appreciatively, though in fact I didn't know one group from another and thought they all sounded suspicious. What I did know was that I was being paid top dollar to save someone from the clutches of these people and my friends were rushing headlong into them.

Before breakfast was over, everyone was on their phones researching the several groups. I looked at COTTEO, Sylvia Rigsdale's flavor—and that's how I thought of it, all these groups side by side like so many ice creams under a glass counter.

"The Cult Conclave starts Monday," said Garrett.

"I'm driving a rental car," said Perry. "There's room. Who's in?"

All hands went up.

Except mine and Allie's.

"Let me guess," said Dara. "You're not going now because we are?"

"I have to," I said, implying they didn't.

"Planes go to Oregon," said Allie.

"But you'll miss out on all the bonding we'll share on the road trip up," said Standard.

"Have fun."

Truth be told, I was then feeling sheepish around Allie. My personal growth had been an underlying, unspoken, long-standing project of hers and I'd come along, because hey, who doesn't want to be a better person? Today however, it had gotten under my skin. The rec center meditation was lame, nothing like the ones Allie had done at home where lame wasn't so public. Then there was the uptight family and their hypocrisy and now my friends jumping into my business. I wanted to be free of them all, even Allie, for a little while. An unspoken commitment hung in the air and she was waiting for me to speak it. So, was wanting a little me time too much to ask? Yep. Of course it was. Luckily, I remembered that such feelings pass and having faith in the way the universe refuses to stay put, I put my arm around my gal and snuggled, and through a smile that I was told would eventually work its way from the outside in, I said, "It'll be great having everyone with me."

With great effort I steered the conversation away from being better people, my progress with the same, and the merits of open-eyed meditation versus falling asleep in an ashram. We talked comedy, the newest idiots on the internet, the oldest idiots on the internet, and the lack of decent mass transportation in America. I carefully also avoided discussing Ted Tessner and Allie's relationship with the billionaire who was now famously divorced and thus single and dating. That, I didn't bring up, since to avoid suffering is noble. Or was it that all suffering is noble? Anyway, I didn't need that kind of comparison right then, me in my hash brown ketchup-stained sweats after I'd abandoned my girlfriend in a smelly community gym and told her she had problems. Therefore, after the bus and train talk, all pertinent subjects were covered. Noting also that all the food had been eaten and the plates taken away, we broke up. The group, not me and Allie. We were still together. I'd shown I was a good person by picking up the tab for everyone which was less than a ticket for the one hour meditation session. In any event, for that gracious act of generosity, Allie and I were made up, if we'd ever been fighting. We went back to my place to pack and arrange a plane to Oregon.

"I can't imagine being in a car with those people for what? Ten hours?"

"At least," I said. "They are best in small servings and never before breakfast."

"They're nice and all..."

"But a little time away from them is also good?"

"Yeah."

"Yeah..." said I, falling victim again to my broken censor, "about that."

We were in the bedroom loading suitcases. Hers was still warm from when she brought it up from Moab the day before. Mine still on the floor from where I'd chucked it after my last trip to Moab, whenever that was. Allie lives in Moab. I have a house down there too. A rental now, a place I inherited and won't—can't—sell. When I go there now, I stay with Allie at her ranch where she trains animals. She's an animal trainer. She specializes in training critters for movies, but that's dried up thanks to cheap CGI. Now she trains critters for people who make movies, rich folk, celebrities and whatnot. Her reputation survived ILM and WETA and she's thriving better than ever. She now has two assistants so she can visit me more often. It's a pain for me to go down there since it inconveniences me. Much better to inconvenience her, the woman with an actual responsible job that benefits from her being around. I'm a private investigator, it says so on my business card: *Tony Flaner, accomplished private detective*. I'm also a maggot landlord letting out a family house in vacationland Utah. Yep. She's the one who should come to me.

"About that?" Allie had stopped packing her suitcase. Actually, she'd stopped folding clothes that would later be put into the suitcase. I skip that step. Quite the timesaver to wad everything up. Probably fit more in too, though I haven't tested it.

I was in it now. New plan.

"Do you think there's any chance I can talk the gang out of going to Oregon?"

"No. Don't change the subject."

"They can get in the way."

"Perry was going anyway and the gang wanted something to do."

"There's something to do here."

"Something interesting," she corrected herself. "You're interesting."

"Thanks."

"And stop changing the subject. You don't want me to go?"

"It's a work trip, honey. I'll be doing my job, dear. Sweetie."

"And...schnookapups?"

"I need to concentrate."

"Pa-lease. I've seen you work."

"Exactly," I said with strained conviction. We both knew she had me. Distractions were never my problem, or they were, but I was the source of them not the victim. "You could be in the way and the trip could be over really quick. A one-night thing. I don't even have reservations."

"*We* don't have reservations. But that's why you need me. I can arrange that."

"Quick trip."

"It'll be what it will be."

"Really?" I said. "You're going to get all wisdom on me?"

"Tony, I want to come. I can help. It'll be fun."

"Mixing work and play doesn't work."

"Pa-lease." She was good at that phrase. It was new to her vocabulary but damn if it wasn't just the ticket.

"You're pretty persuasive," I said.

"I let you help me with my work all the time."

"But you hate it," I countered. An opening.

"That I do. You're terrible at it."

"I don't know about terrible..."

"Remember Mittens?"

"That was an accident."

"You taught her to pee on command."

"Could have been useful."

"The command was 'here kitty.'"

"To be honest, you did most of the work. I just gave out the treats."

"When I wasn't looking."

"When you weren't looking."

"Wolfen," she said.

"Gesundheit."

"Wolfen, the retriever."

"Cutest little beastie, wasn't he? Beautiful lines. Didn't have a mean bone in his body. Very playful."

"You ruined him for duck hunting and that's what I was being paid to teach him."

"He could still fetch. He retrieved well."

"You taught him to rock the boat."

"And..."

"And there's a level of stealth in duck hunting. It's not a log flume."

I remembered Wolfen. Allie would let me take him to a pond and train him to sit in a boat. That was my charge. Sit with a dog in a row boat. I guess I was supposed to teach him to sit still, but you know how you can stand in a row boat with your legs spread out and rock it? Shifting weight from one leg to another until you're almost tipping it over? Dogs love that. And after some encouragement, can do it themselves.

"You could have untrained him."

"That's not fair," she said.

"He'd have paid you. You could have lied."

"I did lie. I told the owner I didn't know how he learned that. And as for training him out of it, you know that would have required violence."

Allie calls physical discipline of animals violence. She'll use it sometimes, on some of the most difficult cases, for specific reasons and situations, but it is a last resort, particularly if it included breaking the spirit of a happy-go-lucky Golden Retriever, smiling from ear to ear, hoping to capsize the boat for the fun that it would bring.

Allie had been good to forgive me for those things. She still hadn't found out about all the Spanish swear words I taught that parrot or the way I taught Tiffy the Tabby to shit in shoes. That required removing the litter box and replacing it with a dress shoe in the same corner, first full of cat litter, then empty. It was never the cat's first choice, but if the box was dirty, she'd go looking for a loafer every time. I'm pretty proud of that one. One day my genius will be appreciated.

"I think I've made my point," I said. "About helping with each other's work."

"Half the reason we're dating is because of your work."

"What? Really?"

"Maybe not half."

"Phew."

"Three-quarters."

"Now you're just hurting my feeling," I said.

"What do you think you're doing to me?"

"Saving you from certain danger."

"Pa-lease."

"It could happen."

"I'll take my chances. Unless you're going to be an absolute jerk and forbid me to come."

I almost spoke, but she cut me off.

"And then you're going to have to have a better reason than that. Jerk or not."

This was the moment I could have said something about needing space, or even, more honestly, that I was feeling picked on for not being perfect. Instead I said, "You know I want you to go. Whatever gave you the idea I didn't?"

She looked at me with those dreamy eyes. Dreamy in a cold accusing way. So, not really dreamy. Cold and accusing, really.

"Actually, it'll be good if you'll play interference with the gang if they get in my way."

"See? I can be useful."

"I know you can."

"Plus I know Ted Tessner."

"He's not who we're going for."

"But he's involved. Could be a lead."

"This isn't a case. It's an intervention."

"Go on." At first I thought she was teasing me, but I saw that she was actually asking me for a plan. Of course she knew I didn't have one, so it was teasing, but it was a good question.

"You're asking me what my plan is?"

"Yes."

"I'll investigate this fake guru, find some dirt on him and confront Sylvia with the truth."

"Why go to Eugene then? Surely your Google-fu can work from here."

She almost got me there. "That goes only so far. I want to meet the guy, and I want to see Sylvia. She was last seen in Oregon and she's sure to be at the Cult Conclave."

"ICOHEP."

"Gesundheit."

"It's a shit plan, but figure it out. I'll be there to help. It'll be fun."

"No promises."

"None expected."

We packed some more, me wearing the smile the meditation books swore was good for me. The contemplative one, like the smiling Buddha wears. Not the laughing Buddha—hell no. Contemplative. A kind of a smug smirk, the 'I know more than you do, punk' expression that's supposed to bring inner peace by feigned superiority. There's also the idea that the physical act of smiling can sink to an emotional level and make you happy. The jury is still out.

After a while, I said, "You know I don't do domestic cases and here I feel like I might have slipped into one. This could be sleazier than even a divorce case."

"Nah. We're the good guys saving an old lady. You like old ladies."

I do, as a rule.

"And you think religious folk are full of shit," she added.

Again, she had it right.

"Push and pull," she said. "This case feels perfect for you."

I'm not sure she got the push/pull thing right in this case. I'd already recognized that familiar pattern at work here, but not in the way she put it. And it was a little weird having someone else—even the love of my life, Allie—telling me how I feel.

6

OUR FLIGHT WAS for Sunday morning. Sunday was a holiday. A real one, not just a war memorial where people get to have hot dogs and beach days. No, this was a full-on guilt-caked religious observance of bunnies and cruci-fixes, closed business and colored eggs. On the drive to the train station parking lot to take the Trax to the airport, Allie and I discussed the holiness of the day.

"Jesus died on Friday, was resurrected Sunday, and thus the celebration," I explained.

"He died on Good Friday?"

"Yes. What kind of upbringing did you have not to know that?"

"Utah."

"We have Good Friday here."

"Good Friday is everywhere if you have a calendar," she teased.

"You know what I mean," I said.

"Look who can dish it out but not take it?"

"Okay, smarty pants, why do they call it Good Friday?"

"Instead of what?"

"Shit Friday where our guy got horribly killed?"

"Propaganda?"

"Touché."

"But what I never understood," said Allie with a mouthful of conve-nience store chocolate-frosted chocolate donut, which is a thing divine, "why say three days? I count two."

"Romans didn't have zero."

"What?"

"They counted the day of. Thus three days is Friday, Saturday, and Sunday. All included."

"But it was Christians measuring it. Or was it Jews?"

"You do know that all the Jesus stories weren't written down for a long time after Jesus died right? And that they were written down by people who weren't even there but were part of the Roman Empire?"

"So propaganda?"

"Three days is catchy."

"And so we celebrate someone dying for our sins—"

"But only for a weekend. Two or three days at most. Could have made brunch."

"I never thought of that before," she said, looking pained. "That kind of diminishes the sacrifice to put it that way, doesn't it?"

"I didn't write the script, I'm just reporting."

"Well anyway, how did we go from saving mankind to bunnies and eggs?"

"Cultural appropriation. It's the name of the game here. And for once, actually accurate."

"What?"

"The three days things was from Egypt. As was the resurrection thing. Ra Ra, he's our man, if he can't save us, we'll use the story again and this time it'll go global. And Ra wasn't even the first. It's a trope. Also the name Easter comes from an ancient pagan English Spring goddess called Eostre."

She stopped chewing and gave me a hard look. We pulled into the parking lot and got out. I put my third and fourth donuts in the bag and put it in my shirt. I'd eat them later. God, they really are good.

We dragged our cases to the platform and waited. We had a few minutes. Taking the train added time, but saved buttloads of money and hassle with the god-awful Salt Lake City Airport.

"The resurrection story wasn't original?" Allie asked after a moment.

"Pa-lease." I'd been waiting to use that all day.

"Bunnies and eggs?"

"Stolen from a dozen fertility rites of conquered pagan cultures. Deliberately, after the fact."

The train rounded the bend and pulled up. I could see that Allie was upset. I figured I should give her some space.

"What's wrong with you?" I said the instant we sat down.

"Sacred things should be..."

"True?"

She shrugged. "Yeah."

"You said propaganda before," I said. "I thought you were on board with the direction this conversation was going."

"Usually I am, but this makes me feel weird."

"Talking religion is a sure fire way to alienate people," I said. "Like if all this flippant talk of mine were recorded and published in a book, it'd probably be pissing off some readers right now."

"How do you mean, deliberately?" she asked.

I hesitated. I didn't want to hurt her feelings. Maybe all the self-help realization stuff I'd been doing was paying off. Then again, maybe not. I said, "It was easier to sell their religion by playing off what the consumers already had."

"Sell? Consumers?"

"Yeah. It's what missionaries do."

"You bashing Mormons again?"

"No," I said defensively. "Not just them. Christianity has a long history of bringing their faith to prosperous people everywhere and ruining their lives."

She looked like she was getting upset again. Or she didn't understand.

"Examples include all of Africa, Central America, South America, North America, Australia, New Zealand, Vietnam, the moon, Trantor—"

"I get it."

"Those places already had some celebration of fertility. Eggs are a symbol of that and since penises and vulvas were out for symbols due to the puritanical nature of the puritanical church, they settled on bunnies. Which fuck like rabbits. And have penises and vulvas."

"How can you be so glib about this? The church has done a lot of good for people."

"Which church?" I never knew Allie to be religious before.

"All of them."

"They've also done a lot of bad."

"Well...so have you."

She turned to look out the window. She was sitting in the aisle seat so she basically turned her entire back to me to take in the Salt Lake industrial areas in all their glory.

We were in a fight.

———

Salt Lake City Airport has been being rebuilt and remodeled and renovated for as long as planes have been an idea. Like Utah's perpetual freeway construction, the airport has fallen prey to a civil job money-machine builders get rich on. I remembered that Tobias Jones, Sylva Rigsdale's dead husband, was a builder. That term used to have a sentimentally honest sound to it, like *Bob the Builder*. Now it fills me with visions of cost-overruns, invoice bilking, tight polo shirts, new tricked-out white trucks with sales stickers still in the window, slow progress, and endless excuses, all this over the whimsical aroma of fresh pine sawdust. It's a scam like no other.

My hatred of flying and airports is well documented. Let me say that it hasn't gotten better. Perfected security theater and brutal baggage costs cannot fail to insult any rational being before the draconian injury of a seat that would cramp a comatose toddler. New wonders of inconvenience and aggravation have been added in modern times, not the least of which is the irate passenger.

Although irate passengers could be seen as a natural byproduct of the airline industry's sadistic treatment of travelers, it has, like many things of late, been appropriated by a brand of screaming victim-complexed idiots who get their news from psyops dark websites and Rupert Murdoch's oozing asshole. I could have sympathy for someone who just had to max their credit card to get their insulin aboard the plane, and split a femur cramming into the seat, but not the no-neck Neanderthal who, just as the plane pulls from the gate, discovered to his horror that when there was no room for his carry-on. He'd been the last to get on the plane, though I'd seen him sitting at the gate cutting his toenails. Really. Cutting his toenails while we queued up. He'd barely made the plane, pushing aside door-closing stewards. Of course there was no room in any overhead compartment and to put it under his seat would require amputations.

He'd be without his bag for the whole flight. His bag "with everything in it."

The attendants sympathized, tried to take his bag, explained that it wouldn't cost him any money and that it'd be waiting at the door of the plane upon landing. He wouldn't have to go to the carousel. I don't even think they were trying to put in the hold, just not with him. The solution was easy smeasy. Logical and neat. The very routine explained at the gate over a scratchy PA before boarding.

Maybe his toe-fungus had distracted him and he'd miss the warning. It could have been an honest mistake—if you were a brain-dead crustacean— but this creep took it a step farther, first by screaming at the poor woman with two children sitting across the aisle from him who'd put her diaper bag in the bin, then by screaming at the first, second and third flight attendant as they tried to calm him down.

I was three rows back of the action. Middle seat. Allie was five and on the other side, also in the middle. Seating choices were limited with such short notice. I saw the man deliberately seek for sibilants to better spatter the spectators with spittle because either moisture would make his point, or it was a callback to COVID days and he was trying to infect people. I tried to think the former, Zen that I was, but it was obvious that it was the latter.

"Stupid sheeple!" he sprayed. "Do you want me to put a mask on too?"

There it was.

"No sir, that's no longer—"

"It's all a hoax to control us!" He held out the last S like a Rainbird sprinkler across the seats.

"I take it you're not vaccinated," I said when the conversation took a lull. I hate lulls in conversation.

He turned on me. "Hell no! It's a short walk from a vaccine to the gas chambers."

That caused another lull, as all the sentient people tried to connect the dots between luggage space, pandemic prevention and genocide. Before anyone could bridge the logic gap, he began singing a medley of patriotic songs.

"*God bless America! At least I know I'm free! By the dawn's early light! Don't tread on my rights!*"

Not sure where the last one was from. Maybe improv.

The plane lurched ominously back toward the gate. But the man was bolstered by all the camera phones pointing at him. He waved a mask he'd produced from his pocket, horked up a really good blob of snot and spat into it. Still not sure why.

He screamed obscenities at a woman with pink hair, more at a mixed-race couple, accused the woman traveling alone with her child of being a home-wrecking whore who probably hung out with Deb, whoever she was. Reaching new volumes and bringing arm motions into it, he swore death upon, "Antifa, the enemies of the righteousness, of democracy, decency and 'Merica." He wanted to see George Soros and Jane Fonda shot. And asked us to "Stop the steal!"

When one of the flight attendants, a frail woman of African American descent told him clearly and plainly to sit down and shut up, and that he was breaking federal laws by his behavior, he calmed down and apologized. Just kidding. He pushed her. She stumbled back a step but was caught by a passenger. The aisle was full of people; the patriot, three flight attendants—one now in someone's arms—and a dozen able-bodied Antifa sympathizers who'd been praying that the jerk would do something like push a woman.

Who says there isn't a god?

The scrum didn't last long and it was well documented. I got some really good closeups of his face turning bright red under the weight of three steroid-enhanced athletes as the Black flight attendant bound his arms, legs, and mouth with a half mile of duct tape. When we pulled back up to the gate, three security men with guns and bad attitudes dragged him off the plane to the applause of the rest of us.

Everyone sat down and the plane returned to the runway as if this kind of thing happened every day. With some chagrin, yes chagrin, I concluded that it probably did.

I put my seat belt on and leaned back. I'd undone it during the event thinking I could lend a good dick-punch if called for, but the aisle was too full by then. Besides, I think someone beat me to it. The child I think, the one with the home-wrecking whore mother. A precocious little seven-year-old boy who I believe—I'd need to check the video to be sure—landed a clean right jab into the creep's shriveled man bits just as the rugby team got involved. Even seven-year-olds love their mothers. Actually, especially seven-year-olds. What the fuck was he thinking?

"He's brainwashed by that QAnon cult," said the man next to me.

"I said that out loud, did I?"

"I like the bit about the shriveled man bits. Good line. You in comedy?"

"Actually…"

"I thought I recognized you," he said. "Caught your show last year. You opened for Perry Whitehouse."

"Always good to meet a fan."

"I'm Bruce."

"I'm Flaner. Tony Flaner."

"That's right."

"Do you have a last name, or should I just call you Bruce."

"I do, but Bruce is fine."

"But you do have a last name?"

"Of course."

"So why don't you want me to know it? Are you hiding something?" It was a bit. Not the friendliest one, fun in the right circumstances. Maybe. Probably. I hadn't found one yet, but it was a bit.

He looked at me warily. "Allenby."

"Do you have ID?" I was deadpan.

He looked sheepish. Glanced over me for an attendant. Then back.

"Oh, man. That was good," he said. "You had me. Nice. Gotta keep on my toes around you."

Looks like I found the moment. Redemption.

"What takes you to Eugene?" he asked.

"I'm checking out the cult conclave," said I

"The what…oh. ICOHEP." His face brightened up. "Me too."

"You were saying that guy was in a cult?"

"Him? Yeah, that QAnon shit gets into your brain. My supervisors say it's a type of brainwashing. Targeted and paranoid. Lost a lot of good people from the bureau to that. We had to purge. I'm sure there are still people there, but the worst ones are gone. We hope."

"What do you do?"

He hesitated just a second, a fraction of a moment of a slice of a smaller moment, a minuscule flash drive vector search and retrieve. "I'm in sales. Industrial supplies."

"Yeah?"

"What do you do?"

"I'm a comic. You know that."

"No. I mean for your day job."

Ouch.

"I'm a private investigator." I gave him my card because that's what you do with cards.

"'Accomplished private detective,'" he read.

"That's me."

"Oh, yeah. I read something about that. Didn't put it together. You on a case now?"

I hesitated just a second, a fraction of a moment of a slice of a smaller moment, a minuscule flash drive vector search retrieve. "Nah, just shopping for a new cult."

"What was your old one?"

"Quakers."

I could tell he wasn't sure if I was joking or not, which put me at ease. Creating confusion is my Zen.

The plane paused for an instant, a second, a moment, and then lurched forward and the cabin filled with the roar of engines. I instinctively raised my arms above my head.

"Hands up!" I yelled. It was my thing. G forces require raised hands. It was in *Prometheus* if you don't believe me, or ride a rollercoaster.

The ascending Gs pulled at my arms, weighted me into my ample ass, and pushed the forward seat into my knees. I glanced around to see if anyone else had their hands up. No one in front. A glance back, and I was saddened to see none there either. Allie wasn't playing along.

7

I'VE HEARD IT SAID, possibly because I said it, that Eugene is where the hippies went when San Francisco got too expensive. Wise words. There is a sixties vibe there and the connection to the flower children and hippie movement is more than just an exodus from gentrification. Ken Kesey, author of *One Flew Over the Cuckoo's Nest*, was one of the original Merry Pranksters, the people who brought you the *Electric Kool-Aid Acid Test*—written by Tom Wolfe that time—and the Further bus that led in a zeitgeist kind of way to the Beatles' *Magical Mystery Tour*. Wolfe's book explains it. Ken lived in a little berg called Pleasant Hill, which isn't Eugene, but is in the same county, Lane County. Though Lane County has Eugene, a university, hospital and bagels, Pleasant Hill is a farm community, barely a zit on a map of the state, so people say Ken was from Eugene. I say it was because Ken died. Everyone dies. It's a thing.

Beyond famous white male writers, Eugene has a long history of political unrest which puts it on the map of activist hot-spots and not always for the good guys. Before the influx of flower children, Eugene was a bastion of hate and racism. 1924 saw a famously massive crowd gathered for a Ku Klux Klan parade which ended on Skinner's Butte, a hill they think is a mountain. Segregation hung on long and hard and even as late as 2017 some asshole vandalized a synagogue. If you ask the locals about Eugene politically, they might well say that Eugene is a liberal island in a conservative sea and sometimes the waves crash in. Maybe they wouldn't say that exactly, but something like it.

Eugene in 1970 was a big year for unrest. With the KKK relegated to Springfield across the river, and Cambodia being leveled in a secret escalation of war crimes, University of Oregon students got good and active. As part of the national anti-war movement, they got up in metaphorical arms over the ROTC being on campus. After much protesting, the school decided they'd keep it anyway, so the unhappy students ransacked the building and broke shit, giving the nascent fascist police state a chance to play with teargas. Later, a group occupied the administration building on campus for a sit-in. They negotiated the sleep-in provided they were peaceful. They would have been, had the National Guard, à la Kent State, not showed up and, again using a weapon illegal in foreign wars, teargassed the folks outside the building. Three hundred chilling people swelled to two thousand pissed-off ones. They blocked traffic and broke more shit. In keeping with a Eugene tradition, they bombed a building. Yes a bomb. Bombs were not always the weapons of the right and the fanatic. Well, okay, always the fanatic, but these years saw the left blowing shit up left and right, particularly in Eugene, by the left. In 1967 bombs went off around the ROTC building and other military-themed edifices, so the 1970 bomb was not unheard of. Good times, good times.

The Vietnam War ended and so did the bombings. Kinda. For a while. Actually arson was now the weapon of choice. Eugenian activists burned down a car dealership and some logging stuff in the name of conservation, Justice for racism, Anti-Globalism and whatnots. All good causes, but damn. Arson? That's dangerous. Eugene reported 125 fire attacks between 1997 and 2001 alone. Shit. That's a lot. Good thing it rains in Eugene. It rains in Eugene a lot. It rains in Eugene a goddamned lot. The annual rains begin in November and don't let up until April. It's the same goddamn storm. Yes I spent some time there and can testify that the rains of Oregon, can, if left to their own devices, wash your soul clean away. Maybe fires would help. Maybe that's why so much arson. People just trying to stay sane.

Eugene was founded by Eugene Skinner. Skinner's Butte, the KKK hill, was named after him. As was the town. He built a cabin above the flood-plain after some local natives, Indians by his reckoning, warned him about floods. This is one of the few historical incidents I have discovered where the white settler listened to the native population and didn't have to learn a hard lesson himself. 'Him,' because it was always a him back then.

Eugene is between two rivers, the Willamette and the McKenzie. Willamette is pronounced like damn-it. Get that wrong and you're marked as a foreigner faster than if you want to know what love is, are cold as ice, or hot blooded. These rivers flood and not everyone was quick to listen to the wisdom of the locals. Before Eugene the place was called Skinner's Mud Hole. It's apt. The mud in Eugene is one part epoxy and two parts tears from broken hearts. You need a pressure washer to clean your boots. No joke.

Okay, I digress in my digression.

Oregon was the first state to legalize mushrooms. Not button mushrooms or shiitakes. You know I'm talking about the interesting ones—Lion's Mane and Turkey Tail. No. Duh. I mean magic mushrooms. Like the magic school bus and the electric Kool-Aid, but with organic molecules. Eugene was key in this. Pot is a staple crop, was even before it was legalized. Mushrooms were never far behind. Ted Tessner, Allie's contact in Eugene, makes his living with mushrooms, all kinds, and now especially the fun ones. He was a force for the legalization of the stuff: *Free the Fungi!* was his rallying cry. Simple. Direct. Surreal. All good. I find all this interesting because back in the day, Eugene was dry even before prohibition. How things have changed. Back in those dark days, people had to go across the river to Springfield, often referred to as Springtucky to get snockered. This was a small inconvenience. The matter of a single bridge. Thus during those years, Springfield thrived on sin and taxi rides while Eugene swam in mud. But they had the university. So that's something. Eugene and Springfield are now so connected that they are basically the same thing, though Springfield keeps its conservative reputation and semi-reasonable rents while Eugene is known for protests and over-excited police retaliation to said protests.

Now Eugene thrives on drugs in one way or another. After the University of Oregon, the biggest employer is the hospital group. Typical of a dying culture don't you think? Anyway, like I said, drugs. Hospitals have drugs, and I've been to the U of O campus. There are drugs there too. Believe me. *Animal House* was filmed there if that tells you anything. And, oh, did I mention the Country Fair? It's an annual event like a hippie Renaissance Festival which caters to the curious with ribbons, music, dancing and clouds of pot smoke, but where invited guests camp overnight and get higher than God after the tourist crowds are ushered away at dusk. There's live music. Bare boobies. Humus. Tie-dye.

My original time in Eugene wasn't long, a few months during college when, on a whim to escape the Utah snow, I transferred. There I learned that cold is relative. There's 'foot of snow cold' in Utah which is chill and then there's 'omnipresent winter rain cold' that seeps past coats, sweaters, long-johns and layers of epidermis to freeze you from the inside out. It's a cold like no other. That and the fact that I never made friends in Eugene meant I didn't stay long. While I was there, I heard all the tales though, saw the sites, hiked Skinner's Butte, and came home just as the rain stopped. I was told the place is nice in the summer, when the bare breasts come out at the fair, but I'd had enough. I'll take frost to mold any day. It was like living in a petri-dish. In Utah you plant something and you get the local bishopric to pray over it that it'll live half a season before drying up. In Eugene, you garden with bulldozers. That says something about life and all, but the place is a cage of blackberry briar, concrete mud, and mold. So much mold.

I was prepared for the worst when the plane landed. I had my raincoat ready, my rain hat, my wool socks and boots, REI branded so I'd fit in, all to fight both cold and mold which is how I remembered Eugene the night before when I packed.

I waited at the gate for Allie to come off the plane and when she did, I gave her a big corny grin that I hoped would make us friends again. She responded with a pained one but took my hand.

"Have a nice flight?" I asked.

"Sure."

"Did you see the asshat get dragged off the plane?"

"Yes. We all did."

"Wasn't that something?"

"Yep."

Conversation extinguished, we found our way to the curb. We hadn't checked any luggage. Perhaps it was our fault the man didn't have room for all his things. We might have checked them, but we hadn't had time for the airline to run a credit check on us for that kind of expense, so we just had one bag each.

"We'll ask the Ridez about a hotel," I said.

"You called for one?"

"No but I will."

"Don't bother," she said. "I have it all arranged."

"You've already arranged a ride for us?"

"Yep." Bouncing on her tip-toes she searched up and down the pickup curb. "I arranged for us to have a place to stay too."

"When did you do all this?"

"On the plane."

"I'm impressed."

"Good," she said. "See? Isn't it good you brought me along?"

I was going to say something about her gloomy mood affecting my concentration, but I could tell she was coming out of it.

"You rock," I said instead.

"I'm not mad at you," she said, reading my mind as she so often does.

"No? Then what are—were—you?" Notice here the power of my applied grammar to get past problems.

"Provoked."

"Much better," I said. "That way I get all the blame." I never said *I* wasn't mad.

"I meant in the sense of facing a provocative question."

"Oh. I guess that makes sense."

"I'll get over it. Don't worry."

"Good," I said. "Because so far you've shown yourself to be a great little helper."

"Oh that's not demeaning, is it?"

"I meant it to be cute."

"You are, but you can also…provoke."

"People are too sensitive," I said. "Comedy is confrontational. I'm a comedian."

"I thought you were a detective."

"I am many things to many people. Some people call me Morris."

The conversation about people being too sensitive was a sensitive subject in the group. By group here, I mean the gang, Perry, Dara, Standard, Garrett and Critter. As comedians, we've all struggled with the new hyper-sensitive milieu of social comment. People are quick to be offended and be really offended when only a little offense was meant. Perry's terrified of being canceled on Twitter nearly as much as he is terrified of being disappeared by men in black suits. Some days it's a toss-up. People need to develop a thicker skin and control their own damn emotions better. John Cleese said, and we comedians listen to John Cleese, that "people who cannot control their own feelings try to control other people's behavior." I get that there's a reason for political sensitivity, but it's really gotten scary. I've heard it called woke aggression, a state where members of the fold who misstep are attacked harsher than the real enemies of progress. It reminds me of how religions go after heretics within their own ranks with more vicious zeal than they do against 'non-believers.' They eat their own.

"You ever think that political Twitter or whatever it's called now, acts like a cult?" I ventured.

She paused then and thought about it. I'd provoked her again. She half squinted her eyes and tugged her lip up to one side as if squeezing ideas out of the left hemisphere of her brain. She tilted to the other side as if catching by gravity the electrical activity, her auburn hair dancing over her shoulder and she pondered.

"You talking about the zealotry?"

"Yeah."

"I can see that," she said.

"Twitter is toxic."

"I think that's their official motto."

I hugged Allie, and she gave me a kiss right on the mouth in front of everyone. I liked that. It was comforting. I was often at my best around her, or at least trying to be. We had our quarrels, this one being a new one. Most often we argued about the distance between our two lives; her in Moab and me in Salt Lake City. Sometimes we argued about the toilet seat. She won't stop putting the lid down. I've noticed in the last little while, however, that our bickering has grown more frequent, sometimes a little heated. Nothing terminal, but a warning sign. She's hinted that she'd like to make our relationship permanent. I think she means marriage, but it could be something else. Entombed together in a pyramid comes to mind. I've done the marriage thing and am a little gun-shy. Don't get me wrong. I love her. She's the world to me, but what would a piece of paper do for our relationship? How would that help?

Seeing Ted Tessner pull up in a shiny black top of the line Range Rover with a dog nearly as large as the bulging vehicle, and then watching Allie run into his open arms and get a big hug by both the man and the beast, I thought that maybe a legally binding contract might be in my interests after all.

8

IF I HAVE A FAULT, and I'm not saying I do, it might be that I'm prone to jealousy. And I eat too much. And have an issue with my internal censor and impulse control. I also don't dress well or take much seriously. I don't mow my lawn except when forced to by the city, and I think God's own rainfall is more than enough car wash for any vehicle. Also, I swear more than I should. I collect things and am a borderline hoarder. I've been known to physically lash out at assholes, with coffee to the face and punches to the dick. I am too honest for most people to take. I'm a go-getter. I used to do drugs. I still do, but I used to as well. I'm afraid of heights. Once I cheated at *Monopoly* because that's really what the game is trying to get you to do. That's how I explained it in fourth grade anyway. The game is a mirror of the greed and inequality of the capitalist system where the rich get richer and the poor poorer until everyone but one blood-sucking landlord leach is brutally bankrupted. It forces the honest player to think outside of the box. Stealing is inferred by the very nature of the enterprise. Why is it okay for the landlord to happily extort hundreds of dollars from me just because I landed on Park Place, where, believe you me, I didn't want to be, but then goes all ape-shit and calls his mom when the bank goes light a couple Cs? He got his goddamn money, didn't he? I mean, really. That game is toxic. The only one I know that's worse is *Life*. Don't get me started about that box of vapid worker-bee proletariat propaganda. Is it any wonder our parents turned to drugs?

But I digress. Where was I? Oh, yeah; if I have one fault, it's that I'm prone to jealousy. Allie's job gives her plenty of opportunity to test this. She rubs elbows with rich and famous folk who are always beautiful people. The rich part of rich and famous always translates to beautiful. You ever see Elon

Musk before he was rich? He used to be bald. I mean ugly baboon-ass bald. Suddenly his hair is back, and he has enough money to fly into space, the better to piss on people from the greatest height. He's still baboon-ass ugly, but in a new and innovative way.

Ted Tessner was beautiful. I knew him from the mushroom wars and his recent rise to rich people after the spores settled. Once Allie confessed that she'd had him as a client, I'd naturally spent an hour stalking him on the internet, learning, among other things, that he was single. Jealousy engaged but in low gear. I figured she'd met him, and would be able to say hello at the ICOHEP cult conclave, but I didn't know that they were on a long, lingering hug basis. Or a pick us up at the airport level. Jealously skipped second for third gear with a quick hi-goodbye as it slammed into fourth looking for overdrive.

The dog was a Saint Bernard called Psilly. It was tall as a horse and as it reared up to slobber on my girlfriend, I had visions of headless horsemen. The big black beast needed a pumpkin, but I could supply the fire.

Tessner pulled the Psilly dog off with a hip check that would have worked on a Ranger forward. He stepped back and, wearing a grin that I thought could be improved by slapping it with a live salmon, surveyed Allie like she was a distant niece who'd all grown up.

"Thanks for coming for us," she said.

His face fell a little, his eyebrow rose. "Us?"

Overdrive engaged.

His eyes searched for someone who'd be traveling with Allie. Allie was dressed nice, I should say, faded jeans that fit just right, comfortable traveling shoes, a loose flannel shirt with buttons undone because women have to do that. His eyes passed over me since I was dressed for a monsoon, and kept going. He looked past me to a very tall Black bald man standing at the curb a few yards up, a chunk out of his ear, apparently waiting for a Ridez. The man stared daggers back at Ted.

"Tony, come say hi to Ted."

I stepped forward. Ted offered me his hand to shake. Mine slid into my pockets.

"Are we going to have a problem here?" I asked.

"Jesus, Tony," said Allie. "What's got into you?"

I tried to mount a steely gaze at Tessner. He was older than me, in his indeterminate sixties. He had silver hair which he famously wore in a ponytail but was today loose in Fabio fashion. His skin was ruddy and tan, an utterly alien hue for Oregon, I might add, and his clothes were impeccably hipster, down to the Birkenstocks and a cluster of friendship bands around his wrist. He had a watch that would function in the Mariana Trench and a unique artsy gold ring clustering emeralds and diamonds that could have paid to feed the Asian subcontinent for a year or cover for the maintenance on the Range Rover for a month, depending on his mood.

My steely gaze shifted from his amused one to Allie's horrified one. Then my gaze turned inward as I'd been taught from hours of doing shit-all sitting cross-legged on a floor, and I realized, sooner than usual, that I was being a dick.

"I meant I hope we're not going to be any trouble." I offered him my hand but Psilly thinking perhaps I had a treat for her, engulfed my fingers up to the elbow.

"That means she likes you," said Ted.

"She's a sweetie," said Allie.

I removed my drool-dripping sleeve and agreed through gritted teeth that she was a sweetie.

"Anybody seen my watch?" I said.

Allie elbowed me to let me know she'd seen through my little tantrum.

"I'm working on it," I muttered.

We climbed into the luxury English jeep and hit the road. I sat in the back with Psilly. Allie in the front, because reasons. Our luggage was somewhere nearby. The vehicle was so vast I regretted having no AirTags on them. Maybe Ted had a native guide I could borrow to find them.

Wafts of conversation floated back to me as Psilly nuzzled my crotch.

"Oh, the detective," Ted said. "That Tony Flaner."

"I get mistaken for Tony Flaner the fletcher all the time," I said. "It's okay."

Allie's smile tensed.

"So you're on a case?" he asked.

"What makes you say that? Couldn't I be here for the ICOHEP?"

"What does ICOHEP stand for?" Ted asked.

"You should know. You're the organizer."

"I think he's quizzing you," said Allie.

"No..."

"He's a sarcastic one, isn't he?" said Ted.

"And adorable. Cuddly and adorable," I added.

I could tell Ted was ribbing me, there was a good-naturedness about him that under other circumstances I would have appreciated, but between jealousy and the immediate crack of my cover, I wasn't in the mood.

"Does ICOHEP stand for 'Iron Clad Olive Hunters Eating Pizza?'"

"No, that was last week."

Allie laughed like he'd just discovered comedy. I could hear my teeth grind in my skull. I tried again. "'Intercollegiate Organization of Heaving Electric Penises?'"

"Eh, no."

"How 'bout, 'Incontinent Cripples Orgasm—'"

"No!" It was Allie, real terror in her voice, a tight grin over her teeth, a forced smile that was not unlike a growl. No, not unlike it at all. To fit the point, Psilly barked at the edge in her trainer's voice. Locking me in a gaze I felt in the back of my skull, Allie said, "It stands for 'Interfaith Congress of Holistic Enlightened People.'"

"No, that's not it," I said.

"What?" It was Tessner and he was confused. Ahhhh...a hesitant confused pause for just half a moment of an instant but I relished that tiny victory, like a rare and arousing fragrance. Floral and musky. Nothing like the panting dog breath splattering across my face.

Ted recovered quickly and said, "The world is full of trouble—climate change, inequality. Hunger. Ignorance. Traditional thinking hasn't worked to solve any of these, in fact, it's only made them worse." I could tell he was gearing into a speech he'd rehearsed. "What the earth needs, what Gaea, deserves—"

"Gaea?" I said.

"Gaea. The earth," he explained. I knew this but interrupting him seemed like the thing to do.

"Okay. Go on," I said. "Gaea has needs and you're the man to fulfill them?"

Allie turned her forced smile to the back seat and got it licked.

"She's a sweetie," I said.

"Gaea." Ted, not noticing or doing a good job of ignoring my tension, went on. "Mother Earth."

"The planet?"

"Yes."

"A.k.a. Terra Firma. Terra to her friends."

"That's the one."

"Needy thing."

"The planet—"

"That's another one."

"Let the man speak, Tony. 'Kay?" I wasn't the only one filling the car with tension. What had gotten into Allie?

Finding yet another way to begin, Tessner did. "It's no secret that the world is headed in the wrong direction. Between global warming, tribalism, gender inequality, pan-social economic éclat divergence..."

That was a new one.

We were on a freeway heading into Eugene. I actually didn't know where we were staying. I had been thinking a bed and breakfast, but hadn't done anything to arrange it. Thank God Allie had been on the ball. Left to myself, I'd be standing on the curb flagging a Ridez and feeling lucky to find a motel in Springfield. Come to think of it, if I were alone, that would be fine. But with Allie, romantically I yearned for a bed and breakfast with a hot tub maybe and prancing deer perhaps. She probably got us into the hotel where the ICOHEP—whatever that stood for—was happening. Or not. I was curious and I thought to ask, but I knew Allie was ready to pounce if I interrupted again.

"Where are we?" I interrupted again.

"Shhhhh." Allie was quicker than I'd anticipated. Tessner didn't miss a beat.

"...Eurasia and Micronesia in particular have shown a tendency..."

This was the Oregon of dreams. A beautiful sunny day, a sky blue enough to swim in, enough green to redefine the word lush. It was not raining. If Oregon always looked like this, people would stay here. I pretended that I didn't know what the state looked like most days, pushed aside the freezing rain that made three feet of snow and an orange inversion look welcoming, the mud that sucked your sock off with your boot, the blackberries bushes that swallowed children whole. It was nice this day. I was happy to be here.

"...homogenesis of enlightened folktales and mythological..."

Tessner took an exit to the city center. Eugene is hidden by trees. Things grow here. Rain is good for something, I guess. Still, there was a verifiable city center that pokes up above a tree line like a mirage in a foliage sea. We snaked exits to the ground level where cars vied with bicycles for right of way and volume. Bikes are a thing in Eugene. Lots of people ride them like they're transportation. The city actually embraces them. It's a natural side effect of disallowing parking places.

Tessner nearly drove over a group of ten-speeders with matching shirts who didn't think traffic semaphores applied to bikes, then he tried to make a right only to have an old man in a recumbent cycle blast him with a handheld air horn that nearly drowned out his flavorful curses. A woman with dreads on a tricycle bigger than a Buick looked on and shook her head.

Tessner took it all in stride, not even pausing his spiel.

"...Cooperation instead of competition. Together instead of apart. We've assembled here the cream of the crop of great forward-focused organizations, linked together by a love of the transcendent, the belief in the brotherhood—and/or sisterhood—of..."

I yawned. The dog managed, somehow, to get her tongue into my mouth. I pushed her away, scraped slobber off my teeth with the shoulder restraint and glared at the dog, giving her my best 'never on the first date' look. Towering above me, she looked pleased as could be.

"...a true brotherhood and/or sisterhood of..."

We drove beneath a banner stretched between two streetlights. *ICOHEP envisioning the future direction of humanity.* The graphic was of the green and/or blue earth held in the talons of white dove, an olive branch held in its teeth like a pirate's dagger.

Up ahead I saw the hotel—a Squire resort, a franchise of decent repute, a skyscraper for this locale with nine floors. Trees. In front of it and flooding out its front doors was a mob of angry people.

"Peace is humankind's natural state. We are all born good. We care. Love is who we are. We are sharing. We are caring. This is a convention of peace-based solutions on behalf of a planet crying for help from its loving children. I present to you this; the first Interfaith Congress of Holistic Enlightened People."

"Don't look now," I said. "But one of those enlightened people just sucker-punched one of the loving children."

Allie didn't shush me because, first of all, Tessner left a natural pause which might have suggested his speech and/or harangue was over, and second, there was a holistic riot going on at the hotel.

Half a block away, Tessner slowed and stopped the car. We all leaned forward to watch. It was a full-on melee made up of at least four distinguishable factions. One group in orange jumpsuits rushed a pack of conservatively-dressed middle Americans in sensible suits and long dresses, who fled holding up crucifixes with too many crossbars in an attempt to ward the coming crush. A man in a leather jacket and gun-metal blue tattoos on his neck holding a knife longer than Psilly's tongue, was cold-cocked by a woman in a black robe with what looked like the statue of Janus, the two-faced Roman god. He fell like unregulated crypto currency, his knife skittering under a lunch wagon. That woman had but a short time to celebrate because she was blindsided herself by a man with leaf-cluttered dreadlocks, leather pants and only one shoe. Grappling, they fell atop the biker dude's prone body and pulled each others' hair.

The scrum rolled out into the street, a mass of bodies which made me ponder why rugby never caught on in the States. Following behind them, a myriad of mismatched men charged a cluster of high-fashioned bodyguards hustling a couple into a limousine that sped off before they could enter, leaving them on the curb like lost luggage. A cloud of white spray erupted as they arrived, and screams filled the air along with it. Someone pulled out a vape pen, dragged it across the concrete, breaking it open, and wielded it like a lightsaber, the tip glowing red. The chemical cloud combusted, and with a flash and a woompf everyone had curly eyebrows over their crazed eyes.

Psilly barked and took a year off my life while testing the acoustic strength of the Range Rover's windows. Her alarm was in anticipation of the wailing of sirens that quickly met our human ears coming from all directions and coming fast toward us.

"Oh, yeah," I said. "I forgot. Happy Easter everyone."

9

IT TOOK about an hour and seventeen police cars, two SWAT vans, a bunch of cops on bicycles and a taco vendor to stop the riot. The taco vendor used a knotted garbage bag to hold back a woman with a leather clutch and murder in her eyes. Ambulances arrived but couldn't get through the police barricades. This being Eugene, a place with a history of social unrest and brutal retaliation—and this society truly looked unrested—the cops had donned their black riot gear, covered their badge numbers, and waded into the mass of holistically enlightened rioters with billy clubs and liberal use of pepper spray.

When it was over, six people were taken to the hospital, most from police reaction, but not all. The one guy who met the wrong face of Janus was carted away and one of the bodyguards, one who used a lot of product on their hair, was taken in for burns after that vape-ignited cloud went up.

As the paramedics guided stretchers between the cop cars, we left the luxury SUV to make our way forward. Or rather, Ted left the car and we followed. An unhappy St. Bernard stayed behind and complained about it with six hundred and ten decibels.

"You should put a barrel around Psilly's neck," I suggested. "Not for first aid stuff; just for wet wipes. Maybe toothpaste."

My witty banter was ignored as we were immediately challenged by the first cop we ran into.

"You from the media?" His helmet was off but his face was covered behind a black balaclava. Maybe it was a turned up turtleneck. In any event. We couldn't see his lips moving.

"No," answered Tessner. "I want to get into the hotel."

"Not media? No cameras? No microphones?"

"No."

"Good. This is a crime scene. No pictures allowed. No reporters. If I see any of you trying to record this I'll be within my rights to arrest you."

"I'm not sure that's—"

Allie elbowed me. "Read the room, Tony."

The cop gave us a good hard look. I noticed his billy club was soiled with something wet. Piss by the smell of it.

"Okay, you can pass," he said.

"Thanks officer," said Tessner.

The front of the building was bodily injury, the lobby was property damage.

I could not see a chair standing upright, no table that hadn't been knocked over, no stand of local brochures intact. The plants had fled their broken pots; a trail of soil marked where they skidded after their first launch and then a pile where they landed.

The walls were intact. Also intact was a big reflective sign behind the front desk reading, in sparkling slanting advertising calligraphy over smoked mirror, *Welcome to the Eugene Squire Resort*.

"Why are you staring at the sign?" asked Allie.

"It reminds me of a mirror in a saloon, you know the very breakable ones behind bars? This wasn't much of a fight if that didn't get touched. Missed opportunity for such an enlightened group."

Ted looked at me like I'd told him sister wore boots. It's a very particular look.

"Sorry, Ted," said I. "I know your KOTEX thing really meant something to you."

Allie jabbed me again. Ted looked through me.

A man in faded blue jeans and a simple tan short-sleeved button-down shirt, stepped out of the elevator with a group of similarly casual people. He surveyed the space, took in the chaos and destruction, the faces of the police, the stragglers who hadn't been questioned or cuffed or bandaged yet. The man lit upon Ted, whose eyes lit up to meet those of this simple man.

He stepped forward and brought his hands tougher, rubbed them and said in a voice as smooth as real butter on fresh baked sourdough, "Let's put this place back together. We got this."

Enter John Smith. The guru who I'd come to discredit. The man who'd stolen the affection of Sylvia Ridgsdale, leaving the poor rich Jones children slightly less rich.

I studied him as he, with the five others with him, moved quickly and deliberately to put the place back in order. I'd seen his picture on the web the night before when I'd done a quick search on the Church of the Third Eye Opened, 'COTTEO.' He'd struck me as very average looking, very simple. Nothing grand or engaging. He didn't have one of those million-dollar smiles you can buy for six thousand and charge on a Discovery Card. He didn't have a stature that would awe the natives, or a face that would soothe a crying child. His voice was something though. Yes, there was that. And his eyes. There was a twinkle in them that didn't show up in the computer, a sparkle that spoke of mischievousness and joy, or maybe just residual pepper spray and an early eye infection.

Ted moved to help him, but paused and said, "You two check in. We'll meet up later."

"Maybe we should help clean up," said Allie.

"No," I said, sensing work. "We didn't do this. Plus I need a shower and a breath mint. I had a #metoo moment with your old student."

Allie went to the desk. I watched Smith and tried to gauge his age. Early thirties, give or take a decade. He was six foot one inch tall, give or take a foot. I reminded myself I needed to get better at that kind of thing if I wanted to keep calling myself a detective. Or not.

"Excuse me." A woman was behind me, gathering travel pamphlets off the floor. I was standing on some.

"Sorry," I said. "I have a thing for—"

My sudden hesitation made her hesitate and she looked up at me.

"Hi," I said.

"Hi," said Sylvia Rigsdale.

"Come here often?"

"No. You?"

"No. Not really."

We looked at each other.

"Do you mind?" she said.

"Mind what?"

"Moving?"

"Oh right." I got off the papers.

"Tony, come on." It was Allie. She waved a paper envelope I suspected in my detective mind of housing hotel room keys.

We went to the elevator just as a porter appeared with our bags from Tessner's Range Rover. Up we went to the fifth floor and found our comfortable economically priced room. I tipped the porter ten bucks. I'm not sure if that was right, but if it was wrong, I don't want to be told about it. I have enough ways to second guess myself.

"Who's paying for this room?"

"I thought your clients," Allie said from the bathroom.

"Oh, yeah." I half expected Ted to have sprung for the room, in which case I was going to accuse him of being a chintzy tightwad. As it was, I was very pleased with the accommodations. Not too much, not too little. A king-sized bed, a desk, a sitting area. A fridge and microwave that I could fit in my suitcase, a safe in the closet and a balcony. It didn't have a tub, but the shower had tile and a wand you could do serious damage with in a close-quarter water fight.

After Allie had unpacked her bag into the bureau. I put mine on the folding luggage rack by the TV and brushed my teeth. She said, "What do you want to do now?"

I pondered the question with a calm and groping mind of calm mindfulness and gropiness. Pondering ponderously, I propositioned that this was a proposition, a sexual pass. Allie once said that vacation sex is the best sex ever. Worst postcard I ever got. Not really. That was a joke. Nobody writes postcards anymore.

Another more important pondering possibility of the first potential proposition was forgiveness. That grand highest form of love and divinity, the other cheek thing that has so challenged wannabe altruists for centuries. She appeared to have forgiven me my earlier religious heresy, and possibly, more immediately, my needling her friend and our benefactor, Ted Tessner. She could have been mad over that. Might have been. Should have been. Here was something I'd actually done that could be held against me, on a personal level. The other was just a disagreement on dogma, and when has that ever escalated to long-term hurt feelings or violence? The Tessner stuff was a byproduct of that one flaw of mine and thus worthy of rebuke. But she was beatifically chill.

"Let's have sex," I said.

"Really?" Surprise.

"We can go to the lobby."

"Really?" More surprise

"Yeah."

"You want to have sex in the lobby?"

"No. It's an either or thing."

"Your phrasing needs help."

"Maybe"

"Besides, you had your chance to help clean up and you ran like a scalded cat."

"I'll do that if I have to, but let's put manual labor on the bottom of the list."

"So you really want to...oh. The case. Wait. Was that them?"

"COTTEO and Smith and Sylvia herself."

"The game is afoot!" she said.

"That's my line."

"No, it's Holmes'."

"So it should be mine."

"You missed it."

"Fair cop."

We got on the elevator.

"I like Ted," I said.

"Bullshit."

"No. I do. I'm just insanely jealous of him."

"I didn't notice."

The doors closed.

"Why aren't you pissed?" I asked.

"At your behavior in the car? You mellowed out."

"Verbally only."

"It was enough."

I said. "Are you being like Zen and stuff now?"

"Yep."

"Ahh, nice one."

"You don't get out of your path to enlightenment just because you're on a case."

"Now I feel patronized."

"What? How?"

"I don't need you to lead by example. I can be chill."

"You ever think that maybe I'm chill because I like being chill?"

"It is good cover if you and Ted had an affair."

Her chill cracked a bit beneath her hot stare.

"That's beneath you," she said.

"I was joking."

"You were probing."

"My thoughts think themselves." It was something we saw in one of the books we read.

"Get a clue."

"I'm working on it."

The doors opened in the lobby. It was a different room. Not a thing out of place. No cops. No pools of blood. Just a lobby.

"Wow," said Allie.

"Wow," I agreed, "but don't change the subject. I'll chill. You just don't sleep with Ted. It'd hurt my feelings."

"You don't either."

"What does that...oh."

"Duh."

That's right. Ted Tessner was famously bisexual. Rich as he is, when he divorced his first wife, it made the news. When he later divorced his first husband, it too, made the news.

"Well, what does it say that you weren't jealous then?"

"Maybe that you just met?"

"Well...well...well...okay."

I have a lot of insecurities, like most people. I hope. It's hard to tell. Everyone seems to have their shit together better than me, but appearances can be deceptive. Sometimes insecurities get the better of me. I could write a book about my recent impostor syndrome issues. That's under control now, mostly, but other issues rise up and I'm not always in control of my emotions and thoughts, and they can all get me in trouble.

I have the idea, or rather instinct, to act on all impulses, that that would be the smoothest way through. After seeing death and divorce up close, I figured nothing else could bother me and I could suffer slings and arrows of people's dislikes. It was on them. Their hangups, not mine. Such thinking is very Zen I've learned after learning some Zen, but it's also sickening. Most people try to be all things to all people, but being nothing to no one is not all that great either, and let me tell you that disregarding others to be yourself is offensive narcissism that crawls up people's backs like fungus. There's a reason most people have an internal censor. Over-sharing is indulgent and off-putting—that's me in two words, one of them hyphenated.

It's a struggle, call it a character arc if you must, but I hesitate there, because that implies a possible resolution, and I'm not sure there is one. Still, I admit I have many insecurities and this is the first step to solving them—or is that the acceptance of a supreme being? Whatever. Stay with me if you can. I'm working on it.

We were standing in the middle of the lobby when the other elevator door opened behind us and three people walked out with some urgency. I fell in behind them. Allie didn't ask why.

The issue at hand was jealousy. Jealousy is not envy, though most people mess them up. Envy is wanting something you don't have, jealousy is being afraid of losing something you do have. I had something to lose. Allie. I actually didn't have that much in my life I was afraid to lose. I collect things like a hoarder, but emotionally, personally, Allie was my prize. Even more than me most times. I'd diet for her. For her I'd meditate and read books on awareness and feng shui, drive all night to a desert town to sleep next to her when she smelled of horses and diesel fuel. For her I'd spar against philanthropic billionaires.

"I'm not attractive enough," I said.

"Pa-lease."

Can't say that that didn't help my mood, but on I pressed anyway. "But if Tessner and I had had a lot of time together, close time, staring into each others' eyes over a gargantuan dog with scented candles licking Spanish Fly-flavored popsicles, then you'd be jealous?"

"Under those circumstances I might be concerned. You have impulse control."

Off the lobby we followed the people into a corridor and up a half flight of stairs which led to the main conference floor, a big area with a bunch of meeting rooms spoking out of it like a dharma wheel. In the hub, there were chairs set up before a raised stage. A podium with a microphone stood unused before a large splashy backdrop advertising *ICOHEP: A Way Forward*. On the brochure placed on every chair, the tagline was *ICOHEP: envisioning the future direction of humanity*. Seems they were uncertain which tagline to go with and so had taken the ever-popular 'use them all, what-the-fuck approach.'

It wasn't a large group but pretty diverse. I noted Allie and I, Ted Tessner and my targets Sylvia Rigsdale and John Smith were present. The others I didn't know but felt they had to be somehow important. One woman had a big iPad and hair pulled back so far into a bun that it doubled for a facelift. She stood next to Tessner looking efficient, worried, and surprised at the same time. Her name, I learned later was Rachael.

"You are the important people here," hollered Ted holding his hands up to draw everyone's attention. Not sure why he didn't use the podium and microphone. "Thanks for coming."

"That's pretty elitist," said someone.

"We are the emissaries of God," said someone else.

"We're of the people people. People Power. People power, people power!" The chant wasn't picked up, but the peanut gallery was alive. Shouts and pseudo-discussions came from all quarters.

"Elitist how?" said someone.

"It suggests a hegemonic hierarchy," said someone else.

"I am important. Don't harsh my self-esteem." More somebodies.

"You are a ragged-ass nobody who needs to learn a lesson."

"I am so triggered right now."

"Om mani…"

"I'll smash your goddamn teeth in, you blasphemous goat-eater. Forgive my language."

"Goat-eater, am I?"

"Holy wrath upon anyone who dares—"

"Shhh." It was John Smith who quieted the room with a single sound. Not even a loud one. Not even accompanied by frantic waving of arms, the podium, or fireworks. Just a single sibilant from the unassuming man. The crowd shushed and waited.

Allie and I exchanged a look.

Sylvia watched me.

"Do I stand out?" I whispered.

"No more than usual."

"I was afraid of that."

"Ted has something to say," said John Smith plainly, "and since he was nice enough to bring us all here and pay for our rooms, I think it's only polite that we listen to what he has to say, not just the way he says it."

A sensible thing to say, I thought.

"There's been a bit of trouble, shall we say," said Ted. "I propose that you all, each the import—*representative* of your respective organizations, join me at my ranch to mingle and mend before the start of the conference tomorrow. It's a chance to get to know each other and bury any…*confusion* that may have arisen."

"Will the Netflix people be there?" It was a male voice.

Ted looked at John Smith.

"No," said Smith. "Friends, that's basically all over."

"Just one episode left?" said someone else.

"I don't know. I think we're done. Sangye? Are we done?"

He was addressing a young Indian fellow—Indian subcontinent, not the misnamed Native American variety. He was in a traditional robe and reminded me of Nero, Indian subcontinent politician, not Roman emperor.

Sangye shrugged his shoulder. "I'm honestly not certain."

This answer didn't sit well with John who turned to the group and said simply. "They're not here. They won't be here. Will they?"

Sangye again shrugged.

"They won't be at the ranch," said Ted. "Will they?"

"No," said Sangye decisively.

"No," said Smith confidently.

"Do we have to go?" New voice, southern accent.

"Do you want to miss it?" asked Sangye.

The crowd went quiet. Almost awkwardly so. Damn, if I didn't sense a threat in the room.

"A luscious dinner is promised," said Ted. The woman with the iPad shared her stretched and broad smile in agreement.

"Vegetarian?"

"Vegan?"

"Gluten free?"

"I'm lactose intolerant."

"I'm doing keto."

"No shellfish, unless it's from the Irish coast."

"Will there be a hot tub?"

Ted lit up to that one. "Yes. Yes, there's a hot tub. I'll have cars for everyone at the front in thirty minutes. Pack enough for tonight. We'll make it a sleepover."

10

"I DON'T THINK we're invited," said Allie.

"So?"

I wasn't keen on a sleepover at Tessner's evil lair, but I wasn't about to miss a free vegan, vegetarian, keto dinner, hot tub party with my quarry. I'm a professional detective, and if sitting in a bubbly hot tub sipping cocktails is what it took to find clues, so be it. I was rugged that way.

Rachael, the stretched-face woman, had taken charge. She asked everyone in a lilting British accent, to form a queue, not a line, a queue and when the Americans milled around instead of falling into ranks, she rolled her English eyes and carried on.

Allie had a program from before with maps of the class rooms, schedules, and bios of the important people. I lovingly took it out of her hands and sidled up next to the British bureaucrat and followed along. It was indeed as I figured. These were the who's-who of the conclave.

She then, ever so properly, called off names and made efficacious checks on her iPad when each person stepped forward.

I'd recognized the first guy from television. He was the head of a Christian Mega Church, ACOG, The Abundant Church of God. They had a syndicated Sunday television show filmed out of a converted arena invariably packed with swaying and weeping born-agains lining up to be saved, healed, and bilked out of only $79.95 for the monthly blessing. The leader, whose name was checked, stood five foot in lifts, had brown parted hair held in place with epoxy, an unnatural orange tan and teeth so reflective you could do your makeup in them. His name was Bartalemuw Benson but some people called him Barty-B. When Rachael called him that, he reported in a southern-esque accent, that he "was not particularly partial to that nomenclature" i.e., he didn't like the nickname. I decided then and there that I would call him Barty-B now and forever and anticipated an opportunity to try it out.

Next in line was a strikingly interesting woman. I'm used to Nordic Caucasian Utah where our racial makeup goes from white bread white to oatmeal white. She was tan and tall and young and lovely and my first thought that she was from Ipanema wasn't far off. Meso-American, maybe, African with strong South American in her. She had that stunning Aztec nose I remember seeing carved on Mayan temples. I guess that would make it a Mayan nose. Or maybe it was an Aztec documentary. I could check, but you get the drift. She wore a smart, dare I say, expensive business pants suit, emerald blue and tailored. She eyed me in my slovenly anti-rain layers before telling Rachael to look for her name, Kaisa Woods, under the Green Tomorrow contingent. I remembered Allie had recognized that organization, but I didn't know it from Blue Monday.

The next woman was the one who had so deftly wielded the Janus statue and clobbered the biker dude on the sidewalk. I could see red handcuff lines on her wrists and made the Holmsian deduction that no charges were being leveled at anyone for the earlier unpleasantness. Doubtless, this was negotiated with some rider about not mentioning the brutal police overreaction. It's an old story, nearly as old as Janus but twice as old as Hecate, the deity behind the crescented silver pendant the woman wore over her hooded black robe. She said her name was Artstar and waved her left hand in the air as if drawing a glyph when she said it.

"Part of the Coven?" asked Rachael.

"What? Do you think she's with the choir?" I couldn't help it. My censor was on a bathroom break and letting stupid question opportunities go unused is not easy for one trained in comedy.

Rachael turned to look at me, seeing me perhaps for the first time, noticing my intimately placed proximity over her shoulder.

Artstar looked at me and I had an electric jolt as our eyes met. Her eyes were…what? Green? No. Blue? No, that's not doing it. They were light, and aqua-ish, but that wasn't it either. It wasn't the color. It was the intensity, it was the reflection. They sparkled. As Rachael tapped her iPad and the hood fell over the pagan's face, it hit me. This woman had dazzle in her eyes. I know that's not a great description, but there it is. I'm sticking with it. Artstar was the woman with dazzle in her eyes.

Rachael cleared her throat. It was obviously directed at me so I said, "I think the next one here is Adam Tuko with the Homecoming Allegiance." I showed her the picture in the program. She glanced at it and then to the young man standing in front of her.

"Hello, and welcome," she said. "Mr. Tuko?"

"Yes."

"Told you."

Adam Tuko was Japanese. He wore a yellow and orange tracksuit that would go unnoticed in the Florida Villages shuffleboard court but didn't look right on anyone under seventy-three. To be honest, track suits don't look right on them either. Florida or Russia, to me there are no other places a tracksuit may be worn. Tuko didn't get the memo and nobody seemed to care. It occurred to me that in this milieu of enlightened minds, such shallow things as clothes weren't a big deal and I was off base bringing my judgmental ways into the atmosphere.

"Move it slant," said the man behind him. Tuko moved, paused, took in the man's leather jacket, racist tattoos, blond buzz-cut and linked steel rings on his fingers. They were effectively brass knuckles but since those things are illegal, even in America, they were rings. Just ask him.

Before turning to go, Tuko bowed ever so slightly and murmured, "You shall not be saved." He then rejoined a group of similarly orange-attired people in the corner. If looks could kill, the racist would be a smoldering mass of over-cooked segmented snake.

It wasn't the same guy who'd been cold-cocked by Artstar the witch, but he was with the same outfit. The Brotherhood of Righteous Action.

"BRA?" I suggested. "Really? You're BRA?"

Augustus Klept was his name and he looked at me with a blank understanding expression.

I explained. "Brotherhood of Righteous Action' the acronym would be B-R-A. BRA. Like a woman's boob holder. A kind of underwear."

I could almost hear the gears turning.

"It's a kind of girly underwear," I went on.

The gears seized up. Heat and anger incoming.

"Whoa." I held my hands up. "A man can wear them too. A crossdresser or if he had moobs," I said. "You know. Moobs. Man-boobs. It's a thing."

I don't like going for sexist jokes. They're cliché and suggest that there's something inferior in the comparison, that women, because they have breasts, aren't as good as men. Or that men with large breasts were icky. I don't think that way, but I knew that the wannabe stormtrooper did, and it would piss him off. That he and his group hadn't figured out this obvious low-hanging insult of their name, was just a bonus.

He took a step toward me but I stepped to the other side of Rachael and introduced the next contestant.

"May I present to your Rachaelness, Stephen Marshall, also known as The Messenger. He's with the Community—not the old show, but the new religious cult."

Augustus left scratching his privates as he went, as if that's where he kept his puzzler. He still looked confused. The Homecoming Allegiance group in their tracksuits followed him with their placid faces.

"We don't use that word here," Rachael said.

"Placid?"

"What? No. Cult. We don't use the word cult."

"You should," I said. "Unless you think there's something wrong with it."

The Messenger relayed the following: "The Community is an organization of friends with similar beliefs and goals. We don't have dues or secret rituals. No handshakes or robes. Cults are evil. It's what we are against."

I observed vocally, "So you define yourself by negatives? Not a very positive outlook."

"We seek truth."

"Lay some on me."

"Our core understanding," said The Messenger, "based on facts and information, is that the Earth has been visited by aliens who now occupy a moon of Saturn and under the leadership of their God Oodrakakam from Mliti Eight, are grooming us for some purpose."

"Good start, poor landing."

"Oodrakakam?"

"No. I'm giving you notes on your presentation. Is the grooming nefarious or beneficial? Sex slave or nice hair cut?"

"To discover that is is our quest."

"So not a cult?"

"Not a cult."

The Messenger, by the way, was a balding middle-aged white guy with a paunch and a Band-Aid on his forehead where I suspect a mole had been recently removed. He wore glasses that were in style in the magical era of *Napoleon Dynamite*, a white undershirt beneath a white short-sleeved button-down top that had pens in its pocket but no protector. Loafers and polyester slacks. Black patent leather belt. He could model for JCPenny.

He waved and stepped back, giving me an eerie smile, his eyes not focusing on me or Rachael or anything in the room, building, state, or planet.

Rachael locked me in her gaze, surely ready to ask who the hell I was, thought I was, was doing, would do, could do, but she was stymied from her nefarious plans by the approach by an entourage, some might say retinue. It was a cloud of fans swarming around a gaggle of bodyguards around the chewy center of celebrity. The burly men peeled back the selfie-afflicted groupies to let Donnopher approach Rachael.

Radiant smiles met her awe-struck one and she checked them off the list without a word being said.

It was Donnopher who'd tried and failed to board the limousine during the scrum. It was one of Donnopher's entourage who'd unleashed the flammable cloud, proved by many of them having thinner eyebrows than before and mismatched one-sided sunburns. Donnopher, however of course, looked glamorous. Him ruddy and rugged in platform shoes; she with her signature Lauren Bacall-esque half peekaboo do over one eye. Her hair color today was black flowing to silver and pink at the ends.

For all intents and purposes Donnopher is one person, but to be pedantic, I guess I should say that their individual names are Donna Hicks and Christopher Mark. Donna + Christopher = Donnopher. Basic math. They'd had a hit movie together a decade before, been dubbed the new Hollywood royal couple, and then slid off the radar into the mire of the Peoples Church of Higher Learning, known as The Peoplists, pronounced, *pee-opal-ists* for reasons only their dark god understood. Donnopher, though not the head of the organization, is the face of the group. The leaders, if I remembered Perry's rant correctly—Perry really hates these guys—was a secret sex-craved cabal of coked-up old cooks living in a guarded compound somewhere near San Bernardino.

Still starstruck, Rachael forgot I was there as the last special guest approached her organized iPad.

"John," said Rachael. "I so want to thank you again for all you've done, especially after this morning."

"Not a problem at all. We're here to help. It's not hard to sweep."

Smith was not alone. The man named Sangye stood beside him pleasantly attending, and Sylvia Rigsdale—the hostage?—was on his other side staring at me.

Tessner stepped up then. I noticed Allie slide into my field of vision.

"Everyone coming, Rachael?" he asked.

"We should have a full house."

"Yeah, about that," he said, rubbing his chin. "Someone will have to tell them that each group gets only one bedroom. Queen and fold-out."

"They won't like that," I said as if I had any say in what was happening at all. "Looks like they travel in packs."

"That's what I was thinking."

Smith regarded me with some amusement, Sylvia stared.

"Have them leave the guards," said Tessner. "Explain that we have perimeter security."

"You're thinking of Donnopher?" I said. "Want me to have a word?"

Allie's eyes went large as she saw my powers of infiltration.

"Sure. Tell them that if they must, they can bring two extras, but they have to stay in their bus. We have hookups."

"They have a bus?" said Allie.

"Who are you?" said Sangye to my girlfriend. Not everyone infiltrates like I do.

"I'm Allison Braise," she said calmly and confidently as I'd taught her. "And *you* are?" Good girl, deflecting the question back.

"I'm with John Smith."

"Is that true?" challenged Allie.

"Yes," said the leader of COTTEO. "He's with me."

"Alright then," she said. "That's cleared up."

"Good," said Tessner who was obviously flustered. His threatening aplomb was a-gone and Allie had only eyes for me. I smiled at how certain I knew this at that moment. She winked at me.

"The question," said Smith to me, "might be, who are you?"

I looked behind me as if trying to find the person he was addressing. Seeing no one over my right shoulder, I tried my left. Seeing no one there either, I shrugged and returned to the conversation.

"Allie and I can share a room without a problem," I said to Tessner, ignoring Smith. It's one of my detective superpowers. "Maybe someone can use the fold-out in our room."

"Oh? Oh yeah, that's very good of you," said Tessner. "Eh Rachael, organize all that." He walked away distracted, but I noticed he'd cast a look over his own shoulder as he did. I traced his sightline. Either he'd been threatened by a potted Pygmy Date Palm, the odd glow of a sunny day in Oregon, or the man talking on a cell phone by the door.

Rachael let out an exasperated sigh and asked Allie about our dining preferences.

Smith turned his warm eyes onto me. "Who—"

"His name is Bruce Allenby." I twitched my head to the cell-phoned man at the door. "I sat by him on the plane. He saw my act once and—"

"—are you?"

"Me? I'm Tony Flaner." I said it with confidence since without Tessner to veto my clever infiltration, I was getting to go to the sleepover.

"The private detective from Utah?" Smith asked.

"Yes. You've heard of me? I don't generally do autographs, but since you're in the business too."

"Business?"

"Being famous."

He laughed. "So what are you looking for?"

I nearly panicked thinking my cover had been so easily blown. Fame sucks for an undercover detective, let me tell you. Luckily, I was prepared. Detectives can be seekers too. This was a convention, and contrary to what capitalism tells you, you are not your job. I was more than a detective. I was more than a comic. I was more than Allie's main squeeze. I could be interested in Truth with a capital T. If anyone should know that, a holy man like John Smith should. In replaying his question in my head before answering, I realized he probably had. 'What was I looking for?' He assumed I was a pilgrim and was offering help. I've got to stop expecting the worst all the time. Assume the universe has only the best for you—

"My kids hired him to bring me back," said Sylvia.

—and you'll usually be disappointed.

11

IN AN ACT OF DIVINE MERCY, just then the cars pulled up to take us all to the ranch and I didn't have to immediately answer the accusation. My stunned silence might have done that already since Sylvia and Smith smirked knowingly and as they left us to fetch their luggage.

"How'd she know that?" said Allie as we rode the elevator up to our room to repack.

"Lucky guess," I said. "It's her own guilt playing through."

"You know you practically admitted it, right?"

"Let's not talk about it."

"What are you going to do?"

"Not talk about it?"

"Are we done here now?"

"You're talking about it."

"No, I'm just wondering what now that your cover has been blown before you've even begun."

"Glad we're not talking about it."

"So?"

"So, we go to a sleepover with mushroom man, a slobbery dog, and half of Homeland Security's watchlist."

"You're saying they're dangerous?"

"Did you not see the riot?"

"But this is a convention of peace."

"Yeah. Funny, isn't it?"

I could tell she wasn't happy with my equating Tessner's ICOHEP cult conclave with Al-Qaeda, but zealots are zealots and today's misunderstanding, blunt force trauma, and pyrotechnic pepper spray suggested that zealots were what we had.

It took Allie a few minutes to repack her bag whereas I approached my unpacked bag of wadded clothes, grasped the handles, lifted, smiled, and said, "Not ready yet?"

She gave me a smirking squint. I tapped my foot and glanced at my watch-less wrist. "Well?"

"I'm going to mash you."

She didn't get a chance to mash me, or finish packing. The cuteness overload of her squint and use of the famous "mash" line was too much. Clean sheets. New Place. Emotional cleansing at hand. I jumped her, pulled her to the bed and nuzzling her neck until all our clothes fell off.

The drive to the ranch was very pleasant. I was sleepy but warmed with an after-sex glow that tickled my toes. Allie snuggled up beside me on the back seat, scanning the messages on her phone.

"The gang just left Bend," she said. "Be here in a couple hours."

"Tell them not to look for us in the hotel."

"Already did."

"Was that what all that beeping was?"

"Yes," she said. "They want details of our plans."

"Do. Not. Tell. Them. Anything."

"Why?"

"They'll crash and it'll get weird."

"No they...okay," she said. It'd happened before.

Thanks to sexy time, we missed any officially sanctioned ride to Tessner's party. Our car was a Ridez and our driver was a local who explained that the famous Eugene Saturday Market was on Saturday in Eugene. You could tell I was in a good mood because I didn't respond to that.

The driver took us south and east on roads claiming to be highways but which would have made John Denver pine. Eventually after passing a half dozen hazelnut orchards and twice that many double-wides, we turned left down a dirt road past bushy pines, lush blackberries, and those really cool orange madrone trees until we came to a tall iron gate on a tall rod-iron fence that extended out of sight into the trees. The fence was easily eleven feet tall and though nicely made and apparently ornamental, the spikes on top looked serious. I could easily envision a spool of concertina wire running its length.

The driver pulled up to the gate and scratched his head. I could tell he was about to ask us what to do when the gate opened and in we drove. I marked the three, not one, not two, but three security cameras aimed at the gate.

I rolled down the window and smelled cool moist moss and detected just an underlying note of spiced clove, the telltale fragrance of a blooming rhododendron. Then, as if I'd sensed the future, the road turned into a long circular driveway and guess what plant was growing along its edges and running up to the humongous red-brick house? Yep, fucking poison oak. That shit is everywhere in Lane County, a curse-level bio hazard that will mess you up good and hard. It's hard to identify unless you know what it looks like, and you don't learn what it looks like until you learn why you have to know what it looks like. I learned about it when I was here before on a hiking trip and had to pee halfway up the trail. I got the bad news before I was back to the trailhead. I still weep just thinking about it. Oh, and there was a big red rhododendron bush by the house too.

I didn't see any other cars, but they might have been parked in one of the many outbuildings, barns and sheds and what nots. We got out and were met at the door by Rachael who almost pretended to be happy to see us.

"Third floor east wing, room with the green door and cantaloupe motif."

"You're kidding."

"Dinner is in an hour."

"Should we bring cantaloupes?"

"Drinks are already happening."

"I don't think she wants to talk to you," suggested Allie.

"Welcome, Ms. Braise," Rachael said politely to not me. "Psilly will be so happy to see you."

"Huh…" I murmured.

We entered the stately manor and I whispered the word "Rosebud" for effect. We had a choice of stairs, the left arc or the right arc. Since I remember something about being the east wing, I took the right arc, hoping that was east.

"It reminds me of the bridge of Picard's Enterprise," Allie said.

"Engage." I made the two finger forward gesture and up the stairs we went.

Our afternoon delight made us the last people to arrive, which surprised me. I don't usually take that long but something about the emotions and events of the day made us linger in reaffirmation. Then again, the others might just have been in a hurry. There was the promise of a hot tub.

Since we were late, I quickly put my bag on the floor and from the foot of a king-size bed watched Allie unpack and freshen up for fifteen minutes. She'd freshened up after the liaison, but cocktails and dinner meant another step. She's not vain, but she wanted to make a good impression. "One of us should," she explained. I'd peeled out of my monsoon wear into a pair of jeans, comfy walking shoes, and a shirt with a collar. I think it had stripes. I ran my fingers through my hair.

The room was bigger than my master bedroom, twice the size of anything in my tiny Moab house. The style was modern suburban, the kind of thing you'd pick up at a decent furniture store, the ones with a sale for every holiday. Mothers Day Sale, Arbor Day blowouts, etc. It was a nice room. Comfortable and unassuming. If I forgot the forty acres of woodland, the three floors and two wings of the house, I might even think it was a regular room.

The window looked out onto an acre of lawn that fed into mossy trees at the back by stone baths under lush rose arbors. The conclavists were down there holding drinks in one hand and aloof in the other.

Farther out, I could see a swimming pool, a tennis court, a barn with horses and—just what everyone needs—a helicopter landing pad off to the right. Just like home.

"Let's go," said Allie.

"Hold it there, miss porno," I said.

"What?"

"I can see your shoulders."

"I know," she said. "I'm so very naughty."

I should say that where we come from, in a certain state there is a certain religion that thinks it immodest for a woman to display her shoulders. Really. It's a thing. Seriously. Shoulders. This one baffles me because even in Victorian times when ankles turned men's heads, shoulders were cool.

"Whoa!" I exclaimed dramatically. "I can see your ankles!"

"It's to draw attention away from my cleavage," she explained.

Yep. Cleavage. There it was. Right atop her black strapless knee-high cocktail dress, just below her chin. "I can't believe I missed that."

"My clavicles confused you."

"Must have."

She grabbed a matching black clutch and took my arm to be escorted to the party.

"I feel underdressed."

"I hope so. Better you under than me though. I've got contacts to make."

"You're working?"

"These people are rich. Tessner will talk me up. Everyone has a pet. I bet I get at least three job offers to train something tonight."

"Probably to teach goats to lie still."

"I like goats."

"Were you thinking for sacrificing or copulating?"

"Ick."

We'd not been given directions from our room to the party, but by careful use of our ears and wandering around the bottom floor, we eventually happened to find a door that led out the back.

Allie punched me when she caught me dropping flakes of potpourri behind us to mark the return trail.

"Did you get that from the foyer?"

"The minute we walked in."

"So you've been planning this gag since we got here?"

"Yeah."

"I admire your foresight and dedication."

"Thanks."

"Now stop it."

I stopped it.

The backyard was the same group who'd checked in for the sleepover in the lobby. They huddled in cliques and threw glares around like they were frisbees. Allie was surely happy that Donnopher had also dressed up. I was happy to see orange tracksuits. On this spectrum, we were fashionable neutral, but then again anything short of a space suit could find a niche.

"So," I said from the middle of the yard in a loud carrying voice. "What was the fighting all about?"

Rachael rushed up to me with a champagne flute in her usually iPadded hand. "Mr....Mr....whatever. We're letting bygones be bygones. This is a new beginning now."

I reached for the glass. She kept it like it was hers.

"New beginning. Sounds like a good idea," said Allie, slowly retreating from me.

"Begin in a moment. I'm just curious. I wasn't there, and if I'm to be of any use, I need some context."

"Nazis!" came one voice.

"Heathens," another.

"Heretics," a third.

"Blasphemers," a fourth.

"Litigious fucks," could have a been a waiter.

"Fuck around and find out," a woman, actually.

"Clear the way or be cleansed." That one I looked for but couldn't place.

"Intolerance," said John Smith in a low cool conversational tone that silenced the assembly.

"Oh?" I said.

"Our host has asked us to put that matter aside for now, Mr. Flaner. Let us respect his wishes."

"Of course."

Allie brought me a glass of champagne as Smith and Sylvia shared a whisper and glanced at me.

"You gave up quick," Allie said.

"I don't know what came over me. I was thinking of stirring the mud to sour whatever milk of human kindness was being brewed, and one suggestion from Smith and I'm all in agreement."

"That's a hell of a mixed metaphor before mixed drinks, but, yeah. That's what it looked like to me."

It did and I'd meant it. That had been my plan, if I'd had one. Of course I was curious why the scrum had happened, but I also saw Sylvia there and remembered how my current job crossed with my bullshit intolerance. I thought I'd muck everything up. But then Smith, John Smith in his casual logoless polo shirt, asked me to behave, and hell if I didn't fall in line.

If it isn't clear yet, I thought this entire ensemble was a bunch of idiots at best and devious evil con men at worst. I felt obligated to bring the entire thing crashing down for the health and happiness of the world, which I realized was very much in keeping with the event's goals. I'd fit right in.

"Look out," whispered Allie, so I did. Sylvia and Smith ambled over to me. Sangye, I noticed, was chatting with Augustus who looked at him like he was something on his shoe.

"Is it a requirement in your cult that everyone has a name with an S in it? Asking for a friend," I said.

Sylvia looked pissed, Smith thoughtful then smiling.

"No," he said. "We have an Arron Allenten and a Bea Green."

"Be green and be seen," I said.

"That's the motto of the Green Tomorrow. Kaisa Woods is over there." Smith gestured. The Meso-American beauty from before noticed us looking at her and looked concerned. "They've had a tough year. Just last month some of their people were murdered."

Smith raised a glass. Kaisa smiled, raised her flute in reply, and returned to a conversation with Donnopher.

"You all know each other?" I said. "What? Is there a circuit?"

"Just met," said Smith.

"Well?" said Sylvia.

"My rash is clearing up," I said. "Thanks for asking? Yours?"

"You have to excuse my friend here, Mr. Flaner," said Smith. "She's currently fixated on the idea that her children sent you here."

"Answer the question," she said.

"I didn't hear one. Now or before. I heard cruel accusations and innuendo, gossip masquerading as truth. Vicious speech. Shameful...shameful."

"Did Sylvia's kids send you?" asked Smith.

"Yes," I said, and to this day I don't understand how or why.

"I knew it," said Sylvia.

"We're guests of Ted's," said Allie, trying to rescue me. "I trained his dog."

"So what's your plan?" asked Smith.

"Like he'd tell you," Allie said.

"I'll observe for a while, dig a little, expose your con, and bring Sylvia back to her grieving children."

"Ha!" said Sylvia.

"I have no con," said Smith. "But I suppose that's exactly what a conman would say."

I can't remember a time in my life I'd been more flustered by the mere presence of someone. I felt like I was under truth serum, not that I've ever been under truth serum, but it might have been like this. Allie elbowed me and I tried to recover.

"Yes," I said. "Yes."

"Yes?"

"Yes, that is exactly what a conman would say. You've outed yourself, Mr. Smith. Now remove your mental hooks, relinquish her treasure to their rightful heirs, and let this poor innocent woman go."

"Go fuck yourself," said Sylvia.

"Now, now," Smith said. "I don't think Tony here is a bad sort."

She stared daggers, but that didn't bother me. Smith, however, yeah, he was in my head.

"We're Ted's guests," said Allie again. "You can't kick us out."

"It's all good," said Smith. "You can work in the light. Ask me anything."

"How did you know why I was here?"

"You're not the first, and Sylvia said that eventually they'd use you."

"Who else was here?"

"Not here, but earlier this year, a guy named Chris Traard poked around."

I knew Traard. He was a straight-laced PI from Provo, Utah I have a tolerate slash ignore relationship with.

"What happened with him?"

"He wasn't very subtle," said Sylvia. "He left when I told him to leave me alone."

"Quitter," I said.

Smith smiled. "Does that mean you're staying on?"

"Are you asking me to leave you alone?" I asked Sylvia.

"Yes. Leave me alone."

"You have a compelling argument. I'll consider it and get back to you in a couple of weeks."

"Subtle is not your suit either."

"I don't mind," said Smith. "I've got nothing to hide."

"Just what a con man would say."

"What would a non-conman say?"

"I don't know," I said. "I've never met one in your profession."

12

RACHAEL TAPPED the side of her glass with a pen and announced that dinner was served. It wasn't as good as Magenta in *Rocky Horror*, but it got everyone moving.

Allie and I followed the group back into the house. Sylvia and Smith were ahead of us, just behind Rachael, the rest of the cadre following in a silent shuffling line. A mood-matching funeral dirge wouldn't have been out of place. If I'd known any, I'd have chimed in. Best I could do was the dour part of *The Song of the Volga Boatmen*. I used grunts instead of words because who on this side of the Caucasus really knows the words to that old chestnut? I got it across though, and my heartfelt rendition earned me many stares and a tug from Allie.

We were taken to a formal dining room with a decked-out oval table. Floral arrangements full of birds of paradise and baby's breath stood sentinel every three feet, guarding butter trays and bread baskets. Lots of silver silverware and china place settings, crystal wine glasses, crystal water cups and folded eggshell name cards with swirly blue-black calligraphy. There were plenty of padded tall-back chairs and a wall of waiters to pull them out for people if they stumbled upon their places.

Allie and I circled the table twice before we realized we didn't have little cards.

"Let's take a hint," Allie whispered to me. "I'll buy you pizza."

Eugene, in the center of soggy Oregon, is as famous for its pizza as Chicago is for its baguettes.

"No," was my reply.

"Garçon," I said loudly. I raised my hand above my head and snapped my fingers three times to get the attention of an appropriate person. When no one appeared, I raised my other arm and snapped some more. I looked like a hostage who'd lost their castanets.

Rachael appeared when the table was seated and everyone was staring at Allie and me. Or rather, just me. Allie had disappeared.

"I don't want to make a scene," I began and watched Rachael's face curl up like a dried rose petal. "But a party foul is afoot. Where're our seats?"

She looked around, maybe trying to place the plural to my words but her eyes fell on Ted Tessner who'd just come in. He gave her a quick nod and began walking clockwise around the table, welcoming everyone.

Rachael made eyes at a waiter who goggled another who raised an eyebrow to a third, and suddenly there were more chairs and place settings. Allie appeared from behind a curtain and joined me between the three COTTEOs, Smith, Sylvia and Sangye on our left and Barty-B who'd come stag on our right.

Allie was next to Sangye who greeted her with an indifferent nod. Barty was next to me and smiled automatically with a set of teeth so white and square he could model equine orthodontics.

"Come here often?" I asked Barty as plates arrived.

"No."

"Me neither. Let's be friends."

"No."

"Welcome," said Tessner from the far end of the table. I could hear him plainly. The room had excellent acoustics. "Let us break bread." And with that the meal began.

"Short and sweet," I said.

"Don't talk to me," said Barty.

"I'm not talking to you," I said. "Why do you think everything revolves around you?"

He smiled. He had a good smile. The best money could buy but it didn't reach his eyes or even his over-tanned cheeks. All lips and teeth.

"I assumed—"

"Shhhhh," I said. "I'm not talking to you. I know who you are. I've watched your show, followed your career. I've seen you beg for money for a fourth private jet saying God wanted you to have it. Don't take this the wrong way, but you are a repulsive human being and should be ruthlessly slayed for the betterment of the species. No offense."

"None taken," he said automatically.

Allie's elbow tossed me into his side before Barty could register what I'd said and how he'd reacted to it. It would come though. A frontal assault with slow-burner kickback. Classic burn and return.

"Mr. Flaner," said Tessner. "Remember your manners."

"Yes, Tony," said Allie through gritted teeth. "We are guests."

"Sorry."

"The strange man is right though," said Donnopher. "He's just being honest. Is honesty not mannerly?"

"Maybe in your bubble," grunted The Messenger. "A weave of lies in a greater weave of lies."

"Not worth it. None of it is," said Tuku. "Come the redemption."

"The jumpsuit speaks," said Augustus Klept, skinhead, tattoo doodle board. "If wimp had an official outfit, it'd be that orange mess."

"You will not be spared," the little man replied.

Augustus Klept's hand twitched toward his waist as his face reddened. He recovered instantly, looked around the table and then bit a roll in half like it was the head of a squirrel.

Klept's motion more than Tuku's line silenced the table. Kaisa brought it around, "Peace and conciliation are the only ways forward." I wanted to ask her if that was Green Tomorrow's new catch phrase, ready to comment that it would be better than whatever forgettable and forgotten one they use now, but she kept speaking. "Regardless of our differences, we must put them away until the crisis is over."

"At least for the conference," said Tessner. "Let's just try that out."

"That's what I meant."

"Aren't there greater crises though?" I offered. "The planet's cooking for example. Ignorance, bigotry, bad fashion. There's a lot to deal with. Should we ignore it all?"

"Harm no one who does not harm you," said Artstar, the pagan witch. I'd forgotten she was there.

"I haven't heard that one before," I said. "Usually it's—"

"Who is this guy?" said The Messenger.

"I come from Planet Claire," I said. "Where no one ever dies."

He looked confused so mission accomplished.

"He's the public," offered Tessner. "Who we're all here for."

Several moved to speak, but the most minuscule motion from Smith, who sat at the opposite apex of the table, shushed them all like a stun beam. All eyes turned to him and waited. Even the waitstaff halted and turned to watch.

"We're here seeking truth," Smith said. "Some of it is subjective. Best we can do is present it as best we see it, and let the public here"—he nodded to me and I felt the gesture like a dart—"decide for themselves."

I couldn't help thinking that he was speaking directly to me, commenting directly on my mission to remove Sylvia from this mess, probably because that's exactly what I thought he was doing.

It took a second to recover and find a retort but before I did, Barty-B spoke.

"From a bully-pulpit lies can be sold as truth." His accent thick and homey, his stare at Smith venomous. Barty-B then shifted his gaze across the entire COTTEO collective and then returned to Smith with aggravated hate.

"The power of publicity is not to be underestimated," said Donnopher. "A baseless accusation told loud and far cannot be fully corrected, no matter how many crushing lawsuits it elicits." They turned their movie-star stares at Smith and COTTEO. Donnopher were trained actors, so they could be thinking anything, but I felt they too were pissed at Smith and had just made a pretty clear threat.

"Was that a threat?" I asked.

"Not all grievances," said Augustus Klept, letting the word hover like a loogie on his chin, "are settled in court."

"Was that?" I said. "I think that was one, right?"

"We are used to persecution," said Artstar. "We shall take our light into the darkness and wait for the next Aeon."

"That's not a threat. Just whiny."

"A misplaced word can ruin all the good work we've done," said Artstar.

"An observation."

"Death can't come too soon," said Tuku.

"Are we back to threats?"

"Shut up the narration," said Allie.

"No. What's going on here? Am I the only one here who doesn't know what's going on?"

"I think you'd be used to it," said Sylvia.

"Ouch. Nice one," I said. "Look at you acting all sassy and pretending not to be brainwashed. You been styling under Donnopher?"

"Be civil people!" said Tessner, slamming a water-glass-spilling fist onto the table. "Or you will be disinvited from this cult conclave—I mean, the Interfaith Congress of Holistic Enlightened People, happening this weekend."

Everyone found something interesting to do with their plates. There were lots of veggies and rice. Allie and I got tasty sustainable salmon Caesar salads. I crunched croutons. Allie tried to disappear.

Three more bites and I was ready for another round, but again, I was stopped by Smith.

"They're talking, I do believe, about my Netflix deal, Mr. Flaner."

"You're kidding?"

"No."

"Man that's infuriating."

"Why?"

"Because it's as funny as a rusted rake," I said. "I know real comedians—really talented and funny people—and they can't get those people to pick up their phone. What the hell kind of act do you have to merit a comedy special?"

"Netflix does other things than comedy," Allie said.

"Horror? You're doing a horror series? Another remake of a Shirley Jackson story?"

"No. It's a docu-series."

"You raise tigers? You've had personal relations with a cephalopod?"

"No. The series is about belief."

"So you *believe* you have a series?"

"We've filmed twelve episodes," put in Sylvia.

"There's talk about a thirteenth," added Sangye.

Smith gave him a look, but he didn't see it, he was deep into his eggplant. He didn't see the others giving other looks too. Lots of looks.

"Ah, okay," I said. "I get it."

"What do you get, pray tell?" asked Barty-B.

"One of the cardinal sins."

"Greed?" said Barty-B.

"Sloth."

"What?"

"No, you dick," I said. "Read *The Bible*. Remember the line, 'thou shalt not covet thy neighbor's Netflix fame?' You guys suffer from jealousy."

"Envy," added Allie and instantly regretted it. Everyone looked at her. "Jealousy is when you don't want to lose what you have; envy is when you want something someone else has. The sin is envy."

"One of Seven Deadliest, I might add," added I.

"Envy, greed, lust, sloth, pride, over-eating, and...another. *The Bible* says it."

"Actually the seven deadly sins aren't from *The Bible*," said Allie. "They're from *The Canterbury Tales*. 'The Parson's Tale,' to be precise."

I raised my finger and pointed around the table, poking at each of them in turn. "Now don't you all feel stupid."

"Fuck no," began Augustus, but I cut him off.

"Wrath! Wrath I say. Wrath! That is another sin. Can I have a hallelujah?"

Barty-B offered me one and then blushed beneath his copper makeup.

"It's not jealousy," said Donnopher while eating a bread roll. It was a good trick. Donna nibbled on a roll while Christopher talked. It was a really good ventriloquism act.

"Then what is?"

They didn't deign to respond.

"Envy then."

"Please," came their voice.

"Envy, *please*?" I offered.

"Which brings up an interesting philosophical question," said Ted. "Is sin real?"

"It all depends upon who's theology has hegemony," said Artstar.

And so the conversation shifted from me to a lively topic among spiritual leaders. I let it happen. Not just because I was a guest, a rude, party-crashing guest, but because I thought I was pushing too hard without a goal. Sometimes I push like this to see if anything will come loose, a thread or a screw.

There were pa-lenty of loose screws around that table, so it was unlikely anything useful to me, professionally, would break free. I used the lively and friendly debate as an opportunity to suss out the guests.

Rachael had done a stellar job of cleaving the guests from their retainers. Each group was represented by their leader alone, Donnopher who was technically two people, but really, one so they (singular) were at the table. COTTEO however occupied three coveted seats as if Smith, Sylvia, and Sangye were a Donnopher-level integrated singular personality drone. I figured that their assistance in the post-melee cleanup, and the fact that their denomination alone hadn't participated in the mayhem, had earned them the extra plates. On the other end of the niceness spectrum, Allie and I got two places to represent the animal trainer and unwanted snoop sect of Utah tourists. Even our host, Ted Tessner, founding luminary of the mushroom-growing billionaire ministry, was only a single person at that table.

The earlier animosity was softened as each diner got a moment to address this vital and important topic, one of the possible open panel debate subjects, as listed in the brochure. They were trying out their material and kept making eye contact with Ted and Allie and me because we were ostensibly the only non-committed audience there.

I could see instantly that there were two kinds of radical cult leaders. One was showman, the other not. The showmen people who did well, nay, flourished in the spotlight. Donnopher was one of these of course, but so was Kaisa who talked about sin as sin against earth. Good to stay on theme. She sold the ecological science and religion fusion very well. The Messenger also shone, which surprised me because his organization, the one Perry was a fan of if not a devotee, was so conspiracy based. Aliens on Saturn is a hard sell, but he talked about sin in relation to the cosmic laws of 'Dark Forest' peril and benevolent lords. I'd have to ask Perry about that. Or not. Nevertheless, The Messenger was a charismatic speaker, and while speaking, he didn't sound bat-shit-crazy one little bit. Only when you thought about what he was saying, took his reassuring face out of the mix, did the bat shit rise up.

Smith naturally took everything in stride, making an occasional pithy comment, but listening more than he spoke, which was suspicious. Augustus Klept, tattooed Nazi skinhead fuck, was pretty animated and though he slid into offensive racist and fascist language frequently, kept his voice active in the conversation. Ted too was present, moderating like a seasoned Comic Con pro.

Among the non-showmen was Tuku who used his energy to nibble his food and seethe in some unseen reality. Really, the man looked pissed all the time. Maybe it was a cultural thing, resting angry face, but when he looked up at anyone, reacting to some terrible racist or stupid comment, his eyes looked like they were trying to shoot lasers.

Artstar too was passive. At least she didn't will hexes on the participants or throw the evil eye, which would have been her right as a witch and all. She listened distractedly. Her eyes wandered to the place settings, the table settings, the setting settings. She glanced at her watch once or twice. Topped her wine glass not a few times and enjoyed a buttery spiced chicken breast as if she'd blog about it later.

Barty-B surprised me by his taciturnity. That's a word right? I'd think that blow-hard would be blowing hard, but he sat still at his place, picking at a bloodred steak and probably trying to grow a few inches. He was short. Christopher short. Like two foot three inches in lifts. Only once did he speak up and the shock of it, brought me out of observation mode.

"Of course sin is real," said Barty-B.

"You're right," I said. "Before I watched you on television, I didn't know what true sin was."

Here again I split the table. Those that understood the joke and those that didn't. Barty-B, dense Barty-B, thanked me and said he had new respect for me due to my confession.

Ted, Kaisa, and Artstar laughed out loud. Smith covered his mouth with a napkin to muffle his. Sangye stared blankly, Sylvia balanced her animosity toward me with my hilarious burn. Augustus mentally chewed on the moment when he saw some people laughing and tried to figure out why. Donnopher wore a passive face that could have been intestinal distress or erotic bliss. No one could tell.

Dessert arrived and moods were decidedly more upbeat, however, I couldn't help but feel a dark undercurrent, a sinister vibe shown in suspicious glances. I couldn't imagine it being otherwise. Everyone there had a decided worldview that differed from the others. If anyone had been pliable to another's persuasion, it was instant death, spiritual and financial. No metaphysical breakthrough would happen at the conclave, at least not among the presenters. I wondered if Ted expected one and decided, against my jealousy and distrust of anyone more successful than me—most people —that Ted was smart and knew that wouldn't happen. No, he was a realist, a dirty word in that room of high flying dictates about what God, the universe, Gaia, Hecate, Oodrakakam wanted. Any good this convention would achieve would come in the minds of those who witnessed it, the pilgrims who'd come to this new new new new age revival buffet. For that to happen, however, these people had to at least get along to some degree, just long enough to show their angle before being carted off to Bedlam or the Eugene Police Station. Ted had expertly used the "sin debate" to relax everyone, give them an arena to battle that didn't include sidearms. A "civilized," moderated, and respectful debate coupled with good food and good wine.

By the time the strawberries were devoured we all had a nice glow. Everyone talked about the opening events the next day, and how it was auspiciously chosen by star sign, daytime TV viewership, moon phase and venue. There was a moment of digression when Augustus wondered why

Smith got to give the opening keynote address. Ted giving the welcome made sense, but Smith was just one of them. What made him special?

"I chose him," said Ted as if that ended it.

"Why him?" Kaisa wanted to know.

"I think he has the most universal message," came Ted's sudden and definitive response.

"More universal than saving the earth?"

"Yes."

"More universal than—"

"Yes," said Ted, cutting off The Messenger and that line of questioning.

"Sins and stones?" said Kaisa.

Sangye added, "It'll be an enlightening speech."

"Okay then," said Donnopher. "A decision had to be made and it was."

Radiating star-power, the most famous person in the room had to be heeded, though I thought I heard Artstar mumble something about, "Teacher's pet."

"Nightcap?" offered Ted as the waiters scooped the last of our plates away.

"In the hot tub?" inquired I.

"Why not?"

"Now you're talking," was my measured response. But around the table there were pockets of grumbling. Not everyone has the same blind spot to body image shame I do.

"Or you can call it a night. We'll get up early to make the conclave."

People stood up and made their goodbyes to whatever piece of furniture they were nearest.

"A dip sounds like just the thing," said Klept. "You going in, darling?" He was talking to Allie.

"I haven't decided yet." This was alarming because she liked a good soak as much as I did and her body was the after picture of an herbal supplement diet ad.

"Hey Ted," I said. "Do you have anyplace to store Klept's auxiliary penis?"

"His what?"

"My what?"

"Your gun."

Guests halted their exits and turned to look. I was suddenly amazed that I'd been the only one to suss out that Klept was strapped.

"He has a gun."

"I got a permit."

"In Oregon?" said Smith.

"Do you need one here?"

No one knew. That was the kind of crowd they were. Didn't know, didn't care. Carried anyway.

"Well?" I pressed.

Klept glanced around, reading the room, then reached into his pants and pulled out a black revolver with a neon green grip and set it on the table.

"And the other one," said I.

He didn't argue, but retrieved a little silver gun from his ankle holster. It was a guess about the second gun, but a safe one. People who imagine their day will get so bad that they'd need a gun, often imagine the day would be so so bad that they'd need two.

"Is that it?" I asked Klept.

"That's all my guns here."

His response opened up the question of what other lethal weapons were on his body. Knives, brass knuckles, unwashed boxers. I let it alone.

Ted picked up the guns like they were radioactive and carried them to a china cabinet and put them in a drawer beside white napkins and silver napkin rings.

"You can have these back at the end of the conclave," he explained.

Klept seemed to understand, which alarmed me.

"Your reaction is alarming," I said. "How many more guns do you have?"

"Have?"

Imagining a gun room, not a rack, closet or safe, but a gun *room* in his bunker, I said. "Bring?"

"These were it," he said. "This is a conference of peace, truth, love and understanding. I didn't think I'd need more than two guns."

13

ON THE NOTE OF 'PEACE GUNS,' the party broke up. Waiters swooped in to clean the dining room and the rest of us fetching either our swimsuits to convene on the other terrace, or sleep masks to convene in the breakfast nook in the morning.

Allie had a new one-piece suit that made me envision her jogging on a beach with David Hasselhoff. I had my ratty old swimsuit tragically decorated with sagging palm trees that did nothing for my self-esteem.

On the stairs down we crossed paths with Donnopher coming up. They were in a strapless bikini and a Brazilian banana hammock making them both work. I suddenly felt small, limp and fat...ter. Allie's bod however held its own and even elicited a look from them. Up and down, they smiled approvingly at her slim muscular physique. I merited a disgusted glance and a hastened trip to their room where no doubt they rinsed their eyes in Visine.

What does one say to half-clad pseudo-Hollywood royalty on a wide staircase? "Have a good sleep time," didn't quite do it, but that's what came out of my mouth.

"Enjoy the...tub," was their cryptic conspiratorial, snotty response.

"They seemed nice," I said to Allie after they were gone.

"No they don't," she said.

"No. No they don't. They seemed worried."

"Maybe it's your suit?"

I glanced down at my wilted palms and realized to wear such a thing was a flex of epic proportion, since it suggested the exact opposite. Right?

We found the terrace and the steaming hot tub just after eleven o'clock. A single waiter remained to mix drinks at a tiki-inspired bar, a tiki bar. Ted was

there, three drinks in, up to his neck in the tub, John Smith and Sylvia Rigsdale soaking beside him. The Messenger was just off the terrace in the grove,
still in his street clothes, wandering circles, his face cast upward as if
communing with the planets.

"Saturn, I can hear you," I heard him say, so, actually communicating
with the planets.

"You just missed Donnopher," said Smith. "They had a drink but wanted
to make an early night of it."

"Saw them on the stairs," I said.

"They wouldn't get their hair wet," said Sylvia.

"We don't gossip," said Smith.

"It's the truth," she said. Then added, chastised, "You're right."

Allie ordered us sweet frilly drinks that spiked your insulin just by being
in the same room with it. I took a sip of my drink and nearly poked my eye
out with an umbrella. I shifted it out of the way and nearly lost the other eye
on a plastic sword handle.

"Mind if we join you?" I asked.

Sylvia's eyes said no. Smith's said all was welcome. Ted's said, I'm
drunk.

We joined them. All fell silent but the bubbling water and the babbling
Messenger in the distance.

Allie started, "Great dinner, Ted."

"I'm so pleased you liked it, Allie," he said. "I was hoping you would."

"I liked it too," I said.

"That's nice."

"Isn't it?"

That killed the conversation for a few more minutes. Against my instincts
and my emotions, I allowed the silence to sit.

"Well done, Tony," said John Smith.

"How's that?"

"You took Ted's insult and didn't react. That shows strength, especially
from you."

"You don't know me."

"I've heard your quick wit. Ted left himself wide open to a deserved
brutal comeback. Why'd you pull your punch?"

Scandalized, I looked around at the other bathers. Sylvia regarded me
with a hard gaze, basalt or maybe cement. Ted looked sheepish and drunk-
ish, Allie curious.

"Trying to be a better person," I said.

"That's good."

"To be honest," said Sylvia, "The 'isn't it' response was a subtle comeback. I don't think Mr. Flaner is up for sainthood yet."

"But he could have done much worse," said Allie, nodding her head
vigorously. "I've seen him make hardened policemen weep."

"No doubt," said Smith. "You have a gift."

"If only he would use it for good," said Sylvia.

"Nice one," I said.

"So you're here to save Sylvia?" slurred Ted. "Is that right?"

"I'm here to see you and Psilly," said Allie. "And the conclave. It sounds so interesting." Her drink was already gone and she waved for another.

"What did my kids say?" asked Sylvia.

"You assume that I was swayed by their opinions? No. It was their money that brought me here."

"No it wasn't," said Smith.

"It was. This is what I do. I solve cases for money."

"You don't need money. You'd not have taken the case if it didn't interest you."

"You been Googling me? I feel violated."

"You Googled me."

"That's different. Then I wasn't the victim."

Smith laughed. "That kind of self-awareness is another gift."

"It's my fucking birthday," said I, holding up my glass for another intoxicating fruit juice. "What was it that you think interested me in this case?"

"Boredom probably. It certainly wasn't Sylvia's kids. You met them I suppose?"

I nodded.

"Were you impressed?"

I was about to say something about upright caring children and family virtues, but knew he'd see through that no matter how eloquent it was. "No. I wasn't impressed. But...but cults are bad, m'kay."

"Cult plus time equals religion," said Smith, "but we're not even that. We're more like a school."

"Do you serve Kool-Aid after nap time?"

"Ouch."

"That kind of self-awareness is commendable."

"Show some respect, you pig," said Sylvia.

"Ouch," said Smith again. "You're not helping, Sylvia."

"But that's why I'm here," said I. "To help Sylvia."

"Anyone want a hit?" Ted had materialized a magical smoking doobie out of the air. He took a hit and passed it to Allie.

Allie doesn't usually like drugs, but here she was in a stranger's hot tub, ninety percent naked, with cultists taking a hit of potent Oregon Mary-Jane, so she had a toke.

Sylvia passed, John Smith took a polite hit. I bogarted the roach.

"Another?" said Ted and another lit joint appeared in his hand.

We all said we were good. He took about half of it and it disappeared again.

"To think this stuff used to be illegal," he mused. "Lots of people got into a lot of trouble for this little weed." He shook his head and looked sad.

"Bummer," I said. "But, Smith, may I call you John?"

"Sure."

"Smith, isn't the presence of psychoactive drugs in your cult proof it's a cult?"

"No."

"But it should."

"It's not a sacrament. We do some work with psilocybin mushrooms, but that's very little."

"I supply them," said Ted.

"Is that legal?" asked Allie.

"It is now," said Ted confidently. "I think."

Sylvia explained, "COTTEO isn't about that. It's about meditation and cooperation."

"Orgies?"

"Now?" said Ted.

"No, I said 'orgies' as another proof that COTTEO is a cult. Cults always have orgies."

"I missed that condition," said Smith, amused. "But if any of our people have orgies it's on their time. And sheets."

"Is that what my kids told you?" Sylvia looked even more pissed. "That I was doing orgies?"

I couldn't exactly remember, so I bluffed. "I don't remember, but maybe."

"Once pot became legal, there was a push to get pardons for all the growers who'd been sentenced during prohibition." Ted was talking to the stars, maybe The Messenger's aliens. I wondered if they had a vested interest in drug legalization too.

"They must have been pretty old by then."

Ted didn't catch my clever quip. "Some small possessions got pardons, early on, but the growers, they rotted until the recent pardon."

"Did you grow mushrooms before they were legal?" I asked.

Ted remembered I was there and looked shocked. "No," he said.

I thought he was lying and I was pretty sure that Smith thought he was too.

"I don't care," I said. "I think outlawing plants is stupid."

"Yeah," said Allie, perhaps sensing Ted's unease, "Tony's always saying we should legalize adulthood."

"Ha!" said Sylvia. "Listen to yourself."

"Me?" I drove a straw up my left nostril. The pot had hit me, and I forgot I had caltrops in my cup.

"You. Legalize adulthood. Hello." She made a little whirling gesture with her hand.

"First of all, Sylvia," I said, "That was Allie speaking."

"She was quoting you."

"Which makes it hearsay. Inadmissible." I'd got her good there.

"It's a good philosophy," said Smith, John Smith. "I agree with it."

"So you advocate drugs and extramarital orgies and brainwashing and orbital mind-control lasers?"

"What's that about orbital mind-control laster?" The Messenger had stumbled by.

"We all have to find our way," said Smith. "We should all be given the space to do it."

"Space? What about space?" The Messenger was kneeling now at the lip of the pool.

"What say you, Stephen?" said Smith.

"Who's Stephen?" I asked.

"Him." Smith pointed to Messenger. "Stephen Marshall is his real name."

"Don't call me that," he said. "That's my dead name."

"You're trans?" asked Ted.

"What? No. I'm not a freak," he said. "I've been renamed by Oodrakakam."

"Where's he from again?"

"Mliti Eight."

"And that is where?"

"M57, that is the Mliti 57, commonly called the Ring Nebula. Twenty-five hundred light years from here in the constellation Lyra. They contact me through faster-than-light mental formations from their base on…on…I can't tell you that. You'd think I was crazy."

I stared at the rest of the group. Usually I don't read the room like this, not with such low-hanging fruit as this fruit, but I was a guest and Ted was handsome and Allie was weird. Everyone looked at The Messenger like he was the nut I thought he was.

"Well, glad you're not a freak," I finally said. Someone had to.

"Who was talking about orbital mind-control lasers?" he asked.

"I don't remember," said Smith.

"Maybe it wasn't us," I suggested. "Maybe it was from that unnamed moon of Saturn."

Scandalized, he stood up, turned around and left the light of the patio for a return to the woods.

"That wasn't nice," said Sylvia.

"I was only following your master's lead."

"Don't be rude, Tony," said Allie.

"Why stop now?" asked Sylvia.

"Smith. John Smith. He's the one who told a lie—a lie—to that poor hapless misunderstood prophet. What kind of a cult leader lies? Oh, right. All of them."

"It was a white lie. I didn't want you humiliating him," said Smith. "Well, not more than you did."

"Did I? Did I really? Doesn't one have to be self-aware for that?"

"Yes. But it would have been public and we'd have witnessed the violence of your strength against his weakness. It would have shamed him and you both. Don't punch down."

"Ouch," I said.

"He is one of the most 'out there' of the guests," said Ted.

"Don't pick on Tony," Allie said, putting down her empty glass. "He speaks truth wherever it lands. Tony is a living bullshit detector. It's a gift and a power and the world needs more of him."

I almost melted then and there. Not only was I level six stoned, level four drunk, level seven hot tub induced relaxed, but Allie had just proclaimed her love for me and not Ted Tessner, biological billionaire.

Smith put his hands up, which meant lifting them out of the water. They dripped as he said, "You are, of course, right, Ms. Braise."

"You can call me Allie," she said with a smile I wanted to kiss her so hard my nether regions stirred.

"Sometimes kindness isn't kind and bullshit does need to be called out. It's a tough call. I admit I might not be the best to see it."

"Ha! So you admit you're not perfect."

"Please..." said Sylvia.

She got me.

"We talk about it," said Smith.

"Argue," said Sylvia.

"About what exactly?" said Ted. "I think I lost the thread."

"Calling out bullshit."

"That's just speaking truth, right?"

"Like what Allie said Tony said," said Smith with a wry smile that did not lower my erection. There was something about him, and damn, that was strong pot. "Sometimes letting adults be adults is letting them follow the wrong path."

"Or false prophets," said Sylvia. I wasn't sure what to do with that.

"Expose the lies to save people time or let them do it themselves?"

"What are we talking about now?" I said. "Are there cookies?"

"Cookies!" yelled Ted as only a drunk host with waitstaff can do. "Bring us cookies!"

"And bubbles," suggested Allie.

"And bubbles!" yelled Ted. Then, "Oh, here's the button."

Bubbles roared to new heights and the light under the water switched from white to red to green to blue in slow psychedelic transitions. The lights on the veranda dimmed and the stars came into view. We leaned back and watched. The Messenger came over, took off his shoes and socks, rolled up his pants and dangled his feet in the warm water, his neck craned up like ours.

Cookies arrived on, you guessed it, on a silver platter. Iced sugar cookies, snickerdoodles and chocolate chip, all big and attractive, doubtlessly from a boutique bakery.

"After a long while, the bubbles retreated to the stirring it was before. Everyone had crumbs on their lips and peace on their faces.

"I'm not being held against my will, Mr. Flaner," said Sylvia. "I want to be here. And I can spend my money the way I want to spend my money."

"But your kids—"

"Are selfish little shits who have a lot to learn."

"I'm being paid to bring you back to your family."

"How?"

"By calling bullshit where there is bullshit." I turned my gaze deliberately at Smith, who met it with a warm smile. Goddamn, if I couldn't hold a gaze.

"You think I'm a charlatan?" he said.

"Maybe you don't think so? I've heard that some people actually believe the craziest things." I looked at The Messenger and here I could hold my stare. It helped that his unfocused eyes were pointed heavenward.

Sylvia rolled her neck. "What if I paid you to leave me alone?"

"Is that how you got rid of Traard?" I rolled my neck too. It felt good.

"The other detective? No. I told him to leave me alone."

"That did it?"

"Sangye might have threatened lawyers."

"He did?" said Smith, surprised.

"He was trying to help," explained Sylvia.

I shook my head. "No, money won't chase me away."

"So it's not money you're after," said Smith. "See?"

"See…" I mimicked back like a two-year-old.

Smith laughed, a deep laugh.

"Now who's punching down?" I said.

He laughed harder. Others joined in. I had to laugh too. Being able to laugh at yourself is a high mark of self-awareness. Besides, it was funny and I was so stoned.

"So, Tony," said Smith after we all stopped laughing. "What's your path to enlightenment?"

"Me?" I said. "Well, I…I…I'm working on it."

"Perfect!" exclaimed Smith.

14

WE DIDN'T STAY MUCH LONGER in the hot tub. The conversation fell off, Smith very pleased with himself for his declaration of my perfection, and I didn't want to argue with him. It would have been rude. Stoned, drunk, and relaxed, we all kinda just soaked in the hot water and cool night air, absorbing the stars, the Oregon forest scents of pine and fading pollen, listening to the wind in the trees and the mumbling Messenger somewhere among them.

Allie yawned, and I took that as a pass and wanted to act before she figured it out. We took our leave around eleven and found our bedroom right where we left it.

Allie was surprised to find me so helpful getting her swimsuit off, then said, "The yawn? Really? It was the yawn again?"

"Playing hard to wake turns me on."

She couldn't argue more. Her mouth was covered in kisses.

———

The next morning we stumbled down the stairs following the smell of coffee to a kitchen where we were the only ones. A waiter, the same guy from the tiki bar, looked less than pleased to see us.

"Finally waking up?" he said.

"We've wandered into a Mensa Meeting, hon," I said. "Maybe we should go back to bed."

"No no no," said Lewis, according to his name tag. I noticed he was the same man who'd taken the guns the night before and put them in the bureau. I think he was the actual butler of the estate, the others merely hired help for the night. "Have some coffee. The others are already at the event."

We had good coffee and delicious bagels. "Are these from the Daily Bagel in Eugene?" I asked. I remember the cute little shop, from my time before.

"Yes."

"Nummy."

Allie took a bite of one, smiled and then stifled a yawn. Her eyes filled with panic as mine dilated.

"Down boy," she said.

———

Lewis ordered us a Ridez which honked into three-facing cameras at the gate for ten minutes before someone let her in. She told us there'd be a charge for waiting. We told her that's fine and to tack on a fifty-dollar tip. We weren't paying.

Where before there'd been a scrim of enlightened combatants in front of the hotel, now there was a line of eager conference goers all carrying the same gift bags, made from recycled plastics, eye-catching and branded. It bulged with such swag you get at every convention: pamphlets, books, pens, pencils, business cards, little hand sanitizer bottles, notepads, COVID masks, more business cards, coupon books, back scratchers, bottle of water, stickers, coffee mugs (plural), USB memory stick promising cyber wonders, snack bar, breath mints, deodorant, and condoms, all branded by some wonderful group generously vying for your attention and ignorant to the waste they'd created. Green Tomorrow should have a word with them, except the bright green and gold bag was branded by them and the murky water bottle had Kaisa's face on it. Nevertheless, the bag promised to have been made from over forty percent recycled material in China, no less. Woot woot.

Allie left me at the elevator to begin exploring and pursuing tickets. We promised to meet again later, if only to screw again. Love is grand.

The door opened to my floor and there stood Artstar in black robes and a hood. Her eyes that dazzled before dazzled now and held me entranced, but they were now lit up with some strong burning emotion.

"Not who you were expecting?" I said and got out. She stood there staring at me, dazzling me, and letting the elevator door close and carry on its merry way.

"I heard you're a detective," she said. "Is that true?"

"I thought it was common knowledge."

"Why are you here?"

"Why are you on this floor?" It was a regular floor. I knew the good ones were higher up at the nose-bleed Eugene height of nine stories above the grass.

"Looking for you."

"Why?"

"To ask you why you were here. Hell, if I'd known who you were last night, I'd not have broken bread with you."

"That's harsh, especially for one who dines with demons."

Her eyes grew larger.

"That's a good effect," I said. "Been studying with the muppets?"

She recovered herself a bit and after a deep breath, a prayer in gibberish, a hand wave, a turn around on the spot. She looked at me with calmer eyes. I looked back. The bags were getting heavy in my hands. "Do you mind?" I said, gesturing to the hallway beyond.

"Who are you here to smear?"

"Smear?" I said with some indignation. I'd have grasped my pearls if my hands were empty. And I'd had pearls.

"Smear," was her retort.

I opened my mouth to retort, but then realized she was dead right. "John Smith," I said. "I'm hunting COTTEO, hehehehe." She was either too young or too tense to laugh at my superb Elmer Fudd impression, but the news seemed to calm her, nonetheless.

"Okay," she said and nodded as if hearing intel from some outer world.

"Blessed be," I said.

"And to thee," came her automatic response.

"Now move."

She stepped aside and I found my way to my room. When I turned back to look for her, she was gone as if by magic. Or maybe the elevator. Who can be sure?

I'd just put my bag on the strapped suitcase saw-horse when there was a knock on the door. It was Bartalemuw Benson, Barty-B to me and you. "Hey Barty, wha—"

"Jesus, lord, who sent you?"

"I take it you heard I was a detective."

"Why did you not disclose this information sooner?"

"I have my reasons," I said. "Good reasons. Secret reasons, like no one asked."

He stood in the hall, fuming, staring, cogitating. His over-tan face twisted to reveal his over-bright teeth in a growl. He scanned the hallway up and down, then said, "How much?"

"How much you offering," I said.

"I will not be blackmailed," he said.

"Sounds like you will. How about fifty?"

"Outrageous. Who sent you?"

"Inquiring minds want to know."

"What do they know?"

I realized I was on the verge of getting fifty large so played an easy hunch. "You've been dipping into the collection plates, preacher. Not a good look."

He paused then looked me in the eye with his unblinking snake-like stare. Slowly his face relaxed, twisted into an artificially square-toothed grin.

"Who are you really here for?"

"Huh..." Bluff failed.

"I thought it was me when you chose to sit where you did last night, but now I have to wonder."

"They were assigned seats," I offered.

"Please, Mr. Flaner, a man of your skill could easily have arranged to sit wherever he wanted. I've read about you, or rather my people have, and given me an account."

I'm used to being underestimated, overestimated was a new sensation and I felt suddenly exposed.

"It must be COTTEO," he said. "Am I right? The people on the other side?"

"No comment."

His smile got large. I felt small.

"I'll give you your fifty if you gather anything useful against those pricks."

"Deal," I said to end the conversation.

I did not think it possible, but his bright white horse smile grew even larger. I could count molars. "Deal," he said and left.

I returned to the suitcases trying to remember what I was doing, in more ways than one.

The phone rang.

"Tony, I heard this morning that you're a detective on a case. Are you officially sanctioned or working privately? Who are you looking into?"

Remind me never to try to do undercover work again. Ever. Ever ever ever ever.

"Who's calling please," was my response.

"Oh, sorry," she laughed. "This is Kaisa Woods. I was just curious about this."

"Why?"

"My organization has been harassed by many people. I'd like to know if you're one of them."

"Who's harassed you?"

"My organization is fighting for the planet, that means we're battling against modern existence, a lifestyle. There is no end to the people that threaten that."

"That tracks."

"You seem like a decent guy, can you let me know if it's me you're hunting?"

"What have you got to hide?"

"I'm a human being. If you dig deep enough, I'm sure you'll find something to use against me and my group."

"Is there a difference?"

"Some would say there is not. Still. Me?"

I tried to remember anything about Green Tomorrow but kept seeing dazzling eyes and blinding teeth.

"I'm here looking into COTTEO," I said.

"Excellent."

"You don't like them?"

"What? Oh, no...it was just that I'm relieved it's not me."

"Feel a little easier about joining an orgy later?" I joked.

"Which one?" She was serious or really good at deadpan.

"Kaisa, can you do me a favor and tell me how you found out who I was."

"Ted mentioned it over breakfast."

"Go on."

"We all noticed you hadn't shown up and commented that you'd be late for the early classes. Ted said you weren't a presenter. He said, cryptically, I might add, that you were a famous detective and were here on a case."

"But he didn't say who I was investigating?"

"He started to, but was hushed down."

"By whom?"

"John Smith. He said that gossiping was never good. He always says that." She punctuated the last statement with a little chortle.

"Glad my secrets were kept." There was a knock on the door. "Gotta go."

The knocking was timid and nondescript, the peephole was all orange so I knew who it was though. Through the door, I called, "Adam Tuku, is that you?"

"Yes, Mr. Tony Flaner. I would like to speak with you."

"I'm naked right now. Got my dick hanging out and everything. Can we do this another time?"

Through the peephole, I watched him stand confused for a minute. His hand went into his pocket, came out, touched his neck, went back in. "Everyone straight down there?" I asked.

He looked at the peephole then, seeing it no doubt for the first time. "One question, who—"

"Not you," I said.

"Oh. Oh. Okay. Never mind," he said and left for the stairs at a brisk walk, no doubt getting use out of his tracksuit.

I figured a trip to the toilet would be a good idea, lots of shit happening. I didn't make it, however. The phone rang again.

"You've reached a wrong number," I said as way of greeting.

"Mr. Flaner, this is Dmitri Lewandowski, from the law firm of Lewandowski, Drabitovitz, Kovatz, Nozadze and Hansen. This is a formal

warning on behalf of the People's Church of Higher Learning, known colloquially as 'The Peoplists,' to cease and desist all harassing, invasive and
unwanted contact, and investigation with our delegation and/or senior
members of said organization, be that vis-à-vis—"

"Imma stop you there," I said. "So you're Donnopher's lawyer?"

"I represent The Church of Higher Learning, known colloquially—"

"A yes or no answer, if you please."

"Yes."

"Are you the same firm who sued that ex-member who spoke to the
House committee?"

"I really don't see—"

"Answer the question, counselor."

"Yes, we represent The People's—"

"Were you also the firm who sued that gardener who claimed he was
never paid for work done on the headquarters of The Peoplists Plaza
Compound?"

"I'm not—"

"Stop evading! Yes or no?"

"Yes."

"And the firm who sued Donnopher's former bodyguard, Donnopher's
niece, mother, second cousin and childhood friend?"

"Yes."

"That Ridez guy in Tulsa?"

"My clients had reason to believe—"

"Evasive."

"Yes."

"And all those paparazzi?"

"Which ones?"

"All those."

"Yes."

"And that class action of active members who claimed there was wife-
swapping, chicanery, brutality and no-vegan choices in the compound. Are
you defending the organization against those?"

"All our members must sign non-disclosure agreements and each is
expected to—"

"Hostile witness, Your Honor."

"Look here, Mr. Flaner," said the mouthpiece. "I'm calling as a
courtesy—"

"You mean a threat."

"Yes." There was something about the way he said it that crawled up my
back like an infected lizard.

"Yes?" I said.

"Yes, and as you so well showed, my clients will not hesitate to bring the full power of the law and this firm down on whomever they feel has wronged them."

"Did you win any of those cases?"

"We didn't need to."

"Can take the rap, but the ride?"

"You are smarter than I gave you credit for, Mr. Flaner."

"Tell Donnopher…"

"Yes?"

"Never mind. I'll tell them myself."

"I doubt you can get close enough. Perhaps you should leave a message."

"COTTEO. I'm here about COTTEO."

"I'll pass on the message. Goodbye."

He hung up before I could invite him over for game night. I guess I'll be the *Railroad Tycoon* by default.

Before I could make it to the sink to wash the smug off my hands from the lawyer talk, a knock came on my door and my cell phone dinged.

I glanced down at the text and saw it was Allie telling me to hurry up, that the keynote was about to begin and to warn me that the gang had arrived from Utah and were looking for me.

I figured the knock would be them.

"How'd you know what room—" I began when I opened the door.

It wasn't the gang. It was the family. Or at least one of them.

"The hell?"

"Hello again, Mr. Flaner, I guess you're wondering why I'm here."

"Why yes, Josh Rigsdale, son of Sylvia, sibling to Hannah, who hired me just two days ago in far away Salt Lake City—at a Denny's no less—to do the very job I'm currently on, I *am* wondering why you're here."

15

"HANNAH WAS sure you'd be goofing off so she came after you. Have you?" said Josh.

"Been goofing off?"

He nodded.

"Actually not," I said. "I mean, I often do. Hannah's instincts are right, but in this case, I'm on the job. Lots of observation."

"So you've observed from afar?"

"Better than that."

"You've made contact and remained incognito?"

"Yes and no."

Josh pinched his temples. "They outed you?"

"Instantly."

"How?"

"Sylvia suspected you'd send someone."

"Seems thin."

"Aren't you Mr. Detective expert? There were also extenuating circumstances."

"Like what?" Josh wanted to know.

"Lots of prophets and seers around here. Can't rule out divine intervention."

Josh rubbed his temples harder. "I came to warn you about Hannah and you're proving her point."

"Which is?"

"That you're incompetent and weak-willed and if you get close to Smith, you'll fall under his spell because of it."

"Why the sudden drop in her esteem of me?"

"She's just worried. She did her own research and—"

"Imma stop you there. Am I still on the case or not?"

"Yes, we agreed to keep going with you, but Hannah's here also. Be careful. She's..."

"Willful?"

"Yes, but more."

"Angry?"

"Yes, but also..."

"What?"

"She can be a real bitch. Her friends call her Karen, if you get the reference."

"I have the internet," I explained.

"I also think she's reckless. She's in a weird space. Lots of email chains and Facebooking, and this Sylvia thing has been eating at her. Hiring you was an attempt to curb her craziness. It didn't last long."

"Craziness is a strong word."

"Pissiness? Rage?"

"Rage? With possible violence?"

"Yes." He turned to go.

"Wait," I said. "Is the whole family here or just Hannah?"

"Just her."

"And you."

"Yeah, don't tell her you saw me. Okay?"

"Gotcha."

My phone dinged again; Allie wondering where I was. When I looked up, Josh was gone.

I remembered Josh as the most reasonable one of Sylvia's family, probably because he'd married into it. Nearly two decades older than his wife Lara, he had maturity that clashed with the family dynamics. I decided to take his warning seriously and resolved to find John Smith and warn him that there was a crazy Karen out to get him. There was probably nothing in the world able to withstand a full-on Karen assault, but he should be warned and have his cell phone ready to record it. A friendly reminder to use landscape mode wouldn't go amiss either.

Allie was waiting for me in the lobby.

"There you are. The buffet has started, and the gang is already inside."

As a refresher, the gang was Perry White, Dara Sutter, Standard Flox, Garrett Corta and Critter of the felt. I felt immediately uneasy thinking of them here, thinking that I was on a case and had already been wildly successful at infiltration while being completely inept at subterfuge. My friends are a handful at the best of times, grouped comedians struggling with secret tormenting inner demons they play dress-up for inspiration. My position was precarious. I was surprised they'd come. Surprised they bought tickets. This wasn't a cheap conference. Hannah's advance would get us in, but barely. The price was hella steep: $2,500 for the whole conference and $500 for a day pass. This included live access to select recorded seminars. A highlights-only online pass was available for $1,000. The keynotes were transmitted live to the cyber attendees. Cleaner versions with certain curated classes—the highlights would be available later and accessible for a year. What a deal. Who said you can't put a price on wisdom?

"How the hell did they get in? There's no way Standard would pay so much. I never would have."

"Funny story," said Allie, latching a plastic band around my wrist and laying a lanyard around my neck with stanch formality like I'd just been given a lifetime achievement Hawaiian leis. I had flashbacks of *Star Wars* except there was no sidelined Wookiee who'd been racially overlooked for awards howling in the corner in mournful unintelligible wails about how he'd been as brave as the rest of the heroes, had risked as much as the humans. Where was his medal? Such bullshit.

"The gang has their own story, but Ted sprang for our tickets," she said.

"Why?"

I was still thinking about Chewie and comparing my own crop of furry chest hair to his and wondering at the advances of civilization when Allie said, "John Smith insisted."

"How do you know that?"

"I was at the registration desk, looking for a credit card to take the hit for our tickets. When Smith walked up with Ted and suggested that we pilgrims should not be turned away."

"Pilgrims? That did it?"

"Yep. Free. There's something about that guy."

"My quarry?"

"Yeah."

"Where is he?"

"Everyone's inside. Big welcome lunch."

Past the registration desk, I saw Sangye stationed at a door and surveying the crowd. "Sleep well?" I asked.

"What?" It took him a second to place me.

"Tony? From last yesterday?"

"Missed you at the hot tub."

"I was busy." He scanned the room again.

"Waiting for someone?" I asked.

"Sylvia's daughter."

"Ohh, you know about that?"

"Yes, but how do you? Did you bring her here? Of course you did." His congenial face was gone, replaced with anger.

"Actually, I just found out myself. I was coming to warn you, maybe suggest someone be a lookout in case she does anything untoward, like try to attend the conclave."

I'm amazed sometimes at how my loyalties shift so quickly. Ten minutes ago, I was flinging social epithets on my beloved client, now I was defending her to a zealot. Why shouldn't she be allowed in? Couldn't she find something interesting here? What were they hiding?

"What are you hiding?" I said for emphasis.

He shook his head in disgust and went to the registration table, no doubt to see if Hannah Rigsdale had registered.

We went in.

It was a typical hotel banquet hall, a large room made three times as large by the folding away of accordioned walls. Dim chandeliers hung ten feet above a sea of blue-clothed round tables, each accommodating eight chairs. A raised stage stood against one wall with the hotel logo prominently displayed behind it. Two tables were placed on either side of a podium, panel style. I had visions of celebrity roasts and Elks clubbings. Hanging above the hotel logo was a banner declaring ICOHEP, the name of the event I recalled. Sounding out the acronym again, I couldn't help thinking that someone somewhere was chanting it while burning Tana leaves in black and white.

I noticed cameras set around the room. These were elevated on tripods to take in the stage or the audience. Four of them strategically stationed with microphones on higher staves. They appeared to be remotely operated to minimize disruption. I wondered if this had anything to do with the Netflix special everyone was worried about but then remembered that there was an online pass available and figured that was for that. Netflix could probably use some of the footage too. I'm sure the conclave would sell it to them. Not like the philosophy of commerce wasn't in full force.

Around all this, fluttering about like a drill sergeant bee, was Rachael and her iPad. It might be Ted's show, but she was the director. She saw me, I waved, she grimaced.

"Popular as ever." Standard was standing next to us.

"I think she thought I was you," I said.

A banquet line was against the right wall, serving both sides of a typical hotel buffet. We fell in line, collected our plates, napkins and silverware to allow us to practice our juggling skills while dishing up. Allie made the rookie mistake of taking too much salad and cold pasta thus leaving precious little room for the main dish of cold-cut sandwiches. Skipping the bulk, I made three tripled-up sandwiches; turkey, ham, and roast beef, assorted cheeses, mustard and mayo, a bag of chips, and two cookies. It looked like a lot of food, but what if Allie passed out from malnutrition after trying to make a meal from spring mix and fusilli? I'd be a hero to save the day with my Cool Ranch Doritos and iced sugar cookies.

Perry was waving for us to join the gang at a table in the center. I tried to pretend not to see them, but Allie had already waved back. I wasn't in the mood to see them just then. Maybe I'd let her starve.

"Hi," I said, sitting down. "Glad you guys made it."

"Really?" said Dara.

"No. Not at all."

"Why?" asked Garrett. I could see the hurt in his eyes.

"He's soul searching," said Perry. "This grand gathering of enlightened minds will challenge everything you think you know about yourself and reality."

"Yeah, something like that."

"Allie was telling us about your dinner," said Standard.

"You got to break bread with Kaisa Woods," said Dara, shaking her head. "She's awesome. The real deal."

Perry said, "The Messenger is the one to get close to. His knowledge will transform the planet. Oodrakakam as near as the moons of Saturn. Gives me shivers."

"Gives me a headache," I said.

"I can't believe Donnopher is here," said Garrett. "Critter and I have been talking about joining The Peoplists for a while. You should too, Perry. Membership has its privileges."

I rolled my eyes.

"Like what?" asked Standard.

"Career boost. Haven't you noticed how many high-power celebrities are Peoplists?"

"And low-level ones," said Allie. Donnopher's star had been on the descent for decades.

"And those make comebacks."

"You're talking conspiracy nonsense," said Dara.

"Look where you are," I said.

She glanced up at the stage where the big names were all seated with salads and sandwiches behind name cards proclaiming who they were. It was the same gang as the dinner before, albeit only one representative from COTTEO, Smith. Donnopher didn't count. I knew there were other speakers in attendance, other people giving talks, classes, seminars, hand jobs, but it was clear who the big names were. Each would be giving a keynote at some point.

"Conspiracy central," I explained. "That's where we are."

"No," said Allie. "This isn't QAnon."

"Ask Augustus Klept if the election was stolen. The Messenger if the moon landing was faked."

"The Messenger says we were on the moon," interjected Perry. "But that we got there on alien ships. They did it as a favor for giving them water and potassium sulfate."

"Not sure that disproves my point."

"It doesn't," said Allie. "But that was nice of us to give them some potash."

"What about Kaisa and Green Tomorrow, Allie's favorite," asked Dara. "The real deal."

I looked at Allie who had a little blush on her cheeks and lettuce in her teeth.

"Sorry, hun," I said, "but the whole 'planet Earth is a living lady who speaks directly to me' is a stretch."

"She didn't say that."

I showed her the quote in the program.

"Oh."

"But she's doing good work," said Dara.

"They all are," said Perry.

"The orange jumpsuit brigade?" Allie tossed her thumb at their cream-sicle table.

"Keeping fashion under control," I said.

"The Nazi?" Garrett gestured to their little putsch near the front.

"He'd say racial purity."

"That's not good."

"At the risk of sounding too wise," said I, "there are different opinions."

"Fuck off, Flaner," said Dara. "Klept is a fucking Nazi."

"He'd argue Aryan Avenger," I posited.

"What about Bartalemuw Benson and The Abundant Church of God?" Allie was going down the line.

"He offers hope to some people."

"Sells it, you mean."

"They all do."

"What about John Smith?" said Allie. "What's his game?"

"He's in it like the rest of them. Selling a story, trading off his cult of personality."

"He's not much to look at," said Dara. "Though he seems nice."

"He's here promoting a Netflix special for crying out loud."

"You're saying no one here is the real deal?" said Garrett. "I mean spiritually speaking. The Peoplists are undoubtedly the real deal for career advancement."

"Snake oil everywhere."

"At the risk of sounding too wise," said Perry, "there are different opinions."

"Touché."

"Well met."

I ate some sandwich regretting the five cheeses and one ham on a roll before saying, "So what's the funny story about you guys getting in here?"

"Seat fillers," said Critter. He was the only one not eating.

I met the puppet's eyes and he nodded sagely.

"Really?" I said.

"They're filming this stuff," he explained. "All the empty chairs look bad, so they let us in for free. Dara held out for all event passes. It didn't hurt that we had a celebrity among us."

"I do what I can," said Perry.

"Eighty percent of success is just showing up," said Garrett after he'd swallowed his food.

"I bet the empty seats look even worse to the accountant than the director."

"Ted can handle it," said Allie. "He's richer than the devil."

"Speaking of which."

"Welcome, everyone," said Ted Tessner from the head table. "I see we all pretty much have been served. I'd like to thank our generous caterers for such a delightful spread of good and wholesome fare."

"Meat is murder!" yelled someone from the audience.

"Dairy products are oppression!" came another.

"Plastic is killing the planet!"

"Vegetarian is another word for shitty hunter, asshole."

"Pigs are sentient. Don't eat them. Chickens are okay."

"Were the plants ethically killed?"

"Who sourced the salt?"

Ted paused at the podium, the look of unbelieving shock on his face lasted only a moment then he pressed on.

"I just want to welcome everyone to the first annual Interfaith Congress of Holistic Enlightened People. This is a gathering of like-minded, though differently directed, seekers of truth and wisdom from many traditions, old and new. It is a pleasure and a blessing that we can all abide together like this for a short time and share our beliefs with each other. Consider this a one-stop shopping experience for the best and brightest holistic ideas on the planet."

Although it was early and this was my first look at the deep-pocketed crowd who'd come, I didn't get the feeling that there were many people actively there to shop for beliefs or even taste anything beyond the one creed they'd come here to see. Already there were cliques forming. You could look at any particular table of conventioneers and guess who they were there to see. The skinheads here, the orange people there. The Wiccans in black eyeliner across the room. It wasn't a stew, wasn't even buffet, it was at best a vending machine where you could get your Green Tomorrow sandwich. If you accidentally got a side of Saturnian space helpers, you might just send it back. This was my impression then, and to be true to the path of greater wisdom that I was on, I reminded myself that it was still early.

Tessner might have felt the same vibe I did. "This is a rare opportunity you've come to enjoy, and I'd encourage everyone to visit the classes of other faiths—not to argue or ridicule, but to listen. There is a strict no-harassment policy in force, so be nice. Learn what others have discovered, see where their paths have taken them. Rejoice in the quest."

It was a good line, but no one applauded it. I almost did, out of sympathy.

"One simple challenge is to eat every meal at a different table," said Tessner. "Meet new people. Network that way. Share and listen. Rejoice in the quest."

The callback line still didn't have the effect he was looking for. Damn.

"And be respectful of each other." I could hear defeat in his voice and could wait no longer. I stood up and applauded.

I stood alone for a long time, clapping alone, for maybe ten, twenty, thirty, sixty, eighty seconds, maybe three minutes, until finally Allie joined me and then the rest of our table. That was enough to shame the rest of the room to stand and join in finally. Shame or a desire to get back to their food because it's hard to eat while someone's clapping their hands bloody staring daggers at you for not joining them.

After a briefest moment of solidarity, the clapping stopped and everyone returned to their food. Ted sat down. I think I saw gratitude in his eyes. Or tears.

16

"YOU WERE PRETTY HARSH AT LUNCH," said Allie after lunch.

"I got ambushed by the lot of them. Everyone's panicked that I'm here for them."

"Like you're John Wick or something?"

"Pretty much. I'm an investigator and in the world of lies, that makes me an assassin."

I'd filled her in about how I was the subject of conversation that morning at Ted's and the subsequent visits in the room.

"That's dumb," she said. "They knew you were a PI at dinner."

"They didn't. It didn't come up. Everyone just assumed…something."

"I bet they thought you were a priest of the church of the Dude. You dress for it."

"I do abide." Dudeism a real thing, by the way.

The gang had splintered to attend their different classes and Allie went to see Kaisa of Green Tomorrow, her favorite. Perry was homed in on The Messenger, Dara wanted a closer look at Artstar. I always thought there was something witchy in her. Standard braved the paparazzi for a glimpse at Donnopher somewhere and Garrett and Critter, looking to see the most dangerous cult, couldn't decide on Klept's BRA white nationalist boys, or Adam Tutu's Homecoming jumpsuit party. I left them arguing in the banquet room and went on the hunt for Smith. I was on a job and I didn't want to get caught goofing off by a stalking Hannah-Karen.

A quick glance at the program showed he wasn't teaching that hour, but I found him in the lobby sitting amongst and betwixt a small group of people on the couches. He was sitting atop the back of one with the others in a semi-circle around him, three deep, many sitting on the floor.

"Hi," I said. "Mind if I join you?"

"No not at all," said Smith.

Sylvia cast me a repulsed look that was quickly removed. Sangye held his a little longer.

I sat down and opened with, "You know about Hannah?"

"Yes," was all the response I got.

"Am I interrupting anything?"

A young man spoke up. "Smith was telling us about his new center."

"You have a new center?" I asked. "Where? Off to the side? Just on the edge? Can that still be called a center?"

Smith smiled, Sylvia shook her head. Sangye looked away. The rest of the group looked confused.

"It's a new headquarters for COTTEO," explained Smith, still smiling warmly. "We've been working out of random places for years, but now we have the resources to centralize. It'll be a campus with outreach and year round classes."

"You're making a college?"

"We might get accredited, but that's not the goal. People will learn to be happy and mindful. We'll help them find a purpose. It's what we do."

"If you get accredited you can tap into the rich vein of student loans. Lots of good scamming there."

"Hey!" It was Sangye.

"What?"

"Stop equating John with the creeps running around here."

"He's not just another creep cultist?"

"No."

"A wise man once said something about birds flocking together."

Sangye's face went red, he was about to go off, really let me have it, physically I thought, when Smith put his hand gently on his arm and all anger drained away like a flushed toilet.

Smith looked at the others in the group. There were thirteen of us in all, eager curious seekers, the very breed the conclave promised to service.

"Everyone here has some truth to share," said Smith rather diplomatically I thought. "You must forgive us if we think we have the most. It comes with the territory." He winked, a warm friendly wink, that—fuck it all— brought a warm reciprocating grin to my lips.

I shook it off, remembered to be cynical and sharper than the average rube. I began, "Then why—"

Smith raised a single gentle finger and like I'd been stunned by a phaser, I shut up.

"Ted asked me to come. He's donating the land for the center. It was the least I could do. Plus I wanted to meet people—yes, even the questionable ones."

"And the true seekers," said Sylvia.

"The conclave is an interesting idea. Well intended, but..."

"But what?"

"We'll see."

"You question everyone's motives for coming?"

"Not my place to say."

"They're motivated, like you, for money."

"Mr. Flaner, be respectful," said Sangye.

I could feel the crowd shifting against me in earnest.

"It's a necessary evil in our society. But money itself isn't evil. It's the lust for it and how it is used that defines that, and even there it's subjective."

"Society enslaves us," said one of the seekers, a young woman with a pierced brow and short strawberry-dyed hair. "It kills me. I work day after day and all I do is get by. I started doing drugs to make the most of the few hours I got each week. I developed a pretty bad habit and then I wasn't getting by."

"And how are you now?" asked Smith.

"I'm trying."

"Good," he told her and smiled that beneficent smile again.

Her eyes welled up. "There is more to it all, isn't there?" she asked.

"The world is as you make it. Fight the good fights and slow down. Although you're right about society stealing your labor and time, it does this through illusion. There, at least, we have an exit. Value the valuable things and ignore the crap. You'll find your way. Come to the center. We'll teach you how to be silent, and how to roar if you need to."

"Before you get smart, Flaner," Sylvia whispered to me, "internships will be whatever the aspirant can afford, including gratis."

"My parents disowned me," said the girl openly weeping.

Smith just opened his arms and absorbed her into himself. He held her for a good five minutes, never shushing her, never moving, never lowering his compassionate smile.

Finally she let him go and her face was a mess, but aglow.

"I don't know why I did that," she said. "Or told you that."

"I'm glad you did."

She looked around at the others half embarrassed, but then found Smith's face again and settled back.

"I make jokes so I can control how people laugh at me," I said out of fucking nowhere.

"Insecurity isn't a sin," said Smith.

"What is sin?" asked another seeker.

Smith laughed at that. "Subjectiveness incarnate!" and he laughed like Santa wished he could. I found myself joining the others in laughing with him.

"Too big a question to be answered here," he finally said.

My emotions, I admit, were all over the place. Smith, simple, unassuming-looking every-man John Smith, had an aura about him. It didn't glow, but it might as well have. Charisma? Magick? A halo? Hell if I knew, but while I mentally listed my own faults, fighting the urge to confess each one for his personal absolution, I understood the attraction to him. There was power here. No question. Here was something I was unprepared for, something I'd read about, sung hymns about. I turned to Sylvia to remind myself that I needed to save her. She glanced back at me then returned her attention to Smith who was answering another question.

"...Buddhism is the closest," he was saying. "Their concept of Interdependent co-arising makes the most sense and highlights the connections that define us and the universe. Once that's understood, everything else follows quickly. It might even be the door to enlightenment."

"So you're Enlightened?" I asked. "Capital E?"

"That's another subjective term, but I've realized certain things that have helped me and by sharing them, have helped others."

"Will this be on the special?" asked someone.

"We'll be circling the idea," said Smith, glancing at Sangye who shook his head.

"The final edits are still coming in, but COTEEO's ideas are laid out.".

"To the exclusion of other faiths?"

"Not at all," said Smith and there was that jolly laugh again. I wondered then if I hadn't discovered his tell. He laughed when insulted. Now how to use that?

"We examine faith and trends through history," Smith explained, "with particular attention to the internal landscapes."

"What?"

"He means psychedelics," said someone else.

"They play a part."

"Ah, okay," I said. "Now I understand."

"What do you now understand?" asked Sylvia.

"How Smith and Tessner got together. Drugs."

"They're part of many paths, but not the only path," Smith explained.

"You're making a drug commune," I said and the words themselves shattered whatever haze my mind was in. "That's what all this is about."

"There will be something like a commune at the center, and hopefully more, but the image I can see you're drawing is wrong. We'll teach the shamanic ways with care and guidance."

"Timothy Leary clutches his love beads."

"Mr. Flaner," said Smith looking disappointed, and damn if that look on his face didn't make me feel bad. "Tony, you yourself know the powers of psychedelics."

"I've never—" I pulled up, considered, consented and shrugged. "Fair cop. Just wanted to test your discernment."

Smith laughed again. Hell if I wasn't getting more laughs in that lobby than I got at my last sets at The Comedy Cellar.

"Ted is interested in that part of our plan, to be sure. But he's a genuine seeker too."

Struggling to keep some control over my utterly failed cross examination, I said, "What does he seek?"

"Truth. Absolution. Freedom."

"Can you be more specific?"

"I could," said Smith. "But I won't."

I chewed on that while Smith answered questions about charity (good), hatred (bad), sustainable energy (necessary), and humankind's potential (infinite).

"Netflix?" I said.

"What about it?"

"Right."

"Well, they offered me a bunch of money to make a series about belief and we took the money to make the center and made a series about spirituality."

"Twelve episodes?" I said.

"Yes."

"Maybe another," added Sangye. "There's a chance."

"So it's open ended? A cliff-hanger? That's pretty shitty considering how Netflix is famous for killing series just when they get a following."

Smith shrugged and glanced around. Sylvia nodded, the rest of the crowd nodded besides.

"It's a complete thing," Smith explained. "Sangye is pressing for a possible epilogue.

"About what?"

Smith was about to answer, but Sangye cut him off.

"Not decided yet."

"Really? I can't imagine why Netflix hasn't jumped at that."

Sangye glared at me.

"Was that a snarky thing to say?" I asked.

"Yes," came a chorus from the entire assemblage.

"Well someone had to say it."

No response.

Plato would be proud.

"The series is coming out this summer. It'll really do wonders for COTTEO," said Sylvia.

"Too bad the center won't be open yet."

"We'll have something," she said.

"Do you have some kind of building permit?"

Glares.

"Someone had to ask," I said,

"We're not in a hurry," said Smith calmly, soothingly, mellowly. "Everything is fine."

Nods from the group.

Sangye's phone buzzed. He glanced at it and excused himself to talk. I watched him cross the lobby and exit the building and my eyes fell upon Hannah watching us from a corner of the lobby. I waved.

She scowled.

I beckoned her to come over.

She shook her head. I could hear her teeth grind from where I was.

"Sylvia?" I said.

Her eyes followed mine. "Oh." She waved.

Hannah scowled.

She beckoned her to come.

She shook her head.

Out of ideas, I asked Smith what we should do. He looked at the angry woman staring daggers into the group.

He waved at her.

She scowled.

He beckoned her to come over.

She took a step.

"Wow…" I muttered.

I shouldn't have, because it broke the spell and Hannah turned on her heels and went looking for a manager.

"She has to find her own way," was what Smith said about that.

"How do you handle all these creeps," asked a middle-aged black-haired lady.

"She's my daughter," explained Sylvia.

"No," said the woman. "The creeps like them."

She pointed to a group of skinheads, another group of goths, a gaggle of glassy-eyed adoring fans with autographed Donnopher pictures. The classes had just let out.

"We handle them with kindness."

Sangye rejoined us. Her face was flushed.

"No," explained the woman. "The creeps who led those people astray. The false prophets? They're spreading poison."

As if on cue, the skinheads began their Easter caroling. "White Power! White Power! White Power!"

Smith stood up and faced them across the lobby.

"Gentlemen?" he said softly. "If you please."

They looked at each other's sheepish faces, shut up, and then scurried away.

"Wow…" I said again.

"Ignorance is a problem," said Smith, settling back down. "It's one of the three poisons. We have to be on our guard."

"Why not just call them out?" asked the woman.

Smith put on a warm, Nazi-forgiving expression and was about to speak when Sangye spoke instead.

"It's not our place really. What would be the good?"

17

I STUMBLED away from the sermon in the lobby a little rattled. Not that anything that was said was upsetting, upturned my views of the world, made me want to be fishers of men or anything, but spending an hour in Smith's presence was sublime, dare I use that word. Or maybe I should hedge and say it was unlike anything I'd ever experienced ever before. It was like a warm soak in a bubbly tub with the best of British Bake-Off projected via kitten purrs to your inner eyelids. Just like that. Soothing, calming. One felt hopeful just being there. Listening to him suggested positive purpose. I remembered the woman confessing herself, and then nearly melted when I remembered my own. Why had I done that? What kind of witchery did that man possess to get people to do that? If it'd been The Messenger or even Tuku, I might have imagined some alien technology or truth serum gas. But it was only Smith's charisma and warmth. The Dalai Lama came to mind, and other controversial historical figures. I don't think I'd ever met a person with so little guile. God help me, but in a hotel full of fakirs, he seemed like the genuine article.

Why, oh why, did I get involved in another domestic case? It's one of the few rules I have as a private investigator, right up there with don't talk to cops and remembering to pluck that one hair that my razor invariably misses. I reached up and felt the stubbly hair beside my nose and sighed.

I'd gone from one extreme of prejudice against COTTEO to the other one of nearly falling for it. I needed more data, some input from the other side to remind me that there was another side. There are always two sides, regardless of how convincing one sounds at first, and then I reflected, as I've been taught to reflect from hours sitting with my eyes closed on a yoga mat holding in farts, that sides look different depending on where you're sitting.

Bat shit looks normal when your eyebrows are deep in guano, peace, love and understanding are catchphrases for theft, and all Nazis are bastards who forget to include that one good Nazi we all forget about, whoever that was. We can only hope that we get enough clarity to identify the obviously right side and toss the others away like the bat-shit crazy they are.

And right on cue, there came Garrett with Critter on his arm. They were arguing.

"The devil you see versus the one in the dark," said Critter. "Homecoming is much scarier."

"But they have no boots on the ground. BORA has fighters in place."

"BRA," I said. "Call The Brotherhood of Righteous Action BRA instead of BORA."

"Why?"

"It pisses them off."

"They're scary," said Garrett. "I saw half a class with that Augustus Klept guy. He lectured flanked by three skinheads standing menacing with bulging folded arms."

"What was the talk on?"

"Organizing militias for the coming race war."

"Hardly seems in keeping with the theme of the conference."

"He was very inclusive," explained Critter. "There were lots of minorities in the room taking notes. Blacks, Asians, Irish. Some Wiccans. More than a smattering of militant crossdressers asking about the best way to track corporate jets."

"Well, then everything's hunky-dory."

"Homecoming was the scary one," said Critter.

"He's overreacting," explained Garrett. "He talked in gibberish."

"In tongues?"

"No. He spoke of redemption through atonement."

"And?"

"He showed his arms as an example. Tons of self-harm scars."

"Ouch."

"He said his first one was given to him by a saint in a subway."

"It was a long cut on his throat," explained Garrett, showing me with his thumb the cut from his Adams Apple to his ear.

"That was a good thing?"

"Since there's an intermediate existence after this and before the next—"

"There is?"

"According to Adam Tuku there is," said Garrett.

"Stop interrupting," said Critter.

"Sorry."

He nodded sagely, accepting Garrett's apology with his rattling eyes. Critter is a puppet, remember. It's hard to remember sometimes.

"Since there is this intermediate level, according to Tuku," went on Critter, "We are wasting our time here and we should all help each other to 'get on with it.'"

"Get on with it?"

"His words," said Garrett.

"And you were debating who was the scariest of the two?"

"Yep."

"Let me know how that comes out."

I left them and wandered down the hall and caught a bit from Barty-B's show.

"Can I have a hallelujah that God gives gifts?" he roared at the crowd.

"Hallelujah!" came the response to the call.

"So giving is Godlike! Hallelujah!"

"Hallelujah!"

"Be Godlike and God Loves You!"

"Hallelujah!"

And up flashed a QR code on a screen behind the spray-tanned man for a Venmo account that the congregation, I mean conference attendees could use to give ACOG money. ACOG, you'll remember from your alphabet soup program is The Abundant Church of God, located in Beebe, voted the eleventh best suburb of Little Rock, Arkansas. They even have a Walmart Supercenter.

I had to admire Bartalemuw Benson, Barty-B to his teasers. He had no stage, no special lights, no paid chorus, no shills to fall over for feeling the spirit. He had only a hotel podium, a projected square and a microphone, but goddamn if he didn't have himself a revival going on. True showmanship. If he could do so much with so little here, imagine what he could do in a tent. He had, I recalled, a converted basketball arena back home.

He wiped sweat from his brow with a soaked handkerchief and then wrapped his hands together around the microphone and turned his face up in prayer.

"Thank you, O Lord, for the generosity of the generous," he beseeched. "Such noble tithing—"

Here I turned off. The word alone would have done it, but the show was enough. Feeling my COTTEO palate good and cleansed with this snake oil, I scanned the room for anyone I knew. I came up with a single face I recognized; Lewis, the server from Ted's house that morning and the tiki bartender. He'd changed clothes, was more casual now in tight slacks and a button-down shirt with most of the buttons open. Gold chain on his furry-tanned chest. He swayed with his arms up with the rest, following Barty's example from up front. Barty was crying now, full-on bawling, snot running down his face to be caught pre-suit stain by his mop of a hanky. Five thousand dollars of Italian tailoring was thus saved from his globulous mucus.

"Hallelujah!" I shouted and left.

"Hallelujah!" come the response.

Following the earthy smells of sage and firewood, I found Artstar and her Coven in a smoke-filled room calling for the forces of the moon to bless the time of Ostara.

"Hallelujah!" I cried and had fifteen black-lined eyes turn to me.

"Blessed be," I corrected myself.

"Blessed be," came the response.

I wondered if the fire marshal knew about the three burning censers around the chalk outline of a pentacle on the carpet in the middle of the room. Probably not.

It was another show, but this one was more inclusive than Barty-B's. The circular structure of the classroom helped with that a lot. It was intimate, and close was good because it was hard to see through the smoke.

"This is the season of fertility," moaned Artstar.

"So Mote it Be," came a response from some of them, the ones in black robes, I figured. The entire group did, however, sway together and reminded me a lot of the prayer meeting down the hall. People closest to the circle sat together on the floor, their arms interlocked. Farther out, people held hands and sat in chairs. Beyond that, people stood and didn't hold hands but many swayed just the same.

I wasn't sure I wanted to breach the inner circles, so tried my hand at swaying in the smoke.

"Fertility means more than eggs and rabbits," she moaned. Really it was like these were pained words. I wasn't sure if she was about to cry, again to recall Barty, or move into a spirit voice of monotone importance.

"All magic is about sacrifice and the secretions of power." She flashed her dazzling eyes around the circle. Light caught in them, shone, reflected. Dazzled. "Ostara is sex. Copulation. Love."

I thought it interesting that love was the last thing on the list. Made things easier I suppose.

"The festival continues, the joy of life, the excitement of bonding."

"Blessed be."

"Blessed be," I added late with the third wave. Hard to follow the script with these guys. Much easier call and response down the hall.

"Join us in room 918 after the keynote tonight to consummate that festival," she said and clapped her hands. "Any questions?"

And just like that, in an instant, Artstar went from Witch Leader to substitute algebra teacher. She tossed back her hood, waved some strands of hair and incense from her face and looked around pleasantly to explain hypotenuses. It took the others a few moments longer to cotton onto that whatever was happening, wasn't anymore. I was quicker off the line.

"Are you saying that this little event will be continued later on tonight in room 918?"

"Yes, directly after the keynote."

"And what will happen then?" I asked.

"We'll consummate Ostara."

"How exactly."

"Through sex."

"Sex?"

"Sex."

"As in humping sex? Doing the beast with two backs? Making Whoopee? Putting the bread in the basket? Assault with a friendly weapon kind of thing? Bumping ugly sex?"

"A holy copulation for all who'd celebrate Ostara."

"As a group?"

"All are welcome."

"An orgy?"

"Don't be vulgar. This is a magickal rite."

"Sorry," I said. "Okay, just to reiterate, everyone's invited to room 918 after the big speech tonight to Slytherin the Hufflepuff. Is that right and magical enough?"

She scowled but nodded. "That's basically it."

"Will lube—"

"Any other questions?" she asked.

John Smith's COTTEO trance was good and gone as I imagined what a Wiccan orgy would look like. I left before anyone noticed the physical manifestation of my thought processes.

"Happy to see me?"

It was Allie in the hallway.

"Do we have any plans tonight after the keynote?" I asked her.

"No..." she answered warily. "Why?"

"No reason."

"You've been invited to an orgy, haven't you?"

I blushed. "Wait. How'd you know?"

She looked at my crotch and said, "I've been invited to three so far."

"Really?"

"Yeah, this place is a regular brothel. Judging from the smell, you heard about the Coven's one later tonight. There's also a Peoplists 'mingling meet.' No phones."

"That doesn't mean orgy."

She handed me a pack of Donnopher-branded condoms. "They change colors if they detect an STD," she explained. "Cutting edge stuff."

"What's the high score so far?"

She shivered. "BORA is having an all-conference all day kegger. 'Chicks drink free.'" She gave me a flier.

"Checks out," I said.

"The Messenger asked me up for some one-on-one time."

"What?"

She nodded.

"Perry's guy? I'm sure he just wanted to indoctrinate you."

"With his penis."

"How can you—"

"A girl can tell. I have a lifetime of reading the signs."

"Not to defend him, but couldn't he have—"

"Meant something else by the word schtup? Maybe."

"Um, 'you've got to schtup before the power of my loony lunar God?'"

"That was it. I'll head right up. I've got these." She flashed the condoms.

"I just threw up a little."

"Welcome to the conclave."

"Did Kaisa try to get into your pants?"

"I'm not her flavor."

"She has no taste."

"Tell me about it. She remembered you. She asked if we are exclusive."

"That's fucked up."

Allie, because she's wonderful, only shrugged.

"A cult isn't a cult until it says God orders the leaders to sleep with the congregation."

"So you got a date with Smith?" she asked.

"Actually, no."

"So not a cult?"

"Jury's out. But Green Tomorrow fits the bill?"

"No. Forget the sex. Kaisa's doing good work. It's not her fault she's been elevated—"

"Don't drink the Kool-Aid."

"Imported mineral water actually."

"What?"

"It's called Woods Water. It's from the Amazon."

"That seems like a carbon loss."

She frowned. "It was to show how pure the water of the area is, before it's ruined by industrial chemicals."

Because I'm me, I pressed, "You're telling me Kaisa Woods served unfiltered, Amazon creek water?"

"Don't say it like that."

"Sorry. How about Brazilian amoeba soup?"

"I'm sure it was safe."

"Parasite punch?"

"Stop it."

"Giardia broth?"

"Tony…"

"A cholera cocktail?"

"It was fine!" She stamped her foot for emphasis. "I'm sure it was treated."

"With chemicals? Maybe chemicals sourced from some kind of industry?"

"I'm not talking to you anymore." She was mad enough to die of dysentery.

"We should probably get you a tetanus shot or something. Did you purge after lunch?"

"Tony, we were getting along so well."

It dawned on me, in a moment of pure enlightenment, that to some, downriver run-off refreshments are sacred cows.

"Ohm..." I hummed.

"I don't need your shit."

"But Amazonian—?

"Tony..."

"Ohm."

The hallway was suddenly full of people like it was sixth period letting out.

Driven by high school anxiety and not sure we remembered our locker numbers let alone pants, we left the hotel for some air.

We walked sidewalks and paths, dodging bikes, joggers, dog shit and homeless people until we found a path by the Willamette and followed it, enjoying a spring afternoon among lush green plants. Although I'd spent time in this valley before, knew this river, maybe had walked this very path, it was all alien now. I wondered at this, thought maybe my new found peaceful ways had brightened things.

I mentioned it to Allie to show my progress.

"Tony, dear," she said soothingly, "you have no peaceful ways, you have intention."

"No, I'm a new man. I see this place so differently now."

"You're saying you've had an epiphany? A Damascene vision?"

"Well, no. Not like that. But I'm a better person."

"Tony, dear, you're just yourself with just a touch more self-reflective."

"Then how do you explain how I see how beautiful this place is?"

"Because it is beautiful."

I was about to argue, to explain how things looked the last time I was here, when I realized the key difference. Today, it wasn't raining. It was warm, I was dry, and things were bright green instead of soggy-muted green because it wasn't raining. All my memories of before were colored in rain. Incessant rain turned to cold rain become freezing rain become cold rain turning incessant rain, and I was out of there and didn't see what else there was. To me, it was all rain rain rain rain rain rain cold rain, really cold rain, rain rain.

"We should get back," she said. "We don't want to miss Smith's keynote."

"We don't?"

"You're on a case, remember?"

"Yeah, but I can do without the hotel rubber chicken plate tonight. I know a little Mexican joint with great tamales."

So we turned back, hand in hand, friends again, And I tried to remember what I was looking for. A tamer temper? Peace? An epiphany? Keener powers of weather observation? And then I wondered if Paul's vision on the road wasn't influenced by weather somehow and bet it was.

The tamale place was now a Thai place but had breezy outdoor seating, passable pad thai and that cardamom cream drink they dare call tea. We chatted outside as the wind picked up and reminded us that it wasn't summer yet. A cloud passed over and invited friends. In the gloom, Eugene took on a familiar cast.

It was after seven thirty when we returned to the hotel. We'd not missed dinner, unfortunately. People were still chewing the chicken and stabbing at salmon, forking at fruit.

The big wigs from the morning session were now scattered around the room as 'table hosts.' Each had a reserved spot at one of the huge round tables, a card clutched in a brass stand proclaiming their domain. I think this was intended as a mixing thing, but each table was exclusively populated with people of that particular faith, as evidenced by orange suits, shiny heads, black robes, wild eyes, and conservative chic looking adoringly at their guru or menacingly at other tables. The exception was Smith's COTTEO table. I didn't recognize anyone there, they looked to be the mishmash of people the hosting thing was meant to attract, but the space reserved for Smith himself, the evening's keynote speaker I remembered, was vacant. Ted Tessner's table was right under the stage, doubtless because he was MC, but he too wasn't in attendance. Neither could I see buzzing around busy British iPad-bearing Rachael. Allie found our friends way in the back with the other shunned non-believing-enoughs and we were headed that direction when someone grabbed my shoulder and turned me around.

It was Sylvia Rigsdale and she looked upset.

"Mr. Flaner, I fear Hannah has done something…terrible."

It was strange, but I immediately knew what had happened and I wanted to throw up.

"How can I help?" I said.

"They're trying to cover it up. For the conclave."

"Take me there."

She led the way out of the hall through the lobby, to the bank of elevators. I glanced back once at Allie who watched me go but must have seen something on my face, because she nodded concerned understanding.

Sylvia pushed the top floor button and together, in silence, we watched the door close and felt the world grow heavy above us.

The ninth floor was a buzz of people, firemen, police, and hotel staff.

Sylvia took my hand and led me to a room on the left. No one stopped us, questioned us, or seemed to even notice us until at the door, Rachael looked up. Her eyes were wild when they met mine. She blinked and looked down at her table as if seeing if we were on the list. Sylvia pushed past and we were in the suite.

It was a full-on suite, not sensible like mine. There were several rooms, an entryway, bathroom, bedroom and wide sitting room with places to sit, like chairs and a couch. There was a bed in the bedroom. A bath in the bathroom. I noticed these things because I was trying not to notice the other thing. For as many people as were in the hall, I noticed there were few inside. With observational skills blunted by dread, I noticed that Ted was there, along with an EMT with a stethoscope over his shoulders. Bruce Allenby, the man I'd met on the flight was also there. He glanced at me and didn't speak. Ted watched me enter, led by Sylvia, and all of them parted to reveal John Smith face down with a bullet hole in his back.

18

I ABSORBED the moment as if I were out of my body observing it from a height, the world rushing around me, the center deadly still and sharp-focused. I felt a loss that in no way coincided with how briefly I'd known this man, didn't even connect with the idea of death I'd come to recognize upon seeing a body. I've seen a few, and it's never easy, *momente mori* shoved in your face, but John Smith's body was different. It was loss, not just mortal loss, but like a rare opportunity had passed and would not come again.

"Tony."

I looked back and saw Ted leaving the room, Rachael pulling him by the arm.

"Yes?" I said.

No one responded. I looked at Sylvia. "You say something?"

She shook her head.

"What do you want me to do?"

"Save them."

"Who?"

She shook her head again.

"Who is that man?" a policeman finally asked.

Feeling my time in that room was now on a short clock, I took in the scene while Sylvia played interference.

The room was a suite. Smith was facedown in the sitting room. He was near a wall, his head nearly against it. A picture frame above him was askew. Maybe he'd touched it falling down, maybe he'd been straightening it when he was killed, à la Jesse James.

His arms, I noted with some irony, were spread out straight from his sides. His tie was next to his ear. His face was straight in the floor. A pool of blood lay under his chest opposite the bullet hole which was, I was sure, right over his heart. He wore blue slacks and socks. A pair of nice matching black loafers at the foot of a made bed to my right, a sensible blue jacket waiting there besides. I reached down and felt for a pulse. I have to admit, I'm not very good at that, I seldom find the right spot. Okay, I never find the right spot, but I thought I should try. Besides, I wanted to get a closer look at the bullet hole in his shirt.

His skin was still warm, and of course, I didn't feel a pulse. The bullet hole was a black rip, a little blood under the shirt in a star pattern from entry point. There were powder burns circling the tear, two inches from the wound.

"You can't be here," said Bruce Allenby.

"Why are you here?"

He flashed me a badge. FBI.

I flashed him my Maverik Adventure Club loyalty card—good for 2¢ off per gallon at the pump if it has a working scanner. I've yet to find one.

"That doesn't make any sense."

"Glad we're in agreement."

I pointed to some folded papers on the table. "Is that his speech?" Before he could comment, I swiveled my head and peeked at the hand-written pages. *I'm working on it*, read the first line. *A new friend of mine explained his spiritual journey in those four words and here I realized was the purest explanation of the path to enlightenment.*

"Jesus," I said.

"You think someone placed him like that on purpose?" Allenby was commenting on the position of the body.

"I'd say he fell like that," I said. "Dead before he hit the ground."

I poked the pages with a pen. "These pages are out of order. You should check them for fingerprints."

"I'm not the officer in charge," said Allenby. "I was just nearby."

"So was I."

"But I have a badge."

"I earn TrailPoints with every purchase. I'd say I win."

"I know you're a PI in Utah—"

"And now I know you're a Fed. Are you here at the conclave for a case?"

"I can't discuss that."

"Does this fit into your case?"

"I can't discuss that."

"Too early to tell, huh? So who's in charge?"

"I am," said Rachael. "Ted left me in charge for now. I understand a local Eugene cop will be by."

I looked at Allenby. "Allenby—Bruce, may I call you Bruce?"

"We're not—"

"Good, Bruce it is. You need to take charge of this."

"Why?"

"Because you're FBI and here."

"I'm already on a case."

"Undercover?"

"Can't discuss that."

"I won't narc. Is it narcotics?"

He looked pained.

"Involved, but not the main case..." I surmised.

"How—"

"FBI not DEA."

"I'm in charge," said Rachael. "I'm the liaison. Talk to me. What do we need here?"

I looked at Bruce waiting for him to say something, but he shook his head, raised his hands and took a physical step back. So it was up to me.

"Have the cops do a thorough sweep of the room," I said. Rachael typed onto her iPad. "Fingerprint the speech. It's fishy."

"Got it."

"I noticed the doors all have those electronic keys. Get me a complete list of key uses, all openings and closings."

"Got it. Should I share that with the police?"

"Might as well. Make sure that I'm the first to get all the information though."

"What about Ted?"

"No. This is above his pay grade."

"Got it."

"Who found the body?"

"I did." It was Sylvia.

I took one more look at the room and then took Sylvia out in the hallway. "Walk me through it."

She took a deep breath. I was worried she'd break down, I could see tears massing behind her eyes like a scream in the darkness.

"He was late," she began. "John's always late, so Sangye and I are always careful to keep him scheduled. When I didn't see either one of them before the banquet I came looking."

"What time?"

"The banquet started at seven but we were asked to be there a quarter hour early to get to our special tables."

"So six forty-five you came up?"

"I called at quarter to, got no answer so went up Sangye's room. He was on John time duty and I figured he'd spaced it."

"Does he usually space it?"

"No." She refueled herself with a deep breath. "But he's been distracted lately.

"With what?"

"The Netflix thing, I think."

"I thought that was basically over?"

"He's the manager. I'm sure there is more to it."

"So you found Sangye in his room at six forty-five?"

"It was closer to ten to, and no, he wasn't there."

"How'd you know?"

"I knocked on the door. No answer."

"And John?"

"His phone is always on focus. You have to leave a message. People know that if anything's important to call Sangye."

"Or you?"

"Sometimes."

"Okay six fifty Sangye's not in his room. What then?"

"I called him again, got no answer, and then went up to John's room."

"Where is Sangye's room?"

"Sixth floor. Six-one-three."

"Do you have a room?"

"No, I rent a place outside of town. I live here."

"That's right."

"How do you know? Oh. Hannah."

"What time did you get to Smith's room?" I asked.

She took out her phone and checked her call logs. "I texted Ted to get up here and called the police at seven. I guess I'd been here maybe five minutes then. Maybe less."

"How'd you get in?"

She showed me a keycard. "We all had keys to the suite."

I noticed her hand shook as she put it back. "Did you touch anything?"

"His neck to feel for a pulse."

"You know how to do that?"

"I used to be a CNA."

"You'll have to teach that to me sometime," I said.

"Okay."

"Then what happened?"

"That FBI guy was the first to arrive. I'd say five minutes later. Then Ted and Rachael. I passed the first responders in the lobby when I went looking for you."

"Why'd you go looking for me?"

"Because you're a detective and you knew John and you'll keep Hannah out of this if it's not her."

"And if it is?"

I half expected a maternal shake of the head, a knowing smirk and some line like 'I know my daughter, Mr. Flaner, it couldn't be Hannah. It's not in her or any of my children,' but that didn't happen. Instead the tears that had waited so long finally came.

A plainclothes cop appeared. He flashed me his badge from a worn brown wallet and scowled. He looked to be about eighty and smelled like he'd used Camel no-filter dryer sheets on his gray seersucker suit and skipped the ironing stage.

"This who found the body?" he asked me, pointing to Sylvia.

I nodded.

And though she was crying hard and deep he said to her, "So tell me what happened. Step by step."

"Imma stop you right there," I said. "Sylvia needs a minute. And a drink of water would be nice."

"This won't take long," he explained.

"Then neither will her answers, which will rhyme with 'I won't say a word without my lawyer present' if you're not nice. Water's cheap."

I have issues with cops. Not only because I've seen all the YouTube videos, read the reports, and basically been alive these last few decades, but one of them actually shot me once. It takes a minute for me to warm up to any cop and this guy, who'd yet to identify himself, wasn't my kind of cozy.

"Get me an EMT," he called over his shoulder.

In short order, one appeared and wrapped Sylvia in a blanket, gave her a water bottle and waited with her while she calmed down.

"Who the hell are you?" the cop asked me.

"You first."

"I'm Detective Dean Johnson, homicide."

"I'm generally annoying, Tony Flaner, licensed private investigator."

"Get out."

"But—"

"Get out."

I was surprised. I expected to be grilled about why I was there, my relationship with the deceased, if I was an autumn or a summer, but he booted me away instantly. I was at once pleased at not being hassled but worried about this lack of efficiency. If he's the guy the police were putting on this case, it better be an easy one or it wasn't getting solved.

In the hall, I passed Rachael, and we exchanged phone numbers. I then went to the one remaining hotel staffer still about. I guess Johnson had chased the rest away.

The woman was Hispanic, about five foot three, thin, and had a warm but worried smile.

I flashed her my Maverik card really quick and said in a conspiratorial voice, "I need to get into room six-thirteen."

She nodded and signaled me to go follow her inside an unmarked room with tons of shelves but a wide path between them. A big industrial elevator opened up at her push of a button. We got in and she pushed six.

The walls of the elevator were nicked and scratched and the back wall had a moving blanket taped up. I also noticed a telltale black dome in the corner of the ceiling, a camera with a subtle, but accusing, blinking red light.

We emerged onto a deserted sixth floor and went to room 613. I knocked.

"Sangye?" I called.

I had a sick hunch. Usually I like it when my hunches are right, it's affirming. It's an ego boost, but this time I dreaded it. Not only was I supposedly on a quest to quell my ego, but if I was right, there'd be something terrible behind this door.

"Open it," I told the maid, Yesenia, was her name.

She stretched a white card from an elastic lanyard and touched the lock. A red light changed to green with a quiet snap. Using my shirttail and one finger, I opened the door.

I could smell it before I saw it. Gun smoke and not the exciting radio show turned longtime television western starring James Arness as Matt Dillon running twenty seasons and 635 filmed episodes kind of gun smoke. The kind of gun smoke that's tinged with a coppery smell that never means good things.

I pushed the door open with my foot and saw, across the room, slumped over a table, John Smith's manager, Sangye. His face was turned toward me, dead staring down the hall, his head on the table in a puddle of blood. Far as I was, I could see a gaping hole in his right temple. His arm lay straight to his side, hovering over a bloody pool where a gun lay atop it beneath his dangling fingers.

Yesenia gasped and made the sign of the cross and said prayers in Spanish for the Indian corpse.

I checked my watch because a good cop would ask me about it. Seven forty-five. "Stay here and hold the door," I said to Yesenia. "And watch me closely. Someone will ask you about it."

She nodded and continued praying sotto voce.

I crept into the room, careful where I stepped, staying near the walls. I was aware that I was violating a crime scene and would probably lose my license for this, but I also knew that Johnson wouldn't give me access once he was here.

I approached the body and touched Sangye's cold neck, checking for a pulse. My perfect score of finding none continued.

The entry hole in his head was pretty big compared to Smith's. I think the barrel had to have been pressed right up to it. I saw then the spray of yuck on the curtains and knew they'd find a bullet hole in the glass.

There we papers on the table soaking up the clotting blood.

I glanced around the room, bothered by a creeping feeling that I was being watched.

Yesenia waved from the door where she was watching me.

"Oh, yeah."

The room was lived in. The bed was made but covered in papers, folders, and an adding machine with paper tape. How quaint. I've long since given those up for my phone, which does all and knows all and sees all.

Where was Sangye's phone? It wasn't on the bed. If it was on the desk, it was under his gruesomely destroyed skull. Feeling around Sangye's waist, I felt it in his front pocket. It took a minute, but I pulled out his phone, turned it on, and then, grimly, held it in front of Sangye's face and opened it.

I took my own phone out and turned on the video capture. Quickly, I opened his recent calls and scrolled down, filming it all. I opened his text messages and did the same to the last five threads he'd had, for as far as I dared. I opened his notes app and clicked on the most recent. I was moving to the emails when a sound solidly stopped my sleuthing.

"Tony? Oh my god…"

"Is that little shit in there?"

I recognized Tessner's voice accompanied by the soothing swears of Detective Johnson's, but I didn't turn to look. My eyes were fixed on the gun on the floor under Sangye's lifeless hand, a big black revolver with neon green grips.

19

I WAS ARRESTED on the spot. The reason given was tampering with a crime scene which I considered damn kind since I was sure I'd be nabbed for suspicion of murder. In truth I was busted for pissing off a cop which was also a kindness since it's not uncommon for that crime to be punished on the spot with choke holds, knees on necks, taser conflagrations or twenty-eight warning shots into the chest after complying with every order. Some would call this privilege, but I didn't argue the point. Ted was there and had my back. They wouldn't listen to a word Yesenia said, and ignored surprisingly detailed descriptions of my every moment, including time stamps. Nevertheless, I made sure they took down her information. They couldn't get past that she'd opened the door for me in the first place. My bluff might have cost her a job and Johnson was pissed.

I spent the night in jail. The murder and my part in it had happened at an inconvenient time and everything had to wait until the next day.

They took my shoelaces, my belt, my phone, wallet, pride, smile, and patience and stuck me in a holding cell with a bunch of homeless men who'd dared blight the city with sadness. My worries disappeared as I heard one man weep over his dog that had been run over that day, intentionally he was sure, by a Tesla. He found the driver at a gas station and confronted him. Another man was upset that his tent was trashed. He went to work and came back to find his little camp being loaded into a garbage truck guarded by cops in riot gear. Here was a man with a job, but no home. Tents don't count as homes so in the name of beautification, destroying all of someone's earthly possessions is okay. Not like he had a mailing address. Close on the heels of losing all his good clothes and pictures was his worry that now he'd miss work and lose his job. He regrets arguing with the policemen, he told me. I wanted to tell him he should have pissed on his shoes at least.

I was surprised I stayed overnight. People of my class, that is not the lowest, can usually get out pretty quick but that was not the case. People like Ted would never have been arrested, and if for some cosmic reason, he had to be, the cops would arrange things with his lawyer so it wouldn't interfere with his trip to Bermuda.

I hate being reminded of the world we live in, but here it was and with it came a glimpse of why people were angry and scared and reaching and reacting and acting out. No justice, no peace. Was all the craziness going on in the world a reflection of social inequality? Some would say so. From what I knew of Smith, he'd not discount the notion, but was social inequality the cause or the effect of different philosophies. I suddenly wanted a good old-fashioned debate with the conclave, and the pope and the Dalai Lama, maybe Moses and Krishna too to figure it all out, but instead I found a urine-stinking lower cot and went to bed praying not for world peace and the deliverance of the downtrodden, but that my bunkmate wasn't incontinent. There's a lesson there.

———

It was after lunch the next day that I was finally brought out of my cell to an interrogation room.

"I've not had my phone call," I said to Detective Johnson. "That's a no-no."

"You're not being held—"

"Could have fooled me."

He grimaced and glanced up at a camera in the corner.

"You're free to go—"

"Bye." I stood up.

"After I debrief you."

I sat back down, put my hands on the table and adopted a smile I saw on a Buddha once. I wanted to go for peace and calm, but it might have come off as 'go fuck yourself' to the policeman.

"Well?" he said.

"I start? Oh, sorry." I stood up, and keeping my peaceful smile, undid my pants, slid them down, stepped out of them and then lowered my shorts.

"Hey! What the hell are you doing?"

"I'm being debriefed, right? Here they are." Using the elastic waistband, I shot them right at him. He jumped like it was a live snake, not just dirty briefs. "Can I go now?"

"Put your fucking clothes on," he said and stormed out of the room.

I got dressed. I might have mooned the cameras a couple times, I don't recall.

After a while, someone came in with my phone which was dead, shoelaces which were broken, belt which someone had shrunk just last Christmas, and the rest of my junk. As I was reassembling myself Ted Tessner came in with Rachael.

"Hi Tony."

"Hi Rachael," I said. "How you doing?"

"Still a little shaken up. You missed a belt loop."

"Thanks."

She seemed amused but Ted seemed worried.

I stepped toward the door. Ted stepped in front of me.

"Tony."

"What?"

"Before we go, we want to fill you in on what happened and ask you what happened."

"That order's a bit messed up," I said. "But I gotta give it to you, you sure as shit got a lot of pull in this little berg. How long have you known Detective Johnson?"

"Went to school together."

"And the chief of police?"

"Known him longer."

"So who's working for whom here?" I glanced up at the camera.

"We're all on the same team."

"Spiffy. I gotta get back to Allie."

"She's fine. She stayed at my place last night."

"How wonderful," I said, but something in my tone, probably the murderous intent, set him on edge.

"Strictly platonic."

"I want to leave."

"Sit down for a minute. We'll just have a chat."

I did not like where this was going, not one little bit, but I knew that the way out that door lay through the chair. I sat down.

"Thanks." Ted took the seat Johnson had had. I tried to remember they were different people.

"How's the conclave going?" I asked Rachael.

"Fine, better than can be expected."

"It wasn't canceled?"

"No."

"Why not?"

"Why should it?" asked Ted.

"Maybe because there was a murder."

"That was truly unfortunate, but no one is in danger. The storm has passed."

"Are you high?" I asked. "I'm not judging, I just want to know."

"No, I'm not high," he said. "Barely had anything."

"What happened at the keynote?" again I asked Rachael.

"We said that Smith was indisposed and had Donnopher fill in."

"Weren't they scheduled for the big weekend?"

"Yes," she said. "Kinda sucks to have had to bump them up."

"How terrible for you."

She blanched at that.

"We'd like you to go home," said Ted. "For the good of the conclave."

"But what about the murder? I can help."

"The case is already closed. Sangye killed Smith with Klept's gun in the suite."

"And I was sure it was Ms. Peacock."

"Allie tells me that you'll make trouble if you stay. We don't need that. ICOHEP can really do some good, but it's fragile. The last thing we need is someone making trouble."

"Why would I make trouble?"

"Maybe you won't," he said. "But we can't take that chance."

"Sounds to me that you don't buy the murder-suicide story either."

"Of course I believe it. It's what happened."

"Then why worry about me?"

"Will you promise not to tell anyone at the conclave what you saw? What happened?"

"No."

"Then you have to go."

"Wait," I said. "Why do I get the impression that Smith's death is being hushed up."

No one said a word.

"You've got to be kidding?"

"It's for the best. For the conclave. Smith wouldn't want his death to destroy the dream of what ICOHEP is."

"And what is it?"

"Envisioning the future direction of humanity."

"And a little murder-suicide isn't the right direction?"

"Of course not."

"I've seen your conclave. I think it might be exactly where it's going."

"Allie said you'd be disruptive. Please, for me. For Allie, go home. Or maybe go to Hawaii. You can use my house. It's on the beach. I'll fly you out."

I know I shouldn't have been angry with Allie. She didn't know that Tessner would use her against me like a bludgeon, but I was still a little pissed and jealousy was again slithering in the dark recesses of my solar plexus chakra.

"Let me have my phone call," I said.

"You're not being—"

"Phone."

"You have your phone."

"It's dead."

"Bummer."

I scowled.

"You mustn't tell the conclave," said Ted.

"How can one phone tell the entire conclave? There are hundreds of people there."

He thought about it, then opened his phone. Maybe to help, maybe to make a point, maybe to rouse the green monster in my skull, he brought up Allie's contact card before handing it over.

I smiled the smile of the righteous and took the miracle of modern technology.

I closed the contacts app, turned on the phone and called Perry Whitehouse.

"Hello?"

"It's me, Tony."

"Where have you been? We've been worried."

"Really?"

"Well uhm, no. Not Dara. Standard went to check out the comedy clubs but Critter asked about you and I was wondering."

"I'm fine," I said and winked at Ted. "I'll be back soon."

Ted didn't nod but neither did he shake his head.

I said, "I really want to see the rest of the conclave."

"You do?"

"Sure. Why not?"

"Okay. So I'll see you soon?"

"Yeah."

"Okay, bye," said Perry.

"Oh wait, one thing. A Mick Jagger favor."

"Yeah?"

"Let's spread the word that John Smith was murdered in his hotel room last night."

Ted had the phone out of my hand in an instant, but I still heard Perry's matter-of-fact replay. "Will do."

"Hello? Who's this?" demanded Ted, but Perry had hung up.

He redialed. The phone went immediately to voice mail where an electronic voice informed us that it hadn't been set up yet.

"Flaner..."

"What? Whatcha' going to do?"

That's when he hit me.

I can't say it was a sucker punch, but hell if I'd thought he had it in him or he'd do it there and then with cameras and witnesses and me already a known troublemaker. It wasn't a fisted slug but neither was it a slap. Open-handed but hard across my mouth. I guess he was trying to disarm me. He bloodied my lip and put me in that weird physical violence eruption moment when the nonviolent take a long time to process the violence that happened to them.

Before I got my senses Bruce Allenby was through the door followed quickly by Detective Johnson. The cop went to restrain Ted, which in this case was a calm hand on the shoulder. Allenby lifted me out of the chair and dragged me out of the room.

My senses came to me as we were walking briskly down the hall. Allenby gave me a handkerchief and I was holding it to my mouth.

"You carry a handkerchief?"

"You'd be surprised how often I use it."

"Is this covered in snot?"

"Not that one. It's fresh."

"Nice."

He walked me out of the police station and directly to a secluded bench off to the side in a bower of trees. It was quaint. Pretty and green. A hidden little place to sit. Shame it was so close to jackbooted oppression, but where today isn't?

"How do you know about this bench?"

"I used to work in this city," Allenby said.

"Doing what?"

"Same as now. FBI."

"Welcome home."

"Not a lot has changed," he said and I thought I heard some bitterness in his voice.

"You and Ted friends then?"

"Acquaintance."

"Is he the reason you're at the conclave?"

"I can't comment on that."

"But you are?"

"No, actually."

"Okay."

"You probably should leave the city, Mr. Flaner."

"Think the trip to Hawaii is still an option?"

"Actually, I do."

"What if I don't think it was a murder-suicide?"

"What are you talking about?" He seemed generally surprised at the idea.

"Maybe it was suicide-suicide."

"What?"

"Smith paid Sangye to kill him as a favor and then Sangye killed himself."

"What are you basing that on?"

"Not a goddamn thing, but since we're throwing out easy explanations and closing the case on the spot, I thought I'd get in a bet."

"I saw what you saw. Pretty clear. Granted, the motive isn't obvious, but I bet we don't have to dig deep to find it."

"What about keep the secret from the conclave?" I asked. "You good with that?"

"Not my call," he said.

"Will they cancel the conclave now that the murder has been announced?"

"You told one person. How many people can he tell?"

"It's true I told one person who has an archaic Nokia phone to stop stray bullets, but he's an entertainer. I used our secret code. He'll have a billboard by now."

Allenby shook his head disbelieving.

"He also knows Dara who has more social media followers than that yodeling beagle."

"I still don't..." Bruce's phone beeped. He looked at the number and sighed. "I gotta go. I got you out of there now leave before they arrest you for something."

"Sylvia called Ted last night and Ted called you. Am I right?"

"I was closest."

He walked out of the little arbor, his phone pressed to his ear. I dabbed the last of the blood from my face contemplating my next move. After a moment, Sylvia Rigsdale peeked around a bush.

"Hey Sylvia."

"What happened to you?"

"The sound of one-hand slapping."

She sat down next to me.

"I'm just going to say it. Did Hannah do this?"

"I don't think so."

"Did Sangye?"

"The cops think so."

"Do you?"

I recalled the scenes and my stomach did a flip. Once for the loss of Smith, once for lies with Sangye.

"No."

"Can I hire you to—"

"I thought you'd never ask."

20

TED BEAT us back to the hotel. Rachael was already seeing to the next keynote. The tables were set up as before but not COTTEOs. I'd missed all the classes that day by being locked in jail. Not sure I was upset about that.

The gang found me all at once.

"Mission accomplished?" I asked.

"Yep," said Standard. "If there's anyone in Oregon who doesn't know about it yet, they're in a cave."

"So the majority?"

"I'd say so."

We got in line for the buffet and returned with our food to the table they'd had the day before.

"So where's Allie?" Dara asked me.

"I thought you'd know."

"I haven't seen her since last night," said Garrett.

"Me neither," said Critter.

"Should we be worried?"

"Not yet." I didn't go into it and they took the hint.

The room filled up. There was no mingling as Ted had suggested the day before. If anything, each clique had grown denser.

"So tell us," said Perry. "You cost me three burner phones, by the way."

"But got me three hundred followers," said Dara.

"So a wash."

"What price is fame?" mused Critter.

"Three phones," I answered.

"There it is."

"As soon as I got traction," Dara explained, "this was the message to the conference sent out." She showed me her phone.

> We regret to inform our guests that John Smith of the Church of The Third Eye Opened was tragically killed today. A suspect in the killing has been found and he too is dead. There is NO DANGER to the public. Use code MOURNING to get 10% off in the gift store.

I glanced at my phone to see if I got the message too. It was of course, still dead.

"Not a very deep discount," said I.

"He wasn't into materialism. I saw it as a compromise."

"So?" said Perry. "What happened?"

Over buffet fish and chips, I told them what had happened. Sylvia coming to get me and seeing Smith dead and then finding Sangye.

"And the maid's testimony didn't help at all?" said Standard.

"Maybe. I'm out."

"But on a new case?"

"Yeah. I'll invoice Hannah and her clan claiming mission accomplished with John Smith."

"That's cold."

"I'm in a bad mood. I expected this thing to be over by now."

"Why would you want that?"

"Because Ted is a dick. He's the one who hit me." I showed them my fat lip.

"Looks good on you," said Dara. "I'll help you achieve that look when we get home if you like."

"Thanks."

"Why'd he hit you?" asked Perry.

"Because I tried to nuke the conclave."

"That's a circular argument. You got hit for trying to kill the conclave and got mad enough to want to kill the conclave when you got hit."

"I might also think he's hitting on Allie."

The whole table in a single syllable said, "Oh."

"He does have a hot tub."

"And he's rich."

"Powerful."

"Likes dogs."

"Successful."

"Handsome."

"Thanks," I said. "Now I've got something to think about."

Perry shook his head. "It was a bonehead move anyway since you have a case. All your suspects are here. If it'd been canceled you'd be traveling all over hell chasing people."

"I didn't have the case when I sent you the message. Only righteous anger."

"Preach," said Allie.

We all turned to see my girlfriend, the love of my life, standing next to Ted Tessner beside our table.

Critter caught my eye and shook his head in warning. He nodded to the table where I saw my hand had involuntarily made a fist.

"Hi Allie," I said, cheerfully and with the same tone added, "And fuck you in the ear, Ted."

He blushed. I was happy. Allie scowled. I'm not sure how I felt about that.

"Oh fuck, really?" I said.

"What?" said Ted.

"No, Tony. It's not that."

"Perhaps I should go," said Ted.

"Only if you value your sperm count and rugged good looks," I said.

"Earlobes," added Perry. He always had my back.

"Designer shoes." Garrett tried.

"Vision," added Dara. Her threats always carried special weight with us because she was pretty unpredictable.

"Maybe—"

Dara stood up and Ted beat a retreat.

Allie regarded us with her arms akimbo, a hitch in her hip, disapproving disappointment in her eyes. "Really guys?"

Before I could answer, the gang did.

"Yep."

"Absolutely."

"Someone has to."

"He hit Tony."

"He did what?"

"He sucker-punched Tony in the mouth while being held in police custody." I hadn't put it like that, but that was exactly what had happened. Sounded much worse when Perry said it.

Allie sat down and took a chip off Standard's plate—don't call them fries when they're sharing a plate with breaded cod. Dara's was closer, but Allie knew better.

"Ted wants me to tell you to cool it. Let the police do their jobs, enjoy the conclave and he's sorry for what happened before."

"For hitting me?"

"He just said 'what happened before.' I didn't press it."

My guts were in a complete maelstrom. Granted, I was prone to jealousy and childish antics, jumping to conclusions the only regular exercise I get, but Allie not asking Ted about details, doing his bidding, being so completely blind to how it looks with him, made me want to throw up.

"Where'd you go last night?" asked Garrett.

Allie turned, was about to answer and then, perhaps realizing how it would sound, shrugged.

"She stayed with Ted," I said. I was indeed ready to hurl.

My friends looked from me to Allie and back to me then back to Allie, all at different speeds, but finally finally landing on the table centerpiece.

I got up and left the table.

I didn't have a destination once the nausea subsided. I was headed either for a bathroom or Ted's shoes, but like I said it went away.

I snaked through the crowd as Tuku took the stage preparing to give his keynote. I found a wall next to Rachael by the door and stood there glad I couldn't see Allie or the gang from where I stood.

"Did you get that information for me?" I asked Rachael. "The logs and all that."

"Are we still doing that? I thought the police already solved it."

"That's just for the duration of the conclave. Didn't Ted tell you?"

"No."

"He's pretty busy. He put me on it to work in the shadows. In fact, I'm not even sure you're supposed to know. If you see him, don't tell him anything about helping him, even in private. He needs complete plausible deniability."

"I'm not sure—"

"You can send the files to my phone or make hard copies."

"When did you talk to Ted?"

"He found me at my table just now. Escorted Allie there and gave me the go-ahead, promising total cooperation. He also apologized for losing his temper."

"He has been on edge lately. Lots to think about."

"Like what?"

"A murder."

"Oh, right. Before that?"

"Tension from the guests. Old problems rising up. New plans coming together."

"Nothing Allenby can't help him out of," I said.

She didn't respond to that which told me something but I had no idea what.

Tuku adjusted the microphone from the stage. He'd dressed up, that is to say, he was in a brighter orange tracksuit than before. "Our wonderful event has been visited by death," he began. "Let us rejoice."

Tuku sounded like a fun guy, I leaned back to watch.

"Death is the doorway to a better place," he said. "This ancient truth is shared by all religions and beliefs without exception."

"I'm not sure about that," I said.

"Shhhh," said Rachael. "We have initiated a strict anti-heckling policy."

"Don't you vet the speeches before they go on?"

"Vet their speeches? No. But I asked Adam to mention the unpleasantness in a dignified way and he was excited to help."

"One day we all will be allowed to pass through the veil to a much better place. A. Much. Better. Place."

"Did you hear the keynote last night?"

"Not live."

"Where were you?"

"I was in Smith's room with you."

"Before that?"

"Doing my job. Why are you—"

"Doing what exactly?" I put an edge in my voice.

"The banquet of course, looking for Smith when he wasn't around, chasing down a maintenance issue."

"How'd you look for Smith?"

"I called him and Sangye."

"No answer?"

"Right," she said. "They were dead."

"And death can come at any time and we should always embrace it when it does. What good is it to dodge that car, avoid that cliff edge? If we knew how wonderful the next step was, in truth, we'd kill ourselves on the spot."

"Tuku should write Christmas cards," I said.

"There's some beauty to it. A promise of hereafter is nice."

"Usually that line is used to make us suffer now."

She made a note.

"What was the maintenance issue?"

"I got a call from the hotel that a guest was getting into the air conditioning closet."

"Who was it?"

"Don't know. It happens all the time. The hotel is smoke-free, so guests often find odd closets, preferably with good air circulation and smoke there. We found some roaches."

"From reefers?"

"Yes."

"Bogus. Can you get me a tape of Donnopher's speech?"

"Why not just download it?"

"How?"

She sighed. "You're an ICOHEP attendee. You can access all the classes and keynotes online for a month. We recorded it."

I'd totally forgotten about that. "Are all the classes filmed?"

"No. But all the keynotes are. See the cameras and microphones?"

I had.

"I'd like to go through the elevator security footage," I said.

"Why are you asking me?"

"Because if I run into trouble, I'm having them call you."

"And Ted's good with this?"

"This or a lawsuit for assault."

She had choices to make now. She could either choose to believe me and do as I wanted or she could be a pill, call me out, and risk me suing her boss. The threat was against Ted himself, extorting cooperation that way, but Rachael was the bureaucrat behind the throne. Friends in low places. Better used here, because I was pretty sure that Ted was behind all this and he'd welcome an assault charge if he blocked me from getting to the murder charge I'd slap him with if he gave me rein.

"You have my number," was her reply.

I saw Allie across the room, scanning the tables, looking for me. Now was the time to go to her, clear all this up, be adult about everything.

I ducked out and ran to the elevators full speed.

The doors opened and Hannah Hill, Sylvia Rigsdale's abrasive daughter stepped out. She damn near knocked me over, but she didn't see me. Didn't even glance. She made a beeline for the cafeteria. Beeline is a stupid phrase. It means to go straight at something, but have you ever watched a bee? They fly all over hell. Here, there, and forward and back. It's like they really don't have a destination but are trying things out. Enjoying the flight. Bees are great that way. A person could base their entire life's philosophy on that. Maybe even find the French word that coincides with that kind of lifestyle and take it for a surname.

I followed Hannah at a discreet distance, not to hide from her, but from the confrontation coming with Allie. If I was going to lose the out-of-my-league girlfriend that day, she'd have to catch me. Until she did it, the cat was half alive.

Hannah marched into the banquet hall as Tuku was telling how wonderful the buffets were on the other side. She scanned the tables and then walked in with purpose. She slapped a fish on a plate and took it to the BRA table, The Brotherhood of Righteous Action. The table was all men but after she said something I couldn't hear, they made room for her. She sat down next to Augustus Klept and all watched her with suspicion. She stared down the others until they turned back to watch the little orange-clad man discussing the condiments of heaven, comparing the hereafter to vinegar and tartar sauce, little paper cups and squirt bottles. Then, as her table looked away, Hannah smiled at Augustus. I couldn't see his reaction to that, but I did see him jump a little, just a little just at the moment Hannah's hand found his crotch under the table.

21

I ASKED at the front desk for the concierge and got the runaround. First, Trevor 'the well coiffed' said she was gone, didn't know when she'd be back, then he didn't know if they were in at all today, and finally couldn't say who she was or if they had a concierge at all.

"That pretty much exhausts the pronouns," I said. "Perhaps you can tell me where the security room is. I need to see the tapes."

"The what?"

"Where can I view security camera footage?"

"The police already did that."

"Neverthelesssssss." I channeled my best Jeremy Brett.

"Back here." The power of Sherlock sarcasm, insistence, need, and confidence worked again.

The young man led me through a wall behind the front desk to a smaller room with a smaller desk that had a computer on it. Another door led out of that room, I assumed to offices, secret elevators, the bat cave. Holodeck. He jiggled the mouse and the screen came alive with a *Brady Bunch* grid of live camera feeds.

"I want the elevators first," I said.

"Which one?"

"Can you show me how to navigate around and I'll figure that out?"

He minimized the windows and showed me where on their server the footage was kept and how to call up the live feeds.

"How long are the old files kept?" I asked.

"Hell if I know."

"Umkay," said I, and Trevor returned to attend the front.

The files were kept only forty-eight hours on the server I was looking at, then they were overwritten. If there was another server that copied them over for longer storage, I couldn't find it.

By studying the live feed, I found the elevator files from the day before and began watching them from 5:00 onward. It was ridiculous trying to identify everyone who got into an elevator and write down when and where. I tried for a while, using a piece of paper and a chewed pen I found in the drawer. I considered photos, but my phone was dead. Still dead. My son Randy could have used his phone as a steno pad with shorthand, he types so fast with his thumbs. Such modern skills are beyond me. That is an evolutionary advance that appeared just after my generation. I finally just made myself watch for visits to and from the ninth floor and sped up the tapes considerably.

I finally found Smith getting off on the ninth floor at 6:20. I watched the tape backward and saw him moonwalk into the elevator and ride down to the sixth floor where Sangye, put down a call just as he got on, and together they both walked backward into the lobby at 6:18.

I watched the rest of the tapes and didn't see anyone access the ninth floor either coming or going with the elevators between when Smith got out and Sylvia went up at 6:50.

I tried the same trick on the sixth floor and saw a lot more people coming and going, but none looked particular murderous, just the run-of-the-mill religious zealot and cult member. What was surprising was of course that I didn't see Sangye ride up to the ninth floor or ride down.

There were no cameras on any of the floors, only the elevators, the front door, the lobby, and a couple in the back to make sure no one was trying to unionize. There were also no cameras covering either of the two staircases.

I pulled up the lobby angle to the banquet hall and watched people mill for the hour between the conference and the banquet. I saw Ted and Rachael running in and out of the banquet room at double speed. I saw some conventioneers open the doors, peek in and then turn away. Kaisa Woods entered the picture from the direction of classrooms at three after six. She was orbited by groupies. She had a phone pressed to ear but was being bothered by all the adherents. She eventually extracted herself by ducking into the banquet hall. When three people tried to follow, they were turned away by Rachael who shooed them off.

At 6:16 I watched Adam Tuku enter the banquet hall from the lobby, unbothered but with a determined gait.

At quarter to seven, the special guests were let in. Augustus Klept, Donnopher and The Messenger came in one after each other right on time, arriving from the direction of the café, the classrooms and the front door. Their retinues were turned away until general admission. Those people hovered by the door like pickets. Artstar passed through them and entered at 6:55. At 7:00 the doors were opened for the public. Kaisa Woods re-entered five minutes into that, and Barty-B five minutes after her. Allie and I arrived very late at seven thirty. I hadn't seen Perry or any of the gang on the video but there were other doors into the banquet hall that were not watched.

I made a mental note to tell someone to save these tapes if they weren't already. Of course the police supposedly already had copies, but since Ted Tessner was the villain, he could possibly arrange to have them lost.

They were of dubious value in any event, showing only that whoever did this, had used the stairs. Ted was fit enough for stairs, but then again, so was everyone I'd met. I remembered I saw one person with crutches, come to think of it, someone with Barty-B's gang. Unless he'd cured her since then, I could possibly take one person off the list. But it didn't matter. Ted 'the girl-friend thief' Tessner was my man, and I was going to bring him down.

I brought up the camera to see an overhead view of Trevor standing absorbed in his computer solitaire as the lobby filled with people leaving the banquet.

I checked the kitchen for agitators, seeing none, I switched to the front foyer. Several vehicles were parked at the curb. A taxi driver left his vehicle to converse with a Ridez driver also parked there. I couldn't hear the conversation, but the animated finger gestures conveyed a lot about the gig economy. Then Allie walked through the revolving doors and my guts melted into molten magma.

I told myself to be calm.

"What's that?" called Trevor from the front.

"I'm telling myself to be calm."

"Always a good idea."

"Red jack on the queen," I said.

"Thanks."

Back at the computer, I watched as the love of my life, my first kiss, my first love, my best friend, walked up to a familiar SUV. A door opened and a dog leaped out and kissed her. Not Ted, the other one. Psilly. The St. Bernard. He bathed her face in dog slobber until she said something that put the beast on its ass at attention. Allie scratched it around the head and then beckoned it for a walk. The two of them exited screen left.

I poked around the computer for a while, noting the absolute lack of security at this security station and pulled up a guest list, recorded their room numbers, number of nights they'd booked, room service charges, credit card numbers and home addresses. I noticed what movies they'd watched, *Shaving Ryan's Privates, Throbbin' Hood, Abreuvoir 2, the Way of Water-Sports*, and *Barely Legal Slumber Party Threesomes Number 14*. Some degenerate also watched *Soul*.

I switched over to the internet to forget my problems. I threw myself into the stream of social media posts, click-bait headlines, rancid movie reviews from people who admit, in the final paragraph to not actually have seen the movie but still hate it because of something they saw on Twitter. I found places that were suffering the worst drought in a thousand years, another with a matching heatwave, a third with more rain, another with less snow, an industry on the verge of collapse, and I learned through a series of twenty-three bullet points that the problems of the entire world can be squarely placed on people born after 2005.

It took some digging, but I found some good news stories too. A boring site showed the relative violence through history. Contrary to the media, present day is among the least violent times in human Earth's history. Even factoring in East St. Louis, the chances of being killed by violence today is a tiny fraction of what it usually is. Try living during the Crusades or Roman times. Meso-American wars were nothing trivial. Massacres were a way of life or rather death. Part of the deal being born then.

Another site showed the life expectancy of people throughout history. Here we get the famous statistic that a person living in Victorian England had an average life expectancy of about forty years. Of course that's including infant mortality, which is also a shit ton better than it used to be, even in America's dystopian medical hell. Victorian statistics included hangings, which are not as common, plagues which have made a surprise return, and pauper prisons which have declined but until the bail system is fixed, still exist in the US at least. Even so, a person living to sixty-five during those times was considered pretty old in Jolly Old. Sixty-five now isn't even retirement age anymore. Ask Moe at Walmart, eighty-nine and still greeting people in an oxygen-assisted raspy voice. In England at least, the average life expectancy then was about forty-one years, now sixty-five; that's a huge increase from 1841 to 2020 on that island. Such dramatic improvements are everywhere. A shorter example is the United States. In 1966, a very good year, a man could expect to wrap things up at sixty-six, easy to remember. Now he'll need retirement to keep him through seventy-seven. A woman to eighty-two. Moe's rocking it! That's good news. No, that's fucking awesome news. It should be heralded, celebrated, mentioned at least, more than a footnote after a deep dive into statistical purgatory to wash the taste of despair from a jealous comedian's social media-polluted palate. But, alas, good news just doesn't sell—it doesn't play upon the fear which drives insanity and commerce, and dare I say, religion. Even in secular groups—especially in secular groups—there is a doomsday cult of dread, a generation of doom scrollers giving up hope and sleep when things are not *that* terrible.

I surfed over to the ICOHEP website and using the codes provided to me at registration, found Donnopher's speech from the night before. I'm not sure what I was looking for, maybe a clue, but more likely inspiration. Keynote addresses are usually the best part of any conference.

The first thing I noticed was that the clip had been edited. It went from a wide shot of the hall with people eating and drinking happily under the soundtrack of a bustling buffet, to a close up of the podium as Donnopher negotiated having only a single microphone between them. There was no introduction, just went from establishing shot to celebrity. I figured that had to do with the MC and his people being otherwise engaged.

"You go first," said Donnopher.

"No you," responded Donnopher.

They played around like that for a minute with obvious practiced precision. Then together, in harmonic perfection, they began, "Every day, every eleven seconds, someone asks who are The Peoplists."

"That kind of curiosity is a good thing."

"It shows people are willing to improve themselves."

"Eager to."

"Committed to it."

I could tell you which of the pair was saying which line, Christopher or Donna, but what would be the point?

"The Peoples Church of Higher Learning—"

"The Peoplists—"

"The Peoplists are a modern religion. The only one of the major religions to be born within the last century."

I wondered how they came up with that distinction and judging from the crowd in the audience, they did too. I guess it was because "major." It sounded good but the shade thrown out in that setting was subtly visible on the cuts of audience reaction.

Donnopher went on a while talking about the Peoplist history, the genius of their creator, Danielle Jarvis and the meteoric rise of enlightenment she started.

While Donnopher droned on, I researched the cult, er, religion. In short order, I found Jarvis to be an enigmatic figure with dubious educational credentials and a lot of arrests. Her book *People Power / Power People* was an underground sensation in the '80s, a true vanity press blockbuster. It caught on in certain affluent rivers of California. The talent agency, Morice Achievers, embraced it like new Quaaludes and subsequently hooked their entire stable of talent. They notoriously included in their negotiated contracts, contributions to the Peoples Church of Higher Learning, along with requirements to include a certain percentage of other members of their organization in the production. This led to many lawsuits that came and went, one where the complaining actress drowned suspiciously near Catalina and another where a producer accidentally got blown up in Malibu. Then the tech sector found it, Jarvis died of a drug overdose, and the rest is history. Now The Peoplists is a true force in Hollywood and beyond. With a stable of famous people to front the group, and a war chest estimated to compete with the Vatican abuse compensation fund, it's the most famous, litigious and secretive "major" religion out there. They teach by special classes which carry ranks. There's talk of special names and handshakes, (probably), human sacrifices (unlikely) and wild orgies (definitely). Each rank carries with it not only promises of greater knowledge and power but also the threat of hellfire and the most formidable non-disclosure agreement yet constructed by mankind, zealously enforced by their own law firm, Lewandowski, Drabitovitz, Kovatz, Nozadze, and Hansen, which had already contacted me.

"Peoplists are better people."

"But being better carries responsibilities."

"That's right. When we see an emergency, we, as better people, know we have to do something."

"Just last week we saw a terrible accident on the freeway and we called the police to tell them."

"That's who we are."

"We are the people who do it."

"When we see people who aren't doing it, we are sad for them."

"But also are we happy because, since we're who we are, better, we can show others how it's done."

"We're all about doing it."

"That's what makes Peoplists so much better. We do it."

"And that's what we're here to say today."

"We all need to come together to do it."

"Spectatorism, for us, is not allowed."

"We're doing it."

"Doing it is fantastic. It's rough out there, but doing it is a blast."

"Together, we know we can all do it."

Then the two together, "Thank you, and God Bless."

And it ended. The two celebrities took a step back, and holding hands, bowed. The crowd applauded politely.

The video ended.

I was confused. I must have missed something. What the hell were they talking about? I rewound the video and looked for it. I never found it, whatever it was. That was forty minutes I'll never get back.

"I hear ya," said Trevor.

"Glad to know I'm thinking out loud again," I said.

"If you find out what it is, let me know. I heard that too and have no idea."

I switched the screen back to video feeds. Trevor was smiling up at the camera. He was now onto Runescape. The front of the hotel was empty. No Allie, no SUV. No fisticuffs between chauffeurs.

An elevator opened onto the fourth floor. I watched Hannah get in and ride to the ninth where she got off. She'd changed clothes. I tried to remember if there was a pool on the ninth floor, then remembered that was on the ground floor.

Checking the list of rooms, I noticed that all the dignitaries had rooms on the ninth floor and no one else. The big seven; Smith, now deceased. Tuku with Homecoming Allegiance, The Messenger representing The Community,

The Peoplists Donnopher, Artstar and her Coven, Barty-B horse teeth, Kaisa with Green Tomorrow, and the crotch-grabbed Augustus Klept of BRA.

I watched many elevators ride up to nine full of excited people but none leave. Must be orgies going on up there.

"Without a doubt," said Trevor.

I ground my teeth and wondered what all the sex was about.

"Conferences are always like this," said Trevor. "This one is particularly bad though. Organized orgies are new, usually it's just out-of-town hookups. Casual adultery."

And as if on cue, there was Ted's SUV pulling into the frame at the front of the hotel. There was Allie entering from frame left. There was a grotesque dog panting to look at her. There was the other dog, Psilly the St. Bernard. There was a door opening. There was a rush of dog to get inside and a gesture for Allie to join them. There was Allie getting into the SUV and driving off in it.

"Orgies are all on the ninth floor?" I asked.

"Mostly," said Trevor. "Some spillage into other rooms."

"There's always spillage," I said.

"Yep."

22

IT WASN'T the best part of me that got on that elevator to the ninth floor, full of rear and planned retribution for harms not actually done me, for but by the time it arrived, I had at least rationed it. I was researching the cult leaders and their behavior as part of my investigation. Pretty good, huh? If I just happened to find an orgy, that was part of the job. A group-sex-curious lonely guy might have gotten onto the elevator, but a dedicated detective dude got out. At least that's what I was putting into the universe as I stood in the ninth-floor hallway thinking how quiet it was.

I passed Smith's room, noticing the lack of police tape on the door. Maybe it was faith in the hotel to keep people out, or maybe it was another attempt to cover up the crime. Okay, not cover up, but downplay it, ignore it for the benefit of the conference. Not a lie so much as a failure to remind people. What would that be called? Propaganda? Burying the lead? Distraction?

"Distraction is good." I'd not seen the man come up behind me. He was a handsome man, well-dressed in casual khakis and loafers. His shirt was open to the second button from his navel making me wonder why he even bothered.

"You going to the orgy?" he said, and I couldn't help hearing a disappointment in his voice. He scanned my sneakers, comfy jeans and prison-slept-in tee shirt.

"Sure am," I said.

We walked down the hall and knocked on a door. The hall suddenly filled with the sounds of carnal knowledge and the smell of sandalwood as someone peeked out. I checked my purloined room list and identified that door as belonging to the Coven. The man broke into a smart grin, walked up the hall, and knocked on another door. Low jazz music and rhythmic moans poured out of that one as he went in. That one was Donnopher's, I noted.

"That wasn't the right knock," said a hooded figure.

The music coming from the room was rhythmic and chant-like. A gasp or moan on every fourth syllable that could have been sampled for a blue movie ringtone. Heavy sweet smoke rushed out and engulfed me.

"I'm here to see Artstar," I said. "I was invited."

"All are invited."

"Then why a secret knock?"

"Some are more invited than others."

"Oh."

"It's okay Ostiarius," said the Artstar emerging from the smoke.

"Hi and thanks." My eyes locked on to hers. "Are you naked except for a silver amulet necklace and red painted star on your tummy?"

"I am."

"Glad my peripheral vision is working."

"You can look," she said.

"I shouldn't." But I did.

Yep naked, nude, without clothes, au naturel, everything visible, birthday suit, there it was right there. Yep, she's a natural.

"Why don't you come in?" she said.

"I just want to talk," I said to her boobs. They were nice boobs.

"Come in and we will. I'm not standing in the door."

She turned around and I saw she was naked from the back too.

I was on a case so I persevered.

"You take care of yourself," I said.

"I have help."

"And are these your helpers?"

The big sitting room, the match to where I'd found the late John Smith's body four doors down, had been converted to a love nest, illuminated by a dozen flickering red candles casting shadows and streaks through the thick miasma of incense from the same brass censers I'd seen from before. There were mattresses laid out on the floor, blankets, bottles, sex toys and fetish items. The usual plastic things, but also some masks, some belts, chalk, body paints, feather dusters (plural), a framed picture of someone's relative standing in front of a Waldenbooks store in an 80s mall with big hair and thick coat, a loofah, a Luftwaffe cap, black boots with heels so sharp they'd poles holes in corrugated steel, and a Tickle Me Elmo in a black robe. Among all this debris were writhing bodies of every kind. Fat and thin, black, white, brown, yellow, whole, broken, modified, transitioned. Twenty motley people without clothes or inhibitions inserted themselves into others and played and fondled and caressed and made slurping noises. The chanting had come from a couple in doggy style, "We manifest wealth with this thrust!" And there he went, creating a nice response moan from the woman. "We manifest wealth with this wiggle," she said. So, that happened. The man followed the call and response with a moan of his own. "We manifest wealth with this thrust." Happened again. "...this wiggle." Yep on cue. And on it went.

"That works?" I asked Artstar.

"Yes."

"I should take notes."

"You can try it on me," she said. "I like that one."

"Not my scene," I heard myself say.

"Don't be afraid." Artstar subtly tried to seduce me by sliding her hand into my pants and gripping my erect penis.

My eyes left the juicy melee, flashed past her skin and found her eyes. Fuck. I'd forgotten how her eyes dazzled. I stumbled, falling into them.

She said, and I listened very carefully because she gripped me so, "It works because they're making a human sacrifice of a kind."

"I...I...I..."

"We...?"

"I...better not." I pulled her hand out of my pants. "Where were you when Smith was killed?"

Her eyes shifted from seductively shining to brilliantly surprised.

"Oh. Right. You're a detective."

"And a comic and apparently, a loyal boyfriend."

"This isn't about relationships. This is about sex power. Sex magic. The closest thing to the ultimate sacrifice a witch can make."

"What's the ultimate?"

"Duh," she said. "Come with me into the bedroom."

"I told you. I'm not—"

"It's private," she said.

"I said—"

"So we can talk in private."

"Of course."

She walked through the clutch of people. I tried to avert my eyes, tried not to notice that the person in the *Eyes Wide Shut* mask was half of Donnopher, or that an orange tracksuit lay in the pile of clothes in the corner.

"You're quite popular," I said as Artstar closed the door behind us.

The bed was only a box spring and covered with more clothes. I pushed aside a sports coat and sat down. Artstar vanished into the bathroom and returned wearing a plush hotel robe that would cost me $200 if it went missing. Half that if purchased from the gift shop.

"Where do you sleep?" I asked.

"I have a room on the third floor. Under my real name."

"Which is?"

"Irrelevant," said she. "According to the scuttlebutt, Smith was killed right before the banquet Monday. Right?"

"Yes. Where were you?"

After classes, I went to my room—my other room, to relax. I took a nap and went down to the buffet around seven. No, a little before for drinks. Say six forty-five."

"How'd you get there? You didn't ride up in the elevator." Though I'd not specifically noticed her absence in my video surveillance, she always wore a black robe, so I figured I'd have noticed if she'd been there.

"I used magic," she said.

"Really?"

"No, you dolt. I took the stairs. It's only the third floor. I usually take the stairs. It helps me get my steps in."

"So no alibi?" I said.

"And no motive."

"I'm sure if we dig deep enough, we can find one."

Her eyes flashed and a wicked grin spread on her lips.

"What?" I said.

"You sound like Sangye."

"How so?"

"I can see the surprise on your face."

"I can't, but it's probably there. Are you really going to take this opportunity to besmirch the dead?"

"Can't speak ill of the dead? Why not? Is it nicer to talk about them when they're alive, when their sins can bite them?"

I thought about that a moment. "Doesn't make a lot of sense, does it? Okay, whatcha got?"

"That little fucker was a blackmailer."

"What did you do?"

"Told him to go fuck himself."

"I mean, what did you do to get blackmailed for?"

She smiled. "You think I'm that easy?"

I recalled her hand on my wedding tackle and bit back a snarky comment. It wasn't easy.

"I wasn't the only one," she said.

"A group? Are you talking about the conference here?"

"There are some here who also got the shakedown."

"How do you know that?"

"I know things."

"And you can tell me things. It's a great relationship," I said.

"No. The spirits tell me things."

"The spirits tell me things too, like two martinis is enough and Oreos are a poor chaser to tequila shots."

"Not those kinds of spirits."

"Oh really?" I gasped in wonder.

"Maybe it's time for you to go," she said.

"I won't tell anyone how I—*you*—found out, but give me a lead. Who else was he after?"

"No."

"Why?"

"You mocked me."

"I can fuck you but not mock you?"

"That's it." She moved toward the door and opened it. The sounds and smells flushed into the room.

"Whoa. Sorry sorry sorry, Artstar. I fell into my improv routine. I'm a comedian by night."

"An open-mic wannabe at some basement dive where you have to buy your own drinks."

My eyes went wide. "The spirits told you that?"

"Just a good guess."

"You should go on the road."

"I am on the road, and you need to leave now. Soon the real work will begin."

I remembered the special knock and a promise of a later event.

I stayed seated. "Give me a hint."

"There are people who'd say that Smith and his dog had it coming."

"Dog being Sangye and the reason being blackmail?"

"Do you always need it spelled out?"

"If you can't spell it out for me, who can?"

She glared at me.

"Witch joke."

"I got it."

"So you're laughing on the inside?"

She closed the door, and the smoke spun in spirals in the gusts. She sat down on a chair by the bathroom door, resigned for now. "He wasn't after me, per se," she said. "More the Coven. My organization."

"He being Smith?"

"No. I only talked to Sangye."

"But Smith was behind his...dog?"

She thought a moment, crossed her legs. Her robe fell open over her chest. Luckily for noble me, her eyes still drew my stare like a syrupy magnet.

"He said that Smith was, but it didn't sound like him."

"But you're not sure?"

"Smith seemed decent. A real nice guy. Special. Sangye not so much."

"How much did he ask for?"

"A million, but by the end of conversation, he was down to fifty thousand or I'd be exposed in the thirteenth episode."

"That's a hell of a discount."

"Like we have that kind of money," she said and blessedly noticed her robe was open. She left it open however.

"But he backed down?"

"What he was trying to blackmail over wasn't worth a dime."

"So why not tell me?"

She shook her head.

"Okay, I get it. Can you at least tell me how he found out about...it?" My mind went to Donnopher's keynote address and the brutality inflicted upon that little pronoun.

"No," she said. "I wouldn't even if I knew."

"But if you had to guess?"

She smirked, crossed her legs the other way which opened her robe enough for me to see muff. Dazzling eyes versus masculine curiosity in a cuckolded detective is not even a close bet.

"You don't shave," I said.

"Wondered when you'd notice."

"You're trying to get me to leave."

"Just the opposite."

"If I stay, can I learn the secret knock?"

"Sure. Why not?"

"Tempting. Tempting."

She smiled and closed her robe finally. "If I had to guess, Sangye got the information from his old boss."

"Smith?"

"Old boss."

"Who isn't the same as the new boss?"

"You're dating yourself hard with that joke."

"I won't get fooled again."

She shook her head in amused disgust, if I had to name it. She leaned back and assessed me possibly to guess my intent, possibly to imagine me manifesting wealth with her. She said, "Why do you care? Isn't your job over? Your quarry is gone."

"I have a new client."

"Who?"

"Who who, who who..."

"Stop it. I'm just curious who hired you?"

"That's a secret."

"Trade then. I'll tell you who his old boss was and you tell me who your new one is?"

It's a myth that a private investigator's client is confidential. I don't like to tell because my clients pay me to insulate them. Dropping their names like shorts at a Coven orgy doesn't do that. In this case, I figured she'd find out by the spirits and not knowing how else to get her to talk I relented and coughed up a name.

"It was Ted Tessner," I said because fuck that guy.

She looked surprised.

"You look surprised," I said.

"Guess that takes him off your list then."

"I have a list?"

She stood up and went to the door, opened it, stood and looked in at the mass of bodies. I joined her and tried to guess where one body ended and another began and realized they didn't.

"Sangye used to be a Peoplist," Artstar told me. "He worked for their grand wizard poobah in charge of dirty tricks. This wasn't his first run at extortion."

23

I LEFT Artstar to the scrum. Once the door was closed behind me, I was surprised again at how quiet everything became. The hotel was well insulated against sound. The groaning stopped. The smoke was still there, hanging like a fever dream exaggerated by the brightly lit hallway, but a gun could go off in one of these rooms and no one would hear it. I had to ask myself if that fleshly encounter had actually happened and wondered at how a simple thing like a doorway can create two so different spaces. This is the path of wisdom, I'm told. Noticing crap like that and thinking about tit—*it*.

I thought of Allie and felt sick. Things were not well there. She hadn't even called me. I'd been arrested and nearly molested by a Shakespeare troupe and she hadn't even called me.

Mad and getting madder, I looked at my phone to see if she'd texted me at least, giving her, for a moment of peaceful mindfulness clarity, the benefit of the doubt, putting aside visions of her discovering how much better her life would be with a billionaire like Ted ponytail Tessner than me. The screen was blank. No texts. No missed calls. No weather and no time. The phone was still dead.

"Oh yeah…"

It occurred to me, briefly, in the little space of positive thinking I'd edged out for an instant from my raving jealous lizard brain, that when the phone was charged I'd probably find all kinds of messages. Maybe apologies for doing whatever it was she was doing, which I was pretty sure was cheating on me. She might remind me that we never formally agreed to an exclusive relationship in writing. I'd never put a ring on it, as the song goes, but she knew I liked her.

Dammit.

It occurred to me also that she probably at that moment was waiting for me in our room just a few floors beneath me, worried sick. Murder was in the air and maybe a murderer. Or maybe she was imagining me having sex with strangers. Or maybe not with strangers, but celebrities. That'd show her. I determined to get even for her infidelity by boinking Donnopher. Ha! That'd show her.

Looking back on things now, I might have been losing my Zen a little then.

I glanced at Artstar's door and thought to return. Half the famous duo was in there, but not the half my persuasion lusted after openly. Besides they'd switched over to the secret knock entry. Several people had approached the door, and after pushing me away with their stares, lightly used the code to enter.

I went down the hall to Donnopher's room. Oh, sorry. One of Donnopher's rooms. They had five. I began to understand how the whole top floor had been booked.

I knocked on the door with the "secret shave and a haircut" pattern which is better than burger bun jewelry any day of the week.

A man in sunglasses and a suit opened the door and gave me a hard look.

"No," he said and closed the door.

I knocked again.

The man reappeared almost instantly, almost as if he'd not left the door in the half second it'd been since I last knocked.

"I want to come and get some of 'it,'" I said.

"What is 'it'?" he replied.

"No idea, but Donnopher seems pretty excited about it."

"No," and he closed the door again.

Again I knocked.

To the man's credit, not only did he have a superb tailor to clothe the steroids-encased mega-skeleton, he also had an unflappable calm I myself was in search of.

"You're in really good shape," I said. "Do you work out?"

No answer.

"Donnopher knows me. We had dinner together just the other day."

He stared at me, I think. I couldn't see his eyes.

"Don't those impede your vision at night? Or are you channeling Corey Hart?"

He smiled and I braced to for a pummeling.

He offered me his glasses. He had beautiful brown eyes and a chiseled jaw. Stark, tan, exotic. Breathtakingly handsome.

"Damn...ever do modeling?"

"Yes, and I act and sing. A little dancing."

"A triple threat. Or is that quadruple?" I looked at his huge hands. He could palm a medicine ball. "Quintuple?"

He reached inside his coat and I braced for a shooting.

He gave me a business card that mentioned he was represented by the Morice Achievers agency.

"Can I keep this, Matt Hansom?"

"Sure," he said. "Didn't you want to see the glasses?"

I took them and put them on. I could see fine out of them, at least through the areas that weren't open browser windows, GPS coordinates or scrolling text. I blinked to clear my eyes and the windows shifted. *Seinfeld* replaced *South Park*, CNN for Fox News. I blinked one eye and *South Park* became *The Lincoln Lawyer* with Matthew McConaughey.

"Do these get Netflix?"

"Adjust the knob at your right temple," he said.

"HBO, Hulu…there it is."

"Hold it and roll your eyes over the menu to choose your show."

I tried and stumbled. He caught me in his big muscular arms.

"They take some getting used to," he said. He took them off my head just as an alert appeared that Connie was calling.

"Connie is calling," I said.

He put the glasses back on, raised an eyebrow Dwayne, the Rock, Johnson style and said, "Hold on a minute, babe," he said, then added "Bye."

It was only when the door shut in my face, that I realized the bye was for me.

I knocked again.

"Not on the list," he said.

"But you don't even have a…oh…"

"Bye."

This time, before the door closed, I craned my neck around his torso for a glance in the room. I didn't see anyone.

"Where's the orgy?" I asked.

"In the bedroom," he said. "Where do you think it is?"

And the door was shut on me again.

"Amateurs," I muttered and turned down the hall.

Next stop Barty-B's room. I glanced at my shitty non-AR notes and saw that he had only one room instead of a block, at least that's what I think it said.

There was a 'Do Not Disturb' sign on the knob. I guess the orgy was full.

I pressed my ear to the door and listened but got nothing.

Next was BRA, Brotherhood of Righteous Action.

As I approached that door, two young white women in tube tops, Daisy Dukes and, I swear to god, lip gloss, knocked and were let in. Loud country music and cigar smoke poured out like a two-act fart. I jumped to the door and followed the two ladies in before it closed.

"Hi BRA," I said in my best red-neck cum frat boy—'cum' as in the Latin, 'combined with.' Pervert.

Crashing a white supremacist drunken party with a dig at their name might sound like a dumb move to you, but let me tell you, from experience, it is.

"Who the hell let you in?" It was a large man without hair on his head but nearly enough in his eyebrows to make up for it. Over his bare chest, he wore a vest that wouldn't have been amiss in a Frankie Goes to Hollywood video, if he removed the racist buttons. In his hand—in everyone's hands—were red plastic Solo cups, the very symbol of American festivities. Oh, the French might have their champagne flutes, the Germans their steins, the Amish their ladles, but in mainstream America, nothing says we're festive like the red plastic Solo cup. Just thinking about them makes me nostalgic for the smell of warm beer and vomit.

There were many people packed in that suite, many more than I think the fire marshal would allow. Some had overflowed onto the balcony where a silver beer keg could be spied on a wrought-iron table beside columns of red Solo cups. A wooden crate of booze was on the floor, straw packing like tinsel lying around it, making me think of prohibition. A man furrier than a furry snagged a bottle from the crate, opened it with a twist, took a swig and passed it along like a joint. I found an empty on the table and examined it. The glass was ice-white with a circular gold line drawing of a man staring out, uncertain of his company. Beneath him were Cyrillic characters proclaiming who the hell knows what. Maybe the name brand, maybe an address. Maybe the coordinates for a good potato bar. The beverage had to be vodka. The bottle came back to hairy man and he swallowed a bunch more. He paused, wavered, considered throwing up, then pushed the bottle into my chest before stumbling away. I wiped the lip and tasted it. Vodka. I've never been able to tell the difference between good vodka from bad vodka without a price tag or until the hangover the next day, so I couldn't make a judgment. I'd have to ask hairy tomorrow.

The music was coming from a large wall-mounted TV showing a music video. Beneath the TV was a rack of phone chargers, dozens of smartphones hooked up and facing out at an angle. I'd seen something like it before in an upscale classroom for borrowing laptops and on the handle-bars of a Pokemon Go zealot scouring Tokyo for little pocket monsters. At the moment they were all showing the same Reddit thread about some grocery store in Pennsylvania refusing to serve a pantless man with an AR-15. That high-tech niche was firmly counterbalanced by the teeth-edging incongruity of the song playing on the big screen—someone in a cowboy hat, tawny chaps and three-day beard was madly raking a guitar in the back of late model pickup during in a urine-colored dust storm. The cigar smoke was coming from three men sitting on a couch opposite the TV. Each of them had a cigar either in their mouths or in their non-Solo cup-endowed hand. On each of their laps bobbed the head of a woman. It took me a second to register what I was looking at.

"Hannah?"

"Get him out of here!" came a familiar voice.

"You got to leave Flaner." Augustus Klept stepped out of the bathroom and I instantly pined for cigar smoke.

"But, I'm a white guy. Can't I stay? Hair in the wrong places?"

"Get him out of here!" Hanna's shrill voice that could launch a viral campaign.

The vested eyebrow man then punched me in the guts. Not hard enough to kill me, but not far from it. Not for the first time in my life that had happened. I knew the drill. I folded over and searched the floor for oxygen.

"Hey," said Augustus with less enthusiasm and urgency than I thought the attack merited. "I know him."

"So?"

A question that would go forever unanswered because just then Augustus left me to approach the lip gloss twins.

Vested eye caterpillars rolled me into the hall and the door shut behind me. All was quiet again while I contemplated my life and my many poor decisions. Was it the remark about the hair? Hannah's screeching? Both carried certain unspeakable power.

The elevator door dinged and Perry got out with a young Asian woman.

"You okay?" she inquired.

"No. I'm Tony."

"I don't think that's what I asked you."

"Yes, it was. Can you help me stand?"

"Tony, what the hell?" said Perry.

"I'll tell you all about it," I gasped. "When I find my breath. I think I left it in there. Can you go get it for me?"

"Hell no," said Perry. "You looked like someone punched you. Again."

"You're not as dumb as I feel," I said. "What are you doing here?"

"We're going to see The Messenger."

I straightened up and jiggled hoping to put my internal organs back into position. I referred to my room list. "No Messenger on this floor," I announced

Perry pointed. There. That's him."

"Stephen Marshall?"

"Yep. You want to come?"

I remembered The Messenger, a.k.a. Stephen Marshall as being a paunchy man, with hair and no visible tattoos, in tinted aviators. He definitely sported a forehead Band-Aid. "Seems safe enough," I said and joined them in their short walk down the hall.

The door opened and there was the man himself. His glasses were gone, but the Band-Aid was there. He wore the same robe Artstar had worn, well, probably not the same one, but the same kind, the hotel one, a plush terry cloth luxury wrap the better rooms offered. He was barefoot and probably bare-ass naked beneath the robe. We could hear laughing beyond, but I didn't have an angle to see past him. The laughs were feminine.

"Hi Edna," said the seer. "Come on in."

She entered and Perry made to follow, but Marshall's hand came up, found Perry's chest, and pushed him back into the hallway sending a clear message.

"Ladies only," he said and closed the door on us. I heard a lock turn. A chain rattle. A curse put in place. It was another message, I was sure.

"Shit," said Perry. "I really wanted to get in there."

"I didn't know you swung that way," I said.

"Are you saying it's sex in there?"

"What else?"

"Intimate lessons."

"Still works."

"That's what he promised Edna."

"And..."

"And she thought that it'd be okay if I came with her, since I was such a fan."

That gave me a queasy feeling. "Are you saying she didn't know she'd been invited up for a tryst?"

"I don't think so."

I knocked on the door again. When it didn't open instantly, I pounded.

After a moment, The Messenger appeared. The chain was on the door.

"We need to talk to Edna," I said.

"She's busy."

"Bring her to the door or the cops will come and you'll be arrested for rape and kidnapping and bleeding on the carpet."

"I'm not bleeding?"

"Yet."

With some satisfaction, I watched the bullied man retreat from the door.

"Tony? Are you okay?" asked Perry.

"Why do people keep asking me that?"

"Well first you were on the floor, the victim of violence, your usual self, but that is still worthy of the question. Now you're threatening to be a perpetrator of violence, not your usual self which would again attract the question."

"It is my usual self. Have you forgotten my rage-filled dick-punching temper?"

"That was a one off."

"It's happened before too. Once in Wyoming. He had it coming more than the heckler, but your friend behind this door is endangering your friend, Edna, I might turn green and tear my shirt off before kicking some ass."

"But miraculously keep your shorts on."

"Of course."

"Never looks tough to fight with your dick hanging out."

"I wonder how the Greeks did it?"

Before we could posit an answer, Edna appeared at the door.

Perry said, "Are you okay in there?"

"I'm fine."

"He intends to have sex with you," I told her.

"I know."

"And you're fine with that?" I asked.

"Mind your own damn business," she said, and the door was again shut on my face.

Perry and I exchanged glances.

"What now?" he asked.

I went down my list and found the Homecoming room.

I knocked on the door. I expected some level of undress, but it was a woman in an orange jumpsuit.

"Is Adam home?" I asked.

"Yes."

"Can we come in?"

"Invitation only," she said. "Do you have an invitation?"

"I heard there was an orgy happening and just thought you could use a couple of studs."

She looked at us, smirked, but before closing the door said, "If you see any of those, have them come by and make sure they have an invitation."

Slam. Lock. Chain. Curse.

"Orgy?" said Perry.

"That's what all these groups are about. I swear to god."

"Not The Messenger..."

"Were you not with me just a minute ago?"

"But...but...but..."

"At least most of them. Kinda kicks your idea of spiritual purity in the butt butt butt. Could all this talk of God and wellbeing be but a ruse to seduce sexual partners? Could it be? Could this be the truth behind all religions?"

"You're cynical," said Perry.

"I'll tell you about my night after this one."

"This what?"

I knocked on the door belonging to Green Tomorrow. After a while Kaisa Woods herself opened the door for us.

"Nice robe," I said, glancing at Perry.

"Nice to see you boys. Come in. We're just talking."

We went inside. It was not the full-on orgy I'd seen in the Coven's room, but the bedrooms were occupied. No one was nude, but the dress code allowed for underwear. Tops were optional as well. I felt very overdressed.

"Settle in," said Kaisa. "We were just talking about human sexuality."

"How so?" I asked.

"Monogamy is a lie."

My mind flashed onto Allie and my guts, my knotted beaten guts, betrayed me and I went into the bathroom to throw up.

24

"DON'T LIKE THE PARTY FAVORS?" asked Kaisa when I came out. She was in a big plush chair that reminded me of a throne.

I looked at the offerings of candy, trays of chocolate, a bowl of gummies. Maybe later. I put some in a napkin and slid it into my pocket. I took a bottle of Amazon creek water, Woods Water, with a picture of my host's stern yet loving countenance on the label and noticed green moss floating in it. I put it back. "I'm good."

"Those are refilled from the McKenzie River," Kaisa explained, noticing the particulates too. "The real water is filtered."

"Good to know."

She removed a couple of bottles from the table, but only a couple. The others I guess were Amazon river, not Oregon.

Perry had joined two topless women on the couch and was into his kale bit. I'd heard it before. "It's one generation from a sticker bush," he said.

With bleary puke-wetted eyes, I admired Kaisa's classical South American features. "Haven't I seen you on a monument somewhere?"

"Nobody wants to eat kale. It's penance. The vegetarian bear shirt." The girls laughed. Their bare boobs jiggled. This was a good crowd for that bit. Green Tomorrow was all about the environment and kale was part of that. In a way, but let's face it. Kale is nasty. I mean, really, who eats that shit?

"Who eats that shit?" More laughs. More jiggles registering in my peripheral vision. I kept my polite eyes on my host.

"You don't agree?" said Kaisa.

"Kale? Yeah. fuck that."

"No, that monogamy is unnatural."

"Monogamy seems to have its advantages."

"It doesn't though. The usual method of sex was an orgy. In ancient times, all the men and all the women got together and went at it."

"Even in Roman times, the orgy was considered decadent," I said.

"By prudes. But I'm talking much earlier. In prehistory."

"Of course."

"It was a celebration, and jealousy wasn't part of it."

"Okay."

"It was a community."

"People's sexual favors were community property?"

"No, not like that. Everyone had a choice to share or not to."

"Very idyllic."

I noticed she was wearing something under her terry cloth robe. A bra at least. Maybe a slip. Not enough to go to the lobby, but more than was the night's style.

"Monogamy came about when the patriarchy demanded ownership of the child."

"Before it was the woman's only? Wouldn't a father stepping up be a step forward?"

"The child belonged to the community. Everyone shared in the upbringing. It takes a village."

"So no family? Just a village?"

"Yes."

"Was there a special baby hut where newborns hung out or what?"

"You're teasing me."

"Yes."

"Because you're insecure."

"Or maybe I am skeptical when anyone tells me how things were in prehistory, because you know, there's no history of it. People can make up any shit, like we were visited by aliens who impregnated our women."

"That happened," interjected Perry.

"Or that in previous lives we were all Cleopatra."

"I know I was," said one of the women with Perry. "A psychic told me."

"It also infers that there's been no improvement since 'the good ol' days,' which is itself a steaming pile of Wyoming outhouse nostalgia."

Kaisa looked at me like I was a wayward child, with pity and put-upon patience. I felt my ears begin to glow.

"You just don't like that men were irrelevant in ancient societies."

"Were we just pets then? Who did the hunting?"

"Women were more than capable of feeding the community."

"What about wars? Who fought off attackers?"

"War only happened because of men."

"Well we had to find something to do while we waited for walkies."

"Women are better soldiers than men when they want to be. That's scientifically proven. Tougher than men in all ways." More pitying stares. "And don't get me started on white men."

"Oh start," I said.

"The bane of existence. The reason the planet is collapsing."

"All our fault?"

"Yes."

"What about the Chinese?"

"Nope."

"What about white women?"

"Nope."

"Brazilian dictators burning the rainforest down for fun and profit? That doesn't count?"

"All destruction is being done because of white men."

"Enlighten me?"

"They're just following along in the track the white men culture. One has to be white or act white to get ahead."

"White and male," I corrected her.

"Yes. White men culture ruined humanity."

"The white men who gave us philosophy and science, medicine and the fidget-spinner? That culture?"

"Yes."

"But aren't the white men countries now doing better?" I said, channeling Monty Python. "Alternative energies and awareness and all that. Scandinavia places?"

"Only when led by women. It's their game, but women do it better than men and indigenous people do it better than whites."

I was at a strange level of agitation. On the one hand, she was flinging some pretty sexist and racist shit, on the other hand, I'd been practicing my patience. And on the third hand, Allie liked this woman and I wondered if she felt the same way. On the fourth hand, I knew Allie didn't and was not cheating on me, but on the other hand, I didn't know that, and Ted Tessner was a dick. But on the other hand, I was a guest here, and just because my host was insulting didn't mean I had to be, but on the—what hand are we on? Seven? Let's say seven—but on the seventh hand, I'm Tony goddamn Flaner and she was being a chauvinistic hypocrite.

I took a deep breath.

"Don't do it…" warned Perry.

In that moment of hesitation, I hesitated. Then stopped when Standard Flox walked out of the bedroom followed by what I can only describe as a satisfied redhead.

"Bedroom's open," said the girl with a deep Georgia accent.

Standard looked sheepish. Seeing Perry and I he looked horrified.

"That bad?" said Perry.

That remark only made Standard's expression worse and now he shared it with the Georgian.

"Peaches and I were just...uhm."

"'Peaches?'"

"That's your name, right?" said Standard.

"I think that's what I told you," said the redhead. She was dressed in jeans and no bra under a Georgia Bulldogs tee shirt. She carried her shoes in her hands. Her hair was mussed and she fidgeted with an earring. "Gotta go." She pecked Standard on the cheek, waved to the others and left the room.

"I came looking for you," explained Standard, "and things happened."

"Things will do that."

"You were going to say?" said Kaisa.

Perry shot me a glance and tilted his head at each of the women to his sides.

"That I should be going," said I.

"I hope I didn't offend you."

"You aren't going to say something about the fragile male ego are you?"

"Not if you don't want me to."

"Let me think. Hold on. Uhm...let me see...uh...carry the two...and uh...ya know, I think I'll pass tonight. Thanks for the offer though."

"Don't go," she said. "Party is just getting started."

"I've had a long day, what with murder and all."

"Oh, that's right. Smith and his servant were killed."

"Why do you say, servant?" I asked.

"Lackey? Bag man? What do you want?"

"To know where you were when they were killed."

That made the room quiet. Before there had been other conversations happening, but not then.

"I was at the ball," she said.

A couple holding hands went into the bedroom and closed the door.

"What kind of ball?" I asked.

"The keynote buffet. I was down in the lobby."

"Before that. The murder happened before the keynote."

"Still in the lobby. No, wait I took a call in the banquet room about the water deal. I took it there because it was quiet before everyone rushed in."

"Did you see the keynote?"

"Of course."

"Who was it?"

"You're serious?"

"Yes."

"That couple who keep plastic surgeons in business."

"What did they talk about?"

"Not much of anything."

"That checks out. But don't leave town."

"Why not?"

"The party is just getting started."

I had to leave then no matter what. It was too good of an exit line to miss. I nodded my goodbyes to Kaisa and Perry, careful not to say anything until I was out of earshot. Seriously, what a great exit line.

"I'll come with you," said Standard. "Where're we going?"

I nodded to Standard and stepped toward the door.

"Where?"

I smiled and winked and reached for the knob.

"Why won't you tell me? Where are you going, Tony? Why won't you tell me?"

I pulled the door open. He pushed it closed. "What's wrong? Is anything wrong?"

I glanced back down into the room. Everyone was watching.

"What? What is it?"

Through gritted teeth, I whispered, "You're doing this on purpose, aren't you?"

"Yes,"

My exit line ruined, I opened the door and left with Standard behind me. Perry waved goodbye with his hand and his eyebrows.

———

"Why were you looking for me?" I asked.

"Wanted to hang out. Figured that since Allie was a Green Tomorrow gal, she'd probably have dragged you up there."

"We're not talking?"

"Does she know that?"

"Probably not."

"Effective strat as ever."

"Shut up."

"The silent treatment doesn't work if the other person doesn't know about it."

"Tell me about Peaches."

That shut him up.

We took the elevator down to the bar. It was after eleven o'clock.

"I really should crash," I said, "but I'm wound up. Join me for a drink?"

"Drinks were free where we just were."

"Is that a no?"

"No."

"No, it's not a no, or no, it's a no no?"

"No."

We went across the lobby to the bar. Unlike some places under conservative religious control, this bar was open past seven.

We took a booth which offered a good view of the room, out the door and into the lobby, away from the conference center.

I ordered nachos, mozzarella sticks, jalapeño poppers and a Diet Coke with rum in it.

"You want anything?" I asked.

"I'll pick at yours."

"And an order of onion rings," I told the waiter.

"Rum and Coke too," said Standard and the waiter left us to the dim light of a wonderfully dim bar. Why are hotel bars the best bars? I've been to clubs a-plenty but they're noisy and icky. If you want a dark bar, a place you can relax and chill, go to a hotel bar.

"It's dark so people can't see who's hooking up," said Standard.

"I said that out loud, did I?"

"You didn't mean to?"

"Just checking." I leaned back and sudden exhaustion wafted over me like a collapsing coliseum.

"More adultery happens at conferences than anywhere else," said Standard.

"I'm getting a headache."

"Glad Peaches wasn't married."

"Did you check?"

"No ring."

"Would it have made a difference?"

"I'd like to think it would have," said Standard.

"It's a problem," I said. "It's about hurting someone's feelings who isn't there and might never find out."

"But I wouldn't like to be *that* guy."

"Yeah…"

As if on cue, Peaches crossed out of the bathroom and rejoined a friend at the bar. She didn't see us, maybe because Standard was hiding under the table.

Standard is a strange person. Sometimes I wonder why he's in our group, but that is always immediately replaced with the certainty that it wouldn't be our group without him. He's a straight arrow, sees things more like normal people, the semi-tightly wound variety. As much as he gets under my skin, I have to admit he's an upright guy. He's always been there, well as much as many of my friends ever are when I need help.

"Dude," I said to the empty seat. "Peaches has a big ring on her finger now."

He peeked up and gasped. She wore a diamond the size of Hagrid's head on her left hand. It sparkled and threw insults at the chandelier for not trying hard enough.

"It wasn't there before."

"I didn't notice one way or the other at the time, but I'd have noticed that."

"Shit dude," Standard said. "Uncool."

"Did you come out and ask her about it?"

"No. It happened fast. Just kinda happened. Accidentally."

"Your penis just kinda accidentally slipped into her clamlette?"

"Kinda, yeah."

"No offense, Standard, but sounds more like something I'd do."

"That's what I thought." He looked horrified. "If you'd have been there…"

"I was there."

"Without Perry or me. Alone. In the dark."

"*I'd walk alone?*" Shirley Jackson, everyone!

"You'd have been weaker."

"I've already passed on one orgy tonight."

"That's different. That's performance art. Athletics. A mindset far beyond what normal people think of as sex. Boinking in a locked room, even with a stranger, is much more normal."

I thought about it. "Fair cop."

Just then Peaches stood up and took the arm of a man she was with. Her ring was gone again. We watched them go toward the elevators.

"I'm not in a relationship," Standard explained. "And it's been a while. Plus there were drugs there."

"You're claiming you were drugged into having sex?"

"No."

"Peaches?"

"No."

"Then what?"

"It was a heightened moment," he said. "It's an aphrodisiac."

"But you weren't doing drugs?"

"No. Standby high," said Standard. "It's a thing."

I had to agree. "I'm sure it doesn't hurt that every guru is a free love advocate, at least as far their tastes go."

"It's not just Kaisa?"

"Ohhhh, no."

"Maybe tomorrow I'll try another. Do you know if Donnopher is having one?"

"Yes, but it's harder to get into that one."

Standard nodded and sipped his drink which had appeared when my eyes were shutting out the headache. I sipped mine and doubted it would be good for my health in the long run, but maybe it'd get me to bed. The food arrived in sizzling baskets and bubbling plates. I dug in, suddenly very hungry and tired and worried.

"There is something in the air," I said after a minute, biting off the stem of a jalepeño. "Where did you get your data on conferences being adultery hives?"

"It's pretty obvious."

"You didn't see a study somewhere? You acted like your information had come from authority."

"I heard it here."

"Peaches?"

"Someone up there."

"They were using it as some kind of justification for cheating?"

"I guess it doesn't count as cheating."

I gnawed a mozzarella stick and waited. Then some chips. Hot cheese. Is there anything better?

"Peaches."

"Good one," I said, appalled I'd been thinking out loud again.

"Don't worry," said Standard. "We all do it."

I must be tired.

"You look it."

"Fuck."

"That's apparently what conferences are for. Someone said, probably the same somebody who mentioned the maybe scientific study, that such affairs are not detrimental to marriages but may actually help them."

"Who did this talking?"

"I don't remember."

"You've quoted this person twice. You weren't doing drugs. How do you not remember?"

"I was distracted."

"How?"

"Peaches' tongue was in my mouth."

"That would do it."

We snarfed down the food which surprised me. I thought I'd over-ordered, but there we were, picking olives off the plate. The wave of exhaustion had abated, but another wave was setting to do me in. I stood up.

"I'm going to bed," I said. "I've had this room for three days and still haven't tried the bed."

"Shame you have to sleep in it alone."

"For fuck's sake Standard. I don't roll that way."

"But it's a conference…"

"You're just saying that so I do something stupid so you don't feel so bad with company."

"So?"

I left the café and went to my room. It wasn't until I was unlocking it and going inside that I remembered I hadn't paid for the food or drinks. I'd stuck Standard with it all. I smiled.

The room was empty. Allie's suitcase wasn't there. That new smile left me quick.

25

EVEN THOUGH I WAS TRASH-TIRED, I did not sleep well. I'd showered before bed, which usually helps, but if it did this time, I cringe to think what that night would have been like without it. My mind spun the wheel of worry and it landed on Allie, on my case, on murders, orgies, Peaches, fried foods, failed diets, sharks, jail cells, jail cells with sharks, broken hearts, sharks eating broken hearts. Festus holding a green-handled Colt revolver over a dead shark. Miss Kitty pouring drinks for fish-eating football hooligans.

Awake before sun-up, which sucks. If you've ever done that, you'll never willingly do it again. Fishermen only do it because they starve if they don't, and if their girlfriends are staying the night at a billionaire's home, I bet they don't sleep at all, but spend the night sharpening harpoons, collecting bags of concrete and lengths of chain, calculating how far out to sea they'll need to go to drop the body, taking into account prevailing currents. I worked it all out as I lay in bed staring at the ever-brightening ceiling for some hours.

I got up and showered again, hoping for the rejuvenating powers of hot water to put some energy into my muscles and clear my caked eyes. It worked for a couple minutes. I figured I'd be okay that day as long as I could shower every half hour.

I'd done one mature thing before going to sleep. I plugged in my phone. I muted it, but I plugged it in. That morning I found a bunch of texts from Allie and a couple phone messages also from her. I did one immature thing then and ignored them all, the better to inflict the silent treatment punishment I'd decreed. I'd show her.

My goal was to get a goddamn cup of coffee before I did anything. My room had a little coffee maker and fixins', but it was far too complicated for me then. I dressed—barely remembering to—and went downstairs

The lobby was already alive with conference people. I noticed all the main factions, witches back in their robes, cute hippy girls in sundresses and beads drinking bottled Amazonian sludge water and asking for signatures on petitions, skinheads hitting on said sun-dressed hippies, finally agreeing to sign if they got a kiss. What cost planetary survival? A few orange jump-suits looking suspicious as all fuck whispering among themselves in corners. There was a clot Christian people wearing polyester suits and hair that the B-52s made famous, while actual famous people trying to be more famous stood distractedly in three-quarter profile with pouts as people asked if they could take a picture.

"Who is that?" I asked a man after he got a selfie with a bunch of them.

"That guy was in *Cat Killer and Mouse Driver*. He was the third victim. And that woman was the love interest in the direct-to-DVD movie *All My Love I left at the Alamo Gift Shop*. Art film. That Black guy is a model, I think. That woman, a director, perhaps. I think that group are bodyguards, or maybe trying out for it. That other one a secretary or a lawyer. Those people over there are also famous. Or will be."

"Do you know any of their names?"

"Not a one, but their faces are familiar."

If I set an AI to show me composites of famous people I might well get this line up. None were memorable, but all were familiar.

"They're with Donnopher," he said.

"Of course."

"Their class is starting. Want me to save you a seat?"

I took a closer look at the man. He had rugged good looks, and if he got his hair done, his posture improved, his lips Botoxed, he could be in that group.

"Need coffee." To the initiated, those two words are all that's needed. He got out of my way and I stood in line at a Starbucks kiosk built into a wall. Maybe it was once a bellman's station, or a janitor's closet, but it'd been pimped out to corporate coffee now and I was damned happy to find it.

I ordered my usual jump starter, two shots of espresso in a cup of coffee. Cream, sweetener, and joy.

"You shouldn't buy this shit coffee," Lucy, my barista, told me. "It's not properly sourced. Eugene is full of excellent coffee shops with superb beans and enlightened practices."

"You're not going to spit into my coffee, are you?" I asked.

"No. Did you want me to?"

I opened my wallet and surveyed my cash situation. "No. Can't afford any extras today." I took my coffee and wondered what kind of clientele Lucy was used to serving.

Donnopher's class was the only one for a while. It was an early morning thing on breathing and "doing it" that ran for two hours in the big room.

Hard pass.

I found a comfy chair to caffeinate in, feeling my soul return to my body one sip at a time.

My phone silently signaled that a call was happening. Unknown number.

My warranty was probably out of date, so I picked it up.

"Tony."

"Listen asshole, I've had just about enough of your crap."

"Tony, it's me. Ted."

"And?"

Pause on the phone.

Ted said, "Allie is with me—"

"Fuck! Okay, mushy man, you've made yourself an enemy for life." I hung up and blocked the number.

I called Rachael.

"Hello? Who's this."

"It's me Tony," I said. "Is Ted with you?"

"No, he's still at the house."

"What did you find out about the killings the other night?"

"Why are you asking me?"

"Because Ted is still at the house."

"Why would you think I'd know anything about it?"

"Because you're smart, observant, very well organized and you promised to poke around for me and report."

"I don't remember that last part."

"See? You don't miss a thing."

I could hear cheering and clapping coming from her phone, the same sounds echoed from the large room farther on.

"The gun was Augustus Klept's?" I said.

"Yes confirmed."

"What's his story?"

"I don't—"

"Broad strokes."

I could hear Donnopher in the background. "To get it, we need to control our breathing."

"It's hard to do it with poor breathing."

"Breathing, in a way, leads to it."

"You could say that."

"Broad strokes," I said. "And make it quick I might puke."

"He says the last he saw his guns were when you took them away from him at the dinner."

"He mentioned me?"

"Yes."

"That can't be good," I heard myself say out loud. I took heart that I was getting better at noticing that, if not stopping it. Could that be what *it* was?

"Probably not."

"And he hasn't seen his gun since then?"

"Neither one."

"Neither?" I said.

"Both guns are missing."

"Was Augustus arrested?"

"No."

"Was anyone?"

"You."

"Besides me," I said.

"For what?"

"For murder, maybe?"

"No. It was a murder-suicide."

"We're sticking with that, are we?"

"Yes, of course."

"Did you get those door records like I asked? I did ask, didn't I?"

"You did, but I don't know if—"

"Email them to me." I gave her my email.

She hesitated.

"I'll expect them within the hour."

"Fine."

I hung up and waited. While I waited I opened my phone. Two new messages and a couple more texts.

I went to my camera roll and scanned the stuff I'd filmed in Sangye's phone. No suicide note jumped out at me from the text message threads.

In the corner of one frame, I could make out part of the gun on the floor beneath Sangye's arm. Something about it didn't sit right.

An email arrived. I opened the app. I had nine unread ones from Allie the last of which was subjected:

You little shit. I know what you're doing! Pick up, you moron!

I tapped open the message from Rachael and saw the attached files. There I found a schedule of times for both Smith and Sangye's door.

Room key #1 opened his door at 6:05 on that fateful night. Then nothing until the door opened at 6:45. Not a key opening, so someone from inside the room. The door was again opened at 6:50. Five minutes later, room key #3 was used and the door was open again. Stayed open for a while after that.

I remembered that Sylvia told me she arrived around 6:50. I think she'd mentioned they all had keys to the suite. I figured #1 was Smith, #2 Sangye and #3 to complete the S trifecta, Sylvia.

Sangye's room was opened by his #2 key at 6:10. Then it was opened from inside at 6:30, 6:35 and 6:40 and then by key #2 again at 6:55. Then nothing until a service key opened it at 7:45. That would be me.

Nothing in the key logs disproved the murder-suicide. In the detective world of motive, means, and opportunity, opportunity was sitting on Sangye's couch in its underwear asking where the pay channels were. Meanwhile, means is knocking at the door, but I couldn't let her in yet. I'd need to check her references and get first and last at least. A cleaning deposit goes without saying. Even so, should they crash the house with a six-pack of PBR and a bag of Lays, later to pass out in the tub, vomit on their shoes, that ever-elusive third triumvirate member, motive, hadn't even RSVP'd. The party may have begun, but had not yet started.

"Jesus, that was a labored metaphor," I said.

"What was?"

It was Sylvia. She looked about how I felt. She'd been crying and recently. Life tip, if you're likely to cry that day, avoid cheap mascara. I think my mother told me that.

"Sit down," I said.

She took the comfy lobby chair across from me.

"Did Sangye have a motive to kill Smith?" I asked.

"No," she said. "The cops kept asking that and I kept telling them no."

"Think though. Really. If you had to put a motive on his actions, however insignificant, what would it be?"

"It wouldn't be."

"Humor me."

She sat back and thought. I looked at Sangye's text threads.

"Well?" I asked.

"Nothing."

"What's this?" I nearly handed her my phone to read the text, but luckily stopped myself before I did. It was a picture of Sangye's phone screen, but the background was Sangye's bullet wound. "Let me read it to you. This is from Smith to Sangye around six o'clock, 5:56 to be precise; Smith writes, 'I know it's you who've been spreading these rumors.' To this Sangye responds, 'Don't worry about it. I'm just teasing.' Then 'Stop.' And Sangye's response, 'Thirteen is a lucky number. It's good for us.' And Smith's 'I SAID STOP.' All caps. That means he's yelling. He could have put periods between the words for even more emphasis. That's one of my favorites."

"No idea what that could mean," she said.

I shook my head. "You're my client. You can tell me."

She shook her head.

"I've already heard about the thirteenth episode."

Her face went white.

"If it elicits this kind of response from you I suspect you might as well tell me about it."

She took a deep breath. "It's not a real thing," she said. "At least I don't think so. Maybe Sangye arranged for one. He was the manager. But I know that the twelve we shot were all on the original contract."

"Go on."

"Sangye may have teased some of the others here that we might use that episode to expose them."

"Pray continue."

"That's it. Sangye thought it could help. Maybe he was thinking of publicity. Sangye was concerned about the cost of the center we're building. He kept pushing for grander things and the budget wouldn't allow it. There's a rider in the Netflix contract that if it really catches on, we get a bonus and there's a possibility of another series."

"Smith didn't like grand things?"

"Oh he did, but reality was the budget we had. The money just wasn't enough."

"Was money missing?"

"No," she said horrified, and then, "I don't think so."

"Smith didn't approve of Sangye's efforts?"

"No. He said it was cruel."

"Do you know who was involved?"

She shook her head. "But I know some of the people here were."

"Hold up," I said. "Some of the people here? That sounds like it'd been going on before the conclave."

"Yes."

"Long time?"

"Since before the Netflix show wrapped up."

"Was Sangye prone to temper?"

"I see what you're getting at. Sangye wouldn't do that. None of us would. We were all on the same page. We all wanted the center. We lived for it. It'd become our life's work."

"And if someone tried to stop you from doing your life's work? You'd be cool with that?"

She didn't answer.

"Okay," I said. "Thanks for being honest. It's not often I get to ask people questions to which I already know the answer. I feel like *Rumpole of the Bailey*."

"Who?"

"Barrister on a Brit show. Before your time. Before mine really."

"What now?"

"Motive's plane has touched down, but it's stuck in baggage claim. I'll keep poking around."

26

I COULD TELL that Sylvia wasn't happy that I'd not wholly discounted the murder-suicide, but I needed her to be at least open to it. I didn't buy it myself, but I've been wrong before. There was this one time, about the date of the assassination of McKinley. I said it was September 14, 1901, the date he died, but the trivia card insisted it was September 5, 1901, the date he was shot. You win some. You lose some. I might have been wrong at other times, but really, I should have gotten the point.

I was shocked that the conference was still going on as if nothing had happened. I noted on the app that Sylvia was now teaching the classes that Smith had been scheduled for. Was that a motive?

I scanned news sites which in all actuality suck now. In the heyday of the newspaper, you'd be able to read about a fender bender that happened in your neighborhood the next day in full detail and compare it to the march to war in Austria-Hungary. Now a double killing doesn't even rate local pages. Supposedly the rise of the citizen journalist has expanded reporting, but it has not. Lots of opinion pieces telling me which movies to hate and why, which corporations to boycott and which celebrities to cancel. A tutorial and rolling a tortilla on CNN, how anime is turning our children gay on Fox. A story about a new one-act play that opened and closed before the story was noticed by anyone. A report from a sexual-harassing dolphin at a Florida water park. Who's after my guns today? Stories of conspiracy, innuendo, greed, and hate, and none of it sourced. Really. The one thing that the old news had was some semblance of truth. There used to be a thing called the Fairness Doctrine that meant that if you wanted to spout some political crap on the air, the station had to give the opposing side equal time. This meant that, blessedly, they tended to just stay out of it. Opinion pieces were clearly marked and a newspaper could be seriously damaged if a story they published was shown to be inaccurate. People lost jobs. All that went away when Ronald Reagan killed the Fairness Doctrine, made worse with each fascist step media took since then, including a complicit Supreme Court that says lying is okay and that money equals free speech. What could go wrong?

"You look pissed," said Dara.

I looked up. "Do I?"

"Your face is red. Your ears are molten."

My diminutive friend was right. I felt my ears and blistered my finger.

"I was thinking about the media."

"Just from thinking about it? Best you stay off Twitter then." She took a swig of my coffee, made a face and sat down.

"Word."

"See Perry?"

"I left him last night at an orgy," I told her.

"Which one."

"Green Tomorrow's. You?"

"Not my style," she said and looked at me hard.

"What?" I said.

"I know you and Allie are in a fight, at least that's what I gathered when you threw a tantrum and left the table last night."

"Tantrum?"

"Tantrum, and don't fucking interrupt."

"Sorry."

"Okay."

"I won't interrupt you again."

"As I—"

"Because that would be rude."

"I'll mash your man peas into your spleen," she said.

I shut up.

"Tell me you didn't use your spat with Allie to justify a one-night stand?"

"If it's with more than one person, is it still a one-night stand?"

"Intriguing question, but don't answer a question with a question. Have you no fucking manners?"

"According to prevailing ideas, as far as that goes, conferences don't count and free love is enlightenment."

"No, Tony...you didn't. Not to Allie."

"I didn't."

She looked at me and sighed.

"Well you're the only one then! Want to hear about it?"

"No."

"It wasn't an orgy it was—"

"No."

"A cowboy—"

"A cowboy?"

"Fun time."

"Good for you."

"So murders. You on that?" she asked.

"I am."

"Tell me it's Bartalemuw. He's a dick."

"What did he do to you?"

"Sexist misogynistic relic from a best-forgotten century. The reason tar and feathers were invented."

"Can you be more specific?"

She finished my coffee and handed me back the empty cup. "Women are an extension of men, because of the rib thing."

"Just that?"

"Family values shit, mother who works outside the home is a victim of society's failure. Polygamy should be reintroduced to address it."

"Shit."

"Yep, so is it him?"

"Might be."

"Get the fucker."

"Have you talked to BRA and the skinheads yet? They're pretty bad." I remembered the less than egalitarian orgy scene from the night before.

"But they're identifiable. They proudly wear the signs of assholeness. Bartalemuw skulks like a kindly uncle."

"Barty-B looks like no uncle of mine."

"Barty-B?"

"A nickname. He hates it."

Her smile was wide enough to crack her face.

"Welp, time to get to work. First I think I'll get a coffee."

"Breakfast too." Dara took me into the little hotel café and ordered an omelet and coffee. I got coffee too along with three eggs, sausage, bacon toast, a tall stack of pancakes with boysenberry syrup and a cup of cottage cheese because I'm dieting.

Dara tried to tell me more about her cowboy, about his long blond hair, tight blue jeans, buckle with a ram's head on it. I tuned her out but was distracted.

When we were done, the Donnopher thing was letting out and the regular programming was beginning. So far I'd accomplished five things: I'd overeaten, I'd over-caffeinated, I'd ignored the gooey details of Dara's tryst, I'd decided that I needed to know more about Sangye and I'd avoided reading any communication Allie had sent me. Quite a full day so far.

The Allie thing struck at the heart of my insecurity. Her messages were just details to my problem, which was me. I was clinging. I was expecting other people to behave in certain ways. I was unhappy when the world didn't care about my feelings. All the mediation and stuff I'd been doing to calm the inner monster, which is a human being, led, I knew, to me. I must be able to forgive Allie for her transgression even if she leaves me, but more so, I must stop imagining those things. That's a lot to ask someone at breakfast. But I am working on it.

"Come on," I said to Dara when we were done.

"Where are we going?"

"I need your help to get to Donnopher."

"Why me?"

"You're here. You'll be good at it, and you owe me for breakfast."

"I was wondering why you so quickly picked up the check."

"You owe me."

"What do I have to do?"

"When I give you the signal, distract the guard. He's Matt Hansom. Here's his card. He wears these super high-tech augmented reality wraparounds. Can't miss him."

"What should I do?"

"You'll think of something."

———

We waited near the elevators until the crowds dissipated. Eventually, Donnopher emerged with their bodyguard, the handsome, ruggedly built guy from the night before with the *Neuromancer* sunglasses. They walked like they were competing in the Olympics and kept their eyes forward rather than risk eye contact with anyone.

Dara and I took the elevator up to nine before they arrived.

I pretended to be trying the door just past theirs. I think it was Adam Tuku's and the Homecoming gang of fashion rejects. Luckily they didn't seem to be in. Dara had taken the door three before theirs. Forgot who that was.

After a moment, the elevator dinged and out came the power couple and the side of meat that guarded them. They were in the same order as before, the couple in front, the ham a few steps back.

As such, Donnopher arrived at the door first and unlocked it.

I signaled Dara.

"Hey fuckbitch!" she screamed.

The world stopped as a new epithet was born.

Dara, diminutive elfin Dara, is a master of sailor speak. She can make a fishmonger's wife sob and get banned on YouTube before anyone's even clicked her link. Her looks and her mouth were so incongruous, her wit so vicious and penetrating, that all of our gang, and all other sentient beings with any sense, fear her. Even I was taken aback by the volume, content, and edge of her taunt. All attention was back down the hall as little Dara stared venom at the bodyguard. Shocked to stillness, like a vole noticing a circling shadow, Donnopher froze at the open door, poised to go through.

"You. Shitweasel. Much Handjob, I'm talking to you. Show me those high-tech glasses."

"That's Matt Hansom," he said, stepping menacingly toward Dara as I pushed Donnopher through the door and locked it behind us.

They both stumbled into the room, and then, on synchronized servos, they turned to face me. There was the famous duo, Donna Hicks and Christopher Mark, one time B list actors who became a power couple by coupling, now become the face of The Peoplists.

"You guys ever do movies anymore?"

"This is kidnapping," they said.

"Is that the De Palma thing I read about in the *Hollywood Reporter*?"

Matt Hansom, a.k.a. Much Handjob, was at the door. I'd taken the precaution of thawing the little horseshoe bolt that kept out everyone without a pencil. He struggled and swore and threatened and called to Donnopher.

"What do you want, Mr. Flaner?" they asked. "Matt will have that door down in a moment."

"Not if Dara is out there assaulting his manhood. It's he who needs help."

"I'm calling the police!" he yelled through the door. Donnopher regarded me with idle calm.

"...and your shriveled up little man-beads..." came Dara's assault.

"Okay, here it is," I said. "John Smith was murdered."

"We know."

"And Sangye was murdered."

"Not suicide?"

"No." I said it with real authority. I was at that moment pretty sure, maybe sixty percent.

"We're not surprised."

"He used to work for you?"

"He didn't work for *us*. He was a member of The Church of the Higher Learning. To serve the holy community he had certain jobs."

"So you knew him?"

"Yes."

"What can you tell me about this?"

"He left the church. We were all very disappointed in him. Not everyone can handle the truth."

"Why did he leave?"

"We didn't ask him."

"Did the church?"

"That's who we meant."

"Why didn't the church chase him down and destroy him?"

"We don't do that."

"Yes, you do."

They stared, unable to refute my dialectic debate style.

"You're calling the fucking fuzz!" screamed Dara. "What a complete wet diaper wuss you are. Just let me see those goddamn glasses, you son of a syphilitic salamander!" I should note that the sound insulation of the suites was superb. For Dara to be heard where we were, meant she was right outside the door and reaching snow-blower lever volumes. She has a gift.

"Why aren't you surprised he was murdered?"

They stared. Either I'd dazzled them with my Aristotelian reasoning or Dara's imagery had stunned them dumb. Syphilitic salamander...

"Was he a blackmailer? Was he trying to blackmail you?" I said.

They glanced at each other, sharing some kind of Peoplist telepathy. "Yes."

"Did you pay?"

"No, but others probably did."

"Why didn't you and how do you know about the others?"

"We have lawyers for that kind of thing," they said. "Controlling the narrative is what we do best. Even if his slander got out, we could stanch it."

"By killing him?"

"No. He was planning on airing dirty laundry on Netflix. *Netflix*. An entertainment media company. If there's one place The Church of Higher Learning has influence, it's there. And just for trying, we'd sue COTTEO into the Stone Age."

"COTTEO? You think it was COTTEO and not Sangye?"

"The money was to be put into their development account as a donation."

"Okay, but if it all went to court, the 'slander,'" I said using air quotes, "would still get out on The Peoplists."

"There are always rumors about any powerful organization, Mr. Flaner. Comes with the territory. As long as nothing can be proven, no lasting harm can be done."

I didn't know about that. Innuendo in the age of hair-trigger social outrage has been known to mess with lives and livelihoods, but I stayed on task. Very Zen of me, I thought. "That doesn't convince me that you didn't kill him. He'd be believed more than most. He'd been an insider."

I was playing on the idea that what Sangye had was pretty juicy. It'd have to be to compete with the rumors that I knew about them already.

"You missed it," they said.

"What?"

"COTTEO. We'd destroy it."

"You can do that?"

"Compared to us, Smith's little church is a tent show. With a phone call, we could tie up all their assets instantly and for years. Sangye was looking to increase their bank balance, not lose access to it. When we explained this, he understood."

The door opened but the little bolt caught. It was pulled shut and I knew I had seconds before it opened. To buy me a few more, I casually leaned against it.

"I do want to say how much I appreciate you giving me this interview," I said loudly enough to be heard through the door.

"Giving you?"

"I assume since you never asked me to leave and never tried to leave, that I was invited and this was definitely not kidnapping."

They smiled.

The door bucked. Then it did it again. Then opened and wouldn't shut. I was being undone by a foot, I just knew it. In came a pencil. I grabbed it. "Thanks!" I said. "Very nice of you to offer."

Donnopher smirked at me.

"And the others? How do you know they were blackmailed?"

Another glance at each other. I thought I heard subsonic clicks on the theta bandwave.

"Stands to reason," one said.

"Why?" I insisted.

"We have people who learn things about people who threaten us," the other said. "Sangye, after he left, threatened us. He was watched."

"Is that a threat? Because I hope it is. I work well when threatened."

They smiled.

I said, "Don't suppose you could share any of that information with me? Who was being pinched? Who wasn't?"

They stared

I snatched a pen as it poked at the horseshoe lock.

"Limit it to cults in attendance," I said. "Please. Not for Sangye. For John Smith."

Damn if that didn't have a visible effect on the two. Gone was their smug look of uniform contempt, replaced then by an expression of matching dejection.

No shared glance this time. They said. "He didn't say, but you might want to look at their finances. That's what we did."

I assumed 'we' was the Peoples Church of Higher Learning and not the two movie icons I was holding against their will.

A screwdriver poked through. I couldn't pull that away. I was sunk. I slapped the little hook a couple of times but not enough, eventually it cleared the latch and the door burst open.

"Look who I get to arrest again," said Detective Dean Johnson.

27

IT WASN'T JUST JOHNSON. Yesenia, my maid friend from before, was there. And of course Matt Hansom, Fuckbitch to his friends. Surprisingly there too was Bruce Allenby, the Fed.

"What do you want? We're channeling sci-fi writers," I said.

Johnson burst in. I stumbled back because forward was out of the question, and the closet door was closed to my side. The detective pulled out a pudge index finger and jabbed it into my chest. Then he spoke with the breath of someone who has a real garden of tonsil pills. With each syllable, he poked me again and a little harder.

"I've heard about you, Flaner," he said. "For the sake of public safety, you're going to cool your heels for a week."

I coughed, gagged, even threw up a little on his shoes.

"Have you seen a dentist? Or better yet, an oral surgeon?"

He poked me again, no respect for the sick. "I've had enough of your sass."

"Let's stick with the chest Morse code," I said. "It'll probably crack my sternum, but at least I'll remain conscious."

Johnson's face went beet red. He glanced around the room. I think I'd hit a nerve.

.I pushed the finger away. "Detective Dean Johnson, let me say just one thing, or rather, one more thing. You really should dress in pastel suits and lose the socks. You're missing a great opportunity to channel Crockett and Tubbs. A haircut couldn't hurt either. Or a breath mint."

"I'm going to fucking destroy you."

"Why are you so testy, Detective?" asked Donnopher.

"What?"

"Why are you here?"

The man looked like he'd shit himself. It smelled a little like it too.

He pointed into the hall. "But your man—"

"Associate," corrected Matt Hansom.

Johnson looked really confused now. "He said you were in here against your will."

"This is our room. Mr. Flaner was just visiting but now he's leaving."

I felt my chest. It hurt. I raised my shirt up and showed my belly to everyone. "Am I bruised?" Nothing lights up a room like a pudgy white man showing his hairy chest.

"Goodbye," said Donnopher.

Passing Matt in the doorway, I said. "Is Dara okay? You didn't hurt her did you?"

"She's fine, but the things she said…the images she drew…fish, thirty-weight motor oil and gardening tools…"

"I know."

"I'm not even Catholic."

I gave him a hug. "Yes, I know. You should sit down and have a drink."

That left just Johnson, Allenby, Yesenia and me in the hall. Dara was gone.

"Hi Yesenia," I said. "You keeping busy?"

"Oh, yes. Lots."

I glanced at the cops. "You got here fast," I said. "Both of you."

When Johnson spoke, he angled his breath away.

"I was already here, heard your name, and had to come to pay my regards." The fucker poked me in the sternum again.

Quick as a methed-mongoose, I grabbed his finger and twisted it around in a jiu jitsu control-point-bend and had him to his knees howling for mercy before what I had done had even registered.

Not really. I just winced.

"I was actually looking for you," said Allenby.

I showed him my chest again. "See what the bad man did?"

"That'll bruise," said he.

"I wonder if Donnopher will lend me her legal staff to seek reparations from the Eugene police department. Won't be hard to find other examples of violent overreacting."

Johnson said, but didn't poke this time, "Listen, Flaner. It's by the courtesy of some upstanding local citizens that you're still walking around."

"Look at your phone," said Allenby.

I pulled out my phone. Noted a list of messages and ignored them. I activated the camera and took a selfie with everyone in the hall instead.

"Another?" I said. "With my shirt up?"

"Am I getting through to you?" said Johnson.

I cropped the photo.

"I assume you're working the case?"

"I doubt it," said I.

"Why?"

"That would require some deduction."

Out came his finger. I snapped a photo of him poking me again.

"We'll call that exhibit A. Wanna see. I think I have some filters that'll put funny ears on you."

"This is as open and closed a case as there's ever been," said Johnson, unwilling to look at the picture. "Murder-suicide."

I swished right and came to the pictures of the crime scene, the list of calls on Sangye's phone. His lifeless body in the background.

Yesenia retreated to the room Smith had died in and opened the door. She waited impatiently.

I zoomed in the photo.

"No," I said. "It's a double murder and you know it."

"You don't know what I know," he said.

"But I know you know what I know about you knowing."

The finger again.

I dodged.

"You're here taking a fresh look at the crime scene because you've come to the right conclusion," I said. "Finally."

"Right…"

"I don't have all day," said Yesenia.

"You're either playing it cool to catch the killer, or much more likely since it smells of corruption, I think you're covering it up, at least for now. Lord Ted Tessner doesn't want his precious party turned upside down."

"Then why am I here?" said the local cop.

"Some higher power has sparked a need to act while you can. Eventually the truth will out and if you let all the crime scenes go cold, you'll look as bad as you smell."

"Which higher power?"

"Around here? A lot. Take your pick. Donnopher has one. Artstar's could provide one. Barty-B says he has a direct line."

He stared at me like he didn't know who I was talking about, which told me he was either completely out of touch with the case, or a good liar. He was a terrible liar.

"You don't have a clue, do you?" I said.

"Mister policeman!" Yesenia again.

He turned and went into the room.

"The higher power could be a person, you know," said Allenby after Yesenia and Johnson disappeared into the room.

"That was kind of implied," I said.

"Right."

We regarded each other for a moment.

"Enjoying the conclave?" I asked him.

"Not really."

"Try the salmon at the café."

"Is it good?"

"No idea. Figured you could tell me."

"What did your friend do to the bodyguard?"

"Wounded the man's inner child and challenged his belief in a benevolent god."

"I see."

We rocked on our heels for a minute.

"Are you trying to ask me something?" I said. "I'm not sure I fit in my prom dress anymore."

Allenby laughed. "I told you before that I heard of you."

"You mentioned it on the plane."

"Looking at files, I just gotta say, I'm impressed."

"I was young and needed the money. I was told the negatives would never leak out."

He laughed.

"Also, the room was very cold."

"It's a pleasure watching you work. You have style," he said, "And a real knack at solving cases."

"You looking for pointers?"

"Maybe."

"That's why you were looking for me?"

"No."

"What was it?"

"Just gotta wait one second," he said.

"Why?"

"Because you won't look at your phone."

I looked at my phone. Yep. There it was.

Allenby's phone rang. "Yes. He's right here," he said and passed me his phone.

The name on the screen was Ted Tessner.

I began. "Listen here—"

"Don't start, Tony." It was Allison Braise. My Allie.

"Hi, honey. What's new?"

"You're being a complete shithead."

"That's not new."

I could feel her anger over the phone, but my response slowed her a bit.

"I've been at Ted's to help with his animals."

"I don't like Ted."

"But he's a nice guy."

"He hit me."

"Did he really?"

"Yes."

"Are you sure?"

"Yes."

"Ted tells a different story."

"That should tell you everything you need to know," I said.

"You've been known to exaggerate."

I looked at Bruce Allenby waiting patiently to get his phone back. "You going to back me up on this?" I asked the Fed.

I could see the wheels turn in his eyes, scales of truth versus loyalty. He gestured for the phone. I handed it to him.

"This is Bruce," he said. "I don't know what story Tony told you, but if he said he was suck—*touched* with force by Ted while in police custody, he's close to the mark."

I took the phone back. "Well?"

"I didn't hit you," she said. "Why ignore me?"

"I don't like the company you keep."

"I knew you were pouting. You promised to work on that."

"You're not helping."

"Ted asked me, no—paid me, to help him with his animals."

"What's wrong with Psilly? Choke on a Buick?"

"His goats."

"Has it occurred to you that Ted asked you to do this to either, one, get at you, or B, get at me. Or third, both?"

"You're paranoid."

"And you can see clearly now? The rain is gone?"

"I know, Ted. You don't."

"I've looked at Ted from both sides now. You've only seen one."

"You can't use 70s pop lyrics as a viable defense," she said. "His goat, Jerry, is in distress."

"Jeremiah was a bullfrog," I said.

"Arrrgghghhh!"

In a rare moment of clarity, maybe because Bruce was judging me, I relented. "Alright alright alright alright alright. Alright," I said. "If you say I'm off base and that Ted isn't trying to get into your pants, I'll stop."

"I didn't say that."

"Arrrgghghhh!"

"But not very hard and he's been totally unsuccessful."

"Come home," I said.

"I thought you were at the hotel?"

"I am. Come here."

"I was hoping you could join me. You could help me. There's a mystery here."

Ted was my favorite suspect for the murders even though I'd not connected him in any way besides my not liking him and him covering up the crime. And hitting me.

"I don't know how to get there."

"Mr. Allenby will bring you."

I looked at Bruce. "Who sent you?" I asked.

"Ted, for Allie."

"Will you take me to Funkytown?"

"Ted's ranch? Sure."

Back to Allie. "Okay. You make loving fun. I'm on my way."

"Oh Daddy."

"Don't stop."

But we did.

Bruce and I rode the elevator down and then got into his rental car. He pulled into traffic and navigated the one-way streets that riddle the town like a short-sighted skeleton and headed south.

"Oh yeah, you used to live here," I said.

"Yep."

"You worked with Ted."

"I really can't—"

"But you will."

He drove and the wheels turned.

"How do you know that this wasn't a murder-suicide. You seemed pretty sure with Johnson," he said.

I pulled out my phone and found the picture of Sangye. I zoomed into the corner where his hand hovered over the gun. When we got a light, I showed him.

"I was in the room. See here? The gun?"

"What about it?"

"The blood is under it, not on top. It's in a pool of blood but shiny and clean on the top."

He studied the picture until the light changed.

"Nice."

"How'd they figure it out?" I asked.

"No idea."

"So you're not in on the case?"

"The murder? Oh, no. That's local."

"It's time, Bruce. Give me the Ted Talk."

"That's good."

"You want to help me," I said.

"I do?"

"You're a fan."

"I am."

"You've got six minutes. Go."

"Why six minutes?"

"That's how long TED Talks are," I said.

"I thought they were twenty."

"Eighteen in its heyday, now they want three to thirteen minutes. Blame shrinkflation for turning a useful educational experience into a bloated soundbite."

"Check."

"So go," I said.

Outside the car, Eugene spring green passed by in tufts. Rainclouds congregated in cliques but hadn't decided whose lunch money to go after yet, so the road was dry.

"When the killing at the hotel happened, Ted's first thought was that it was done to get at him."

28

"WAS it done to get at Tessner?" I asked.

"How would I know?" said Agent Bruce Allenby.

"Because you're with the FBI. I thought you solved crimes."

"Not my department."

"You're kidding."

"No. I prevent them at best. Someone else sometimes solves them."

"Sometimes?"

"Yeah. Don't get me started on how few bank robbers are actually caught."

"Good to know. But what about Ted?"

"I really shouldn't," he began.

"You know I bet that someone who sometimes solves crimes would do better if people told them stuff that could be helpful. Just a thought. Maybe you could drop that idea in a suggestion box at work or something."

He sighed and took a green exit as rain misted the windshield. "Ted is a successful grower."

"Mushrooms are big."

"He started out doing a different business."

"A puzzle? Now you're giving me puzzles. How do you people ever get anything done?"

"You can figure it out."

"Of course I can. He used to be a male prostitute specializing in aquatic mammal sodomy."

"He did?"

"Fuck, Bruce. Keep up. Okay, so he grew pot. This is Oregon, lots of people did. Even before it was legalized, it was ignored. I was here, or there. Do you say there, for a time shift?"

"It was ignored up to a point. If it got large, the law would step in."

"What's large?"

"A business."

"Ah. So that's how you met Ted. You raided him."

"Yes and no."

"You were working drugs then?"

"Yes and no."

"I'm going to smack you."

"It's the DEA actually, but the FBI helps and Ted was helpful."

"He was FBI?"

Bruce swallowed, braced himself against the wheel, swerved off the road and rammed a tree. Okay, not the last part. Instead of swerving, he said, "Ted was an informant. He informed on a lot of local growers who, if they find out it was him, even after all these years, might be upset."

"That's the problem with snitching. It's hard to keep friends."

"Yes. Can't say that Ted didn't take advantage of the situation. He'd put one person out of business and then take their customers."

"You let that happen?"

He shrugged.

"God, the drug war is a shit show."

"That's why I got out of it."

"What are you doing now?"

"Anti-terrorism."

I thought that was very interesting. "That's very interesting," I said.

He didn't look at me but drove out of the mist into a fog cloud, out of the fog cloud, past bright burning moist sunlight and into another cloud.

"So why now?" I asked. "Something symbolic about the conference, beyond crosses and such?"

"Ted's using it to try to change his image. Even talked about going into politics."

"Still, seems like a weird time to be uber paranoid."

"There's also Vance."

"Oh, isn't there always?" I said. "Who's Vance?"

"Vance Derow. Grower that just got out of prison. I saw him at the hotel."

"What does he look like?"

"Big Black man, six six. Bald. Lean. Muscular."

"Prisons offer the best workout program ever, amirite?"

"It could just be a coincidence," conceded Bruce. "Him at the hotel. We don't know he even knows who Ted Tessner is."

Then I remembered something. "Does he have a chunk out of one ear, perchance?"

"Yes. He got it bit off in prison."

"I saw him at the airport when I arrived. Ted was there. They locked eyes and I could smell sulfur. He knows Ted exists."

"I was afraid of that," he said, coming into the light again. He turned down Ted's road. Fog. "So now we have a real suspect in the killings."

"That's a jump."

"Hardly."

"I'm an expert at jumping to conclusions," I explained. "Like how I know you've been hitting on me for the last hour."

"I have? I didn't notice."

"And you a Sagittarius."

"I'm not."

"See? I'm always jumping, and even I don't like Vance for the killing."

"Who do you like?"

"Honestly?"

"Sure. Why not."

"Ted Tessner."

"Ted?"

"Ted."

"Tessner?"

"Tessner."

"Ted Tessner?"

"Maybe I should write it down for you."

"How can you think Ted would sabotage his own event?"

I stared at the FBI agent and thought that maybe instead of easy bank robbing, with him, terrorism would be a safer bet.

"There's the house," I said, pointing. "Allie said there's a road around the back that leads to where she is."

"I know it."

He pulled past the house and went down a soggy gravel road through a canopy of trees that opened up into an idyllic pastoral scene with pastures. Several buildings that looked like barns but could have been converted grow rooms, were on either side. He drove around one and exposed a corral behind a haystack, not a cute yellow conical haystack of yore, but stacked bales of hay. A poor modern interpretation of a traditional classic. Allie put down a kid, a real kid, a baby goat the size of a cat, small dog, itty bitty farm animal, and waved. Bruce stopped the car and I opened my door, the easier to get out. I had a plan.

"You and Tessner sure are close," I said.

"He gave me some good busts. I owe him."

"Well thanks for the ride and new suspects."

I shut the door and as I walked away, I could hear Bruce's muffled question but ignored it. "Suspects?" he said.

Without turning around, I heard him drive away as I reached my farm gal in the farm yard with farm animals looking on.

"Allie," said I. "It's me Tony. The love of your life. The person you owe your happiness too. Please don't throw it away?"

"Your insecurity is only overshadowed by your idiocy."

"No one understands me like you do."

She kissed me. I liked it, though in truth, she smelled like a barnyard.

"Sweet-talker."

"I said that out loud?"

"Yes."

"I gotta work on that."

"Probably."

"Is this Jerry?" I pointed to the little goat who was staring up at me with strange horizontally-irised eyes. "He's all ears."

"He's valuable. A Kamori goat from the mountains of India."

Seeking enlightenment, I looked at the little guy, he looked back. I noticed his long floppy ears that would put a hound dog to shame. He wore a chocolate-brown body and a very earnest expression. He noticed my tubby middle and bright shirt with head-tilting curiosity.

"What was the problem?" I asked.

"His mother was hurt. She was taken to the vet, and I stayed and kept him company. I just slept in the barn with him."

"Seriously?"

"Yeah. Valuable goats, and as you can tell, Jerry's really young."

I must have made a face because Allie said, "What?"

"Why you?"

"I'm good with animals."

"Yeah but…"

"You're thinking this is about you, aren't you?" she said.

Jerry looked at me accusingly.

"I am," I admitted. "A little."

"You might not be wrong."

"He's hit on you?"

She shrugged.

"First he hits me and then he hits on you."

"Nothing happened."

I pointed to my face.

"What? Oh, right, he hit you. So you say."

"'So I say'?"

"Sorry. He hit you. But you can't see it on your face."

"Look now," I said and filled my eyes with rage.

"Oh, yeah, okay. There it is. I see it now. But nothing happened to me."

"Except a kidnapping."

"Tony—"

"Kidnapping," I said with emphasis.

"Oh, oh, I see what you did there. Very good, but—"

"Kidnapping."

Her smile was the warmest thing I'd experienced all day. I relented. "Are you done here now?"

"Yeah Beatrice is home, just there in the shed. Someone shot her."

"Shot?"

"That's the mystery."

When she put the goat down, it was immediately overcome with a wave of zoomies. He ricocheted from road to corral to pasture and back, made half an ascent up the haystack and added a kick turn off a rail before disappearing into a shed.

"Good timing. We can go."

She took my arm and led me down a wood-chip path between mossy trees and poison oak.

"So will you take the case of the wounded goat? Ted pays."

"He wants me to find the shooter of Jerry's mother?"

"Beatrice. Yes."

"And be out here in Bumfuck Briarpatch, Oregon, away from the conference?"

"Yes."

"Let me think about it for a couple weeks."

"I thought you might say that."

"Ted is looking good for it," I told her.

"You think he shot Beatrice? Why? To get you away from the conference on a trumped-up case?"

I hadn't thought of that, but it was a killer theory. Allie was quick.

"That's what I was thinking."

"No, you weren't." I said she was quick.

"No, but it's a good theory. I was talking about Sangye and Smith."

"Not a murder-suicide?"

"Nope."

"Shit."

"You're not surprised?"

"Disappointed, he's a good contact. And rich. He gave me five K for coming over last night, but I know Ted didn't get where he is without being ruthless. Did you know he was thinking about going into politics?"

"Says it all, right there. Tell me 'bout the FBI agent."

"Bruce? He's a sweetheart. He's how I finally got a hold of you, you shit."

"Yes, that was very clever." The canopy cast moist murky shadows which matched the murders. "Why did Bruce do that for you?"

"I asked him to. I was insistent. I told him Ted would want him to do it for me."

"That's what I'm talking about," I said. "Bruce and Ted are tight. Bruce could have done it for him."

"It being the killings?"

"He has a gun. I think."

"But why would Ted want to kill Smith and why would Bruce agree to help?"

"They seem to have history, some of it shady."

"And Ted's motive?"

"Blackmail."

"Blackmail?"

"Blackmail."

"Over the shady history?"

"Could be," I said.

"Wait." She stopped.

"What?"

"Have you been beaten up yet? Attacked?"

"Ted hit me."

"That doesn't count."

"It did to me. But what are you getting at?"

"You never finish a case until after you've had some real physical harm. That means there's still lots left in this case."

I blinked for a moment or two. "I'm not sure about your logic," I said, "but the facts do kinda support you."

"Aha!"

"But Ted did hit me. And Bruce was there."

"But you're not done yet," she said, taking my arm and walking again.

"No, not even close, which is kinda scary for how long this book is already."

"Yeah."

"Yeah."

"I'm sure you'll manage."

"I'm working on it," I said.

"What's next?"

"I have no idea."

"I've a couple," she said

We emerged from the woods behind the house at the base of the lawn. I glanced back thinking that we were being followed, watched. I saw nothing but green.

Before us, the wings of the mansion spread out before us, and the hot tub was just visible off the lawn. It was covered and no one was serving drinks or handing out towels. I could have used both. I was tired and soaked. The walk wasn't bad, but it was long and hot and the moisture in the air had be-sogged me.

"I said I have a couple of ideas," said Allie.

"On how to get in?" The door was locked.

"The case."

I've known for a while that Allie wanted to be more involved in my sleuthing work. She's dropped subtle hints like, "You should use me as an operative in your sleuthing work."

"First let's get in."

She knocked on the door. After a moment, Lewis opened it.

"Lewis, my man," I said, getting an idea. They do come to me, you know. "Just the man I wanted to talk to."

"Oh?"

"I want to talk to you about who had access to those guns we took off the Naziman."

"Naziman," he said. "You make it sound like he's a superhero."

"I'm sure he thinks he is."

Allie pushed her way inside and I followed. Why didn't I think of that?

"Is Ted still here?" she asked.

"No. He left for the conference. Wish I could be there."

"Why can't you?"

He shrugged.

"Who's keynoting tonight?" asked Allie.

"Barty-B," I said.

"The Holy Reverend Bartalemuw Benson," corrected Lewis with feeling.

"Him," I said.

He blushed. "I already told the police everything."

"Tell us," I said.

"Why should I?"

"Because we're guests of Mr. Ted, maybe-I-kill-people, Tessner, and we asked you to."

The sound of Allie's hand slapping her forehead echoed through the halls.

Lewis's expression was unmoved.

Allie said, "You can tell us as we drive to the conference to catch the keynote. I have an extra ticket."

He brightened. I raised an eyebrow at Allie who smirked knowingly.

"Okay," Lewis said. "I actually made a list of people who could have taken it."

"Superb."

"I'll pull the car around and meet you out front." He opened a door we'd just come through, indicating to leave that way. Allie, leading the way, did. Lewis disappeared in the house after locking the door again.

We followed the path around the house and I again had the feeling that we were being watched and followed. I peered into the trees and saw only trees, moss, mold, and poison oak. Ah, Lane County, Oregon.

I rushed to catch up to Allie. "You mad?"

"You know what I want."

"A hickey-belly with whipped cream?"

"That's what *you* want."

"Oh yeah."

Around the front of the house, we meet an electric SUV. Lewis was in the driver's seat, the back doors were open. I raced around for the front, the shotgun position, calling it at a dead run.

"We gotta hurry," said Lewis. "We'll be late."

Allie climbed into the back but just as she closed the door, I heard it. A near and plaintive cry followed by the sound of inhuman scratches and then the door shut.

"I guess we can go," said Allie, and Lewis floored it out of the driveway.

Looking into the back seat, I beheld standing next to my girlfriend, on what I had to be a grade or two better than even the best Corinthian leather seats, was a chocolate-brown all-ears goat baby.

Like the void, it stared back at me, but unlike the void, it bleated in triumph and tilted its head.

29

"YOU SAID WE WERE IN A HURRY," she said. "And Jerry's fine. He's just having a little adventure." Babies of all species elicit the baby-talk response.

Lewis wasn't sure about the etiquette of transporting farm animals in his employer's vehicle but neither did he slow down the electric behemoth.

"What are we riding in?" I asked.

"A Rivian. Ninety-five K."

"Ouch," said Allie, maybe about the price of cars, maybe about cloven hooves on sensual thighs.

"Could it have uglier headlights?"

"No," said Lewis.

"Blaaaaah!"

Lewis drew the line at allowing Jerry to steer so Allie held the beast on her lap the rest of the way.

"So tell us about the guns."

"The cabinet wasn't locked," he began, "but the room was at eleven thirty. Dinner ended at ten fifteen."

"How do you know these times?" asked Allie.

"That room has an electronic lock. The dinner I knew because I was there and watching the clock."

"Do all the rooms have those nifty locks?"

"No, only a couple. Not the guest rooms, if that's what you're hoping."

"That would be too easy," I said. "I love a challenge."

"Blaaaaah!"

"Go on," I said to Lewis.

"I was in the dining room cleaning up until I shifted into the hot tub.

That means there was at most twenty minutes between me not being there and the door locking."

"What about the other staff?"

"They were already leaving or in the kitchen. I'm permanent. They were hired for the dinner."

"So, a list?"

"When I got to the hot tub, there were people in it. Those people obviously couldn't have taken the gun."

"Who were they?" asked Allie.

"Mr. Tessner, Mr. Smith, and his woman associate."

"Sylvia," I said more for you guys than us.

"And the Reverend," said Lewis.

"Blaaah!"

"The Messenger was wandering the woods when I got there," said Lewis. "And Donnopher were mixing their own drinks. They might have done it, since they left when I got there."

"We passed them on the stairs," said Allie from the back. "They were coming from the patio, not the dining room."

"If you say so," said I. I honestly didn't remember.

Lewis nodded. "You two arrived later, so you could have taken them."

"Barty—*the Reverend*—B wasn't in the hot tub," I said.

"He was milling around, had a drink and left before you got there."

I glanced at Allie who raised an eyebrow. Jerry tilted his head.

"I don't remember him being a drinker."

"Like you know him," said Lewis.

"This doesn't get Tessner out of the picture," I said. "He could have gotten to it someway. It is his house."

"He's an agricultural billionaire, not technology," said Allie. "He wouldn't know."

"He can still point and click."

No one argued. Not even Jerry.

The conversation faltered then, and the road opened up into patches of sunlight and sleet alternatively. I felt like I'd spent the day in cars, where I was the safest of all, but was relieved when downtown Eugene appeared between the trees. You gotta look for it. It's forest and farmland then boom, civilization. But I was a detective and trained for that kind of thing, so when the trees gave way to buildings, I knew where we were.

We parked and entered the lobby as folks were filtering in for the evening's banquet and keynote. I'd never been to a conference with so many banquets and keynotes. I had a feeling that it was in the contract for the big presenters that they would get to the keynote. I thought also that when everyone keynotes, no one does. Syndrome would understand.

Allie produced a ticket to the buffet for Lewis, who was very pleased to have it. He rushed past us to find a seat.

"Ted give you those?" I asked.

"Yes. Lots of people left the conference today. It's why he's so mad at you."

"Me?"

"For telling everyone about everything."

"It was Dara," I said. "And Perry. And the gang. And stuff."

"It was you, and you know it."

"People have a right to know."

"Ted thinks they could have known after the conference." I couldn't tell where she was on this, and that bothered me.

"But there is a murderer on the loose."

"Yeah, there is that," she conceded, and I felt better.

"Blaaah." Yes. Allie still had Jerry in her arms.

"You better do something with him," I said.

"See you inside." She pecked me on the cheek and went to the elevators.

It was true. Many people seemed to have left. The banquet was going, but there was no line and lots of empty seats at bare tables. I found Rachael talking earnestly into her phone by the kitchen doors. I saw my friends at their usual table. Comics like to be in the shadows when not in the spotlight. Barty-B was with Ted at the front table, all square teeth and fake tan. The Messenger had a conglomerate of people near the middle. Passing by, I thought I heard the words "transfixatoriamusation displaying entricum" and kept walking. Artstar was in a formal black robe and witch's hat. She was trying to catch Barty-B's eye but he made sure not to glance the sixteen degrees to his right to view her. She instead noted me looking at her and gave me a wink.

Augustus Klept was in attendance and actually sitting with Kaisa Woods. Not sure what they were talking about it, maybe how to smuggle weapons to trees in the Amazon. I had no doubt Klept had a connection. Sylvia was there, several people talking to her at the table now marked only COTTEO. She saw me, and I could tell she wanted to talk, but couldn't get away.

Adam Tuku was not there, though his orange jumpsuit acolytes were all over the place. They'd chosen not to share the same table tonight, but instead to spread out. I knew that was good networking, but no one was talking to them and they seemed dour. Their mission to mingle apparently not popular even with them.

Agent Bruce Allenby was not there, but I knew he was nearby. An ebony egg drew my attention to one side and there was Mr. Vance Derow, bald man from the airport, who Ted had sent to jail and now, maybe, hopefully? was out for revenge. I tried to catch his eye, but he was interested only in the potato salad. Lewis had found a table but had forgone the buffet and only had a glass of iced tea. With lemon.

I made a plate of food—meat, carbs, more meat, sugar, carbs—and sat down with my friends.

"Dara told us all about operation celebrity kidnapping," said Perry. "Why didn't you just ask me to introduce you?"

"You know them?"

"No, but I'd have pretended to."

"Dara was what I needed. She has a certain style."

"I noticed they haven't come down to the buffet," Standard said.

"Neither did Critter," said Garrett forlornly.

"You two fighting again?" I asked.

"Someone complained," explained Garrett into his mashed potatoes. "Said he triggered them."

I waited for the punchline, and when it didn't come, I said, "Really?"

"I tried to argue, but when I failed to produce a ticket for him, his fate was sealed. He's up in the room watching who knows what smut on TV."

"You didn't leave him your credit card?" Dara asked.

Garrett nodded.

My mind reeled, first at wondering what could have happened to someone that just the presence of a hand puppet in a dimly-lit five thousand square-foot banquet hall would upset them so much they'd have to call the authorities and have it removed, but also at what kind and how much pornography an empty hand puppet might consume in a day through hotel streaming services.

"You should have bought him a ticket," said Standard.

"I might tomorrow," said Garrett.

"Did you get what you needed from Donnopher?" asked Perry.

"I'm working on it." Before anyone could challenge me there, Ted was up at the stage introducing the Reverend Bartalemuw Benson from The Abundant Church of God for the keynote address of the evening.

There was a smattering of applause as the man adjusted the microphone and put on his blinding grin. I noticed Lewis beaming from his table on a similar but warmer frequency. How bad can anyone have it when there's someone in the world who looks at you the way he did Barty-B?

"I have come here today, to this gathering as the only spokesman for the one true God. I am here like Daniel among the lions, to preach truth to you pagans in an attempt to save your souls."

If he thought that was a laugh line, he needed to do a lot more work-shopping. He raised a gold-edged Bible above his head while looking malevolently out at the crowd. My brain took this as a sign from God to tune out.

I opened my phone and played the video of Sangye's crime scene. The list of recent phone calls was suspicious. Three from John Smith, one from Sylvia but thirteen from either blocked or unknown numbers. Considering the heinous amount of robocalls I get every day on my unlisted number, that wasn't a shock. The strange thing was that he answered them all and had lengthy chats with each. I noticed specifically on the day of the murders, a call came in to him at six twenty and lasted ten minutes. Next call was from Sylvia at six forty-five. That went to voice mail.

A fist pounding on the lectern brought my attention back to the room. "God has a simple plan for his children. And ye have forsaken it. This is a conglomeration of idols, golden calves and demons."

The notes on Sangye's phone were more interesting. I paused the video to read that he needed to buy new shoes. He had the address of a Nike outlet store at the mall pre-programmed and ready to navigate. It'd be a short walk from the hotel. With it was a note of John's shoe size, ten and a half suggesting that he'd buy his boss a pair too. He'd copied a recipe for a potato curry from somewhere and another for no salt naan. There was note listing a few color ideas to send to the architects for the new COTTEO center but also a wish list of possible upgrades including three new buildings on the site and a helipad. On the next page was a cryptic list that I took to be a clue since it was the last note he'd modified before his death. A column of letters under the heading "Donations; A, G, B, Cm, P, Cv, H, and T. The A and B had smiles and an exclamation point, the G and T had smiles but no exclamation point. The P and C had frowny face emojis, while the Cm and the H had question marks following those letters. The time stamp on the note was 6:40 the day he died. Five minutes before he didn't answer the call from Sylvia.

"And the worst sin is homo-sex-you-ality." Barty's labored pronunciation of the word drew my attention again. "It is the vile rot that has rotted the vine."

"Now there's a labored phrase," said Dara. She wore the expression all my friends had on, one of disgust and disbelief.

"Was this vetted?" asked Perry.

"No," I said. "I asked already."

"Shit."

Barty's smile was gone, replaced with a scowl. "All the horrors of today can be placed upon the shoulders of the degenerates who lie with their brothers!"

"What about sister lying?" cried Artstar. "Is that okay?"

"Hecklers. He's got hecklers," said Standard.

"Good," said Garrett.

"The man can speak a storm but sure as shit can't read a room," observed Perry.

I looked around and saw he was right. Outside of the BRA skinheads and maybe two tables of clean-cut middle-class AARP members, everyone else was staring daggers at the man on stage. Ted was visibly uncomfortable, shifting in his chair. When he turned his back squarely on the table Vance was at, I wondered if the discomfort might be something else.

That's when I saw Lewis at his table. He sat still as a statue. His hands folded on his lap, his posture straight, his face grave and blank. Only the tears rolling out of his eyes suggested anything other than equanimity.

Alarms went off across the room. Not fire alarms, but watch alarms, phone alarms. I glanced at my own and saw it was indeed exactly 9:37 p.m. The sound was coming from everywhere, from all angles and all directions of the room.

In a motion, an orange motion, all the Homecoming cultists rose as a single unit and rushed to the door they were nearest. To the sound of electronic dings and bings, chirps, dongs, and whistles, they barred each one with chains and locks, pushed chairs and tables against them. It was done so quickly, so expertly, that one had to imagine that it'd been practiced, nay —choreographed.

No one moved to stop them. Everyone was too surprised to see danger. It was only when they began chanting that things got serious.

"Embrace death!" they said. "Embrace death!"

Up went their hands as if reaching for a floating rope ladder.

"Embrace death! Embrace death! Embrace death!"

This went on a long time. Maybe three minutes before one of them reached into her pocket to silence her phone. It slackened a little then.

"Embrace death. Embrace death."

She was followed by the others in ones and twos, alarms went silent as each reluctantly turned off their alarms, lowered their voices and eventually dropped the chant altogether. Then they stood, each at a door, looking at one another. Someone tried to get in from the outside and rattled some chains. Still, the jumpsuits waited and stared.

The door to the kitchen, which hadn't been chained but barricaded, burst open and six armed men rushed forward.

The Homecoming folks didn't resist as they were led away.

Ted Tessner returned to the stage.

"Enjoy your desserts while we find a pair of bolt cutters for the doors," he said. "And let's have a big round of applause for the Reverend Bartalemuw Benson from The Abundant Church of God!"

30

"SOMETIMES THE RAPTURE WORKS, sometimes it don't," said Perry.

"It's never worked," said Standard.

"I was ready for the last one," said Garrett. "I had my eye on my neighbor's new Prius. He's a really nice guy, so I didn't think he'd mind if I took it after he was gone."

"But he didn't go?"

"No. Goddammit."

"Fucker."

"I know, right?"

Dara was not as calm as the others, reflecting my own feelings. "What the fuck was that about?" she said.

I shook my head. "I think I need a drink."

"The bar here is a rip off," said Standard. "I snuck in some Everclear if you want some." He offered me a hip flask of paint thinner.

"Are we in high school?" I said.

Dara took the bottle and swigged.

"Germs," said Standard.

"Bear-molesting anchovy," was her response, which I think got her point across.

The doors were cut open and all the waiters wearing the cheeriest of smiles held them open for all to see. They couldn't have been cheerier if their jobs depended on it, which I'm sure they did.

"I'm beginning to feel sorry for Allie's new boyfriend," said Dara.

"The fuck?" said I.

"Not boyfriend?"

"No. Allie and I are made up."

"So you were fighting?"

"I was."

"Over Tessner?"

"Yes."

"Because you're threatened by him and he's hitting on Allie."

"Your point?"

"The poor guy tried to put together something nice, and it's all gone to shit," said Dara. "Now he has the waiters doing a *Mulholland Drive* in damage control."

"The cab scene," said Perry. "Good reference. I wondered where I'd seen that glassy-eyed grin before."

"In your nightmares," said Garrett.

"There too."

"Club?" said Standard, wiping the rim of his bottle with a napkin.

"Club," said Perry.

"Club?" said I.

"Perry found an open-mic comedy club. Thought we'd see what's what."

I thought of Allie.

"Kh-Ohhhmmmm!"

The room jumped as if electrocuted.

"Jesus fucking Christ! What was that?"

"My ringtone. Hi Allie."

"Where are you? Is everything okay?"

"We're just leaving the banquet. Going to a comedy club for drinks. Wanna come?"

"Sure, but you're alright? Nothing really horrible happened?"

"No, Why?"

"The lobby is crawling with firemen and cops."

"Failed Rapture," I said.

"Oh, just that? Okay. Meet you in the lobby."

She was right. Eugene's finest were there en masse. Billy clubs were drawn but not being swung, firemen were ready but not on fire. We weaved our way through them while the rest of the guests waited, cowered, or skittered to elevators, doubtlessly remembering the police beatings that began the conference.

Bruce Allenby seemed to be in charge. He spoke into his sleeve and nodded at other people in casual wear, suits for the men, sensible slacks and blazers for the women. All had nice bright gold badge necklaces that really set off their ensembles. They'd be the bad-ass in the room at any formal business meeting arrest.

Also dressed for success, were the appropriately orange jump-suited Homecoming Allegiance members who were being perp-marched out of the hotel into a waiting bus. Eugene has a great mass transit system, but not all the buses have bars on the windows like that one. I had to admit it was strange to see it there so fast, but then remembered the city's over eager police force and figured they had to have a fleet of these somewhere parked alongside the dozen armored vehicles they'd purchased from the army who had got rid of them to be in accordance with the Geneva Convention. The orange men looked as dangerous as Oompa Loompas but they were taking no chances. Patented plastic cuff restraints, the kind sold at January 6th reenactment days, were doubled up on their wrists. The cultists looked not guilty and not scared, but rather confused and entered the bus in an orderly manner, a feat Southwest Airlines has yet to imagine.

"Blaaaaaah!"

"Jerry?" There was Allie and there was a goat. "I thought you were going to put him down."

"What?"

"I meant like sleep."

"Oh. Well, he's too young to leave alone, so I thought we'd bring him with us for a night out."

"You can't bring livestock into a nightclub," I said. "This is Eugene, not Springfield."

"This is my emotional support goat." She held him up and showed me. Draped over his back was a little cape that read *Emotional Support Animal*.

"Where'd you get that?"

"Etsy."

"You keep them with you at all times?"

"I've used them before. Psilly wore one of these for a while."

"Don't you need a permit or something?"

"In some places for actual service animals, but the emotional support thing is gray."

I remembered a time I was at a bookstore and someone brought in a dog claiming it was a support animal and it nearly ripped my arm off before going for the children's section.

The gang ogled at little Jerry who seemed absolutely thrilled at the attention. He demanded to be put down and then did a leash-limited zoomies session that included high hops with darling little head tilts and heartwarming bleats. It brought the entire hotel to a standstill and smiles to everyone's faces. He couldn't have done more adorable if he'd farted rainbows that played *The Carpenters*.

"The club's just downtown, we can walk it," said Perry, eyeing the heavy police presence. Perry is by nature paranoid, but a healthy fear of cops is not a bad thing to have. He'd missed the first day riot or else he'd never have left the banquet room, probably would have turned around and gone into hiding. Again. He has a cabin in Wyoming he pretends no one knows about.

Dara led us out through a back door and around a rental car lot to a tree-shaded sidewalk. "Where now Magellan?"

He pointed. Jerry was again in Allie's arms. He was calm because Allie was herself an emotional support animal.

The name of the club was Funny on Fifth. I'd never heard of it, but Perry told us he'd performed there a couple of times. We all call ourselves comedians, but Perry is the only one who's had real success. He's put in time doing the circuit, performing in clubs and bars that don't pay enough to cover the gas there. I'm always amazed that he'd done so well, considering he's half crazy. I finally figured out that he wants to be famous so he can't be so easily disappeared. Fame and riches sought as a deterrent to government over-reach. Made sense, in a focused conspiratorial kind of way. The rest of us wanted fame and riches for the fame and riches. No ulterior motive. We sometimes think that's why we haven't achieved it. This argument makes more sense after a couple of drinks.

Perry though is on the verge of televised standup which will put him into the next league. He had three minutes on a cable random standup survey, but now Netflix is interested. He's putting together an hour to offer them, planning a tour for the summer to work out the kinks, with the hope of having cameras on him at the end.

We arrived at the door and Perry stood there expecting to be ushered in, but the doorman didn't know him.

"Twenty dollar cover and two drinks plus an appetizer per table," said the man at the door.

We are cheap people. Artists aren't rich. Comedians, painters, writers, none of this says big money, but we weren't getting by the man without paying, so we paid.

"I thought you said, they knew you?" said Dara,

"They do. They did," said Perry. "My signed headshot is on the wall, three from Aziz Ansari and two from Bill Burr."

"Times must be tough," I said.

Perry stopped in the foyer and looked forlornly at a blank wall.

"Where are all the pictures?" he asked no one in particular.

"Redecorating?" suggested Dara, but we knew that wasn't true. The wall was pockmarked with nail holes, torn paper and phantom squares that showed where pictures used to be. The wall spoke of absence not change.

We found our way inside. It was a bar with a stage and we were between acts. We found a table in the blue shadows off the side where a booth could be if they committed to permanent furniture. Above us was another barren wall of once something, now nothing.

A waitress with green hair and steel in her face welcomed us with a laminated menu of house drinks, beer lists, appetizer choices, and even promises of whole sandwiches should we want to get crazy. Then she produced a laminated document entitled *Disclosures* and told us we'd need to agree before she could serve us, mentioning also the two drink, one appetizer minimum.

"We have to agree to these terms and conditions to get drinks and food?"

"Yes."

"And if we don't get food and drinks, we have to leave?"

"Yes."

"Even after the cover?"

She shrugged and offered us an electronic tablet with a page open to *Table 9*. "Just initial there," she said. "Each of you."

"Can we read it first?" asked Standard.

She rolled her eyes. "I'll be back to take your orders. Don't hurt my pad."

She left us and we watched Standard skim the document, scrolling through no less than five screens before saying, "It's a list of trigger warnings and a promise that we won't hold the club or the artists responsible for anything that might be deemed offensive today, yesterday or tomorrow. There's also language here that's taken straight from a corporate non-disclosure agreement that says that if we speak out on social media about the acts or the club in a derogatory manner, we can be sued to Suez."

"Suez?" said Allie.

"Thereabouts," said Standard.

"What the actual hell?" said Dara.

Garrett, I noticed then, was sulking. He'd been sulking since dinner, but I'd not paid him attention before. "Your thoughts?"

He shrugged.

"What's wrong, smookie?" I said.

"I wish Critter were here. He'd know how to handle this."

He was right. Critter would know how to handle this, or maybe at least explain it.

Garrett gave a long sad sigh and I felt bad for not telling him to go get him when we left. It was an oversight, probably brought on by Perry's rush to leave the cop show.

"Allie?" I said and nodded to Jerry.

She understood and handed Garrett the goat. He looked surprised and a little startled, but then as Jerry examined his ear with his lips, my friend warmed into a smile.

In the rush of getting in, of paying too much, of Perry's confusion and picture problem, I'd not noticed how easy it had been to bring a goat into a nightclub with a food license. True, Allie had put a cute little baby-blue cartoon-character diaper on him, but really, doesn't Eugene have a health department, or does all the money go to the cops? Looking around however, I saw that Jerry was just one of the menagerie of creatures wearing capes and coats proclaiming in Etsy-furnished lettering that they were emotional support animals.

There were four dogs, a ferret, a parrot, two cats—one in a backpack with a dome window, another hiding under a table—a pink pig and a boa constrictor. The snake wore a collar and not a cape and seemed scarily restless. The cats kept an eye on it. The pig didn't care.

"Well?" Our waitress was back.

We each dragged a finger over the pad indicating our agreement and ordered nachos and a pitcher of local IPA called *Rainy Days and Mondays*. Jerry seemed pleased enough to fart a rainbow, but we wouldn't have been able to see it with the diaper on.

Perry was in shock. He had the kind of look one might have if when returning from a long vacation they found that someone had replaced their precious belongings with wet oatmeal and their house with a piece of artist's foam board. You know—*that* look.

A thin, droopy-shouldered, twenty-something white guy in a beret and black-framed glasses approached the stage mic and read off his phone. "Funny on Fifth would like to welcome to the stage Richard Moensis!"

Perry perked up. "Richard's great. He's a regular here. He has this killer bit about girls named Jyll, with a Y, and a tale of living with hippies for a summer that ends with tie-dye dysentery."

"Don't spoil it," said Garrett.

Onto the stage trotted the comic waving at the crowd and reaching for the microphone, but before getting it, the man in glasses went on. "For those of you visually challenged, Richard Moensis is a thirty-one-year-old cis white man, presenting as described. He has dark-brown hair combed neatly with a part on the left side. He's in faded black Levi jeans, a plain black tee shirt, and New Balance running shoes. He has an imitation leather belt with a chrome buckle. I'd say he has a BMI of about one ninety, one ninety-five pounds at six foot tall. He wears no visible jewelry."

"Is this a bit?" asked Allie.

We waited for the punchline. Moensis rocked on his heels, waiting with us.

The weaselly man on the stage went on. "Trigger warnings: PG-rated cursing, monetary disadvantage, mild to mid-level gender differences, death in the background, disease with lingering side-effects, reference to religion—Christianity; holidays—Christmas; drug use—caffeine and alcohol; ableism in vocabulary, 90s cultural references and male profession sports; sleep deprivation, sibling rivalry, school lunch, recess trauma, airports, cultural differences between city and country—specifically San Francisco California and Garwin Iowa, prejudice against culinary tastes and three fart jokes."

We all stared, even Jerry's mouth hung open.

The announcer stepped back to check his work examining the comic and then the audience for a moment. He nodded in satisfaction before, finally, handing the microphone to Moensis. The comedian took it but waited, watching, as the little man exited the stage and disappeared into the depths of the club.

Turning back to the crowd squinting against the lights, Moensis smiled broadly. "Hullo Eugene!" he yelled, trying to create some kind of enthusiasm in the dead dead dead room. "What's up with airplane food anyway?" he began.

"Jesus wept," said Perry.

31

WHAT FOLLOWED WAS a ten-minute set of pablum. No jokes about a girl named Jyll, with a Y. No jokes about hippies eating manure for the vitamins, which Perry said was beyond hysterical. He went down a list of the safest most inoffensive and spoiled jokes I'd ever witnessed. The strongest joke, and this should tell you something, had to do with a barista at Starbucks getting his order wrong and him having flashbacks to his brother opening up his present by mistake at Christmas. Laughing? Neither were we, but the audience seemed content, amused. Placated.

We all felt sick when the act was over.

Jerry was the first to speak. "Blaaah." He was a wise little goat.

"Richard was never edgy, but what the actual fuck?" said Perry.

"Excuse me," said a woman at a nearby table. "Can you please not speak that way?"

"Blaaaah," said the goat.

"My friend has Toxic Obscenity Syndrome," said Dara. "We all fucking do. It's a fucking tragedy, but we're fucking dealing with it the best we fucking can. Thanks for your fucking understanding." She spoke in a soft sweet voice like she were speaking to a toddler wanting more cotton candy. Dara's hand shot to her mouth. "Oh," she shrieked every so sweetly. "I fucking did it again, didn't I?"

She threw herself into my shoulder, sobbing.

"You did," I said comfortingly, softly stroking her. "Titty-fuck cock-sucker ass."

"Shit," said Allie.

The woman shifted in her chair as Dara took a deep breath to speak, but before she could, the woman stood up and changed tables.

"Hey Perry." It was Richard Moensis. "I thought that was you. You going to do a set?"

"I might."

"Really? Okay. You'll have to have material screened first. Matt!" Richard raised his hand to signal the be-spectacled man from his introduction.

Perry reached over and pulled his arm down. "Nah, I'm good."

"Oh?" He looked at us. "You guys want to do some?"

"How'd you know we were comics?" said Garrett softly petting Jerry whose smug expression made clear he enjoyed it.

"I didn't," he said. "It's open mic."

"Aren't you full?" I asked. In my experience getting on an open mic night needed the kind of skills one reserved for Walmart Black Friday TV sales.

"No. Just run your material past the management." He tossed a thumb at Matt who waited nervously and alone by the stage door.

"Not a lot of takers?" said Standard.

"No. But it is a weekday."

"Better on the weekends then?" said Perry.

"Not really."

"So what happened here?"

He took a deep defeated breath and was about to speak when a wild red-headed Georgia peach appeared.

"I thought that was you!" said Peaches. Peaches, if you remember, was the woman Standard slept with at the Green Tomorrow orgy.

"Hi," said Standard. "How are you? Look everyone, it's...my friend."

"Peaches!" I said much to the relief of Standard. "What are you doing here? I haven't seen you since the conference after-party."

"Looking for some laughs."

"Find any?"

"Eh, no."

Richard Moensis's crest fell.

She pulled a chair from the table where the insulted woman had been and sat next to Garrett and Jerry. Jerry surveyed her with those weird horizontal eyes and proclaimed her welcome. "Bleeeeah!" She scratched his head and he beamed caprine contentment.

"That little guy has a lot of personality," I said.

"Oh, yeah," said Allie.

"You didn't like my set?" Moensis asked.

"Like?" said Peaches. "What's not to like about it? Love? Laugh? Sorry no, darling."

"You didn't notice the lack of laughter from the stage?" I asked.

"Well it's a small club and not a huge crowd," he explained. "I figured... you know. I figured."

"What happened here?" said Perry. "Funny on Fifth used to be..."

"Funny?" offered Allie.

Moensis looked around conspiratorially and then moved in close.

"Keeping up with the times, I guess."

"What happened to all the photos on the wall?" asked Perry.

"They got complaints. First too many white men, then too many men, then too many whites, then one of the black comics got caught reading *Harry Potter*, so she had to come down. In the end, it's less hassle just not to have them."

"And the joke screening?"

"Shows goodwill toward the release forms. Lawyers put it in place. They haven't had a single Twitter trend since implementing the changes."

"And probably not many acts either, I'd bet," said Standard.

"You'd be surprised."

"Horrified, is the word you're looking for, if you're the measure," I said.

"Hey."

"No offense, but that set was safe enough for a children's birthday party." It was Allie making the comment but we were all thinking it. She'd been around me and the gang long enough to have an appreciation of our sick hobby of standup comedy.

"Perry said you had a dynamite set. Girls named Jyll with a Y, and hippies."

"A girl named Jyll with a Y was in the audience one day. She had sixty-five thousand followers."

"And no sense of humor?"

He nodded. "My agent won't answer my emails anymore. This is the only club who'll show me and you've seen what I have to say."

"Aren't there other clubs in town?"

"Not anymore."

"Jesus wept." Perry was finding religion today.

"It's scary what people get mad about these days," said Peaches. "Green Tomorrow lost a couple people in São Paulo last month. Assassinated in their hotel room. A timber company practically admitted to doing it. No repercussions. Can't find the foremen accused. You know, the one on the video? So it's an isolated incident and if he shows up for work again, they'll let someone know. But what? Look over there—it's a Christmas-themed latte. Time to picket."

"Two people killed at the conference and no one's brought that up," said Dara. "What the fuck? Hours of classes about being better people led by the fucking cream of the fringe, and no one has a fucking word of sorrow or comment about one of their number being shot."

"It's not like the killer's running around," said Peaches.

"Bheeeefh!"

"What's that you say, little guy?"

"He's saying that there is a killer running around. It was a double murder," I said. "No suicide involved."

"Oh," said Peaches. "Any timber people around?"

"Good callback," said Standard.

"Why haven't they made any announcement about that?"

"Why haven't we?" said Dara, waving her phone around. "We let them get the last word."

"No," said Allie. "Don't. Ted's trying so hard to keep this thing together."

"Why?" said Garrett. "Not like anyone's being converted to anything else."

"The answer is not censorship, but more dialogue," said Perry.

"Are you talking about the Interfaith Congress of Holistic Enlightened People or the state of comedy?"

"Both," said Perry. "And more."

"I love your goat," said Peaches. "Can I hold him?"

Garrett reluctantly nodded and offered the goat her to her.

Peaches missed the handoff however, her hand falling instead to slide down Garrett's thigh where it lingered, wiggled and shifted, pulled back, went in again. Rubbed, caressed, and finally withdrew before collecting Jerry.

"Bwwwaaaa!"

"You staying at the hotel?" said Garrett through rosy cheeks.

"Room four-oh-six. Should be back in by eleven."

Standard's crest fell too.

A woman took the stage and told a story about her toddler ripping her clothes off and running through a department store. It was cute, innocent and funny, we got a couple laughs, but we were alone. Instead of applause, many in the audience had their phones in their hands, taking video and scowling while tapping away.

"Fuck," said Moensis.

Matt rushed onto the stage and told the woman to get off before apologizing for ten minutes for the egregious act.

"I'm out of here," I said.

"Yep."

"I think I'll head back to my hotel room 406 now," Peaches said to no one in particular who wasn't Garrett.

"Uhm," he said. "Do you mind if I bring a friend?"

Peaches surveyed the group. Her eyes fell on me, fell off when she saw Allie's warning expression, came to Perry who shook his head, Dara who shrugged.

"Not one of these people," said Garrett. "Not a person at all, really."

She looked at Jerry.

"He's with me," said Allie, taking him back.

Peaches looked confused.

"Just say yes," I said.

"Yes," she said.

Garrett, smiling instead of sullen, left the club with Peaches.

"Say hi to Critter for us," I said.

"Will do!"

"It's too early to go back," said Dara. "What else is there to do in this town?"

"Riot."

"Okay."

We left Moensis to do his next set which he said was sadder than the first but would pay for his gas that week. He had a Prius. The rest of us went in search of a riot, but alas, that Thursday in mid-April, Eugene, Oregon didn't have one. We thought of trying to start one, an idea that took on more and more merit as we finished Standard's flask of Everclear, then dropped off when Dara mentioned it sounded like work. We walked the streets of the little town, admiring that they had trees and glad it wasn't raining and only threatening too.

We passed the place where the famous Eugene Saturday's Market was held. Without the tents and tie-dye it was just a dark city square with only a handful of people, probably the kind without permanent addresses, chilling on the benches.

I had good memories of the market, more than it deserved, since I'd never actually experienced it. The Saturday Market when I was staying in Eugene was called Holiday Market and held across town in a warehouse at the fairgrounds. It was nice. Lots of knickknacks and such. Even then though, I couldn't help but think that it would have been better outdoors with green trees and sunshine, a luscious farmer's market cross corner, which is the usual way. A note on the bulletin board proclaimed that the market was again here and outdoors, rain or shine, but not today. It was, as I said, a Thursday.

Jerry was getting antsy. Allie suggested we find him some milk. We wandered on, found a Dari Mart trying to close, but which was kind enough to let us in when we held up Jerry like he was Simba on the rock. Dari Marts are a local phenomenon, a homegrown 7-Eleven knock-off specializing, you guessed it, in dairy products. I think they're related to a farm somewhere. Probably a dairy farm. These are the kind of hunches that make me the great detective I am.

A bottle of whole milk and a rubber glove and we could bottle feed Jerry.

"Do goats sleep?" Perry asked. "Maybe we should go back."

"I want to see one thing," I said. "See if it's still there."

I led them a block up and another over directed by my phone. "There it is," I said. "Behold, *The Storyteller*."

"A stature of a guy reading to kids. Wow," Dara said.

"That's Ken Kesey, or it's supposed to be." I didn't think it was a very good likeness, but it was bronze.

"So he's reading *One Flew Over the Cuckoo's Nest* to those kids? I hope it's the part about the lobotomy," said Dara.

"Maybe it's his other big one," said Perry.

"What's that?"

"No idea."

I did. "*Sometimes a Great Notion*. Never got a movie, though it is a contender for Great American Novel status."

"Is it good?"

"It's like an Oregon river," I said, "Dreary, wet, turbulent. But good."

"Wrestling with the big problems," said Allie.

"He was a wrestler, so it fits," I said. "Also I love the controversy about this statue."

"Too ugly?"

"Part of it. Kesey was a hippie, one of the original, if not *the* original Merry Prankster. See the previously mentioned *Electric Kool-Aid Acid Test* by Tom Wolfe."

"Mentioned where?"

"Never mind. Wolfe was an author and along with many other notable scribes of the time, helped pay for the statue." I read the names on the plaque. "Jean Auel, Tom Robbins, Nike founder Phil Knight, the other big Eugene alumni, actor Paul Newman and several members of the Grateful Dead."

"He doesn't look like a hippie here," said Standard. "Is that what the controversy is about?"

"Buckle up. It's about money and real estate." Gasps all around. "At first the businesses around here were okay with it since it was a tourist attraction in a place without any tourist attractions."

"It's no Bryce Canyon," said Allie.

"Bleaaaachh."

"Here," she said. "He wants you." In what felt like a baby handoff, Allie gave me Jerry. It was the closest I'd ever been to him. He looked me over, took my measure and rested his head on my shoulder. I melted a little.

"Kesey Square? I've never heard of it," said Standard.

"I'm sure some people made a pilgrimage to this place, but the open space was the real draw. Right in the heart of the city. It began bringing in the wrong kind of people—homeless and drug users who don't have cars and won't spend money on glass art." There was in fact a small group of wrong people in a doorway of a glass art studio just across the square. "They want it gone so the right kind of people will come here more often. This riff and raff is bad for commerce."

"The spirit of the '60s lives on," said Allie.

"Why don't they just send the police in to chase them away, tear down their homes, hit them with their sticks like they do in Salt Lake City?" said Dara.

"I'm sure they do, but this town is liberal and if they beat one hobo they might have to beat an entire graduating class of IT engineers who rise up in protest."

"Good on them," said Dara.

"The most prominent idea is to turn this whole square into an apartment house with shops on the bottom floor," I said. "Like in Sugarhouse back home."

"How very fucking gentrified," said Dara. "Fuck. Can't we have any public spaces at all?"

"What about the crime?" said Standard, eyeing the group eyeing us. "That's a real thing."

"A fucking symptom of a greater problem," Dara said. "Capitalism."

We all agreed. I went on. "The city is schizophrenic about all this. They know their heritage is the counterculture, but they're materialists by main culture. A lot of suggestions on how to best use this space are submitted anonymously."

"Everyone's a fucking sell out," said Dara. "These asshole developers suck. Where's a riot when you need one?"

"It says something that the statue is still here. It's still city property. The battle continues."

"Everyone has a price," said Perry wistfully, "to sell out your ideals."

"You're thinking of the comedy club?"

He nodded.

The attackers came from around the big red-brick wall that was the sculpture's background. Three of them, all in black hoodies. They walked three steps toward us then rushed me, in what I can only describe as the mugging version of a crash and grab, those storefront robberies where someone drives a car through the front window and then everyone grabs shit quick and gets away. A shock and awe crime that would warm Rumsfeld's dead heart.

The first one smashed into me, making me lose my balance. The second ripped Jerry out of my arms, the third slugged me upside the head so hard that, already-off balance, I teetered, turned, and hit the brick pavement where I decided to take a nap.

32

IS THERE A BETTER experience than waking up in a hospital? You open your eyes and behold the clean white surfaces, medical equipment, drapes, and nurses. You smell the comforting scents of antiseptics, hear the reassuring sound of professional medical personnel comforting and soothing. You know you're in good hands. You are safe.

Or...you lose your shit.

Confusion leads to panic when you see the wires leading from your body to machines. There are bars on the bed, you're strapped down, your vision is gauzy. Find level eleven on the panic meter as the smells remind you not of cleanliness and health, but of COVID, anthrax and tuberculosis germs. Convince yourself you can taste them. Wonder if you're in the morgue. But not so lucky. The air is full of bings and beeps, booms and moans that place you squarely in one of the better-lit rings of Hell. You tell yourself to keep it together, not to freak out, to remain calm in a *Johnny Get Your Gun* kind of way, else you'll summon Nurse Ratched who'll shoot you up and prepare your forehead for a little reassembly. Is Chief around to save you? Have you befriended him yet? Fuck. Drool city. Keep your shit together. Why all the *Cuckoo* references?

Slowly I remembered the nightclub, another trip to hell, Kesey Square and the kidnapping. I followed the drum beat to the back of my skull and then, reaching up with a unrestrained arm—I guess the blanket had felt like straps—felt a bald spot with a pokey caterpillar in it. Stitches, I concluded.

"You're awake," said Allie.

I turned to see Allison Braise sitting in a chair. She looked tired, unslept and relieved.

"What time is it?" I asked.

"About nine in the morning. The day after the *kid*-napping."

"I see what you did there," I said.

"That means you have your brain," she said. "That's good."

"Why wouldn't I have my brain?"

"Concussion. You smashed your noggin on the bricks. That's why we had to wake you up every hour."

I had a vague recollection of that happening, at least I think it was this time, and not the concussion before. Or the one before that.

"So what'd I miss?"

"Do you remember the attack?"

"Three thugs rushed from the shadows and grabbed Jerry out of my arms, putting me into the hospital as they did."

"They got away," said Allie sadly. "Stan followed them for half a block before he was winded. Dara damned their children's children six generations deep to cesspools and boils. But the ambulance was quick to come. And cops."

"Cops?"

"They weren't much help. Best they could do was suggest we not walk around dark neighborhoods at night."

"So we should walk around dark neighborhoods during the day?"

"That's what Perry said."

"Did he get a laugh?"

"Cops. Of course not."

She took my hand and squeezed. I squeezed back. "Sorry to put you through this. Again," I said.

"I'm used to it. So you are getting close to solving the case."

I thought for a second. Touched my lucky caterpillar and frowned. "It had to be random."

"Being mugged for a baby goat is random?"

"What could be more random than that?"

She admitted I had a point, but wasn't ready to give it up. "It's too weird not to mean something."

"Maybe. But it was absolute happenstance that we had Jerry at all, let alone with us then. How could anyone have known?"

"Everyone knew."

"What do you mean?"

She scooted her chair in close, glancing around to see that no one was watching. She could do this by looking under the curtain that surrounded my bed. I was apparently in a ward of some kind. No hard walls. I could hear murmurs and shouts and moans and hellish beeps, but unless someone was close enough to expose their loafers we should be safe to whisper.

"I had Jerry at the banquet," Allie said.

"You weren't at the banquet."

"No, but I had him before and was trying to get in when the doors were locked by the creamsicle people. Afterward, everyone coming out of the banquet would have seen him with me. All they'd have to do is follow us and wait for the chance to take him."

"You don't think it was just some random hicks looking for a good time?"

"Tell me that wasn't a bestiality joke."

"Okay."

"Well?"

"Assume I did."

"Jerry was valuable. Maybe hicks would recognize that."

"How much?"

"Un-papered, they're maybe a grand. Maybe less. But Jerry was papered from India. I think Ted said he paid three thousand for him, plus shipping."

"Doesn't seem like enough to risk the crime."

"No, but I found out something. I didn't realize it, but Jerry could be here illegally."

"You mean he's taking a job from an American goat? Anti-immigrants always make for good suspects."

"It's something like that. The FDA forbids the import of goats from outside the US except from Canada, Australia, or New Zealand."

"I'm sure he pulled some strings."

"He'd need a special reason."

"Or toss money around."

"If someone had the goat, they'd have proof he'd circumvented the law. Could use it against Ted. He's pretty jumpy right now."

"That's not bad."

"See? This is why you need to include me in your sleuthing."

"I could use someone to take a few concussions for me," I said, feeling my heartbeat in my skull.

"Hush up or I'll have them give you another enema," she said.

"What. The gave me—"

"Jerry wasn't the stolen goat. Jerry is a newborn. His mother, that's the trick. I found out that a goat from the Birbhum district of India was recently stolen."

"How the fuck do you find information about a lost goat in Birdfoot India? Are you on a mailing list or something?"

"I went looking for it, because of ICHOEP."

"The bad guy from *The Mummy*?"

"Interfaith Congress of Holistic Enlightened People. The cult conclave as you keep calling it. Maybe you are still concussed."

"No. I just hate that acronym. Go on."

She looked around again to make sure no one was near. "The Tarapith Temple, dedicated to the Goddess Durga is in Birbhum."

"Duh."

"Smart-ass."

"Just commenting on your grasp of the obvious."

She hit me and I probably deserved it.

"The religion they follow is called Shakiism," she said. "Guess what one of its tenants is?"

"Obscurity?"

"Goat sacrifice. When a prized goat meant for sacrifice gets stolen before a big event, it makes the papers and the eighth page of a Google search."

My eyes stretched in astonishment. "You went eight pages deep in a Google search?"

"I did."

"Fuck me."

"Here? Now? Your kinks..." She began to take her shirt off. But pulled it down when the doctor came through the curtain.

"Mr. Flaner," he said, looking at Allie. "I see your strength has returned."

I gave him the squint. Allie the blush.

He was a youngish doctor, maybe thirty. He looked absolutely knackered, to quote the Brits. Worse than Allie. I wondered how many consecutive shifts he'd had. You could smell the fatigue on him.

"You have a slight concussion," he said without anyone asking him. "Eight stitches in the back of your head. The stitches will dissolve on their own, but I recommend a follow up with your own physician in seven to ten days. I'll have someone bring your paperwork. You're free to go."

"So I can leave the ER."

"ED."

"I assure you I've never had a problem there. Well, once, but I was drinking. You've no right to assume—"

"We call it ED for Emergency Department. Not ER for Emergency Room."

"So nothing to do with my massive erections then?"

"No."

"Okay then."

And he left.

"Wait! Will I ever be able to play the piano?" I yelled after him.

The sigh from beyond the curtain was heartfelt and long. "Could you before?" he asked

"No."

"Then no."

"Nice one."

We were alone.

"So the goat is valuable on a symbolic level," whispered Allie. "Religion is involved. Cult stuff."

"For the mother, but not the kid."

"I don't know how things work, how these twisted minds twist. Maybe

Jerry is even more valuable for having been born of a holy goat that avoided sacrifice."

"That's some twisted thinking," I said.

"Have you *been* to the conclave?"

She had a point.

"I still don't see how it figures with the killings," said I.

"*We* don't. Yet."

"Yet," I said.

"We?"

"We."

She kissed me warm and wet and my ED was cured then and there.

"So what do you have so far in the case?" she said.

"I have motive."

"To take down Ted?"

I thought about that for a second, then said. "Motives. Plural. That is one, but not a great one. The only people actively trying to get at Ted are me and some guy named Vance. No, I think the motive is self-defense."

"A double homicide and kidnapping in self-defense?"

"I don't know what else to call it. I think Sangye was blackmailing people, thus pushing them to murder. Is there a name for the crime of avoiding blackmail?"

"I don't think so. There should be. It appears in enough mystery books."

"Not a lot in real life, though, have you noticed?"

"I don't remember any. Maybe that means that they usually get away with it."

"Like bank robberies," I said, remembering my talk with Agent Bruce Allenby.

"So what was he blackmailing people about?"

"I have some inklings, but nothing concrete."

"A conspiracy? Those are always so creepy."

"No, actually, I think they were all different. "Donnopher, for example. Sangye tried to bring up old rumors about sex parties and murders. They dismissed it."

"Even if he had proof?"

"From what I know about the Peoples Church of Higher Learning is that they're immune to proof. There's no novelty in trying to go after The Peoplists. They're experts at dealing with it after so many hushed scandals."

"So they're off the list?"

"No one is, but strangely enough, I can't see them doing it. Too ugly and obvious for them. Stolen gun? Narrow window to do it? They kill you where it really hurts. In court."

"So who else is off the list? I assume Smith's group, COTTEO, since they were the victims."

"Yeah, I guess, but I can't help wondering if Sylvia benefits financially if her boss and his manager died. Did die. Will benefit. Grammar."

"So how are you going to weed out suspects? The ICOHEP only goes a couple more days."

"I'm working on it."

"How?"

"I gotta figure out all the secrets, figure out which one is worth killing over. Then I have to figure out who had the means—access to the gun, and the opportunity—no alibi for the time of the killing."

"Detective Obvious has his methods," said Allie.

"Hey, you asked to be part of this."

"It's just, that's what you always have to figure out. That's how all mysteries are solved."

"No. Sometimes detectives trick villains into confessing."

"Hidden microphones?"

"Surprise accusations."

"*The Pink Panther* method?"

It was a great call back, and I recalled cuddling with Allie as we watched the old Peter Seller's movies. She'd never seen one before and I'd been worried she'd think it was stupid. That had been a while ago, but she remembered it today and I loved her for it.

Allie really was a treasure and at that moment, I recognized the truth that I really needed to make our relationship permanent, my commitment to her lasting. In light of my feelings, to quote the song, I really needed to put a ring on it.

I said, "Have you heard anything about the weird lock-in last night at the hotel?" And coward that I am, I dodged the moment.

"I've been researching missing holy goats and waking you up every couple of hours. Hadn't gotten to that."

"We should see what's going on then," I said. "Garçon! Pledge pins please."

"'*Animal House*'?"

"When in Eugene."

"I don't get it."

"It was filmed here."

"And 'Garçon'?"

"I want the nurse. I guess I cross-referenced *Pulp Fiction*."

"You should have that looked at. I don't think it'll work here."

A nurse appeared with a ream of papers.

"Ha!" I said.

"You're a child."

I filled out the forms, cringed at my deductible, and handed over a credit card. I dressed. My shirt was a scab from the blood on my head, but my undies were unsoiled. Score one for me. When that was done, Allie arranged for a car and walked beside me as a CNA with arms hairier than mine wheeled me to the curb. I guess she was concerned I'd fall over from a concussion on hospital property.

We saw the Ridez driver double mask as he pulled up, slapped on some rubber gloves, sanitized them and turned off the air. Hospitals are scary. I showed him my owie to put him at ease. "Violence, not disease," I explained. "All good."

I'd like to tell you that put him at ease, but I had no idea what his expression was behind his masks. It might have been relief, might have been rage. Maybe colicky. Yeah, I think I'll go with colicky. He was colicky.

Fifteen minutes later, we were again in front of the Eugene Squire Resort. It was just before eleven o'clock and the last classes for the morning were beginning. Lunch was at twelve thirty. I note this because I was hungry.

The usual groups were in attendance and giving each other dirty looks. The housewives from the Bart's ACOG stared suspiciously at The Peoplists, who all looked like they had an audition later and would be quick to use the name of God in vain if it meant a speaking role. The Coven were out of robes but still sported dyed hair, necklaces and enough eyeliner to fulfill Robert Smith's Christmas list. Green Tomorrow tree huggers looked askance at the Messengers' followers who had a hard time focusing on anything. BRA skinheads looked like they wanted to beat the shit out everyone. What was missing were the traffic cone contingent. Not a single orange jumpsuit was in evidence. Either they'd changed them into something less conspicuous like feathers and chains or they were gone.

Agent Bruce Allenby, my one time chauffeur, saw me across the lobby and made a bee line for me, which contrary to common sense, means straight at me. Not the flighty path a bee might take visiting flowers along the way hither and yon.

He moved right into my personal space, inches from my face and thrust a finger up my nose. I don't think he meant to do that since he pulled it out quick and wiped it on his pants. Undeterred, he stepped even closer in.

"Tell me the truth," he demanded. "You did this."

"I did! I did! It was me. Forgive me. Mercy."

"What's going on?" said Allie.

"The sudden accusation. It's terrifyingly effective," I explained.

"What is it you're confessing to?"

I shook my head. "No idea. But I must have done it."

Allenby produced a rolled newspaper, so I must have shit on the carpet.

He opened it to reveal the headline: *Murders and Mayhem in Eugene—Inside Ted Tessner's, Goat and Magic Show.* The deck, or the headline below the main headline, was a little more informative, and inflammatory. *Ted Tessner's Big New Age Conference Nothing But a Whitewash for a History of Criminal Activity and Betrayals.*

"Tony didn't do this," said Allie. "Did you, hun? Hun?"

33

IN FACT, I had not done it, but I could have. I would have, maybe should have, after he hit on my girlfriend and smacked me.

"I don't think so," I said. "But I was concussed."

Allie asked, "Mr. Allenby couldn't that other fellow have done it?"

"What other fellow?"

"The man Tony saw at the airport. The Black guy Ted informed on and put in jail."

Bruce looked at me like I'd just spilled state secrets at a caviar and vodka mixer in the Baltics.

"See," he said. "Loose lips."

"She's my partner," I sputtered. "I mean—she's helping me with the case."

"You're not together as a couple?"

"We are."

"So...?"

"I mean...uhm. We're not like, you know..."

"He's afraid of the M word," said Allie and I thought I might have heard an edge there. "Dickhead."

Yep, there it was.

Bruce turned on Allie. "So it was *you*? Who else knew about the goat?"

"What do *you* know about the goat and when did you know it?" I countered, pushing right up in Bruce's face. He jerked his head away before I could get my finger up his nose.

"What about the goat?" said Allie.

"The paper says he has illegal goats at his ranch. Jesus. What a shit show."

With my hand so close to his head, I pulled him into a compassionate embrace, and said. "Do you want to talk about it?"

His face brightened at the gesture, but only for a second.

"Fucking Vance," he said. "Some people..." And he left.

"I thought he was on terrorism?" Allie said.

"He might be on other things too. He seems to be team Ted, if you know what I mean."

"Lovers?"

"Maybe, but I sense something else."

"Like?"

"Like that." I pointed.

Detective Dean Johnson burst through the door accompanied by three uniformed policemen. They were met by one of the hotel staff who led them to the elevator in a hurry. Allenby rushed to meet them. Johnson tried to lose him, but the FBI agent boarded the elevator and the doors shut with the whole unhappy group going up.

Walking toward the stairs, I watched the elevator lights stop at four.

"You coming, Watson?" I said to Allie.

She grinned and trotted after me.

Together we climbed the stairs to the fourth floor. The well was traditional industrial with concrete and painted steel beams, blue in this case. Cigarette butts were the accent of the day. No smoke alarms here, no cameras to narc out the sneaker smokers finding infrastructure-based loopholes to the hotel's 'strict' non-smoking rules.

On four, the action was happening two rooms from the stairway. Room 403 had a policeman at the door. I ducked back before he could see us.

I whispered to Allie, "You've got to draw that cop's attention away from the door so I can go in."

"I want to go in too."

"Do you know a way to do that?"

"We could ask?"

"Next."

"Walk in like we own the place and bluff it out."

"That's plan B."

"So what's plan A?"

"You'll think of something," I said.

"Will I?"

"You have to," I said. "Go. Go-go-go-go."

No one can resist the go-go-go-go spell and Allie bolted through the door.

I paused a second hoping that my rash decision that rash decisions were a good idea and that necessity is the mother of invention instead of stress is the father of disaster. She'd taken maybe three steps, maybe five when I had visions of her either streaking topless past the cop to get his attention or rushing him in a linebacker tackle and taking him down, thereafter to receive the prescribed police beating.

A thousand detective stories flashed through my head remembering how each, when they formed an attachment to someone, had a sudden and exposed Achilles heel. My business was crime and crime didn't play by the rules. That's what makes it crime. I'd sent Allie on a dangerous mission and if anything happened to her, I'd be...

I ripped open the door expecting to see the cop hovering over naked Allie simultaneously beating her, raping her, and making her sign up for monthly essential oil deliveries.

What I saw was Allie well past the door fiddling with a keycard and acting all confused and helpless, and the cop watching her.

She spoke just before the cop would have seen me in the stairwell door. "Can you help me with this stupid key? Please." She puffed her lower lip out. It was burlesque but it worked. Allie is cute and the cop sauntered down the hall, leaving his post unguarded.

Still feeling guilty, but also strongly aroused, proud, and excited, I went for the door and slid inside room 403 before the cop noticed.

Detective Dean Johnson and Agent Bruce Allenby were not getting along.

"I cannot tell you what kind of deep shit you are in," said Johnson.

"Bring it flatfoot," said Allenby. "You'd need to quintuple your salary before your pay grade could even glimpse what I work on."

"Quintuple?"

"It's a word," I said.

My voice had the desired effect, both men stopped and turned to me. I used the opportunity to slide between them and past the other uniformed riot-beater to the crime scene.

It was a regular room, no suite. Simple bathroom, two queen beds instead of the one king. A narrow writing table. A TV on a dresser that cleverly concealed a refrigerator at the cost of drawers for your drawers. The room had been made up. The beds unslept in, though Adam Tuku was lying on the farther one. He wore his orange jumpsuit and white tennis shoes both of which clashed with the red paisley bedspread. One hand was over his chest, a flip phone clutched in his fingers. His other hand was raised by his head, not far from the bullet wound that sprayed gore across the pillow, strangely this time matching the bedspread. Poor color choice for a hotel room. The decorator should have seen this coming.

Tuku was good and dead. I could see powder burns on his temple, the other was, thankfully turned from me. There was scorching on his fingers which still held the gun, a gun I recognized. It was the other pistol, the little sliver one Augustus had given up from his ankle holster at Tessner's party.

"Was he flying a drone?"

"What are you doing here, Flaner?" said Allenby.

"How'd you get in here?" demanded Detective Dean. "Officer, see where the other man is."

The uniform threaded his way past us and out the door. I kicked the door shut behind him.

"What makes you think you can stay here?" said Johnson.

I opened my wallet and showed him a buy-one-get-one-free coupon to Michaels Craft Store. "Same as you, chewing bubble gum and taking up space, and I'm all out of space."

"What does that even mean?" asked Allenby.

"Like I'd tell you."

My verbal distractions allowed me to notice Tutu's serene face and a black and white card sticking out of his breast pocket. Which I casually plucked out and looked at.

"Hey!" Dean reached to snatch it out of my hands but I pulled it away.

"You'll contaminate the scene with fingerprints," he said. His face, already warm when I came in, was cooking hot now.

"And you grabbing it out of my hands wouldn't get *your* grubby little fingerprints on it?"

It had no words. It was a picture of a maze. I held it up to take a photo, but once my phone focused on it, it opened a web page.

"'The Homecoming Allegiance Liberation Manifesto,'" I read.

"I guess that's the suicide note you were looking for," said Dean. "It was online. FBI really doesn't have its shit together."

"Go beat up a baby!" was the retort.

"Something I don't know about?" I asked.

Dean made another grab at the card. I let it go.

"Whose room is this?" I asked. "Tuku has a suite on the ninth floor."

Johnson nodded, "One of the oranges."

"A man who can make a comment on attire sound like a racial slur," said Allenby.

"I have a gift," said Dean.

"How'd you find him?" I asked.

"Agent numb-nuts has been looking for him since last night."

"The maid," said Allenby. "When she came to clean."

"Why were you looking for him?" I asked.

Dean put on a smug expression and waited for Allenby's answer.

"Because of the stunt last night," he said.

"Tell him what the stunt was about?"

"We think it was some kind of suicide attack."

"And tell him why you thought that."

Allenby stared daggers at Johnson. "Because we've been following this cult for a while and figured they'd do something here."

"Something?" said Dean.

"A mass suicide."

"Just suicide?"

"Killing possibly too. Mass killing."

"And why would you think that?" egged on Johnson.

"That's above your pay grade."

"That's the case that brought you here?" I asked.

Allenby nodded.

"I was beginning to think it was Tessner all along."

He shrugged noncommittally.

"Sure would have been good to know there was an imminent terrorist attack in my city before, you know…it happened," said Johnson.

"Nothing happened," said Allenby.

Together the three of us looked at the phone in Tutu's dead hand.

"Nothing happened," repeated Allenby.

"You need to leave, Flaner," said Johnson.

There was a knocking on the door, insistent would be a good word to characterize it.

"But, I can help you," I said.

He shook his head.

"The gun," I said, pointing to the little silver gun. "That's the—"

"The other one missing from Tessner's cabinet," supplied Johnson. "Got it."

He waited for me to share some other deep insight that his years of training and experience had missed.

"Uhm, well, uhm. I talked to Lewis, a bartender at that dinner, where I was at, so I'm a witness, see…"

"Go on."

"Well, if I remember right, Lewis said…uhm…"

"That Adam Tuku could have accessed the room during the brief time it was unattended that night, as could have Kaisa Woods, Augustus Klept, Emily Stowe, Stephen Marshall, you, and Ms. Braise."

"Who's Emily Stowe?" I asked.

"Artstar," said Allenby.

"Stephen Marshall?"

"The Messenger."

"I thought he was cleared," I said.

"He said he went for a walk around the house after dinner. No one can verify. He could have grabbed them and come back to your hot tub."

"And Donnopher?"

"According to a maid, they were up in their room getting dressed."

"How long does it take to get dressed?" Then I remembered how glamorous they looked that night, even in swimsuits they had fresh makeup and perfect hair. "Well, I haven't ruled out Ted Tessner," I said.

"We have."

"You noticed the blood under the gun in Sangye's room?" I asked.

He nodded.

"And the coroner's report showed he'd been killed before Smith," I said with some authority, though in fact, I had no idea if the coroner had even supplied anyone a report or what it might say should said report be a thing.

"Inconclusive, but probably."

"And still you hushed it all up?"

"No need to panic people," he said.

Allenby took that. "So, you're saying, that sometimes it's a good idea not to alarm the public?"

"Public," said Dean with venom. "Not local law enforcement."

"So who was secretly solving the crime after you 'pretended' to shut the case."

He blanched.

"You can't be here," Detective Dean said.

"He's right," said Allenby, maybe to offer the local cop an olive branch. "We have work to do, Tony." Allenby gestured me to the door. "Let the boys in on your way out."

I was surprised I was being let off so easily. "I'm not being arrested? Smacked?"

I could tell by the snaking grin that the idea was appealing to Detective Johnson.

"You can go home now," said Allenby. "Your case is solved."

"You think this is related to the COTTEO murders?" I asked.

They both looked at me like I was a blathering idiot chewing on a rubber sandal.

"Yes," they said together.

"But..." I said.

"But?"

"Maybe not?" I offered.

"Bye," they said.

I looked again at the gun and the dead guy, the clear suicide this time and had to admit, they might be right.

At the door, Allenby called to me. "Oh, Flaner. Ted's looking for you and Allison. I don't know why."

"We do," I said.

"Why?"

"Like Vance," I said

"How's that?"

"We got his goat."

34

"THEN I SAID, 'We got his goat.'"

"Good one," said Allie.

We were in the banquet hall. The classes had ended and people were filing in, lining up to fill their plates with Italian today. Trays of lasagna, garlic bread, Alfredo pasta. I'd skipped the line to find a good table close to the front where Allie and I could decompress after room 403.

"Where'd you go?" I asked.

"After the other cop came out," said Allie. "I figured I should get out of there. I said I'd get a new key made and bolted for the elevator."

"That's a great story."

"You're just saying that so I won't feel cheated for not visiting a crime scene."

"A little, but you wouldn't have liked it."

"I've seen death before."

"You wouldn't have liked it," I said again. Truth is I was feeling a little sick myself. At the time with the cops, I was in an adrenaline rush of sleuthing. The burglary bug had insulated me. Now, sitting in the banquet room, Adam Tutu weighed heavy on me. I was no longer hungry. I was sickened by the scene, the smell of blood that somehow eluded me then, had followed me downstairs. I felt sad that someone—anyone—would kill themselves. I felt ill thinking what that device was on his chest. Recounting it all to Allie had helped, softened, and organized it as only sharing a trauma can, but it was still there.

"The man was a believer. Gotta give him credit for that," I said.

"Don't they all?"

"Oh no. I'm hunting the real deal, remember?"

"Is that what we're doing?"

"I'm multitasking."

"Tuku?" said Allie. "He believed his story so completely that he'd...you know."

"That's commitment. Call him a believer, but not the *real deal*. I'd think the real deal was someone who showed actual contact with...something."

"A metaphysical connection?"

"Sure."

"Presupposes the commitment component."

"Obviously, but I'd think the real deal would demonstrate miracles and such."

"Couldn't they just be right? Not every cult here claims miracles."

"Who doesn't claim some divine connection?"

"BRA, the skinheads."

"No," she said. "Theirs is a God-given place. They claim him among their number."

"But they don't rely on miracles."

"Kaisa Woods is like that. Green Tomorrow's religious side suggests a universal intelligence that has certain laws but no particular exclusionary place for humankind. If we screw up, we get the switch. God loves us, but he loves all of creation. If we're in the way, she'll push us aside."

"God's a she in Green Tomorrow?" I asked.

"Yep. Sometimes they call her 'Gaia.'"

"Didn't know you were such a fan," I said.

"She's the second least crazy sounding of all the cults here."

"The first being?"

"COTTEO," she said, pointing to the sign on our table. "Smith's doctrine was humanistic, environmental, spiritual, altruistic, covered in chocolate and served raw."

I'd not noticed the sign when we sat down. I probably wouldn't have chosen this table if I had. Maybe it was a sign. "Do you think Smith was the real deal?"

"If only for his teachings, I'd say he was."

"I wonder if others thought that too," I said. "Could you have just found another motive for his murder?"

I could see the chill spread down Allie's neck. "That would make him a true martyr, right up there with Jesus and Gandhi. All we need now is someone to write books about it."

"That might not be for years if we follow precedent."

"Sooner, hopefully." Allie looked wistfully at her napkin. "I hope Sylvia keeps COTTEO going."

"How do you know all this stuff about COTTEO? You've been stuck in a barnyard."

"I've been following the conference on the app. Some of the classes were broadcast live, not just the keynotes. Some were rocky, but you could get what was happening. They'll edit them later and re-publish them. Also, there's all kinds of links and such."

I'd forgotten about that. I hadn't been to a class since the first day, but this room should have given me a clue. Looking around the banquet hall, I again noticed the strategically placed cameras aimed at the stage, pivotable to catch audience reactions, tripods topped with foam balls to capture applause and questions from each quarter. Some classes were held in this room too, I remembered. Donnopher had filled it, whatever 'it' was.

I also noticed a good-sized contingent of people today. My earlier idea that conference goers had fled the show was wrong. Apparently, they'd fled Barty-B's homophobic keynote, not ICOHEP. Good for the gods, I thought.

Sylvia Rigsdale sat down at our table, which made sense. It was COTTEO's table. Without Smith and Sangye, she was the host.

"How are you doing," said Allie, putting her hand on Sylvia's.

"This is Allison," I said to introduce them. "She's with me."

"But not married?"

I blushed. She took the hint and turned at Allie. "Thanks for asking. I'm doing alright." She carefully unfolded a napkin and placed it on her lap.

I have an absolute soft spot in my heart for dear little old ladies. My mother was one. My lovely aunt Vicky was one, my new aunt Sophie is. I don't see them as frail and out of touch, but wise and caring. Sylvia carried such a stature. Knowing what trauma she was facing now, her friend, mentor, and guru killed, her future upside down and broken. Here at least, she was alone to carry on the work. But she was doing it. Gotta admire that.

As if she could read my mind, she said. "Death is part of the game. It was sudden, but no one should ever say that death is unexpected. John was a good man, the best I've ever known. I'll miss him, but it was always a temporary relationship. I figured I'd check out first, but it's the same thing. The living carry on. The dead? They have other things to do."

"You will carry on then?" asked Allie.

"Of course. John was a magnet, but he was not the force. There are thousands of us worldwide. And once the center opens, there'll be thousands of us here to match."

"What work will you do?"

"Missionary work comes to mind."

"Oh no," I said. "I was beginning to like you."

"I'm from Utah, too," she said. "Not like that. We'll share the ideas. Boots on the ground to share the vision. That's all. Also, we're stepping hard into politics. We plan to run a slate of COTTEO candidates wherever we can."

"Sounds creepy," I said.

"I know," she agreed. "But the church of consumption beat us to it. We're just offering alternatives."

Couldn't argue with that.

She stabbed some pasta and tasted it before dropping a ton of pepper on it. "You're at my table," she said. "You have news?"

"I do." I told her about Tuku, about the gun, about the cops now, again, wrapping up the case.

"Do you believe it?" she asked.

"There's a ton of things I don't know."

"Is that an answer?"

"Maybe."

"Stay on it until you're satisfied," she said. "It won't bring him back, but I am curious."

"Could you do something for me?"

"Sure."

"Does this mean anything to you?" I produced my phone and found the list I'd seen on Sangye's. "It's like a code. What do you think?"

She examined it. "No. Where's it from?"

I told her.

She shook her head in a way that conveyed the emotions of negative response, sorrow, and disgust.

"Do you have access to COTTEO's financials?"

"I do."

"I'm sure they're heavily convoluted, but could you see if anything stands out to you."

"Why would it be convoluted?" she asked.

"Taxes. Shelters. Holding companies to hide trillions of dollars from the SEC," I offered.

"We don't work that way."

"Oh," I said, looking around the room at the other cults' tables. Kaisa nods knowingly to a bearded Birkenstock wearer with designer sunglasses holding an investment portfolio. Barty-B smiling his over-bright smile to an elderly woman, probably from Florida, scribbling out a check. "Sure you're in the right place?" I said to Sylvia.

She smiled broadly.

A cluster of five others joined the table and any more private conversation would have to wait. We listened as Sylvia explained the center's scheme for community outreach the medical insurance plan it was already working on. Every member of the church would get access to affordable health care. She talked about the meaning of rain and how a lotus leaf cleans itself with each raindrop, never to be truly wet from the worldly downpours.

Allie squeezed my hand and whispered. "Your mouth's open."

Indeed it was. She was captivating, and what she was saying was making me a believer. I hadn't felt anything like it since I'd heard John Smith before in the lobby.

Like bad news, a figure approached behind Sylvia.

"Hi Mom," said Josh.

"Honey. What are you doing here?"

"And where's your pass?" asked eagle-eyed Allie. "How'd you get in?"

"I snuck in," he said. "Hannah's here too."

"I know," said Sylvia.

"She bought a ticket," he explained to Allie.

I'd forgotten some of Sylvia's family was still running around. I'd not seen Hannah since—I had to stop and think about it—since the orgy shopping night in BRA's room. Was that real? I asked myself. Did it happen?

"Was what real? Did what happen?"

The whole table was looking at me.

"Hi Josh, what's up?" I said.

"You didn't tell me my son was here," said Sylvia.

"You didn't ask."

She glared at me.

"Mom," said Josh, "I just want to say how sad I am about your friend dying. I know he meant a lot to you."

She regarded her son a moment, then smiled, stood up and hugged him.

"I thought you were here to take me home or some such."

"I will if you want me to," he said.

"I've got more work here than ever." She cupped his cheeks warmly in her hands. She was a good twelve inches shorter than Josh and looked into his face with her graying eyes full of love and pride. And he beamed back reminding us all of greater goals and gratitude. The real deal. Grace.

I melted a little and thought of my own son, Randy, back in Salt Lake. I hadn't talked to him since I came to Oregon. I was overdue.

"Where's your sister, Josh?" asked Sylvia.

"I haven't seen her."

"She's right there," said Allie, pointing to the table next to us.

There she was. Detective me had missed seeing the arrival of my original client. Hannah Hill, né Rigsdale. In my defense, she looked totally different. Gone were her conservative polyester slacks and sensible blouse, replaced with jeans and plaid men's shirt sizes too big with rolled-up sleeves. Her hair was cut differently and revealed a new tattoo under her ear. It was still red and swollen, there was a hint of adhesive still clinging to her head where a bandage had just come off. A compass rose. No—a two-tone eight-pointed star. I pondered a moment, trying to remember where I'd seen it before. Then I recalled seeing stars tattooed on the chests and knees of Russian mobsters. She was sitting at the BRA, né BORA—Brotherhood of Righteous, né Racial, Action table. She hung on Augustus Klept's arm like moss. How she hadn't noticed us sitting so near could possibly be explained by the fact that she was obviously high out of her mind. She stunk of alcohol and weed, and when she finally noticed all of us looking at her, her eyes shone with the glossy glow I'd often seen created by strong amphetamines.

Her eyes found her mother and widened in a child's panic before narrowing. "Mom, you're making a spectacle of yourself," she slurred.

The table of onlookers compared the face of the woman sitting with them and the drunk at the next table, saw the resemblance, and blanched. Shared embarrassment is a thing. The other table, the one with Augustus Klept and his scary Nazi friends, looked on bemused.

"Hannah, honey, where's Mark?"

"Don't you throw that woke guilt at me," she said.

Josh stared at his sister in complete disbelief.

Sylvia tried again. "Hannah, honey—"

"You're undermining America," Hannah said. "You and your pronoun police, transgendered environmental reactionaries. You're taking orders from Russia to erode the fabric of our country. You're no patriot. You're no mother."

The rant was amusing up until the mention of motherhood. Sylvia's calm expression weakened then. I had a vision that John Smith could have handled it. He'd have found the right words to soothe the moment, to teach and inspire. A healing smile like sunlight. Sylvia possessed an echo of that, a modicum of the peace I'd witnessed from the dead leader, but not enough to overcome such a direct and personal attack from her child.

With as much grace as she could, Sylvia wiped her mouth, nodded to everyone at the table and excused herself.

Josh wanted to follow, but Sylvia shook her head. He, with us, watched her go, disappearing among the tables and then out of the room. He, like us, then turned and looked hard at Hannah, who to her credit, and I may be stretching it a bit here, looked ashamed. A little. Maybe.

Seldom at a loss for words, I was the first to speak. "What the actual hell, Hannah?"

"You were supposed to get my mother out of that cult. You failed. She's so far gone. The cult brainwashed her," she said, drool spilling out of the corner of her mouth. "I'm just trying out some tough love. You failed. Even killing the guy didn't save her."

"You killed John Smith?" I asked.

"No," she said. "I thought you did."

35

I LOOKED around the table at the staring faces of the COTTEO fans.

"She's joking," I said.

"No, I'm not," said Hannah.

"She's drunk," I said.

"So?"

"She's wrong."

"Am I?"

"Yes."

"Really?" Is there anything more charming than a slurring drunk saying 'really?'

"Pretty sure," I said.

Klept was smiling amusedly at me.

"Fuck off BRA," I said. "Your man-boobs are showing."

He gave me a hard, threatening look. I think he was about to stand up and come after me when Perry appeared.

"Hey guys," he said to our table and gave us a little wave. "Hi fucking Nazi assholes," he said to the other table and gave a Hitler salute which drew eyes across the room and brought the entire table to their feet.

"Joking, joking," Perry said, shaking his head. "Man, the right can't take a joke, can they?"

"I thought it was the woke left that destroyed comedy," said Josh.

"We should have a panel," I suggested. "Nazis, Wokesters, and comedians; why can't we all just get along?"

"That's an idea," said Perry, taking the seat formerly occupied by Sylvia.

Ted Tessner passed our table and gave us all a stern look usually reserved for middle school vice principals. As conditioned, we all shrunk back and tried to act cool. He left us for The Messenger's table farther on.

"You two are in a mood," said Allie. "I know what got into Tony, but you Perry?"

"I was trying to save Tony," he explained. "He has a history of violence. I didn't want him going off on that skinhead gang."

I looked at the hundreds of pounds of muscles at the next table, and then back to my friend. "One dick-punch into the groin of someone who had it coming and I'm branded for life? I'll have you recall there was no bloodshed at all at the last comedy club we visited, or any since then."

"Do you even know how to fight?" asked Allie.

"I know Kung Fu, Jiu Jitsu and several other words of Asian origin," I said. "Do you really think I was looking to brawl?"

"'Man-boobs'?" said Allie. "Them's fightin' words in that group."

She was right. My mood had changed. I was pissed at that table. My fury had been kindled by Hannah's cruelty to her mother, but it had spread to the whole table and drawn out the less than clever 'Fuck off' retort. It was an insult far below my usual caliber. My Zen had been punctured.

"Fair point," I said. "And thanks for the backup, Perry."

"I was coming over anyway. A better seat for The Messenger." His eyes lit up.

Tessner escorted The Messenger, real name Stephen Marshall, to the stage. Ted looked agitated. Marshall looked like a woodchuck caught illegally ripping *Harry Potter* DVDs.

"I'd like to welcome to the stage, The Messenger, who'll give us...a message," said Tessner.

The audience gave him polite recognition, but several, notably Perry sitting next to me, whooped and hollered and cheered like Led Zeppelin had reunited.

The man didn't try to hide his paunch nor the Band-Aid on his head— hopefully not the same one he'd had all week. He wore '80s Bob Lazar aviator glasses that, though clear, still gave a Jim Jones vibe and that, no one who knows the story of Jamestown, would ever willingly wear.

He adjusted the microphone, glanced at the retreated Ted, and began. "Hello," he said too close into the microphone. "I'm The Messenger."

Perry whooped again in true groupie fashion.

"And I have a message."

"Tell it, preacher!"

We were very close to the stage, and Perry's exuberance drew the speaker's attention. He focused on Perry for a moment and then a wave of recognition crossed his face. It wasn't necessarily a positive look.

I leaned over to Perry. "You gotta calm down," I said, "to let the man get his talk out. He only has until tomorrow morning."

"Oh, right," he said.

The Messenger composed himself. He had no notes. This was going to be an ad-libbed speech, a notoriously perilous path from my limited experience. The man took a deep breath, composed himself and spoke with clear conviction.

"The world is at a pivotal juncture," he began. "Our atmosphere and our water is in peril, and with them, life itself is threatened."

The Green Tomorrow table was now paying attention. Kaisa Green looked miffed. Her keynote was scheduled for tomorrow but here was someone speaking her talking points today. There's a terrible thing in comedy where someone going on before you steals your best material. It's the taboo of taboos in that world. It's ugly. I've seen it. Violence ensued. I've seen comics get banned from clubs, canceled out of tours, hated and black-listed. This wasn't that, but the vibe Kaisa was giving off reminded me of it. I glanced at Perry and tilted my head to the Green Tomorrow table, but he didn't get it. I began to whisper my insight to Allie, but she shushed me. "I'm trying to hear this," she said.

It's hard for me at times when I'm not the center of attention.

The Messenger went on, "Our world is depleted and dangerous like never before. Humankind has to rise to the occasion. Together."

Kaisa squirmed. I sulked.

"It's change. It's the Great Change. We have to pay attention. We have to take action. There is a time limit. We all have heard it. We know it. The oceans define our planet. Let us start there. The statistics…"

His statistics were as usual terrifying. His timeline familiar, his call for global action to save the planet was clear and concise, well spoken and timely. Nothing I hadn't heard a thousand times before, each without summoning much action to the cause.

Kaisa was stone-faced. The theme couldn't be usurped, but I wondered if her talk didn't have the same statistics. From what I knew of The Messenger he was a crazy space alien prophet, not an environmental crusader. I could feel for Kaisa. The environment was her bailiwick.

"I have been sent to oversee humanity during this great change," he said. "God himself or herself, themselves, genderless until required—has told me what to do."

Here I thought Kaisa would relax. The crazy was coming out. Nope. Her face flushed.

"Humanity will splinter or unite during this great change. That's only logical," The Messenger explained.

"Aristotle would be proud," Allie murmured.

"If we fail, we fail. We fail big time." He paused to let the sink in, if it could. "If we succeed, we will be ready to join the intergalactic community of intelligent life."

That was an applause line in some quarters, The Messenger's believers I assumed since Perry clapped and beamed.

"I have been contacted by this intergalactic community of intelligent life through PCP, my patented psychic connective procedure. By this means, I have learned that they have representatives monitoring us as we speak from a moon of Saturn. They won't interfere as long as we have a chance, then when we don't have a chance, they will harvest the planet for their own needs."

That quieted the room. The threat of an alien apocalypse can do that.

"That is the nature of the universe. It's very competitive. The struggles we have here in microcosm, on our planet, are renewed and rehabilitated out there."

"Is that the right word?" Allie said to no one in particular.

"Shhhhh," said Perry.

"They are waiting to show themselves."

Applause.

"Nay!" he said.

"Did he just say 'nay?'"

"Yay, verily," said I.

"Shhhhh."

"Nay, this visitation shall be terrible. An intervention like the one that will come will destroy us as a people, as a species perhaps. I know this. They told me."

"Who told you?" asked Kaisa, resorting to heckling.

"Oodrakakam is the name," said The Messenger. "That is the name of the universe's true god. Oodrakakam resides on Mliti 8 in the Ring Nebula."

That did it. Kaisa smiled and settled back. She even sipped her cocktail, something with cranberry by the look of it.

"Representatives of Oodrakakam have visited us. God has sent us angels, but remember the stories. Angels are not always kind. They are actors for the truth of the universe."

In the pauses, I could hear cutlery on plates, see people moving around. He was losing his audience.

"It is my task to prepare as many people as possible for the coming contact. This contact will be traumatic like nothing the world has ever seen. It has taken me years myself to understand this coming event. Our current crisis harkens the moment soon-coming."

"Harkens?" said Allie.

"Soon-coming?" said I.

"Shut the fuck up," said Perry. "Your life depends on it."

"Not mine," said Josh. I'd not noticed he'd stayed at the table with us.

Perry's angry look suggested the threat to Josh's life might be closer than he'd imagined.

"We are the Olmecs when Columbus arrived," The Messenger said. "We are ignorant. We will not be able to even comprehend the visitors who come to exploit us. Slavery, death, theft. Death. Death. Death Death Death."

"Space capitalists," I murmured. "Shit. That is really scary."

Perry looked at me. I expected the same 'shut the fuck up' threatening stare, but he just nodded vigorously. "See what I mean?" he said.

I didn't have the heart to tell him that the Olmecs were two thousand years dead before Columbus was born and that when that explorer did land in this hemisphere it wasn't even on their continent. The Messenger was probably going for Aztecs and Cortes and wanted to sound cooler. He would have done better with a prepared talk, editors, and a fact checker. Luckily for him maybe, few people have even heard of the Olmecs so maybe it worked on some level—a famous invader and a forgotten civilization. The fact that they had nothing to do with each other...eh...fuck it. I turned to Perry.

"You know that the Olmecs—"

"Shhhhh."

Allie patted my leg and nodded. She understood.

The Messenger went on. Some people had tuned him out as his talk wandered a bit, another mark of not having a prepared speech, but others were watching with rapt attention. As he talked about how the Spanish had used the infighting of the local peoples against them, finally getting his history right—his talk began to take on a darkening mood.

I recalled a science fiction series I'd read, Liu Cixin's *Three-Body Problem* trilogy, where one of its premises was that intelligent life should stay as hidden and quiet as possible because in a competitive universe, showing oneself would lead to disaster from more advanced civilizations. This "Dark Forest Hypothesis" was echoed by Stephan Hawking who suggested it would behoove humanity to be very quiet and not attract attention in the cosmos. A YouTube video I remember called *Shut the Fuck Up Friday*, suggested the best course of action is to shut the fuck up. My then agitated mind equated this to corroborating evidence, and a chill shuddered my bones.

Here I realized was an actual doomsday preacher. He'd overleaped the environmental collapse horror which society is already, horribly, coming to grips with, and landed squarely on existential extermination from outside forces, compounded by our disunity and weakened environment. Science meet spiritual in a truly paranoid fashion. Maybe he was using this to unite the world, a *Watchman* kind of threat to bring everyone together, or maybe he actually believed it. Fuck, maybe he actually had messages from an alien being warning him of the coming catastrophe. I'd have to buy the book, however, to find out.

"The *Big Book of Messages* book contains the direct communications I've had from the angels sent by Oodrakakam," The Messenger went on. "It's on its twenty-sixth edition now. Most of the typos are gone. It's thirty-five dollars from my website or twenty-five during the conference at my table in the merchant cove."

He gave a web address. I saw several people typing it out on the phones, two of the COTTEO groupies at our table among them. So it was possible to influence the other cults at ICOHEP after all. Ted should be proud.

He wasn't.

He stood in a far corner with Rachael, surveying the crowd and looking like someone had lost his favorite goat.

36

THE TALK WAS OVER. It'd been forty minutes of fear turned to terror turned to book pitch. I was exhausted. Ted Tessner returned to the stage and announced that classes would resume on the hour. I sensed a lot of people had seen the day's newspaper and now looked at him differently. I think he thought so too and left the stage in short order.

"What's a merchant cove?" I said.

"It's mentioned in the app," Allie said. "Merch from the presenters. It's down the hall."

"I'll go check it out. Allie, see if you can get me a chat with The Messenger."

I'd have asked Perry but he was gone already from our table, joining the throng of people fawning over The Messenger after his speech.

"What are you going to do?" Allie asked.

"Rachael," I said and bolted after her as the conference director disappeared around a corner.

When I got through the people to the lobby, Rachael was gone, but Kaisa Woods was there surrounded by her groupies.

"Where ya' headed?" I asked her.

"My room to freshen up, then I lead a class," she said.

"What did Rachael want?" I said. "I missed her."

"Calling a meeting with all the presenters during the afternoon snack break."

"Oh, that's right," I said. "She told me all this earlier." For effect, I slapped my forehead to show how silly I was to have forgotten. "Where is it again?"

"The conference office."

"Right, right," I said. "And that is…where?"

"Room two-oh-five. Second floor."

"Yeah yeah yeah. I can't believe I forgot all that. What's your name again?"

She smiled, but it wasn't warm.

"So what's your next class about?" I asked.

"Local activism and the place of religion."

"That place being you?"

She ignored my baiting.

"Who is this corporate shill?" asked one of her adherents.

She didn't answer.

"You want me to fuck him up, Ms. Woods?" the adherent persisted.

That made me take a closer look at said persisting adherent. He was young, twenty-two maybe, white, brown hair braided to mimic dreadlocks beneath a knit cap. Two shirts, an open flannel over a faded concert tee proclaiming the band Metric. Distressed jeans and flip-flops. His glasses were narrow rectangles, practically slits. He had a scruffy beard. That is to say, Eugene hipster to a #7.

"Don't fuck me up," I said. "I don't give you consent."

That confused him but bemused Kaisa. I made my exit before he could recover by walking purposely across the lobby. Walking purposely anywhere is a powerful totem. Kaisa got in the elevator and left.

I blended into the crowd who were moving toward the class rooms. A black shiny head in the distance drew my attention. I followed that into the Merchant Cove.

It was a big room. Around the outside walls, tables had been arranged with various swag and marketing information. It reminded me of Comic Cons I'd been to, bright eye-catching displays of blue and orange backgrounds, but instead of heroes, there were cult leaders. Some had symbols and banners suggesting that the organization might be more important than the person fronting it, but those were few. COTTEO was one of those, as was the Coven, Artstar's merry band of witches. Their table had big black silver crescents and glyphs that would give John Dee a hard-on. A man with a long beard and black robe shilled incense and jewelry. A couple of self-published books by Artstar were also on offer, *Sacrifice, the Power of the All-In, Old Rites for New Times, Lust in the Moonlight; A guide to Wiccan Sex Magic*. Remembering I had an expense account from someone—Hannah hadn't officially fired me yet—I bought the lot. Research and date night.

Kaisa Wood's face stared out from a huge portrait at the Green Tomorrow table a Big Brother meets Meso-American Greta Thunberg kind of way. A face that radiated power, guilt and accusation, but doing the good work, it reminded me. It didn't quite work. It spoke of cult of personality more than purpose. Peaches was there manning the table giving out free flyers, with Kaisa's face on them and the famed Woods Water bottled Amazon river.

After checking the seal was intact and nothing visible was swimming around, I bought one of those and took some pamphlets before I remembered I already had them as part of the conference swag bags upstairs.

Donnopher's booth had professional headshots of the couple, signed or not. The signed ones were at a premium. I wanted to buy some of those STD detecting condoms but they didn't have any for sale. Not sure what I'd have done with them, but seemed like a good souvenir. There were lots of copies of The Peoplists's bible *People Power/ Power People*, being sold at cost I figured since you could get twenty-five books for the price of one unsigned picture of the Hollywood power couple. Their backdrop was, of course, their famous faces, but also the restless sea motif which adorned the cover of their founder's book. The founder herself, Danielle Jarvis's face was nowhere to be seen, but it's the message not The Messenger that counted.

Speaking of The Messenger, there he was all alone at the simplest table in the room, just a stack of his books on a hotel-provided tablecloth, and him taking credit cards and signing books for a long line of people. I waved to Allie and Perry. They waved back.

I sidled up the man I wanted to talk to.

"You're Vance Derow aren't you?" I said.

He froze, turned slowly to face me.

"I have every right to be here. You try to expel me or lay a hand on me and you won't know the level of shit you'll face," he said.

"I'm not The Man."

"What the fuck?"

"I'm trying to talk Jive," I said. "Is the accent wrong?"

"Is that some kind of racist shit?"

"It was more of a callback to *Airplane*," I explained.

"That movie was funny. But you gotta watch yourself, Cracker."

"Oh, now who's racist?"

His smile broadened and I saw a twinkle in his eye. He could have been pushing sixty but he was fitter than I'll ever be. I remembered he'd just been let out of prison and figured I knew why. He was dressed in very nice clothes, shimmering black shirt and slacks. A tailored steel-gray jacket. A gold chain that spoke of a bygone era at Studio 54.

"And to be honest," I said. "The Man is still a thing. You don't have to be black to be oppressed by The Man."

"That's true. So who are you?"

"I'm Tony Flaner." I offered him my hand to shake.

He checked it for eels then shook it.

"You know who I am," he said.

"I do indeed and I also know who The Man is."

"Who?"

"Ted Tessner."

He regarded me a moment then nodded. "Yeah, I saw you with him at the airport."

"And I saw you killing him with your eyes."

"If only," he said,

"Can we go somewhere and talk?" I gestured around to tables of commerce and crowds of consumers.

He looked at me suspiciously. I looked suspicious.

"I think I want public," he said.

"I'd like quiet. Can we compromise?"

I led him away from the money changers to the lobby. We sat at the same sofa John Smith had held his impromptu philosophy talk.

"I'm investigating the murder of a couple of people here," I said.

"I was in Springfield in the company of a very beautiful woman with very reasonable rates that night," he said. "And I can prove it."

"You have a receipt?"

"We were not quiet."

I sat down across from him. "So what do you think of the killings?"

He removed a folded newspaper from his jacket pocket and sat down. "Sure would be bad for something to stop this big PR stunt."

"You don't think this conclave is worthwhile?"

"In what way could it be?" he asked.

"Bringing diverse opinions and beliefs together in search of common ground."

"That would be a hell of a thing, but nowhere is that happening. It's one soapbox after another. No debate, no discussion. Sales pitches. The only intermixing I see are the brawls. And besides these are all fringe religions."

"Cults."

"That is a word," he said.

"So why are you here?" I asked.

"You're not the police so why should I answer anything?"

"I'm a fancy dancer."

"Harlan Coben would be proud."

"A well-read ex-convict."

He tilted his head. "So it's like that. You know all about me, huh? I suppose Ted told you."

"Actually it wasn't him, but I do know something of your situation."

"Do you know who caused my situation?"

"You."

"Me?"

"Weren't you doing crimes?"

He flicked his fingers to dismiss the idea. "Even then it was gray. Growing grass? How can anyone think a plant is illegal? A plant. A thing God put on this earth. Making a living thing illegal? It's ludicrous. It's the epitome of hubris."

"Even so, it was illegal and you knew the risk you were running."

He nodded. "That I did, but when your competitor turns you in, it's a different thing, particularly if you think that person was your friend."

"How do you know it was Ted?"

"A man finds things out."

"Just that?"

"You ever been to prison?"

I shook my head. "Jail plenty of times."

"That's not even the same, but good on you. I can tell you're something of a hustler which puts you in the crosshairs of someone. I'm sure people have tried to put you in prison."

"Only the police. And my victims. Their families. Friends. Pets. That one guy at the drive thru."

"Well, one thing you learn in prison is that snitches get snitched on."

"If she'll cheat with you, she'll cheat on you."

"Something like that."

"You fell into Ted's crosshairs, and now he's in yours?"

"That's a vexed question."

"Enlighten me."

"Why should I?"

"I want to know."

"What's your relationship with Ted?"

"He's paying for my room and wooing my girl."

"Sounds like him."

"Come on, Vance. I can tell you want to tell someone what's going on."

"I already did."

"Agent Allenby isn't neutral like me."

He blanched. "You are plugged in," he said.

"So what's the story?"

He stretched out and rolled his neck, thick and muscular. Could break walnuts with his throat.

"I used to live here between the rivers. I came here to this hotel to see the dog and pony show," he said. "I know something of faith. That long in prison, betrayed by a friend, will make one look at the big picture hard in the face. I see religion as a way to excuse bad behavior more than not. It's all a show like *Hamilton* or something. Makes you feel a certain way and you pay for it, like any show. The piper gets his coin. Maybe you buy a book or go on an installment plan they call tithing. Get the man a new airplane. You get a show now and again, join a fandom, get to be part of a long-running book club."

"A long-running book club?" I laughed. "Damn, now there's a description for religion."

"It's not mine, but it's not wrong."

"There are believers here though. Book club or no, there are true believers here."

"Belief is the key and it's important. Someone without belief is sailing without a rudder, in my opinion. Belief steers you. It doesn't matter what the belief is generally, what matters is that it gives meaning to a life. It can be a solo belief, self created and nurtured. A quiet belief. The kind of thing one finds sitting in solitary for a month. Or it can be communal, supported by others. That belief is different, has many advantages over one man's darkest discoveries. It doesn't have to be a big group, just enough to form that echo chamber the news is always talking about. In fact, I think, if it's too big, it loses something. There's a lot to be said about being an underdog. It's a righteous position, one that justifies things that larger, more dominating groups, have a harder time with. Seeing yourself and your group as the victim is powerful armor. It legitimizes, somehow, all kinds of terrible behavior."

I thought of the Weather Underground and the Rajneeshees in Rajneesh-puram just a few miles east of here, underdogs who bought up a whole town and then poisoned the residents.

"You're talking about yourself?" I said.

"Talking about everyone. I spent a lot of time finding religion in prison. In many ways, I'm a better man coming out of the clink than I was going in. I could thank Ted for that, but I'm not going to. I'm trying to figure out why he did it. Was it him or me? Or was he playing a long game, a game that leads to Washington? Hypocrisy knows no bounds. Turning in a fellow grower isn't a big step."

"Why didn't you turn him in?" I asked.

"I wish I would have. Would have loved seeing him dance and duck, but when it fell on me, I was a good soldier. I honestly don't think I ever did anything wrong, only illegal. Then, when I realized it was Tessner who punched my ticket, it was too late. He was untouchable."

"Do you still think he is?"

"We will see."

"So you did come here for revenge."

"I wanted to see what God looks like in so many different eyes. Revenge was another thing." He tapped the newspaper beside him. "A bonus opportunity."

"How does God look?"

He thought about that for a minute. "Religion—organized religion doesn't always have to have a god, a devil will do. Some of these groups have that, others have something of a God. An alien or a bearded bigot on cloud nine. There are a couple that intrigue me though."

"Which ones?"

"COTTEO and Green Tomorrow."

"I thought so too."

"COTTEO is reaching for the whole enchilada, a humanistic near-Buddhist compassion for all things. Green Tomorrow, well they have a devil but their God is the god of survival, so maybe Ms. Green's time is neigh."

"Allenby knows you spilled the story," I said, pointing to the newspaper. "He's pretty pissed."

"Ten thousand dollars doesn't buy what it used to."

"What? He bribed you?"

"Two packs of new hundreds. Yellow band, consecutive numbers. He told me he was on the inside working with Tessner back in the day and wanted to give me a hand getting back on my feet. 'Just doing his job,' and all that. He asked that I let bygones be bygones with Tessner, explained how it was the agency that made Ted turn me in. I didn't believe it. My land was adjacent to his. When I was gone, sold all I had for a shit lawyer, he bought it the second it went up to auction. He's since built a mansion with a goat house on it."

I was going to ask him if he'd been back to visit but I shut up and listened instead.

"I said thank you very kindly for the money and was on the phone within the half hour. That weekly rag was already wary of Tessner. I wasn't the only person he turned over, all the while having the biggest growing operation in Lane County, if not Oregon all with government assistance."

"Musk made his money from the government too," I said.

"And how's that working out for everyone?"

"I'm not defending him," I said. "Just pointing out the bullshit myth of the self-made man."

"Different categories. Musk wants to be emperor. Buy it. Ted wants to be a senator. Maybe even president. Get elected. Maybe the same thing. He wants to be liked. Maybe he's the same as these cult leaders here, or wants to be. Power, you know? Maybe you do, maybe I don't. Hell, hell hell. And if Ted can make it—good on him if he can, but we'll go ahead and shake a few skeletons out now and see how he handles them."

"Ever thought of just killing him?"

"I was in prison for decades, my friend," said Vance. "Nah. That thought never even crossed my mind."

37

VANCE HAD places to go and so did I. The classes would soon be emptying out and the prophesied secret meeting to take place up in room 205. I figured I had a better chance of crashing it if I were already in the room. A trick I learned from a rabbit in a John Travolta movie.

The talk with Vance was productive. I lowered him on the Smith suspect list, but upped him on top of the Jerry kidnapper one. He might have found belief in prison, but forgiveness had escaped him. That's always a hard one. How does one balance right and wrong without protecting one and attacking the other? Turn the other cheek is a quaint concept, but I always think that sometimes the good guys gotta get guns. The equal rights movement with Martin Luther King Jr. was only successful, in my opinion, because Malcom X was on the other flank with rifles. If the feminists had had a bomb chucking, assassination wing of covert housewives, I do believe the Equal Rights Amendment would be law today.

That isn't to say that sometimes a movement can't take over by sheer change of perception. The new environment of acceptance of LGBTQ people says a lot, as does the meteoric rise of women in society despite having no armed cohort. It just took longer. They're not done yet, but it's a far cry from Gloria Steinem's day. The zeitgeist has changed. Decades of work, often in colleges, altered notions of equality and traditional roles. It's mostly good, great even, but sometimes, in my darkest most secret thoughts I see a pattern I shouldn't voice out loud. There, under my covers, I wonder if one of the driving forces behind this change isn't the devil that Vance mentioned. I don't mean a supernatural being—though he's often portrayed that way, exaggerated beyond reality, but a Big Brother's Goldstein that unites all in common hate. I speak here of men. The left has so demonized men that they've become the one group that it's okay to be prejudiced against. Yeah, it's an unpopular opinion in the world I live in, socialist left, but I've seen it. I've felt it. The right has its own takes on this, but I don't know that world, so I'm speaking about us quiche eaters. Forget personal experience, I worry about the falling rates of male college attendance and graduation. They're startling. Worse still are the "deaths of despair"—suicide and drug overdose deaths which are seventy-five percent male in this country. Men learn to hate themselves. They give up. This is where Augustus Klept and his Brotherhood of Righteous Action collect followers from. Men are unmoored, unwanted, prime subjects for fringe and radical groups. This issue is ignored because, well, fuck those people, right? They're men. Maybe even white too. But elevating one group on the bodies of another doesn't seem like a solid foundation for the inclusive society that's sought. I have a son and I worry. It's a blind spot in much of society and now that I've mentioned it here, let us never speak of it again. Never blaming the victim doesn't count if the victim is a white man.

I took the elevator up to level two. It wasn't a floor with regular rooms, but a suite of offices and hotel utility closets. Storage spaces, wiring arrays. The kinds of places usually put in the basement, but basements are rare in Lane County due to flooding. There are two rivers here and the place used to be called Tanner's Mud Flat for a reason.

I found room 205 without much hassle. I heard voices within and since inside was my goal, like an EST graduate, I reached for it with gusto and made it happen in my reality without having to resort to a vision board or mental imaging first. I was that powerful.

"Look who just walked in the door." It was Agent Bruce Allenby, FBI bribe-giver. He was with Rachael, her hair once again pulled so far back that her resting face was half grimace. They were the only ones there. She was sitting at a computer monitor at a desk and he was hovering over her, ready to say "enhance" at any moment.

Allenby turned to the computer screen and said, "Can you zoom in there?"

"Close enough," I said.

The room was big, wide open, and bright. I could tell it had been designed to accommodate modular furniture should such be called for. Plugs were set regularly in the floor. There were several desks there now, but no 'privacy walls.' Two desks with papers and phones, businesslike, one a high-end computer station with Rachael and Allenby in attendance. I noticed a table with a good assortment of single use coffees cups to speed the demise of the climate while personally caffeinating someone. There was a sad empty donut box.

Not taking his eyes off the screen, Allenby said, "What are you doing here, Flaner?"

"I'm here for the secret meeting."

"There's no secret meeting."

"Oh? Oh...oh, you don't know about it. Oh, well, uhm. No. No. You're right. There is no secret meeting. Nope, nothing like that. No secret meeting where you're not invited."

"You idiot," he said, squinting at the monitor. "The meeting isn't secret."

"Not everyone was invited."

Here he looked at me. "It is, however, exclusive."

I stepped forward to look around him and over Rachael's shoulder. A video editing program was up on the screen, and in the main window was a scene of the banquet room.

"Whatcha doin'?" I asked.

"Dammit, Flaner!" He reeled on me.

"Hold up there, cowboy, I thought we were friends. Why the sudden hostility? You and I both know I wasn't the one to diss your dude in the paper."

He sighed, ran his fingers through his hair. Took a deep breath, thought of the queen, and said, "I've got a lot on my mind. If you're here for the meeting—and God knows why Tessner wanted you here—please stay out of the way."

"Rachael, do you feel the same way? Am I limp and hard to manage?"

"Whatever," she said, reminding me of a British valley girl, a rare and wonderful beast for the depths of my imagination.

I withdrew a step but kept close enough to see what was happening.

"Okay, now run it from there," said Allenby.

I noticed the date stamp on the tape. It was the first night of the conference, the night Smith was murdered.

Allenby had asked Rachael to rewind the tape to six fifteen and then let it run. The main window showed the overall banquet room, tables and place setting, a few waiters shuffling about. The other windows showed the stage from three different angles. I recalled seeing four cameras in the banquet room, so that checked out. The video was very good, no grainy Bigfoots here, but I couldn't help but wonder why they were recording so early.

"I had plenty of storage and knew I might be away for the beginning," Rachael said, "so I just started all the recordings in anticipation of the night."

I'd apparently spoken my thoughts out loud.

"Yes, you must have," said Allenby. "Now shut up."

"What's a valley girl?" asked Rachael.

"Tell you later. Mr. Short-temper is having a tantrum-time."

Surprisingly, that didn't calm his mood at all.

I watched with them as Tuku entered the room with the same firm determined step I'd seen on the other side of the wall when I'd watched the security footage for that day. He crossed the screen and waved to Rachael, who waved back before falling again into her iPad. He said something to Kaisa who was sitting at a table talking on her phone. If she said something, we couldn't hear it. There was no sound. Tuku ignored the staff, because, staff, and walked like an entitled prick directly through the door that led to the kitchen.

"What's in the kitchen?" I asked.

Allenby shook his head. "Kitchen stuff."

Just then people began arriving. Ted Tessner, looking flapped, as opposed to unflappable, Barty-B, Kaisa, Augustus, The Messenger and even Donnopher in the flesh. Artstar and Sylvia were last. Sylvia had been crying. I offered her a nod. She forced a smile.

Allenby straightened up, Rachael reached for her iPad sitting beside her. She opened it and scanned down, taking roll probably.

Donnopher went to the Keurig machine and began bleeding the planet as people milled around. Ted consulted with Rachael in low tones.

"Miss Woods?" said Allenby.

Kaisa removed her scowl from The Peoplists and put on a not injury-inducing expression. "Yes?"

"Do you remember what Tuku said to you the first night of the conference?"

"What? When?"

Allenby pointed to the monitor. She moved over and studied it. Allenby fiddled with the mouse and reran the minute of Tutu's cross into and out of the room.

"No, I don't think so."

Rachael appeared back at the table and carefully and intentionally moved Allenby's hand off the controlling mouse. "There's a microphone stand right there," she said, pointing to the video. "I have a sound file for that somewhere. Let me look for it."

Kaisa said, "I think he said something like, enjoy the show. He might not be there for it."

"What did you think he meant by that?" asked Allenby.

"I thought maybe he was boycotting it. The way a lot of people did the Reverend the other night."

Barty-B flushed.

Allenby asked, "And what did you answer?"

"I think I said something like have a good night. I didn't want to get into it with him."

"Tuku's speech was on the terrifying side," I said.

"His people ruined my sermon," said Barty-B. "Mr. Tessner, I'd like to make an official complaint against The Homecoming Allegiance group and their disrespectful leader, Mr. Adam Tuku."

"Tuku is dead," said Tessner. "That's why you're here."

As if on cue, and I had to think it was, Detective Johnson entered the room then. He pulled the door closed behind him.

"Hello everyone," he said, but his eyes glowed for Donnopher. I half expected him to ask them to sign his badge. "Mr. Tessner is correct. Adam Tuku was found this morning dead by a self-inflicted gunshot wound to the head."

"Like Sangye," said The Messenger.

"No," I said. "Not like Sangye."

"Why not?"

"Because Sangye didn't kill himself and Tuku might have."

"Is that true?" asked Kaisa.

"Yes."

"So who killed Sangye?" asked Barty-B.

"And Smith," added Sylvia.

"Tuku," said the detective.

"And who killed Tuku?"

"Himself."

"How do you know this?"

"We found the body."

"But," said Donnopher, "you found the bodies of the COTTEO people and said then that was murder-suicide by Sangye. Perhaps you better bring us up to speed. Things have obviously been kept from us."

"Naughty naughty, Ted," I said. "This kind of thing might look bad in the paper."

He looked at me with a rage that surprised me. I thought of my Zen, of Allie, of just plain manners. "Sorry dude," I said. "That was uncalled for."

The apology caught him off guard. "It's…it is what it is," he said.

"And sorry about your goat."

That triggered him again. New righteous fury flooded his features. Confidently in the right now, he said evenly, "We'll talk about that later."

Johnson said, "The motive for the crime is most likely a philosophical difference between the Homecoming group and uhm…"

"The rest of humanity?" I suggested.

"The COTTEOs," said Johnson after a glance to Allenby.

Something in the exchange bothered me. No, scared me.

"Forensics has shown that Mr. Tuku was in his room alone when he shot himself, last night during Mr. Bensen's talk."

"Reverend Bensen, and it was a sermon," said the man.

"The gun used was the second missing one from Mr. Tessner's home."

"What guns?" asked Artstar.

"You better unpack that, Detective," I said. "It is key."

"At our dinner party the other night," said Ted. "Remember we took two guns from Mr. Klept?"

"You took nothing from me," said Augustus. "I surrendered them voluntarily. You'd never have taken them from me while there was still breath in my lungs if I wanted to keep them."

There couldn't have been more macho NRA vibes if he'd had a check from the Russian State Duma in his breast pocket.

"Those guns," I said. "Those two. That's key. Sangye was found with one of them. That gun had killed John Smith and Sangye. Left to make it look like a suicide."

"Which gun?" asked Klept.

"The big one."

"Good choice," he said.

Sylvia shook her head. It was that or *his* mindless head.

"So both guns were stolen?" said Artstar.

"That night from the bureau in the room."

"And one was found with Sangye?"

"Yes."

"And the other wasn't located?"

"Not until this morning."

"So why did you think for an instant that Sangye killed himself," Sylvia said.

"I don't follow," said Johnson.

"Wouldn't the absence of the second missing gun from Sangye's effects be a big fat red flag against shutting the case down and claiming it was a murder-suicide and we were all safe?"

That shut everyone up. Me too. I hadn't thought of it. I should have. I'd had a hunch, discovered the blood under the gun to show the timing that pointed to Sangye being killed before Smith but the second missing gun would have gone a long way to backing me up there.

"Well, it's found now," said the detective.

"But we were always in danger," said Kaisa.

"We didn't think so."

The group looked around at each other, maybe for the first time understanding the peril they were in.

"You all knew there was a killer on the loose," I said. "Chill the fuck out."

"How did we know?" asked Artstar.

"Social media."

"That didn't mean we were in danger."

"Why not?"

"We'd done nothing to deserve killing," said Artstar.

"What is that supposed to mean?" Sylvia stormed at her, more of that righteous anger in the room.

"Nothing, nothing." The witch stepped back.

I went to Sylvia and put my arm around her. She rested a moment, then let me lead her out of the center where she stared down everyone.

"John Smith was a good man. It wasn't his...him...that...he was a good man. A wonderful man. More than a man. More than..." She fell off and caught herself beginning to cry but stanched it. She instead straightened her back and faced the world again like the hero she was.

"The threat's over now," said Ted. "We had a nut with us. He's gone. His people are still being questioned by the authorities. We'll make an announcement at the dinner keynote. Not sure what I'm going to say, but our last days here will be under a pall—a great pall, greater than even before."

"You going to cancel?" I asked.

"No," said Ted. "We only have a day and a half yet."

"Is that what the group wants?" I looked around wondering who among them would stay on this sinking ship. Not surprisingly, they all did.

"It is what it is," said Ted.

38

"I'M UNCONVINCED," I said loudly to everyone.

"Why?" asked Kaisa.

"I don't know."

"Shut up and go home, Flaner," said Allenby.

"First, where was everyone the night Smith was killed?"

"Now?" said Sylvia. "You're getting around to asking your suspects this now? What have I been paying you for?"

"I'm working on it. Kaisa, where were you?"

She pointed to the screen. Classes, a call, and then cleaned up for the keynote."

"Run the tape, Rachael."

Surprisingly, she did. Everyone leaned in to watch Tuku cross the room, exit the kitchen. After a moment, Kaisa stood up, made a step for the door, turned around and exited through another door.

"Why'd you leave that way?" I asked.

"I'd been harassed by followers. It's why I ducked in there in the first place. I took the back stairs."

"Did you see anyone?"

"The Messenger."

"Is this true?" I dramatically turned on The Messenger and put a finger in his face for effect.

"Yes. I was sitting in the stairwell."

"Why?"

"I'd rather not say."

"Spill it or I'll get the hose," I said.

"Can he do that?"

Johnson stared. Allenby said, "Why don't you just tell us."

"Smoking."

"Is this true, Kaisa?" I was aghast for dramatic effect, I even threw an arm over my forehead.

"No?" she said, looking at The Messenger.

"It's okay," he said. "I release you from your promise."

"It's true," she said.

"So why the hesitation to tell us?"

"I promised him."

The Messenger said, "The angels told me years ago that smoking was killing me. I rail against, but I'm weak. Forgive me."

I felt he was about to go into a whole Jimmy Swaggart rift, so I cut him off.

"How long?"

"Since I was sixteen."

"In the stairwell," I said.

"Oh, uhm, maybe three or four."

"Hours? Minutes?"

"Cigs," he said. "Don't know how long."

"There he is," said Rachael, pointing to the monitor. "He entered through that back door at six forty-five. Right when he was supposed to arrive. Thanks for being punctual."

"My pleasure," he said. "Manners are important."

"Okay," I said. "Where were you Augustus?"

"None of your goddamn business," he said.

Detective Johnson said, "We cleared him for the night of the killings."

"How?"

"He was with a young lady, a Ms. Hannah Hill."

"Mrs.," corrected Sylvia.

Ouch.

"There he is entering the hall at 6:46." Rachael pointed to the monitor. "There also is Ms. Artstar a few moments later."

"That's about when the murders took place," said Johnson. "Six floors away."

"What about Mr. Barty-B?"

"Reverend," he corrected.

"Reverend Barty-B."

"Seven ten," said Rachael, and I remembered that I knew that already. "After Ms. Woods."

"Exactly," I said. "You, Barty boy, could have killed Smith and Sangye."

"And Mr. Tuku? While I was giving my sermon?"

"That's a pretty good alibi, I admit," I said. "But we'll check the finger-print DNA to be sure."

"Fingerprint DNA?"

"It was a shitty sermon," said Kaisa. "I was there and saw it. You can check if you like, Mr. Flaner."

Rachael said, "You want me to pull up—"

"No," said Ted. "Mr. Flaner was just leaving. The only persons not at the opening keynote were Tuku and Smith. Let's get back to work everyone. The threat is over. The killer is…gone."

"What is all this equipment for?" asked Augustus. "What are you doing here?"

Rachael looked surprised and then looked at Ted. "We're making video content for the online conference. Keynotes and classes. Maybe even a two-hour special to pitch to streaming services."

"Do I have a say in this?" he asked.

"Not if you signed your contract," Ted said.

"It'll be very professional," added Rachael. "Music, background ambiance, only the best highlights. We don't want to make anyone look bad."

"But you will if it suits your purpose," said Klept. I could have been wrong, but I thought I saw a flash of neon green under his jacket.

"We all signed a contract," said Artstar. "Didn't you read it? There are even royalties if it sells."

"There are?" He lit up then. Not the room with gunfire, but with a smiling countenance. I had to think that was an improvement, but his smile was crocodilian and toothy.

"When will we be able to see it?" asked Kaisa.

"I have hundreds of hours of audio and video. It'll be weeks. I've got lots to go through."

"Are you the only one?"

"I'm the director," she said. "I wouldn't trust anyone else."

I said. "A director in more ways than one, I see. Nice."

"Yes."

"You don't think it was Tuku then?" asked Donnopher. "You think whoever killed Smith and Sangye killed him? And is therefore still on the loose?"

"It's a possibility," I said.

"No it's not," said the detective.

"Goodbye Mr. Flaner," said Ted. "And the rest of you, have a great day."

"Bayeeeeee," I bleated to him, just to see his face redden.

Donnopher was met at the door by their bodybuilding bodyguard. The others waiting and left one at a time, apparently afraid to be alone with anyone.

"I should sue you to oblivion, Flaner," said Ted. "You're a human wrecking ball."

"I have been known to swing naked on chains."

"Where's my goat?"

"Didn't Allie tell you? It was kid-napped. Get it?"

"You can thank my respect for your girlfriend that I don't sue you for grand larceny."

"And you can thank my laziness for not turning you in for having illegally imported livestock."

"What are you talking about?"

"You can only import goats from New Zealand and Canada. Jerry, and his mother, come from the subcontinent."

"You're right, but I got a permit."

"Prove it."

"I can and will if necessary."

"I don't believe you."

"I have more pull than you know."

"Oooo, look at Mr. Powerful with his inside connections at the USDA."

He paused for a moment, thought of punching me again, saw The Messenger watching him with big eyes, held back, and then walked away.

From the office, I saw Allenby shake his head in disgust. I'd lost a fan. Rachael wrinkled her forehead. Two. Detective Johnson looked like he would smack me in front of a crowd of defense lawyers and smile doing it. Three. Well, two. Johnson was never Team Tony.

"Your friend Allison said you wanted to talk to me," said The Messenger when we were alone in the hallway. "You're a very lucky man. She's one hotty. Would you mind if I had a little one-on-one seminar with her?"

"You asking my permission to sleep with my girlfriend?"

"I'll give her back," he said.

I almost threw up in my mouth. "I don't think she wants to."

"She said she would consider it if you gave the okay." The man looked hopeful. I prayed that Allie had given herself a polite exit instead of an actual in to this man's slacks. Slacks.

"Ehm, no," I said. "We're committed."

"Nothing needs to change that. It'll unite us too. We'll be sharing the greatest thing two men can share."

"A woman?"

"Yes."

That time I did throw up a little.

"You're not the jealous type are you?" he asked.

"Actually, Mr. Marshall, I am. Sorry. One of my failings, I'm afraid. I just have to live with it. My burden. Alas."

"Nothing cures a fear like facing it. Let me have Allison for an hour and then return her to you. It'll clear your fear now and forever."

I tried to see Allie, my Allie, my first kiss, my childhood crush, the woman of my dreams, with this pudgy nutcase and nearly fainted. It wasn't that he wasn't attractive, he wasn't, at least not to me, but the idea of sharing my intimate partner went to the core of my socialized male behavior. Possessiveness is a thing. As is not wanting to be compared to other men, who despite their physical appearances, might possess attributes that could threaten my confidence.

He looked at me with friendly warm, alien-crazy eyes and I realized that this man had made this same proposal before and it had worked. He honestly expected me to acquiesce, to give him permission to sleep with my girl. This was a cult leader, I remembered. If there was any doubt, the "I get to sleep with your woman" test was a clincher.

"Still no," I said. "Thanks for the offer, but I'll just have to work through it in therapy."

"A waste of time," he explained, "and opportunity. Women who've slept with me are blessed."

"I'm sure you think so."

"No, God told me. If they've been marked by my seed, then when the aliens come, they'll sense I was there and leave her and any offspring she may have had—regardless of the biological father—alone. No guarantee for you, I'm afraid. I don't do guys."

"Oh, that's a shame. I really would have liked that alien insurance policy."

"So I can—"

"No."

He was about to argue some more, and I was about to get really sick, so I changed the subject. "What I wanted to talk to you about was where you were when Smith was killed."

"You know that now."

"I do."

"You're not going to tell anyone about that, are you?" he asked. "You promised."

"Actually, I didn't, but I don't see it coming up."

"Good. It is a failing and I am ashamed of it. But sometimes, you see, I get scared and the nicotine helps calm me down."

"Wouldn't want you to be scared."

"No."

He went to move around me.

"Wait, one thing. Did Sangye ever approach you at all?"

"About what?"

"About anything?"

"Like?"

"Like maybe blackmailing you."

"For what?"

"Smoking?"

"Smoking?"

"Smoking."

"No."

"What's the name of your 'group' by the way?"

"We call ourselves the Community," he said. "In anticipation of joining the greater community of the galaxy."

"And they're coming like conquistadors into Mexico?"

"Yes. That's it."

"Scary shit," I admitted.

"We have God on our side," he said, and I think he actually thought so.

He left down the hall. I turned back into the control center.

As I got there, Johnson was at the door. I ducked, expecting the afore-mentioned smack, but he just closed the door. I tried it, but it was locked and my will was not strong enough to overcome that obstacle at that time. I committed to positive visualization and went in search of magazines to find pictures to cut out for my vision board.

In the lobby, I found Allie.

"See Ted?" she asked.

"How'd you know that?"

"He appeared from the elevator red faced, but cooling. He saw me, thought about you—I just know it, and went bright again."

"Did he say anything?"

"No."

"That's probably for the best."

"I talked to The Messenger," she said.

"Me too."

"What did he say?"

"He wants to sleep with you."

"I know."

"Were you going to tell me?"

"He said he would."

"Checks out."

"And?" She gave me a wide eyed 'are you going to let me' look.

"I don't like this subject one little bit," I said.

"A comedian who can't take a joke. That's funny."

"Success then," I said.

She kissed my forehead. "You men really don't have any idea what it is to be a woman."

"I tried on stilettos once."

"I get propositioned all the time."

"All the time?"

"Most aren't as forward as The Messenger, but yes, all the time."

"What keeps you from falling for it?"

"Seriously?"

"Yeah. If some woman came up to me and threw herself at my feet, I'd be tempted."

"I've known that to happen to you and I've seen you resist. Don't sell yourself short."

"I was tempted."

"If you want an open relationship, just say so."

I know she was teasing, at least some upper consciousness part of me thought—hoped—she was, but to be sure, I let the lowest language-skilled caveman brain frame my reply.

"I don't want an open relationship," I said. "No on the open. No. No. Nope. Nope. Please God no. Not. I'm against it."

"Why?" all innocent, still playing.

Me, struggling not to cry. "I'm not strong enough."

"I know."

I looked at her and that impulse to make it official hit me like an alien stun gun, but again I balked. Commitment is a four letter word. In some languages. Maybe French.

"Did we miss snacks?" I said after a long-hanging obvious and unused moment.

She sighed. "Yes, we missed snacks. Afternoon classes are starting."

I bounced a second or two on my heels, thinking what to do now. I opened the app on my phone and checked the schedule.

"Let's go get some testosterone," I said. "I could use a fill up."

"Not sure what that means," she said. "Is this some kind of new boutique café in Eugene? My, this place is trendy."

"No, BRA is having a little class on white privilege."

"Why would you deign to give that man and that organization any legitimacy at all?"

"I'd give it legitimacy by attending?"

"Yes."

"Because the official line now officially is that Tuku of Homecoming killed himself and also Smith and Sangye of the Church of the Third Eye Opened. The case is closed. The Interfaith Congress of Holistic Enlightened People can continue without delay or threat."

"So you're done and you want to spend your free time and free ticket to learn how to become a white supremacist? What you need is a new hobby? Where was The Messenger when you saw him, by the way?"

I gave her my best furrowed eyebrow disapproving stare.

"His suite, maybe?" she said. "He gave me a key."

"He was going to get a shot for syphilis," I said. "It was really flaring up."

"Just asking," she said.

"Just telling."

She kissed me again. "You don't buy the official line then?"

"Too much I don't know."

"And why would you think you might find something with The Brotherhood of Righteous Action?"

"Because," I said, "Augustus Klept has a new gun."

39

"DO I have to come with you?" Allie asked.

"I thought you wanted to be a part of the investigation."

"Isn't there something else I can do?"

"Like what?"

"Anything."

"You're white. They'll love you."

"I'll be the star of a racist misogynist hour-long rant? Sign me up."

"There might be firearms training."

"Please."

"Okay. There is something you can do, if you don't mind."

"What?" she said warily.

"Talk to Ted for me."

"You want to apologize for something?"

"Nah, I did that earlier. Not that I shouldn't do it again and often with that man, but I'd like to know if Sangye hit him up for blackmail money."

"How do I do that?"

"I don't know, but I bet you'll have an easier time with him than I would. Try battling your eyelashes."

"Batting."

"Not battling?"

"No."

"Oh."

"And you think that'll do it?" she said.

"Or you could come with me."

"I should talk to him about Beatrice."

"Who's Beatrice again?"

"Jerry's mother. I'm sure she's upset about Jerry being gone."

"And being shot," I added.

We kissed—on the mouth!—and I left her to wander toward the conference rooms. The classes had already begun and I had to dig around the conference app for ten minutes before I found the right place, so I was really late.

I paused at the door to listen and heard Augustus Klept's voice. He sounded reasonable, so I dared enter, trying to remain unobserved.

"The liberal elite come in many guises, not just the pink-haired nose-ringed type," he said. "Take Mr. Flaner there."

So much for unobserved. All eyes turned to me.

The audience surprised me. There were maybe forty percent skinhead types I'd expected to find, but the rest were a good potpourri of the conference goers, including folks I'd label from the outside as the dreaded "liberal elite." One woman had pink hair, another man had a pierced nose. One woman had both, though I think they used to be a man. There were also half a dozen people of color, all were there and listening.

"Hi," I said. "I'll be your straw man tonight."

"There ain't nothing wrong with looking as you want," said Klept. "That doesn't matter. The matter comes when we forget the natural order of man/woman, white over darkies."

I expected an exodus at that. I myself turned to leave, but when no one else joined me, I found an open chair next to Peaches. "Why are you here?" I whispered.

"He's paying us."

"What?"

She nodded. "One hundred fifty dollars to anyone who stays the entire time and hears him out without comment or complaint."

"You're kidding?"

"He does this every class," Peaches said. "This is my third from him. I'm getting new earbuds after this."

A man next to her with pink hair and a nose ring whispered. "Better the money with us than him."

I counted forty-five people in the audience and did the math. "That's… uhm, a lot of money."

"Yeah."

"The alt-right was all about money," Klept went on. "We don't care about that. We care about the races. How we work together, how we work apart. Philosophically, we differ from some people in that we don't want a society of soup, but a well organized dinner plate, with steak and potatoes separate from the vegetables. They're all part of a balanced meal, just recognizable from each other."

I recalled I hadn't eaten, and was okay with that.

"You should be proud of your portion. Steak pride is real. All food groups matter. That's what I'm saying. I just happen to believe that steak is the best food, because I'm a steak. That's how the world works. I work for better steak. Go ahead and champion your creamed corn or your grits or what have you, but don't tell me that I've got to like them as much as I like my steak. A big juicy dripping juicy juicy steak."

He was talking to Hannah who was in the front row.

"It's important—no, vital—that the races unite under their own flag. That is what Russia is trying to do in Ukraine, uniting all the Russians together."

I was going to raise my hand and mention that the Ukrainians were Ukrainians not Russians, but then thought about the juicy juicy one hundred fifty bucks and waited.

"The effeminate leftist elite has led NATO to get involved there, which is, first of all, none of their business, and second risks thermonuclear disaster because Russia is in it for the long game of survival. They're uniting themselves against a common enemy, the existence of which is proved by Ukraine's resistance to join with them voluntarily. Is there any parent in the world who would not resort to violence to save their child from evil? That is Russia for the Ukrainians against the evil of the Jews and the gypsies and the homosexual agendas..."

Money or not, I was ready to leave. It was only my desire to figure out the BRA boys that kept me there. It was also my quest for equanimity after dick-punching a Nazi before, that kept me from dick-punching this Nazi now. I hesitated, mentally stepped back, let it go, packaged my visceral outrage into a little box I let drift away on my mental cleansing river clogged with leaves and food wrappers. I would be still and observe like Buddha under a fig tree at Nuremberg.

Since there'd been talk about the real deal and real believers, not necessarily the same thing, I measured Augustus Klept on those scales and found him wanting. He'd changed out of his branded clothes, i.e., he didn't look like a Hell's Angel *American History X* castaway. He wore a sensible pale-blue dress shirt today over a white tee. Jeans. Boots. Always boots. Nothing but the ink creeping up his neck and down his sleeves to suggest his alternative lifestyle. He was handsome if you didn't listen to him, auburn hair, blue eyes. Firm chin. A poster child for 'good' genes. His speech was matter-of-fact, even, worryingly convincing in the way he framed dubious arguments, erected straw men, went ad hominem, played the no real Scotsman to take a slippery slope to vacuous truths in ipse dixit. There was the dinner guest Augustus, the orgy hosting Augustus, the Augustus in public with the other cults, and now this one, each a variation. His tattoos showed large and permanent commitment to his cause and yet he reminded me of speakers I'd seen before. Not just at TED Talks, though there was a sense of that happening, but more of a manager kind of thing. I felt that this was a job to him, at least this part. Maybe he was playing to the room, softening in the face of the people he'd so casually slurred, but he seemed on the fence a little. He spoke fluently but almost sadly as if his emotions didn't match his scripted words. He was businesslike and rehearsed, and considering how much this was costing him, his demeanor suggested one thing to me: he wasn't spending his own money.

Like most of the rest of the room, I put my attention into my phone screen. I'd been behind in my Google fu and thought, with the right concentration, mindfulness and intent, I might tune out Klept and tune in the AI overlords.

I went first to Homecoming Allegiance, the late Adam Tutu's group. The front and only page was a lengthy suicide note. Of sorts. It echoed the brutal firebrand speech Adam had given at his keynote. Reading it through, I could see how law enforcement wasn't looking farther than Adam's right hand for his murderer. One thing struck me though, when talking about the release of death, the freedom to join the hereafter universe yada yada, it read like they weren't going alone. A mass event seemed to have been planned. I remembered the confused orange people at the locked doors. People waiting for the rapture to be freed from this world along with "the lucky few who'd be welcomed to join them at the appointed time."

I poked around links mentioning Green Tomorrow and found Kaisa Woods at the center. It was an environmental movement, but it had her face in the center of it. She appeared many times in native dress being quoted about humanity's responsibility to the earth. It was a good sentiment, but it was nearly overshadowed by Kaisa putting herself all over it. She spoke of her ancestral and recent spiritual links to nature, how the forces of the planet spoke to her personally, telling where she hurt and what to do. She bemoaned several setbacks she and the earth had suffered recently, not always differentiated. A reef had been lost in the Caribbean to a tourist destination, an oil field was lost in the Arctic, and most recently Green Tomorrow activists had been killed in Brazil leaving the way open for a lumber company to take a huge swath of the Amazon. There were successes too, Everglades defense, air regulation in Canada, a pro-environmental movement rising in Argentina despite economic hardships.

Being a religion by definition allowed her to use all funds she received to benefit the cause and not pay the governments who subsidized the planet's destruction. Very smart. Of course this meant that there was no official tracking of where money came from or went. I remembered she had the newest Apple phone and her clothes weren't from Dillard's. Her new water company worked under the same umbrella and was headquartered in the Cayman islands, but bottled in Brazil. Nothing suspicious about that. It took me a minute, but I found what I was looking for, yes, I was looking for something. The water was bottled under license by Nestlé. For those in the know, this is a red flag. Nestlé is the poster child of corporate malfeasance in the progressive world. Bedfellows, however, needs must. In the previous year, Woods Water had brought in millions of dollars for the cause.

I searched around and couldn't find it locally. Online, it was available at prices that rivaled Cristal. I found it listed as a line item of expenses for a Green Peace meeting last year and ironically for a drilling company in Helsinki. Someone on the inside getting good digs into the corporation, filling their fridges with the enemy's revenue source to the tune of five million dollars last year according to their financial statements. Activism comes in all shapes and sizes. Respect to the insider there bleeding that company for the cause.

Augustus Klept had a digital fingerprint Elon Musk would be threatened by. There were the usual retweets of Fox News, a ton of talking heads from YouTube spouting conspiracy theories under the header "something to think about." The topics were far wider than just race, though there was a fair amount of that, but also politics in general, all of a hard right bent. Not surprising. Millions of followers, many of them no doubt Russian bots. Klept would make five to twelve social media posts a day and they'd be instantly shared into the hundreds of thousands. One post stuck out. It was an attack on a senator who'd been accused of insider trading. Nothing new, or even illegal I'm afraid to say, about that, but the timing was suspicious. It appeared on his timeline twenty minutes before the Voice of Moscow dropped the same information from an insider in the senator's camp. Klept didn't have the informant, but he did have the information. The Voice of Moscow's post was shared widely and instantly by bots across the world, both the electronic and meat puppet variety.

I remembered the wall of screens in Klept's room. After about half an hour where Klept proclaimed that the free market would have dealt with the race problem if the bleeding hearts hadn't interfered, I thought I had it figured out. They were in fact, dummy accounts. His own echo chamber where he took on different flavors of fanaticism. There was one who quoted him frequently pretending to be a mom in South Carolina, 'just looking out for her kids.' There was another who claimed to be a software engineer in Silicon Valley complaining about the woke tyranny of his company. He was careful not to give any identifying information because they were watching. All of this sounded true enough, but by context and timing, and the flashes of images I'd seen before, I figured they were all Klept. Those other identities told me a lot about what his game was and I surfed away from the hate right to the conference app to see if it'd been updated to make it any more useful.

It hadn't.

I shuffled around until I found the schedule for the rest of the conference. It was then Thursday afternoon and the conference ended Saturday. Keynote tonight was Artstar from the Coven. Bring your broomsticks. Tomorrow's lunch keynote would be this jerk, Augustus Klept. God help us. Dinner would be Kaisa Woods. Saturday was supposed to be Donnopher in the afternoon, but they'd already gone, taking John Smith's spot. That left a hole.

The farewell address Saturday night had Ted Tessner scheduled with an important announcement. Press will be in attendance.

Everything was falling into place. Everything except who killed John Smith and Sangye and who took Jerry the goat, you know the stuff I was supposed to have figured out.

40

I FRESHENED up after the BRA meeting by exfoliating, mouth-washing, new clothesing, showering and trying to take a nap. Conferences are overwhelming. Sensory overload with new people, places and ideas, flashy colors, myriad sounds, inputs of all kinds short circuit the little gray cells. As I lay on the bed being lazy, my usual go-to strategy for life, let alone sensory overload, I remembered I was trying to be a spiritual savant and spirit savants count tarot cards and meditate. They don't nap.

I set a stack of pillows on the floor, sat upon them, and tried to empty my mind by focusing only on my breath.

In out. In out.

In and out.

That burger place. With the Christian french fries.

I was hungry.

Tony. Back to breath.

Breathe in and out. In out.

Inhale. Exhale.

Sangye was kinda sleazy.

Back to breath.

Smith seemed like a really nice guy, though. I wonder what would have happened if he'd fulfilled—

Back to fucking breath. Breathe. Breathe. Breath.

I wondered where the gang was. Garrett's having a terrible time. I bet Standard has the clap.

Goats have too much personality. Probably why we don't eat them.

Usually.

There are places that eat goat. Probably the same kind of places that export scorpions in suckers to sell at gas stations.

I think I have a blister forming on my right foot. Maybe one on my—

God dammit!

In out.

In out.

In out.

Jerry needs my help.

In out. In out.

Jerry will die tonight, if you don't do something.

Oh, yeah? Who says.

Me.

And you are?

John Smith.

Really?

Yes.

Is he the only one in danger?

You know he isn't.

Who else?

Everyone. You have to save everyone.

Well I'll just get around to that after I breathe.

In out.

In out.

In, fucking out.

I gave up. I put the pillows back on the bed, laid down for a minute, trying to sort out my new schizophrenia. Next I figured I'd be Napoleon. He was of normal height, by the way. The short thing was British propaganda. Strange how that kind of smear can stick so long.

I began to doze off with the image of John Smith smiling benevolently at me from atop a rearing white horse crossing the Alps. I was about to ask him a question when *Satan Stabs Your Eyes* growl-screamed "Hommmm!" and shot me to my feet like triggering landmine. A phonemail.

"Tony." It was Allie. "Are you coming down for the keynote?"

"What time is it?"

"Time for you to come down. I ordered you a steak plate. Standard is eyeing it."

"Tell him if he touches my food, I'll have his ears for cock-rings."

"Will do." I heard her relay the message across a noisy room. "Now Dara is looking at your cake."

"I'm on my way." Standard could be threatened away, but Dara was unpredictable. I figured if I got down there in five minutes, there was still an eighty percent chance I'd not have cake when I got there.

———

There was no cake. Dara smiled and told me, "The cake was a lie."

I said, "The menu suggests there was something."

"Nope."

"Everyone else has chocolate cake."

"They're special."

"And you have two plates."

"I'm special too."

I looked over at Allie who was licking the last of the frosting off her fork. "It wasn't very good," she said and then licked the plate

My steak wasn't hot, but it wasn't stone cold, so that was something. The garlic mashed were tasty, the carrot medley was half butter, so tasty. Ice tea was on the table, and blessed be to the gods, the pink sweetener. I usually like the yellow ones, but they don't dissolve in cold beverages. The pink ones do. Pink for cold, yellow for hot. That's my motto.

"We know," said Critter.

I should say that the gang was all at the table. Mischievous Dara, roll-munching Standard, sullen Perry, giddy Garrett and even Critter.

"How'd you get in here?" I asked.

Critter glanced at Garrett and both of them smiled, one a fresh-faced friend, the other his hand covered in a felt envelope. Also a friend.

Critter slowly turned to reveal a black and red cape, red with a black triangle. Within the triangle were the words *Support Animal*.

"I had an extra," said Allie.

"Nice."

"One person tried to give us shit," said Dara. "We shamed the fuck out of her until she apologized three ways from Sunday and swore to the spirits and her ancestors—really—that, going forward, she'd endeavor to be a better person."

"Sorry I missed that."

Standard pointed to the camera and microphone by the table. "Maybe it got recorded," he said. "Who do I ask for a copy? It was primo."

"That'd be Rachael." I pointed to the iPad toting woman on stage at that moment. I couldn't help noticing that Ted was not there.

"Where's Ted?" I asked Allie.

"He's laying low so the buzz about the article today can die down. He'll be back Saturday. He's doing the final keynote."

"You think people will have forgotten the scandal so quickly? Forty-eight hours?"

Standard said, "In a sane world, they would."

"Point taken."

"ICOHEP would like to welcome you to the penultimate evening keynote of our first ever, uhm…ICOHEP," said Rachael. "Let's give a warm welcome to Artstar of the Coven."

A lot of applause, some polite, some enthusiastic, some in a strong rhythm that suggested ancient rites and fires. The good-sized crowd was reinforcing my opinion that Barty-B's keynote was boycotted, not the conference. I wondered what Augustus's would look like the next day. Would he be handing out money?

"Welcome seekers," began Artstar. "Blessed be."

"Blessed be," came the response from several tables, notably, the ones with folks dressed like witches.

"Tonight is a full moon and so power is in the air."

"What's wrong with Perry?" I asked. He'd not said a word since I'd arrived but had rearranged his vegetables on his plate six times. Now seven.

Garrett said, "Allie told him about The Messenger hitting on her."

"It's worse," I said. "He hit on me to let him hit on her."

Perry's head fell a little lower.

"And he smokes."

"Oh, for fuck's sake!" Perry slammed his hand on the table, rattling the glasses.

I said to the gang, "Did Allie tell you that if she took his seed, she'd be blessed for generations from the alien—"

"Yes," said Perry. "Yes. Yes, yes. And he smokes?"

"Yes."

"Dammit!"

"Never meet your heroes," said Critter.

"That's the truth," said Perry. "It's just...just..."

"Creepy?" said Garrett.

"It undercuts the rest of his message."

I was going to ask how it did that. Marking the woman he's had sex with for special treatment from telepathically contacted alien overlords wasn't much crazier than telepathically contacted alien overlords.

"It does it by being so salacious," answered Perry, informing me again that my censor was out to lunch and all my thoughts were leaking out of my head like smashed pumpkin guts.

"I'd have said jelly from a squished donut," said Standard.

"Puss from a herpes sore," offered Dara.

"Vomit at a frat party," said Critter

"Blood from the heart." It was Artstar on stage. "Metaphorically now, once literal, it demonstrates the ultimate commitment of sacrifice. And that is the greatest power in the universe."

"I talked to Ted," said Allie.

"I talked to Smith," I said.

"Huh?"

"Nothing. What did Ted say?" I busied my mouth by eating, lest my thoughts ooze out again.

"Though he's already a big donor to COTTEO, Sangye had approached him with some allegations he'd heard about his past."

"Wha did Thed thay?"

"Don't talk with your mouth full."

"Why did he say that?" said Perry. "Hahahahahaha!" Then he put his head in his hands and moaned. "I'm a professional comic. God, forgive me."

"Only if you swear on your goddamn grandparents you will hereafter strive to be a better person."

"No."

"Fair enough."

"Ted said he thanked Sangye for the information and when asked about a further donation for an upgrade to the cultural center at the same meeting, he pulled out a checkbook and gave him another fifty thousand."

"So it was a shakedown?"

"Ted didn't think so at the time," Allie said, "But after I told him that Sangye had pressed some of the others here, he conceded it could have been."

"Is he stupid?" asked Dara

"He just thinks the best of everyone."

"Pa-lease..." I said.

Allie blushed. "Well, he thought the best of Smith and COTTEO. He'd already donated the land for their new place and given money before. This was just some more."

"So Tessner's affiliation is COTTEO?" said Critter. "So why this whole thing?" He gestured with his wired arms around the room.

"Ted wants to give back," said Allie.

"Pa-lease..."

"He's not that bad," said Allie, getting defensive. "He's not pressing charges about Jerry."

"He still hit me," I said.

"Wait?" said Dara. "What blackmail?"

"Sangye was blackmailing some of the people here," Allie explained. "Tony thinks that's why he was killed."

"Some but not all?"

I nodded, mouth full of steak and potatoes.

"My money's on Benson," said Critter. "Garrett told me about his homophobic rant."

"Wait until you hear Klept tomorrow," I said.

"Let's not."

"Peaches said that Kaisa's people are going to picket the conference for allowing Klept to speak at all," said Standard.

"Why?" asked Perry, coming out of his funk. Gotta love bipolar disorder. "I thought her schtick was the environment."

"It's a broad humanitarian philosophy dedicated to living in peace and harmony. Hate and violence creates divides that distract from the real problems, so they're going to riot."

"No argument with that," said Dara.

"Adam Tuku's the guy," said Allie.

I shrugged. Chewed and shrugged. Swallowed. I'd gone five minutes without my thoughts spilling out.

"Four."

"Fuck!"

"So if not Tuku who?"

"The place is full of suspects with motives," I said, wishing I had some cake to finish the meal. "I just have to figure out who has the best one, one big enough to justify a double, if not triple homicide."

"So Tuku didn't kill himself?" said Critter.

"I'm working on it."

"You don't need to look to new gods," said Artstar. "The old ones are the best, reformed. The pure strains of the holy and powerful are to be found in nature."

Cheers from the Green Tomorrow Group.

"And in the old books."

Cheers from Barty-B's gang.

"In the power of the greater powers we cannot see but feel."

The Messenger's mass had a moment to agree. I was lost.

"Fed by our devotion. Be it time or money, the sounds we make in prayer, the thoughts we share, the hopes we have, the actions we make, the work we do, the pain we suffer, the blood we spill."

An uncomfortable cheer from the Nazi wing of the room.

"It's all in what we're willing to give. The bigger the gift, the greater the reward. It's a simple equation; what and how and when." She paused for general applause and got it. She wasn't a bad speaker. Her eyes glittered almost as much as the shiny pentacle choker around her neck.

"Tonight is the full moon," she said, leading into the finish. "The Coven have work to do now, so we will leave you. Blessed be." She bowed and stepped back to applause before leaving the stage.

The dinner broke up. The day's events concluded.

Artstar shook hands with a few people in the crowd like a politician after an announcement speech and crossed the room to an exit as dishes were collected and goodnights offered around.

We watched her join a group of followers at the door, and as a bunch, pull their hoods up over their heads and leave.

"Did you see that?" I said out loud.

"Yes," came the response from the gang.

"What did I miss?" asked Critter.

"That's right," said Garrett. "You weren't there when Jerry was kidnapped by a gang in black hoodies."

"Not hoodies," said Allie.

"Robes," I said.

41

"I'VE GOT a bad feeling about this," I said.

"What do we do?" Allie said.

I looked around for good ideas, found none. "We'll follow them."

We snaked through the crowd to the lobby just as a chartered bus pulled up and the Coven began to board.

I said. "Perry, you have a car. Go get it."

He was gone in a flash.

"We have to stall them until Perry gets here."

"How?"

I looked at them. "Eh, I don't know. They'll recognize us from the square."

"Not me," said Critter. "I wasn't there and I have an idea."

"What is it?" asked Garrett.

"You'll see," said the puppet, and led Garrett out the door to the loading area.

The rest of us hovered just inside, curious what Critter had up his sleeve, trying not to think about him literally being Garrett's sleeve and Garrett not knowing what he was up to either.

They approached the line boarding the bus. Critter said something and half a dozen people turned to look. Critter waved his arms, he didn't used to have arms, an upgrade Critter demanded after seeing Randy Feltface in Las Vegas, so his were a little jerky. He engaged them in conversation, pointing to the hotel, the bus, the sky. The ground. They nodded in agreement, all eyes on him. Even Garrett seemed spellbound by what Critter was relating. He swayed like a convert, threw his arms up in supplication, rolled his head like an ecstatic and then locked each listener in his googly-eyed stare. They listened, transfixed. A sage imparting wisdom. I'd expected a comedy bit, but it was a sermon on the mount.

Then Artstar stuck her head out of the bus and broke the spell. They all said warm goodbyes, boarded and left. Perry was nowhere to be seen.

"What did you say to them?" I asked when they came back.

"I didn't understand any of it," said Garrett.

"*Nichomachean Ethics*," said the puppet. "I engaged them on the nature of the soul and Aristotle's idea that a freed soul is happier than a trapped one, ergo, killing is fine. They were very interested in the subject, which goes far to confirming what I think we all fear about that goat Garrett told me about."

"When did you read Aristotle?" asked Garrett.

"Strangely enough, when I was in the room the other night alone, you dicks having left me."

We all stared.

"Then I debated the idea of possession of a soul and the heat that binds body to soul, again Aristotle, and asked them to explore the idea that receiving gods had an unseen heat to attack freed souls on the other side. The notion of heat sealing flesh and soul is fascinating and worthy of a cult itself. I was going into my theory of quantum level radiation as a possible heat source when their queen witch took them."

"Well, you tried."

Lewis came out of the hotel then, saw me, took a step toward us, but then changed his mind.

"Hold up," I said and trotted over. "You wanted to talk to me?"

"It's nothing." I could see he was upset.

"I collect nothing," I said. Perry rounded the corner. Lewis was at the Rivian. "I'm a good listener."

He looked at his hands, the road, the streetlights. "I was going to sin."

"I'm flattered."

"What?" He laughed. "No, not that."

"Now I'm insulted," I said.

He slapped his arm around my shoulder. "I needed that. Been a rough couple of days."

"Tell me about it."

"Tony!" It was Perry waving me over. I waved him off. The bus was good and gone but I was concerned with Lewis.

"I was going to tell you that the Reverend could have taken the gun."

"I know he could have."

"But he couldn't have. Really. I talked to him past the lock time."

"You're mad at him?" I said. "I get that."

"I was also going to tell you he could have killed Smith. I was going to deny his alibi."

"I haven't pressed Barty-B—er, the Reverend, for an alibi yet. But it's on the list."

"When pressed, when really pressed he might have told the truth and I'd have denied it."

"What would you have denied?"

Allie trotted over.

"Critter knows where they're going, James Creek Park, but we don't know how to get there and Perry's rental doesn't have enough seating for all of us. At least one of us will have to stay back. Garrett volunteered, but Critter is adamant he not be left behind this time."

"Hold up one second," I said. "Lewis…"

"That's out by Walterville," he said. "Past Springfield up the canyon."

"The Reverend," I said. "Did he kill Smith?"

He looked up now. The sky was clear and cold. There was a bright moon rising from the east but light pollution from the city allowed only a few stars to peek out, to those he said, "No. Not personally. When they were killed, I was with him. In his room. If you know what I mean."

I recalled the fiery keynote sermon the man had spat out from the podium and Lewis's face while he did.

"I'm sorry," I said.

"He's a hypocrite," said Lewis. "Closeted hypocrite."

"Yep."

"Tony…!" said Allie.

"Hey Lewis, remember Jerry the goat?" I asked. "Artstar and her group of Goth goblins are on their way to sacrifice him by the light of the moon at James Creek campground. We're trying to save him. We need a guide and another couple seats."

"Sure, why not? Hop in."

"Follow us!" yelled Allie to the gang and the chase was on.

Not much of a chase. We never even caught sight of the bus, but we made good time. I didn't press Lewis for any more information. He'd confirmed for me what I'd suspected Barty-B's secret was. He was a closeted homosexual. In his position that was a blackmail-worthy detail. It would come out eventually, I was sure. Eventually he'd find a lover with lower ethics than Lewis, but for now, I figured Sangye had scored his money. That took him off the suspect list.

I really couldn't explain why I didn't buy the Tuku theory for the COTTEO murders. It was a hunch I had, a big one. And unlike the previous hunches that had shaped my career this one didn't have a lot of foundation. It was attractive because it went in the face of what the police were saying, always a good staring point for my work, but it hadn't cemented the way Sangye's non-suicide had. He could have purloined the guns the night of the dinner party. He had definite homicidal motives, as evidenced by his web page and, yes, I have to admit it, his suicide. He led a suicide cult—what else was he to do? Nevertheless, I had this feeling, dare I say in retrospect, an otherworldly suspicion that the truth lay elsewhere. I pondered this on the dark weaving roads through Eugene, Springfield and Thurston, promising myself that I would make a goddam chart of times and alibis and see if I couldn't assign the killing to Tuku or give myself something better than a scratchy scrotum to dismiss him.

"As a joke, when we were trying to figure out seating," said Allie. "I suggested that Critter should ride in the glove box. The look on his face. You'd think he could take a joke, being a comedian and all."

"Critter has always been sensitive about being insentient."

"Lesson learned."

"Are you talking about your friend's puppet?" asked Lewis.

"Maybe."

"This has been a very weird conference," he said.

Perry and the gang were all in his rented Jetta and following us closely.

"Here's the turn," said Lewis and pulled off the highway.

I looked up. It was all trees and blackberries in the headlights. Low traffic on the McKenzie Highway had become no traffic as the road snaked through forest. A sign welcomed us to James Creek Park. Closed at nightfall. It was past nightfall. Crimes were being committed.

"Fuck the sign," I said. "Take us in."

"I was going to," said Lewis.

"Oh."

"I know this park," he said. "Mosquitos can eat you alive in the summer."

"If it were you, where would you conduct a secret witch coven goat-sacrifice meeting in this park? Asking for a friend."

He slowed and thought for a moment. "Probably around the other side and up the trail," he said.

"Take us there."

He drove past a play area and down a little hill to a gurgling creek with a lawn and a couple of tables on the bank. In the parking lot were four other cars and one big little bus. Two cars were vacant; two had necking teenagers in them. The bus was empty.

"The trails there." Lewis pointed. We parked. Perry and the gang pulled up beside us and got out.

"Leave your keys in the cars in case we have to make a fast getaway," said Perry.

"What's the plan," said Standard.

"Is that a tire iron?" I said.

"The car didn't come with a crowbar."

"Imagine that."

"So?" said Dara. "What's the fucking plan? Eight of us against thirty of them?"

"Eight?" said Lewis.

"Hello," said Critter, shooting Lewis a skin-scorching stare with his piercing plastic eyes.

"Sorry."

"Show us the way, Lewis," I said. "Oh, everyone, this is Lewis. He seems to be okay, now that he has an alibi for the killing of Smith and Sangye."

"I was a suspect?" I could see the shock on his face in the bright moonlight.

"Insulted?"

"No. Just never occurred to me."

"That's very suspicious," said Dara. "Do you have a girlfriend?"

"He plays for the other team," Allie said.

"Pay up," said Dara.

Standard reached into his wallet.

"Wait," he said. "Exclusively?"

"Yes," said Lewis.

Standard counted out some bills and gave them to Dara.

"Now I'm insulted."

"Don't be. Dara has enhanced gaydar."

"How it works," explained Perry, "is that if she finds a man attractive, he's either gay or married. When she didn't see a ring on you, she figured it was the other."

"Shut the fuck up, Perry. I did not find Lewis attractive." She was blushing.

I took another look at Lewis, noticed his muscular arms, his solid jaw, firm butt. "I find him attractive," I said.

Lewis looked at me in a new way.

"He's with me," said Allie.

"Can we put this rom-com shit aside and save this magical goat of yours?" said Critter. "I'm freezing my felt fangs out here."

It was chilly. The James Creek, which would have been called a river back in Utah, a stream in Ohio, was gurgling along and sapping what little heat there was left.

Lewis led the way.

"Be vewy vewy qwuiet," I said.

And we were.

We walked carefully and quietly up the trail for about fifteen minutes before we heard the voices and saw the firelight through the trees.

I signaled for the others to spread out. No one understood my improvised hand signals, so in a bunch, we crept closer until we were just outside a clearing behind a thicket of bushes. I pressed my way forward, parting the plants until I could angle my face in to see what was happening.

The bonfire was big and mature. I deduced it had been started before the group arrived, tended by minions who'd no doubt later be murdered by

Artstar to show how evil she was in accordance with the stupidest movie trope ever. Really, I absolutely despise that trope. And it's played all the time. It totally ruined *Blade Runner 2049* for me, there when Jared Leto kills the replicant. *Ooooo, isn't he a baddie!* It's the reverse 'save the cat' moment—the 'kill the dog' scene, if you will, and it's stupid stupid stupid stupid. Stupid.

The newcomers were arranging themselves around the fire, positioning themselves in certain ways. Artstar was near the center fiddling with what looked like a large box in silhouette against the light. She lit a candle and then another and by their light I saw and a knife among other things I couldn't identify.

I pulled back and the gang followed me as I moved to farther cover to make a plan.

"Okay," I said. "I'll go to the left with Allie and Lewis. You guys go right. We're looking for Jerry, the goat. We'll meet back here in ten minutes."

"I don't want to go that way," said Critter. "There are bears out there."

"You want us to split up?" said Lewis. "What is this Scooby Doo?"

"Can I hang with you guys?" said Perry. "I'm really sick of you know who."

"Who put Tony in charge?" said Garrett.

"I want Lewis to come with me," said Dara. "For reasons."

"I want to go right," said Allie. "It's higher. Less mud. I'm ruining my shoes."

"I think we should go back to town," said Standard. "Get some black robes and then infiltrate the group, like in *The Ninth Gate*. Or was that *Eyes Wide Shut?*"

"Dammit!" I said as loud as I dared. "There's a life at stake."

That quieted them for an instant, but only an instant.

They all spoke at once and the noise was rising. I was losing control and we were going to be discovered.

Lewis finally waved his arms to quiet everyone down.

"This is stupid," he said. "We don't even know the goat is here."

That's when we heard him.

"Bleeeeemph. Bleeeeemph."

42

I POINTED RIGHT; the gang went right. Lewis and Allie followed me to the left. All it took to get some cooperation was a child in distress. I guess they weren't all bad.

"Bleeeeeemph! Bleeeeeeeeeeemph!"

We crept wide around the circle, crossing the trail toward the other side where the sound had come. A robed figure stood on the path as sentry, but their attention was directed toward the light where the ceremony was beginning.

I could hear Artstar "Places, places. Wardens take your positions. We shall soon begin!" What little murmuring there was slowed and stopped and we pulled back farther into the trees to avoid being noticed.

The tree cover was surprisingly thick and the going was rough. Brambles, ferns, rotting logs and mud, lots of mud, made passage slow and slurpy. This being Eugene, Lane County Oregon, it had rained recently and a lot. This moment of clear moonlit sky was the aberration. My feet were soaked up to my shins and my shoes were mostly potter's clay as I trudged forward. Lewis, a native, was having better luck. Allie was watching where I was failing and hopping from stump to log in an attempt to save her already ruined shoes.

I got my foot stuck in a surprisingly deep mud puddle. I signaled Lewis to scout ahead while I fought to pull my foot out. The suction was otherworldly and I envisioned demons from hell nervously chewing on my foot waiting in the underworld wings for their cue to join the rite. "I summon thee, oh, New Balance Nibbler, and Sock-Sucker, come to our soiree!"

"Hey Allie," I whispered. "I just thought of a joke about devils seeking soles instead souls. Want to hear it?"

"Didn't I just?"

"Oh. Yeah, okay."

"Do you need any help?"

"Nah." And no sooner had the word escaped my mouth than I fell face-splat forward into the muck.

It is an ancient soil, fine and strong. I wasn't kidding about the clay. I got a mouthful of suffocating china-worthy muck that I sucked up my nose. It found paths into my ears, and oh, yeah, tried to smother me outright.

When I was growing up, I saw a lot of cartoons about quicksand and expected it to be a much bigger problem in life than it turned out to be. I'd kind of been disappointed by how little quicksand there actually was in middle-class American suburbia, but I had some now and my quick thinking child's brain immediately knew what to do. I reached out for a vine that was invariably just inches beyond my reach. I'd have to kick and fight, and nearly slide all the way down to doom, only my eyes and nose still above the surface, but just at the last moment, the nick of time, I'd grab it. A few moments of hard pulling later, I'd be on the shore, probably surrounded by spear welding cannibals, but I'd be out of the quicksand. I knew what to do.

There was no vine of course. Instead I rolled over and spat mud out my mouth and scraped it out of my eyes. I slithered on my stomach to higher ground and then tried to stand.

My shoes were gone. My socks a memory. My pants looked like I'd shit them for a year, and my shirt looked like it had tried an unsuccessful intervention to save my pants and got the worst of it.

"You look like shit," said Allie, confirming what I already felt.

I took a step forward and realized I could hardly move. I was wearing a half ton of Oregon's finest silt.

"What happened to you?" It was Lewis. "I was only gone two minutes. Tops."

"That long?"

"What are we going to do?" asked Allie.

"There's a table with extra robes on them. I grabbed a couple," said Lewis, holding them out.

"Hallelujah," I said. "Maybe there is a god."

"Which one?" said Allie.

"Let's see, this is the Coven, so Baphomet?"

"Sure, let's go with that."

Artstar's voice rose from the clearing and carried. "Oh Cernunnos, horned god of the Underworld, hear our prayers!"

"Or Cernunnos," said Allie.

I began stripping my clothes off. Allie, and Lewis wiggled into the robes.

"Stan is going to be so pleased when he sees us," said Allie. "This was his plan, right?"

"He'll be insufferable."

Once my muddy clothes were off, I felt like a new man, newborn, naked, and three hundred pounds lighter because that's how much goddamn mud there was caked on my clothes. Newborn is a state of mind and all the mindfulness and meditation I've done has taught me that each moment is an opportunity for rebirth. One only has to slow down and—

"Bwwwaaaaaaaapph!"

"Cernunnos, our lives we would lengthen, our fates we would improve."

We couldn't see the circle from where we were, but the light from the bonfire flickered above us in the treetops. Jerry's plaintive call had come from where that light was.

Lewis and Allie moved toward to circle and I, still fumbling with my robe, followed, finding every sharp stick and bramble branch with my bare feet and buttocks. I bit my tongue to keep from screaming as new scrapes and stabs decorated my chilled flesh.

We paused just at the tree line behind some bushes. The Coven held hands in a wide circle around the center altar and bonfire, where Artstar stood—her eyes which always dazzled, dazzling the brighter in the flickering firelight. Oh, to have those eyes. With her were three others, one held a knife, another a bowl, and a third, Jerry, his big floppy ears unmistakable.

"Hail Cernunnos, diablerie Cernunnos. Hail Cernunnos, diablerie Cernunnos." The chant rose like a miasma from the forest as the circle of robbed figures began to sway and then move in step counter clockwise.

To my horror, the three in the center moved, the one with Jerry pulled the little guy's head back, exposing his throat. The bowl was placed beneath that, and Artstar, with a wide flourish, took the knife.

The chant rose, the steps sped, the circle wove.

Across the way I could see Perry and Dara similarly placed just in the trees. Critter, Garrett and Standard were nowhere to be seen.

"Horned God!" called Artstar. "Horned God, Horned God of our ancestors, protector who thirsts. Let us bargain!" The knife came up.

Jerry bleeped, "Bwwaaaaa…"

A scream to our right, "Ahhhh," and "What the hell?"

There was Standard with the sentry guard that we'd snuck around before.

The circle paused mid-step, Artstar scanned the woods for what the commotion was.

The sentry, whose attention had been toward the circle, dropped his hood and turned to look at Standard.

Standard's reaction was to drop a karate chop on the man's bicep.

"Ouch!" the man yelled.

Standard grabbed the man's other shoulder and pinched it.

"The fuck?" he yelled and pushed Standard away.

"Was that an attempt at a Vulcan neck pinch?" asked Allie.

It was, but I didn't answer. Instead, with the distraction, I bolted into the circle, breaking my way in like some demented Red Rover player. In the center, I pushed Artstar down, knocking the knife out of her hands where it flew into fire. Without missing a step, I ripped the little goat from the hooded menace's grasp and broke the bowl with my knee. I used my momentum to carry me forward into the next line of witches, toward my gawking friends. The distraction of Standard's assault, the suddenness of my act, and the sheer shock of seeing a pasty naked middle-aged man charging through them bought me enough time to clear the Coven and make the tree line.

"Run!" I yelled.

Perry and Dara darted in opposite directions, Standard took to his heels. Allie and Lewis were out of sight, but I knew they'd make it out. I bushwhacked in the direction I hoped lay the parking lot and passed Critter and Garrett hiding behind a pine holding the tire iron from before.

I waved.

They waved back.

Jerry bawled.

Clouds covered the moon and the forest found a new level of darkness. I'd been cold before, but was warm and sweaty now, dripping perspiration from exertion and fear. When I paused to catch my breath, the air turned me into a pale popsicle with bleeding feet and body scratches.

Behind me I could hear the oncoming witches. "Stop them!" "He must suffer for this desecration!" "Curses!" "Curses!" I was a little disappointed by the shorthand there. I mean, they were witches, they should have been able to come up with something better than "curses." Maybe it was just a placeholder for now and they'd get around to boils and baldness later. Who knew? I guess I'd find out later. Later, being the operative word, if I was lucky.

I plowed forward, visions of countless horror movies playing in my mind —*Omega Man, Children of the Corn, Race with the Devil*. I tripped. I fell. I scratched my scrotum. I began to hallucinate.

"This way." It was John Smith's voice.

Having lost all sense of direction and having no better plan than to follow a disembodied voice, I followed the disembodied voice.

Jerry was surprisingly calm now. I'm not sure I'd have been able to hold him had he tried to escape. But he didn't. Such a chill trusting little guy.

I broke through the tree line, bleeding, freezing, scared to death. The sound of oncoming cultists sharp in my ears. I glanced back and saw dancing torch flames rushing toward me. Of course they had torches.

The Rivian was the closest vehicle. I sprint-limped toward it, giving the good ol' full Monty to the neckers in the Corolla.

We'd left the keys in the cars on Perry's paranoid suggestion and not for the first time did I appreciate my friends' insanity.

I swung my clammy butt into the vehicle, slid behind the wheel as Jerry leaped into the passenger seat taking shotgun like a boss.

I stared at the black screens. This was a modern car. All information is related to the driver through repurposed iPads. I tried to remember how to turn it on and recalled that I never actually knew.

From the forest came a flood of black-robed maniacs, orange torches and dark silhouettes. I had a vision of hornets attacking, not the nice ones from Utah, but the bald-faced bastards Oregon spawns in the mud around rivers. If you've ever met one of these guys, you won't forget it. They live in holes and are as territorial as they are vindictive. They sting first and second and third and never bother asking questions. They've been known to follow picnickers home to sting their babysitters, shoot out their porch lights before SWATing them from behind a VPN.

"Bwaaam! Bwaaam!"

"Couldn't agree more," I said.

I found the door locks and engaged them with a satisfying click just as the mass surrounded the car.

"Let's see..." I said as they pounded on the hood and tried the doors. "If I were a starter, where would I be?"

Someone smashed a torch against the windshield and all was orange sparks.

"We're going to kill you!"

"Spoilers," I said.

"You will suffer for this outrage!"

"What ever happened to do no harm?"

Rock meet glass and the back window exploded.

"I guess that's some other Wiccans, eh?"

"Bwaaaaamp."

The vehicle started. I would have preferred a throaty muscle car menace, over an electric hum, but I was grateful that the dash was lit.

"Warp speed, Mr. Crusher," I said.

"Bwaa, bwaa."

As I switched it into reverse, the center screen showed Mathias's minions in the way. I gave a quick tap of the horn, waited a beat, then floored it. They got the hint and dove for cover without me having to kill anyone. "Blessed be," I said.

I did my best Rockford bootlegger reverse into a forward spin, which looked more like a three-point turn, but in short order, as flaming torches landed all about the car, I was heading out of the park. In the rearview mirror, I saw the lights of the little bus turn on.

"You've got to be kidding me," I said.

"Bwwaa."

"Point taken."

I spat gravel back and raced toward the road wondering how far they'd chase me. As I did, I felt a certain calm that was unwarranted for the situation. It was as if I was at peace with the world and though challenges—deadly challenges—were set before me, I was composed. I'd even made jokes. I remembered struggling for half this much clarity in the endless sessions of meditation. Stress-induced enlightenment? Or maybe I was just in the groove of awareness. But not so aware that I saw the truck that T-boned me as I tried to join the highway.

I don't remember the truck itself, just the headlights to my left as time slowed to an impossible frame rate. There was a crash, airbags deployed and the big expensive electric SUV went head over tea kettle in a sidelong roll that lasted about a week.

I remember distinctly thinking, oh, this is happening. This sucks. And then, oh, this is still happening. I think it's worse now. I'm upside down. Oh, still here. Still happening. God, I wish I hadn't pulled into traffic just now. Still happening, there's Jerry trotting up the ceiling trying stay ahead of the roll. Look at the airbags. So many. Oh. Still happening. Still here. My side down now. Oh, look there's the road. Gravel and everything. Jerry's on me, sharp hooves trotting away. Can't wait for this to be over. Nope, not yet. Still happening. Sliding now, another turn. Hey, I'm back on the wheels. I wonder if Allie's okay. Is that glass in my arm? Still here. Oh, another turn happening. This is really going to slow me down. Good seat belts in this car. Very strong. Gravity shifting as the whole vehicle slides over on the passenger door. Ted's going to mad about this. I hope he doesn't take it out on Lewis. Lewis is a nice guy. He's too good for Barty-B. Jerry's airborne, his ears float. Weightless he flies, elephant style. Why do I not think Tuku killed Smith? Was that really John Smith in the forest? The car slows slides and stops, now everything is just long slow rocking back and forth as I hang sideways from the driver's seat. Don't have to worry about the broken window anymore. What's the sound? Sound everywhere. Is that the horn? My horn? It is the horn. It won't shut up. It's been blaring forever. I can't shut it off. Noise, noise, noise everywhere. Jerry bleats. He's landed on his feet like a horizontally-pupiled cat. Does that mean it's over and the next moment can come? Can I find a retreat into a memory or a future projection? Nope. This is the longest moment of my life. Now is it over? I really want it to be over. Do I really need to notice every cracked panel, every shard of glass, every drop of blood dripping from my arm in slow motion? Apparently I do. It's not over yet. Now? No. How about now? No. How about—. Nope, nope, nope. Still happening. Still here. Still in the crash. Yep. Here we are. I swear to god, it's been a year. Now? Nope. Now? Now, maybe? Nope.

43

IT WAS the car itself that called the police and fire department. I could have done it if I'd been able to find my phone, which I didn't have. I could have crocheted a call for help and trained a husky to deliver it across the tundra in the amount of time I hung there, suspended by the seat belt listening to the drone of the horn. I could have grown the cotton for the yarn, mined the minerals for the dye.

It was only after both my seat belt and the horn cable were cut that time even began to return to its normal progression. I climbed out of the wreck under my own power, though three men had to pry the door open for me to do it. Jerry skipped right out after me. One man was kind enough to give me a blanket, which I draped over my shoulders before being reminded that I was all-over naked and shifted the covering to include my man bits.

I told everyone I was fine but I asked several times who was president and if the climate thing had been fixed. My arm had a nasty patch of glass cuts and a nice man with blue hands helped with that while two not-so-nice ones led me into the back of an ambulance and quizzed me about drug use, family history of insanity, headaches, and hallucinations.

"Does hearing the voices of the dead people count?" I asked.

They thought so.

I was taken to a hospital in Springfield. Where shock and a kind doctor tucked me in for naptime which finally, blessedly, brought time to a blissful pause for a while.

———

I woke up with that wonderful disorientation that only comes from a trauma-induced sleep and hospital waking. I'm actually kind of familiar with it. Seeing the instruments of human repair was at now comforting and panic-inducing. I took in the white ceiling, cables, tubes, smells of disinfectant and human oozes, the humming of machines, the murmurs of staff, and was about to close my eyes again for another try at waking when I saw Allie watching me from a chair across the room.

"Hey stupid," she said.

"Yeah? Well, your hair is silly."

She brushed some behind her ear. Allie had magically straight auburn hair. She could no sooner mess it up, she could put curls in it.

"How do you feel?" she asked.

"Like I got hit by a truck."

"Funny you should say that."

"What did I miss?"

"The teenagers called the cops and they broke up the melee between the Coven and the gang. After you left, they chased us. We retreated to the river bank and were cut off. We took turns swinging the tire iron to find out who was the most intimidating."

"Who was it?"

"Garrett actually. Iron in one hand, Critter trash-talking on the other. They bought us time for the cops to arrive."

"Was Artstar arrested?"

"Oh no. She got a ticket though, for being in the park after hours. That'll teach her. So did Perry, by the way. His car. That'll teach him. The teens knew enough to book it out early to avoid the twenty-dollar fine."

"I got in an accident," I said.

"We saw the cleanup as we left. You got smashed by a Toyota pickup doing eighty in a fifty-five. Not a scratch on the other driver. You had no business joining traffic, but he got the ticket. His POS was totaled by the flat tire. The Rivian, maybe not. Takes a lot to total a car that expensive."

"Bully for me."

"But you probably did."

"Bully."

"You saved Jerry. I collected him from the wrecking company. He could have run away but he stuck around, like he knew I'd come for him. He was in good spirits."

"Tough little goat."

"Streaking through the middle of a satanic sacrifice was the perfect amount of shock and awe to get the job done. Who'd have thunk?"

"You have to use the tools you have, right?"

She rose and came over. Puckering up, she hesitated to kiss me, looking over my forehead with some concern. I puckered and the kiss landed there, tenderly, on my lips.

"Why the hesitation?" I asked but had figured it out before the words had left my mouth. "How bad am I?"

"No broken bones," she said. "Lots of bruises. *Lots* of scratches. You split the stitches on your head from before. They replaced those. Your feet are messed up from all the thorns you walked on. Your elbow looked like hamburger meat, but you didn't need stitches there. Lots of little cuts we think came from the driver's side window breaking."

"I remember it well," I said wishing I didn't. "So why the hesitation? What's on my face?"

"No concussion, though the medics said you were acting disoriented."

"That's just me."

"Yeah and being naked didn't help."

"So..."

"You're still on pain meds," she said.

She was holding back, probably for my own good. Still, I reached up to feel my brow when I saw my arm was encased in white bandages.

"What's all this?"

My other arm was too. I lifted the sheet. I was mummified.

"Allie, what's going on?"

"The bandages are just so the ointment doesn't ruin the sheets."

"Ointment for what?" Then it hit me, or rather it crawled down my legs, coiled up my back, scratched at my neck, tickled my taint like a coming storm. The promise of hell. The coming itching hell. "Poison oak."

"Head to foot, and even the places you really don't want it to be."

"Not again," I recalled my previous encounter with this noxious weed and wanted to cry.

"The witches and warlocks were thwarted though. You saved the day."

"But their curses worked," I mused. "Boils it is."

"Sorry sweetie." She kissed me again, really lightly.

"Pain pills are working," I said. "I do feel kinda funky."

"You slept a long time. You missed the morning conference."

A niggling feeling came over me then. In my state, I was aware that it could have been the raging rash all over my body, but I suddenly got the terrible tickling sensation that I had to get back to the conclave and fast.

"I have to get back to the conclave, and fast," I said. "Can I leave?"

"Do you want to?"

"Hospitals are expensive."

"Ted's already taken care of it. You're good for days."

"Really? Why?"

"Because he's a nice guy, Tony," Allie said. "Like you, he has a temper sometimes, acts out, and is an ass, but deep down inside he's nice."

"I dick-punched a Nazi who was interfering with a friend's act."

"And he slapped an ungrateful interloper who was interfering with his friends' acts."

She was right. There was a parallel between the unforgivable slap he threw at me and my nightclub antics that led me here. The rest was probably —no, definitely, mostly jealousy.

"Tell him, thanks."

"You can do that," she said.

"I still have to get to the conference."

"Why the rush?"

The question brought to my mind John Smith's serene face. It wasn't a spectral vision, not auditory like the previous night's possible poison-oak-induced sound hallucination, but the idea of the man, his desire for people to be safe, to save many lives, and for Sylvia to have closure, was an over-whelming idea I had to act upon.

"I gotta get back for Sylvia and for...something else."

"You've got the mystery figured out, haven't you?"

"Why do you say that?"

"You've never solved a case where you weren't in bandages. Look at you now."

"True that, but there's something else."

"What?"

"Something urgent." I wanted to tell her that Smith was filling me with fear of death, but I couldn't. Pain pills and analgesic creams play chemical hell with the little gray cells. Instead, I said only, "I don't know." Which was true. I didn't know. I felt.

"That's also a sign of nearing the end," Allie said. "This is how you act when all the pieces are falling together."

"I'm working on it, but this feels different. It's something else. Let's go. Where are my clothes?"

"Ruined, unless you want to chisel them out of the block of clay they formed when you left them in the forest. I got you clothes from the room. They're not clean, but it was the best you had. They smell like incense and perfume."

I'm glad that that was all they smelled like. She handed me the clothes I'd had on during my orgy shopping night.

"I got your phone though." She handed it to me. It had dried mud on it, and was dead.

"You had a call from Sylvia," she said.

"Urgent?"

She shrugged. "Dunno. I just saw it on the screen before it conked out."

"Help me get dressed."

It's not very often I exit a hospital not against doctor's orders, so things went smoother than usual.

"If the itching gets too bad, you can come back and we can help."

"How?"

"Put you out, so you can get a night's sleep."

Allie pondered what kind of god would put a plant on the earth that required an induced coma after contact with it as a Ridez arrived to take us back to the Eugene Squire Resort.

"You're working under the assumption that God is benevolent," I said. "There really isn't a lot of proof for that."

"Don't say that."

"Religion is a myth we want to believe."

"Don't say that either," she said. "Let's just enjoy the ride." She gripped my hand and smiled at me, taking me in like a tourist.

It occurred to me that Allie must have been through hell the night before. Chased by a satanic mob and then rounding a corner and seeing the vehicle I was last seen in twisted into bloodied scrap metal. She'd not said anything, but she'd been with me all night, and that look was long and meaningful. She was glad to be alive, she was glad also that I was.

"I love you too," I said.

I sometimes stumbled on that phrase. I'd said it many times to her, and I'd always meant it, but it also carried with it an unfulfilled promise I was unwilling to commit to. This time was better somehow.

"We got this," I said and snuggled up to her. Snuggling, by the way, rocks! If you're not a snuggler, your relationship is always incomplete. Learn how to snuggle. Guys really respond to snuggling. Really. Ladies, snuggle. Please.

The clouds were back, the rain had returned. It went from misting to raining, back and again in the course of a half mile as if a noncommittal atmosphere was trying on new clothes. Rounding a corner near the hotel, the heavens let loose in a burst, which was appropriate because we had driven into another riot.

It had been a protest. I could tell by the rain-smeared signs: 'Go home Nazi!' 'Snowflakes grow up!' 'White supremacy is the enemy,' 'Be proud of who you are!' 'Bring back Seinfeld.' 'Meat is murder.' 'Bacon is delicious, eat pigs'—a picture of porcine policeman on that one. 'Save the earth; slug a Nazi.' 'My pronouns are "fuck off."' Real classy stuff that had somehow turned free speech into a free-for-all as scrum spreading out from the center. I recognized the BRA boys and also some Green Tomorrow people among the masses. The affiliated groups were the minority though. Most of the people looked like everyday folk, not wearing matching tee shirts or shaved heads. The right wing was decidedly outnumbered. The scrum, which might have been going on for a while, favored them for now but the left, in Eugene at least, knew how to fight and riot like the best of them. The tide would soon turn by sheer numbers as incensed latte-sipping hipsters found designer cudgels and put them to use. And then, if this wasn't contained soon, I had little doubt the violence would spread to the city and shops would go down and cars go up. If it did, there were plenty of news people there with cameras to record it and share the mayhem across the world.

On cue, thunder rolled and rain fell in buckets as the police arrived in newly surplus military vehicles. They poured out bristling with teargas launchers, nightsticks, and shields. They set up a phalanx and waited, rain running down their helmets. The scrum went on but protestors nearby who'd noticed the new arrivals began to prudently melt away.

An ambulance blared and forced its way through the masses. Hats off to our drivers who drove down the center of that melee and through it to the front of the hotel to let us out.

"Oh, shit," I said.

"Used to it," she said.

Allie and I got inside the building just as a sedan pulled up and Detective Johnson got out. He looked at me and shook his head. "Oh, all's well now," he said. "The soggy mummy has arrived. We're saved."

I was still in all-over body bandages. My jeans, tee shirt, and sandals did little to make me look otherwise. My face was exposed and would have been white splotches of ointment if the rain hadn't washed it away. The rising red rash there was probably worse.

"Hi, how ya doin'?" I said and offered him my bandaged hand.

He shook his head. "I really want to hear all about what happened to you," he said. "I need to be cheered up sometimes, but not now. Stay out of my way, Flaner." He pushed past us and went inside.

"You heard the man," I said. "Let's get in his way."

"That's how I heard it too," said Allie.

Leaving the rain and riot behind us, we followed the detective inside. Worried employees pointed him along until we all saw ambulance people standing outside the door to the stairwell.

Johnson marched forward, the EMTs moved aside for him. We came behind like we belonged.

Inside, the first thing I saw was Ted Tessner squatting against a well, his face wet with tears. The next thing I saw was his assistant Rachael lying upside down on the steps, her hair wet with blood.

44

THE EMTS STOOD awkwardly by with sheepish expressions, embarrassed perhaps, that they'd been unable to help her. Johnson took in the scene for a long still moment. I could hear Allie's breath catch.

"I got this," I said.

She nodded and went back into the lobby.

My speaking drew everyone's attention away from the horror of the stairs. I had seconds to act before Johnson tossed me out.

I walked over to Ted and kneeled next to him. He looked up at me with soaked eyes. I looked back and felt his pain wash over me like a salty ocean wave. Wordlessly, I put my arm around him. He hesitated just a moment then fell into my shoulder and sobbed. Snuggling is magical.

Johnson watched this happen, his expression softening. He turned back to the body and took a few pictures with his phone.

Tessner's sobs took on a new level of urgency and Johnson nodded for the EMTs to do something.

"Come on, Mr. Tessner," said one. "Let's leave the detectives to do their work."

He reluctantly let go of me and stood up. He looked lost and broken and I nearly cried myself, not for Rachael but for Ted. For all of us.

"It'll be okay," I said. "Eventually."

Without a word, he followed the EMTs out the way Allie had gone. The door shut.

"She was struck from behind," I said. "Fell face forward. Made no attempt to break her fall. See how her arms are?"

I expected a tirade, but Johnson nodded instead. "Blunt force trauma on the back of the head. Square. Deep. There's water on the steps which might suggest one of the rioters from outside came in to do it."

I hadn't noticed that. There were indeed small puddles drying up fast. I thought of the cameras in the lobby and remembered this was a blind spot.

"The victim isn't wet. It couldn't have been her."

"Yeah."

"I don't see her iPad," I said. "She always carried an iPad. It was an extension of her arm."

"Maybe it's under her."

I bent down and looked. "Don't see it."

Johnson took a step back on the landing to see the stairs and the door at once. "She was just coming down, about to enter the lobby. That's the last turn where she got hit," he said. "She knew the protest was happening and getting heated. She had to. It's been happening for hours. Wouldn't that put you on guard? Screaming people outside your door? Wouldn't you notice a stranger in the stairwell? Would you turn your back on them?"

"She struck me as a trusting person," I said, "but not stupid."

"If the wound had been on the front..." he said. "With the missing iPad..."

"Random theft."

"Could still be."

"Smith was the same," I said.

"How's that?"

"Remember he was shot in the back. He too turned away from his killer."

"Well...he knew Tuku. He had no reason to think the man was going to shoot him."

"Then who killed Rachael? And why?"

He regarded me a moment. "You really don't think it was Adam Tuku?"

"If it makes you feel better, I think he killed himself, but I'm not convinced about COTTEO."

"What's COTTEO?"

"The Church of the Third Eye Opened. Smith's group."

"Can you prove it wasn't Tuku?" He was asking, not accusing.

"Maybe."

"How?"

"I dunno. Stuff and things. Clues, probably."

He rubbed his temples. A forensics team arrived, people with paper booties, disposable gowns, masks, and blue gloves. Fogged goggles.

"Flaner, that's your cue," said Detective Johnson. "Bye."

I took one more look at the face-down woman and ground my teeth. Four deaths this week and all I had to show for it was saving a single minia-ture goat with ears that would shame Dumbo. It was something, one life saved. Just one. Sure didn't seem like a lot just then.

I moved into the hall, past the EMTs who admired my bandaging, and into the lobby. I was starving and upset. In my pocket, I found some candy and ate all of it. It wasn't enough.

Allie and Ted sat together in a quiet corner. For the first time, I did not feel jealousy when I looked at them together, and when Allie opened her arms and he fell into them crying, I was glad she was there.

I caught myself beginning to cry, out of sympathy or maybe a break in the dam I'd erected to work a case and not just mourn the dead. It took all I had to swallow it back.

The protest/riot seemed to be ending. The rain was hard and cold and the drops big as duck eggs. Under the awning, outside by the driveway, police had cornered Augustus Klept on one side and Kaisa Woods on the other. Several plainclothes people were with each group. They seemed to be interviewing the ring leaders.

I closed my eyes and took a deep breath. Two in, one out, a trick I learned to calm myself. It sometimes even worked. When I opened my eyes a few moments later, I felt better, calmer, clearer, still sad and frustrated with the murders, but able to move forward. My face began to itch and I scratched it for a minute before remembering not to.

Sylvia stood beside me. I'd not seen her approach, probably because of my eyes being shut, nor heard her, possibly for the cloudburst.

"Hi," she said. "What happened to you?"

"Livestock roundup gone bad."

"What's going on with Ted?" Even from this distance, across the wide lobby, it was clear the man was a mess.

"Let's sit down."

I found a couple chairs by the window, and in low tones told her about Rachael. Sylvia's face went still, her eyes stared through me, her breathing stuttered, slowed and then fell to the familiar four in, four out of a calming meditation.

I thought to ask her if she knew the double in and the slow out, but figured this wasn't the time. Instead, I waited.

"Is it related?" she said after a while.

"We don't know."

"That poor man," said Sylvia, looking at Tessner. He'd come to himself a bit. The waterworks were off, he'd wiped his face. Someone had brought him a glass of water with a whiskey chaser. Allie glanced at me with a sad expression. I returned it.

Sylvia's eyes fell on Kaisa and Klept. "This is supposed to have been a place to find common ground and peace, instead we get those goons."

"Do you know what happened?"

"Woods called a very public protest of Augustus's keynote." I looked at my watch. It was past four. The day had truly gotten away from me. "The keynote was at twelve thirty, right?"

"Yes, but the Green Tomorrow people and their allies blocked the door since eleven. Nobody coming in, nobody going out. Not a big deal since most conventioneers are staying at the hotel. Augustus got up, gave a speech calling for White people not to be shamed and to support their own interests. In all honesty, it was surprisingly low key. I expected a call for concentration camps. Instead he just painted the white patriarchy as a working social system that has served society well."

"Sorry, I missed it."

"It'll be on the app later."

"I really didn't mean I'm sorry I missed it. What do you call one Nazi giving a speech to a hundred people?"

"A hundred and one Nazis?"

"Yep."

"That's what the protestors thought. They burst into the hotel right when he finished, yelling slogan, taunts. I think someone had some red paint."

"How'd the BRA respond?"

"How do you think? They chased them out of the hotel *tout de suite* and then launched their counter-protest. They already had signs. If I didn't know better…"

"What?"

She looked at Kaisa out the window. I faced Klept. Both seemed calm and reasonable. I could tell the police were nearly done with them.

Sylvia said, "If I didn't know better, I'd think they'd planned it together?"

"Huh," I said.

Several black-robed people came inside escaping the rain. They saw me, gave me a look of hate, saw my rash, and smiled with satisfaction.

Agent Bruce Allenby came in. He at least had an umbrella. Staff pointed him to the stairwell.

"Did you get my call?"

"My phone died. Tell me it wasn't important."

"You tell me." She opened a laptop she'd had with her the whole time and I shook my head for not noticing it before. Then again, I'd not noticed her shoes. I looked at them. Yep, those were shoes. I giggled.

"What's so funny?"

"Your shoes?"

"What's wrong with my shoes?"

"You have them."

"That's funny?"

"It is to me now. For some reason."

She was at a banking website. She offered me the computer. I shook my head. "Explain like I'm five," I said. "What did you find?"

"Several of the other groups have made tax-deductible donations to us," she said. "Big ones and recently."

"How big."

"A million dollars each."

"How recently?"

"Within a week or on its way."

"Who?"

"Ted Tessner, for one," she said.

I thought about that. "I'm sure he made donations to each group. A sweetener to get them here. Plus, I think I heard that COTTEO was already his favorite."

"We're contracted to get a hundred thousand dollars for coming to ICOHEP."

That's the Interfaith Congress of Holistic Enlightened People for those of you playing at home, the cult conclave.

"That I knew about," she went on. "But there's a note to expect also another million dollars from that account in the coming weeks."

"Who else?"

"ACOG."

"These abbreviations are murder. Who is ACOG?"

"The Abundant Church of God. Reverend Bartalemuw Benson's outfit. A million this week."

"Is that it?"

"Brotherhood of Righteous Action." Sylvia pointed to Klept. "BORA for the crossword. Also this week."

"Also a million?"

"Also a million."

"Is that it?"

"There is a memo, like the one saying to expect the million for Mr. Tessner. This one says to expect a million this week."

"No idea who from?"

"That was all it said."

"Did the Tessner one say when to expect it?"

"Yes, within the quarter, but not that other one."

Just then, Josh, Sylvia's son, rushed over from the elevators. "Mom, Hannah's been arrested."

"For what?"

"She was in the protest. Cops grabbed her. Something about racial slurs, physical violence and brandishing a weapon."

"Give me strength," said Sylvia.

"You gotta go," I said.

"I'll see you tonight," she said and followed her son out of the hotel. They had to wait to exit, though, because all the rioters, er—revelers, were coming back now. Tie-dye everywhere in movement that reminded me of an electric stream. Against the gray day, the flashes of colors—yellow, orange, a violet deep enough to get lost in—struck me as extra vibrant.

"Tony."

I turned and saw no one.

Allie caught my eye and I went over. My feet seemed heavy. My skin crawled. I popped another pain pill.

"Hey, Ted," I said. "I am so so sorry."

"What a nightmare."

I sat down.

"Ted's thinking of canceling the rest of the conference," said Allie.

"What's the point?" he said. "The reason I organized it was for John and he didn't make it to day two. John…" He was on the verge of crying again, but he swallowed and shifted his color palette toward blue.

"I can't run this without Rachael," he said. "She was more than my campaign manager. She was my right hand, my soul. She's the only one who knows the app. No matter what else happens, I can't deliver the edited content to the streamers now. She's the editor. She's the director." He laughed a sad, broken laugh. "Least of my worries. Thousands in refunds. Refunds. Refunds. Refunds. Refunds. Refunds…"

"Tony."

I turned and looked, again there was no one.

"Who're all these people?" I asked, for indeed the flow of folks coming into the hotel had not diminished. I do not remember this many people being here at all.

Ted explained. "Green Tomorrow bought out the rest of day tickets. I heard she was offering them free for keynote to anyone who'd march with her. March? Jesus, can't people agree to be civil for one damn week? Week. Week. Week. We all agreed to hear each other out. Out. Out. Out. Out."

His electric blue auras shifted to green but were sliding toward red now.

"That's a fast-acting pill," I thought.

"Did someone kill Rachael to get to me? Kill John Smith? Adam Tuku?"

"Don't get paranoid," I said. "Not everyone is out to get you."

"Only takes one. One. One. One. One."

Allenby came out of the stairwell. He throbbed with light, orange, and blue. Green waves, crackling arcs. I could see his worry like a shadow even across the wide lobby. He glanced around the room and his face grew even grimmer as he noticed all the new people.

"Tony. It's serious."

"What's serious?"

"What are you looking at, Tony?" asked Allie.

"I'm looking at Allenby."

"Okay, who are you talking to? To. To. To."

"I'm not sure."

Ted leaned in close and looked at my eyes. Fractals formed around his head, like Allenby's auras but more mathematical.

"Tony, did you take anything?" Ted asked.

"I took a pain pill a minute ago."

"Tony. Get up. We have to hurry."

"You look like you're on mushrooms," Ted said.

"How can you tell?" asked Allie.

"I'm in the business."

"Oh right. Right. Right. Right. Right."

Ted again, "Tony. Tony. Tony, you probably need to lie down. Down. Down. Down."

"You need to get up and follow me," said the voice.

"I need to get up and follow him," I said.

Ted and Allie both traced my line of sight. "Who?" they asked.

I stood up, my legs wobbly, my vision glazing in radiant pulsing lights. A shimmering man waited for me to follow him. "Who else?" I said. "John Smith."

45

THE ROOM FOLDED, twisted, and erupted into levels of traced visions. Sounds echoed, amplified. My skin crawled in waves of itching made worse by the electricity emanating like a Tesla coil from my brain. Sound merged into color as Allie rose and spoke to me.

"Tony, what's going on with you?" she asked in yellow and pink.

"Synesthesia," I said. "It's real." Violet mist evaporating.

The candy I'd found in my pocket and eaten, I remembered, had been purloined from the treat table at Kaisa's party. One had probably been a solid hallucinogenic dose. The five I'd just consumed on an empty stomach mixing with the several melting prescription-strength painkillers I'd munched on like Pez, was probably the upper end of human tolerance. Somewhere around suicidal Hunter S. Thompson at a Grateful Dead show, or Terence McKenna on a Wednesday.

"Tony." The shimmering hallucination of the late John Smith beckoned me forward.

"You're not real," I said.

"What is real?" he responded.

"Good point."

The shape signaled me forward and I followed.

"Tony?" Allie speaking technicolor concern.

"I'm good," I said. "Hold on a second. I just gotta...do...do what, John?"

No answer. My hallucination was big on urgency but small on details.

He faded in and out. I was afraid of losing him. I'm not sure why.

I sat down and stared in the middle distance. Allie had left me alone, Ted was saying something, probably explaining to her what was happening. I didn't think Allie had ever done mushrooms. Or did I?

Agent Allenby came into focus. He was standing by the reception desk now. The ambulance was gone and with it Rachael. How long had I been sitting there? Had I seen the cleanup? Where was Detective Johnson?

The halls were empty now. People no doubt going to the afternoon classes. Allie was sitting across from me. Where had Ted gone?

"You've taken hallucinogens," Allie said in pastel green. "It'll pass. Go with it."

"A true trip sitter," I said. "Not that I know what that is."

"Right," she said. "Right. Right. Right." Green glowing light. "Right."

Allenby had moved. He was now by the doors to the banquet hall.

I tried to imagine what he was doing, what he was looking for. Lightning and lights all around him. A glow of urgency, the same kind that the now missing John had had.

I thought of my son back in Salt Lake and was overcome with emotion and started to cry. I loved that kid so much.

"Tony, focus. Not much time."

I opened my tear-moist eyes but saw nothing.

Allenby was gone.

Where had he gone?

I stood up and moved toward the banquet hall door, feeling my way forward as if I were in a stream and this is the way the current led me.

Reality and dreams flowed in and out of my control. Sometimes nearly overwhelmed by the trip, vertigo and dreamscapes of electric gnomes inviting me to linger. Other times, sitting at a distance, in a strange third-person limited perspective, I watched myself move with direction. At those times I was hyper-lucid. Ideas and worries of dangers and threats informed my steps which followed the flow deeper into the hotel.

Allenby sat at a table in the far corner. I could see his breath, sense his angst. He looked at me but didn't see me.

I waved. He was all waves.

I was out of body floating in a corner looking down on the tables. There was a déjà vu, and I remembered the same angle from Rachael's video.

I saw Adam Tuku, orange and black, those fucking hornets again, walk past me and through a far door. To the kitchen, I think. He left behind him a wake of rippling flashbacks.

A wake was like a flow. I followed.

The door swung both ways, I noticed as I entered the kitchen. Hell of a symbol, that, I said, as I watched myself trip harder than God.

"What is?"

It was Allie.

"The door swings both ways."

"Nice one," she said.

She glowed in the brightest green, and seeing her here now, nearly overcame me. Emotion and love swelled like an eruption. Tears formed and my legs nearly melted beneath me.

"Tony," came the voice of John Smith. "Stay with it."

"I gotta stay with it," I said to Allie.

"All good," she said and gave me a smile that threw me hard off balance with its power.

"Whoa there, cowboy," she said.

"I gotta stop looking at you. At least for now."

"Okay. So, where are we going?" she said excitedly as if we were exploring a new European city.

The waves led on past the tables where workers piled plates, cut vegetables, stared at us like we were wraiths.

"I never saw where Adam went after he disappeared into here," I said.

"Okay."

"But I know he went this way." At least the wake went that way and I followed it across the kitchen to a back door. No one stopped us. How do you stop a wraith with a spoon?

It was a concrete hallway, windowless. Doors on both sides. A service corridor, a place for the staff to pass through unseen on their way to other places. The afterlife in architecture. The wake went forward.

"Flaner?"

"Shhh," said Allie. "He's on a mission."

Allenby had joined us.

A lit exit sign showed an escape farther on. An unlit one pointed toward the employee elevator around a bend. The wake moved to a door marked *Air Conditioning*.

"Rachael said something about this," I said.

"What?" said Allenby.

"Tony, hurry."

"I'm working on it," I said.

I tried the door. It was locked. I wasn't flummoxed. I was high as a gale kite, but I wasn't flummoxed. I turned to look at the FBI agent and knew then why he was here. "Open this door, Bruce. I know you can." And I did. I knew he could. And I don't mean, kick it in. I knew he had a goddamn key that would open it as clearly as I knew my feet were just the tops of roots that extended to the center of the earth.

Allenby moved past Allie who watched with some surprise as he dug a ring of keys out of his pocket and opened the door.

"I already searched this room," he said.

"What were you searching for?" asked Allie.

He blushed, at least that's what Allie might have seen. I saw him burst in red sparking waves. "We didn't find anything," was his response.

I felt for the light switch I knew would be there and flicked it on. The room was full of heavy environmental machinery. They rumbled and vibrated while fans whirled and motors spun. I felt the vibrations of the machines in my bones like it was a bass speaker at a Deadmau5 concert.

"People still listening to deadmau5?" I asked.

"They broke up, I think," said Allie. "But I still listen to them."

"So not so dated?"

"It's current affairs compared to your usual references."

"I am the very model of a modern major general."

"And then we're back in the Stone Age."

"Fifties."

"Try the 1890s," said Allenby.

"Stone Age," said Allie.

"Shhhh, I'm communing with ghosts."

Allenby made to speak again, but Allie shushed him with a finger to her lips. I followed the motion in electric tracers as it flowed from her green radiating body to her auraed head.

"Tony. Up here."

The vibrations were gone—the ghostly vibrations of the air that had led me to this room, were gone, but the voice had returned and had come from the upper right wall in front of me.

I looked closer at the machines and the wall of lights and control knobs. It was old, not as old as my *Pirates of Penzance* joke, but not computer-age either. I saw that room had been mislabeled. There was a furnace in here. The air conditioner would be on the roof. The controls for both, however, were here, so maybe it all worked out.

It was a cold day and the industrial-sized heater was blowing warm into rooms with serious pressure which I felt in my condition as ants biting my already rashed body.

The upper right corner where the voice was had a large outgoing conduit.

"We need a ladder," I said.

Allenby was gone in a flash and I stood there alone with Allie and waited.

While we waited, Allie took my hand and even through the bandages, it felt like living lightning.

"Tony!"

"Where's Allenby?" I said.

"You sent him for a ladder," said Allie.

"No time. Tony. Now!"

I let go of her, it was not easy, and went to the furnace.

My mind focused on purpose and though my eyes were filled with fractals, and my body shook with fear and itching, I climbed like a mummied monkey to the top.

"Aren't you afraid of heights?" asked Allie.

"Don't remind me of that," I said. "Just…wait. Allie get the fuck out of here."

"What? Why?"

"Get out of here. Out of the hotel. Get everyone out. Right now."

"You're high."

"No I'm not."

"You're twelve feet physically and eight miles mentally."

"Great reference, but still…"

"Tony!"

The pieces had all come together in my mind. The timing, I would forever wonder about, but where and what and why, was clear as sunshine as I, hanging from one hand, my sandaled feet slipping on the metal sides of the machine, I ripped the duct off the wall and exposed the bomb.

"What's that?" asked Allie.

It was an orange bucket of alcohol, about half full. A reinforced handle curved over it. Hanging above the liquid was what looked like a large waxy tea bag, a coated bundle the size of a fist. It dangled menacingly by a last single thread of an otherwise severed piece of twine. It moved in the breeze my stuttered breath stirred up, and hovered over the bucket, rocking back and forth. Back and forth. Back and forth. Slipping down. Down.

An exposed circuit board was taped to the apex of the handle, a wire reaching up out of it. Under it were a pair of snapped-shut scissors attached to a servo connected to a square nine-volt battery. Kirkland brand.

Barely perceptible, back and forth, the bundle swung. My senses seeing molecules. Deeper and deeper the scissors cut, the waves a scent of danger.

Allenby burst in then accompanied by several white-aproned servers. They had a ladder.

"Jesus, God!" he proclaimed, seeing me and the hole and the bucket of doom. "Don't touch it!"

And in that moment, perhaps from the vibrations of his voice, or the tread of the steps, or the phase of the moon or fate, gravity and sharp metal conspired to cut the last thread of the half cut twine and send the bundle downward into the waiting pool.

And reality contracted again.

For the second time in as many days, an instant stretched toward eternity before me.

I existed in preternatural time, my eyes focused on the falling bag, a cascading line of tracers showing me its path, down and down and down.

All at once and all together and for all time, it seemed, I thought of death —my death here and now, and damned myself for every mean thing I'd ever done.

I thought of all the people in the hotel about to die, for I knew this would kill them all, and damned myself for being too slow.

I thought of my friends dead in their rooms and damned myself for not appreciating them more.

I thought of my son, Randy, my dear lovely son who I'd not talked to this week, and damned myself for being a bad father.

I thought of Allison Braise, my love, my future wife, glowing love-Chakra green, watching me from below, her life in my hands, my happiness in hers, and I caught the goddamned bag mid-air, a millimeter from the edge.

46

THE REST of the trip was pretty mellow. Policemen took me to the hospital, sirens and lights, where I was sent through sixteen de-contamination routines before being re-anointed with salve, re-bandaged with dressings, and offered a nice nap in an oxygen tent while my blood work came back and the tracers faded. My clothes were burned.

Allenby was nice enough to drive us back to the hotel. I met Allie in the car. It was after dark.

"Have a nice nap?" she asked me.

"Yes. And you?"

"Wonderful."

Allie got much the same treatment as I, but I think only five decontaminations. She got the nap though, which made me happy. She'd stayed up late the night before and needed some shut-eye.

"Methylphosphonyl difluoride," said Allenby, pulling into traffic.

"Gesundheit."

"That's what was in the satchel. It's a binary chemical agent. Sarin nerve gas," he explained. "The stuff that Japanese terrorist group used in the Tokyo subway."

"Ouch." I was not wholly sober yet. The lingering effects of the mushroom candy coursed through my veins and clotted my muscles. I wanted another nap. What I didn't want was someone to harsh my buzz. Nerve gas is a buzz harsher if ever there was one.

"The batch you grabbed can be traced to a Syrian stockpile. We got most of it, but it's been hell chasing the rest of it around."

"That's what you're really here for," said Allie. "Tony says you're on the terrorist squad. We wondered what you were doing in Eugene."

"Yes."

"And Ted," I said. "Don't forget the Tedster."

"That too."

"How close were we actually to being killed by it?" asked Allie, stoking the harsh.

"A millimeter," said Allenby. "The satchel contained the two elements for the reaction. Had it dropped into the alcohol the barrier between them would have been instantly melted away, the chemicals would have combined, reacted and filled the room with nerve gas to kill everyone there instantly, the whole hotel within a minute or two, and then linger waiting to kill anyone who came inside. It would have been the worst terrorist attack since 9/11. Comparable to Oklahoma City. No. Worse."

"Can we have some music?" I moaned. "Some Steely Dan would be good. Maybe The Doobie Brothers?"

Allenby glanced at me through the rearview mirror.

"The coating was effective at preventing contamination. It's how he transported it without sensors finding it. It's why you guys are clean."

"Enya?"

"So Tuku set a bomb to kill everyone in the hotel, but it didn't work?" asked Allie.

"It worked. The signal went out, the mechanism fired, but the string caught. It gave us time to find it."

"You mean for Tony to find it."

"Yeah, how'd you do that?"

I whimpered.

Allie said, "That's what the Homecoming people thought was going to happen when they locked the doors during Barty's speech."

"Yes. They didn't know what would happen, but they were certain they'd die then with everyone else, or as they put it, be 'translated on.' They were quite disappointed."

"King Gizzard and the Lizard Wizard would be perfect," I said. "Surely they're playing on some Eugene station right now. Can you look?"

"He's serious?"

"He's had a hard day."

Allenby fiddled with the radio station but Allie took out her phone and paired it to the Bluetooth. Soon the gelatinous chords of Jerry Garcia's guitar popped out of the speakers, soon to be joined in a little bit by the man himself. I smiled a deep spiritual smile and leaned back.

"And Tuku?" said Allie.

"He didn't wait for the gas. If he had, he'd have realized it hadn't worked. My feeling is he was a coward and shot himself rather than suffer the effects of the gas, which can be pretty harsh."

"Harsh is the operative word," I said.

"But he still killed himself, so he believed in what he was doing," said Allie.

"How's that?" asked Allenby.

Allie touched my bandaged hand. I saw it more than felt it. "It's something Tony has been pursuing, the nature of true believers and 'the real deal.'"

"I also think he wanted us to know that he's the one who killed Smith," said Allenby. "Using the missing gun cemented that."

"No it didn't," I said.

"What?"

I couldn't believe I was joining this conversation. "Tuku couldn't have done it."

"Why?"

"Because when Smith and Sangye were being killed he was planting the bomb to kill everyone else."

"How do you figure that?"

"Shhhhh," I said. "After this song."

Allenby shut up, and let the music play. Allie leaned over and kissed me softly. She knew as well as I did that this song was over thirty minutes long.

We arrived at the hotel long before it was done.

"Thanks for the lift."

We got out and found an empty lobby. For all the death and near death that hotel had hosted recently, it held its head high in snobbish tidiness and sparkling floors. "Welcome back Mr. Flaner," said Trevor at the desk.

Allie looked up from her phone. "Banquet with Kaisa Woods' keynote," she said.

"Food sounds good," I replied. "Let's go."

The hall too showed no signs of the near apocalypse I'd stopped. Probably for the best. At the hospital, Allenby had asked us not to talk about the bomb with anyone. He'd not made us sign anything, which was cool, but he had mentioned in passing that Gitmo was still operational, which was not so cool.

It was plated meals that night and so Allie disappeared to find a waiter while I found the gang at their usual table. Most people were politely watching Kaisa at the front. The few who noticed me, mummified, dressed in green hospital scrubs, understandably stared. The gang hadn't saved us seats, but a kind waiter, maybe sensing an ADA violation, summoned a pair and made everyone scootch over.

"Whatcha been up to, crasher?" said Standard.

"Saving ignorant animals from certain death," I said. "And rescuing a goat."

"Poison oak?" asked Perry.

I nodded.

Each of my friends showed me someplace on their bodies with a rash. Hand, neck, face, arm. Tongue. The last one was Critter.

"Lewis wanted us to let you know that the car was insured," said Dara.

"You talked to him?"

"Spent the day with him," she said. "We helped apply lotion on our poison oak."

"How'd that go?"

She smiled.

"But I thought..." said Standard.

"The wine and not the label."

"What does that mean?"

"It means you fall in love with the person, not their orientation," said Garrett. "Right?"

"Right," agreed Critter. "I heard it first on *Schitt's Creek*, but I think it's older."

"I missed that one," said Garrett.

"It's about love, not sex."

"Eh."

Kaisa's keynote had slides and so pictures of coral reefs and rainforest, arctic tundras, and savannas faded subtly in and out behind her as she spoke seeking converts to her cause.

"The planet has put us on notice," she said. "In times like this—critical, urgent times—the lines are clear. You're either with us or against us. 'Us,' being life on the planet."

"That's a hard sell," said Critter. He still sported the emotional support animal cape.

"To think there's still an argument over the climate issue," said Perry. "Absolutely ridiculous."

Allie joined us. "Steak for you. Mahi-mahi for me. On its way."

"Hardly an environmental meal," I said. "Shouldn't it be seaweed and road gravel?"

"She obviously didn't pick the menu," said Allie, gesturing to the sad white face of a baby seal behind the speaker.

"The dominant culture, let's call it white men, is in control," Kaisa said.

"Let's not," heckled Augustus Klept from the front. "Let's call it civilization."

Kaisa offered him a crocodile smile and went on.

"They know we're in trouble, but that doesn't matter. They face it with the only tools they have ever used, greed. They think money will buy them an exemption from extinction. They'll cheat and lie and kill—yes kill, to get richer at the cost of the planet. Good for them; not for the rest of us."

"They suck," said Perry.

"Don't they?" said Dara. "Don't get me started about them."

"Who's them again?" asked Standard.

"The simplest terms, in the most convenient definitions…" quoted Perry.

"*The Breakfast Club?*"

"Well caught," he bowed.

At the front of the room, I counted the usual suspects, Ted Tessner was here, Rachael notably not. Barty-B was at a table populated with septuagenarians. Artstar was back, which shocked me. Her table ringed in robed goat menacers. Donnopher were in attendance, sitting with their bodyguard and several runway-worthy groupies. Sylvia represented COTTEO sitting next to her son Josh. The others there looked like they were ready for a Buddhist retreat, lots of beads around necks. Sylvia's daughter, Hannah, was not with them, but she was out of jail. She was with Klept at the BRA table. The Messenger's group looked like a D&D game could break out at any minute. But by far, the greatest collection of followers was for Green Tomorrow. Handing out free tickets was a good idea. Getting them to riot to piss off the neo-Nazi hate group, probably also a good idea.

"Ted Tessner is speaking tomorrow night," said Dara. "For the closing event. Media will be in attendance. That's interesting." She was reading from her phone. "Donnopher was scheduled for tomorrow afternoon, but took COTTEO's slot earlier so it's empty. Just another buffet. Anybody else ready to go home?"

"The price of life is measured in dollars to these people. They have no qualms in murder to line their pockets. We just lost two activists in Brazil. I'd just talked to them right…" Her voice broke. She turned away to wipe her face. After a moment of grief felt by the entire room, she turned and went on.

"The fate of our rainforest initiative there is now very much in peril. I need your help to save those woods. Don't let it become another Siku plains, where last year, after the disappearances of five Arctic activists working with us, big petrol gained the rights to drill practically without oversight."

"She makes me pine for The Messenger's aliens," said Standard. "At least they'll be quick, right?"

"Oh no," said Perry. "Slavery for everyone."

"Unless you've slept with Marshall," said Allie.

"Don't say that. I'm trying to forget."

"All these people have scary stories and nasty underbellies," I said as my steak arrived.

"You need help with those bandages?" said Garrett. He reached over and exposed my lips so I wouldn't be eating medicated gauze all night.

"Thanks."

"We're leaving tomorrow then," said Dara. "I'm sick of this fucking place."

Perry argued to stay. "But…but…but…"

"All good points," said Critter. "Would you like to respond, Dara Darling?"

"I'll fucking end you. Don't call me darling."

"We paid for it," said Standard. "We must receive consideration for our money."

"You doing homeschool economics again?" I asked.

"Maybe."

"I think you'll get a refund. At least partial," said Allie. "It doesn't look like the online stuff will be done."

"Why?"

"Rachael."

"What about her?"

Allie and I shared a look. It made sense. No need to advertise yet another high-profile murder, even if the high-profile person was a low-profile person.

Allie gave them the rough outline as I ate. My stomach felt like a new organ, reborn and experimenting with solid food for the first time. It approved.

"It's not all bad news," said Kaisa from the front. "I'd be remiss if I didn't also share with you the advances we've made. There is hope. There is goodness. There is generosity."

"That's fucking terrible," said Dara. "Who'd want to kill that nice English lady?"

"The IRA," said Standard

We all stared.

"What? Centuries of bad blood there."

"If we're polling countries that have a grudge against England," said Garrett. "We're going to have a lot of suspects."

Critter nodded in agreement. "The sun will never go down on the number of suspects we'll have," he said.

"Woods Water is bringing in significant funds to Green Tomorrow."

I looked up and saw a big close-up of her face on the label of a plastic water bottle. Clear, moss-free for the picture. Must have been Photoshopped.

"So far this year, we've made over two million dollars from Brazil alone, just in this first quarter. The people in Brazil are generous and understand the need to support the efforts that support them."

Applause.

"I thought Brazil was poor?" said Standard.

"Don't generalize," said Perry. "People who do that, all suck."

"Tony, you're ready to get the hell out of you, aren't you?" asked Dara.

I ignored her.

"Well, screw you then. You didn't come with us anyway. You're on someone else's dime."

"That argues to stay," said Standard. "Let's get our money's worth. There's a lot of buzz about Tessner's speech tomorrow."

"What buzz?"

"Buzz."

"I think he means the notice about media in attendance," said Garrett.

The last of the electric drugs coalesced in my forehead, the very place where the third eye is said to reside. I noticed this and smiled in warm appreciation as if watching a shadow play formed in fractured holograms shone into my skull. I, a witness to my own thinking. You had to be there, I guess. But still, patterns were forming, ideas, strings coming taught.

Allie's fish was gone and she was working on her potatoes and carrots. She looked up at me, concern in her eyes. Then, slowly, a twinkle, as the corner of her mouth plucked into a smile.

"You two aren't just getting back from the hospital?" said Critter.

"You said he wasn't hurt."

"No we got back earlier," said Allie, watching me. "We went back though, after we defused a bomb."

"Oh is that all?"

"And we listened to the Grateful Dead."

"Which one?" asked Critter.

"Nassau Coliseum, November 1, 1979."

"Fire on the Mountain?"

"Yep."

"Great song."

"It's wonderful."

I listened for the otherworldly voice of John Smith, wondering if I wasn't on the verge of another full-on hallucination, but none was there. I was alone. I might be chemically impaired or more accurately, chemically enhanced, but it was all me. The ideas and connections that fit like four-dimensional puzzle pieces were shaped from my own experiences, things I'd witnessed, heard, and connected. In short, the clues were coming together. Fair play.

"Allie, back me up here," said Dara. "It's time to blow this chicken stand."

"Chicken stand?" said Perry. "Where's that reference from?"

"My ass. I want to sleep in my own bed again. I'm sick of these freaks." She said the last bit surprisingly loud I noticed, but not enough to shake me away.

"We can't leave yet," said Allie.

"Why not?"

"Tony hasn't solved the case yet."

I smiled at her.

"Oh. No wait," she said. "He has."

47

PEOPLE BEGAN ARRIVING for the Saturday afternoon keynote right after the end of morning classes. There was a half hour break but seating was in demand. Early that morning, the app had sent out the message of a replacement lunch speaker, *The Real Deal Tony Flaner, injured detective*. The title was my suggestion, one of the top contenders for the name of my comedy show if I ever got around to putting one together. I'd already had business cards made. The speech title was *I've been working on it*, and promised to reveal the killer stalking the conference. *ICOHEP is all about truth*, it read. *Come get some.*

The line to get in was long. The problem being there was only one door open and that door was warded by the handsome Matt Hansom, Donnopher's own bodyguard. He was backed up by half a dozen private security guards the hotel had finally got around to hiring—four bodies too late. Hansom's physique and warm Hollywood smile made the line a little more bearable, the metal detector a little more palpable, and the paperwork a little more doable. That's right, to attend my keynote one had to sign an industrial-strength NDA made specially for me by Dmitri Lewandowski, from the law firm of Lewandowski, Drabitovitz, Kovatz, Nozadze, and Hansen. It was eighteen pages long. We had three tables of notaries to witness the signings, collect and hand out claim tickets for cell phones. I was taking no chances. I'd seen the state of comedy today.

I'd stayed up late doing research and preparing my talk. I only had notes; I'd have to improv some. Allie would keep me straight on time and run the AV. We needed to remember to allow time at the end for questions. I'd surreptitiously and blatantly arranged for all the persons of interest to be there. Persons of interest is the kind of thing legitimate detectives say, and I had a note to use it in my speech somewhere to add credibility.

It was a Mexican buffet, with taco fixings, hard and soft shells, several kinds of beans, pico de gallo, salsa. Guacamole. The gang, for once, occupied a table close to the stage, the very one reserved for Ted Tessner. He'd been less than thrilled with my idea for such a public airing of the conference's horrors, but when I told him that if he denied me, it would look worse, he relented. My theory of Tessner's ambitions played well there.

"Is there something untoward about a Mexican buffet?" asked Standard. "Is that cultural appropriation to have it here, in Oregon, at a resort? To serve it at a buffet, also known as a smorgasbord?"

"Some people no doubt would say it was wrong," said Dara, "but fuck those people. Tacos rock."

My face was rashy, my scalp still stitched up, but Allie had stripped me of most of my visible bandages and I could sport a long-sleeved shirt and slacks without looking like Imhotep in disguise. I still had mediated maxi pads all over underneath, but they didn't show if I kept my pants on. I made a note to keep my pants on.

"Good idea," said Perry, reading over my shoulder. "Bert Kreischer can do the no-shirt thing, but even that's iffy. Not certain you've got the legs to one-up him."

"Do what feels right, honey," said Allie. God, I loved that woman.

"You do have great calves," said Critter, still in his cape. Garrett looked at him shocked. "What? You never noticed? He does."

"Thanks." Sometimes I worried about those two, but they seemed to get along, so...

Across the table from them, Tessner, watched the exchange with tired glassy eyes. He'd had a hard week.

Lewis checked in with us to see how I was doing, two plates of tacos balanced with an iced tea in his hands.

"Make room," I said to Ted who seemed surprised to hear his name. He scooted over and Perry brought another chair. Lewis sat down with us. "I'm good, are you good?" I asked.

"Did I sign what I think I signed?"

"Yes. But I owe you one. I could find another way."

"Nah, I'm good," he said. "We're here for truth."

"The tagline is *envisioning the future direction of humanity*," said Ted.

"Let's put that one aside after everything that's happened? Go with *we're here for truth*."

He thought about it. "Smith would agree. Okay, truth it is." Ted bit into a taco and the hard shell exploded in his mouth, dumping meat and cheese and salsa and lettuce all down his lap. He sighed resignedly and just picked up another taco and bit, careful to eat this one over his plate. It exploded too.

"Hard shell tacos are an American invention," said Standard. "A way to use stale tortillas. Maximize profit."

We thought about this and munched on. The room filled with convention goers confused about the forms, but happy about tacos. Who doesn't love tacos?

Artstar waved at us from her Coven table of witches and warlocks suggesting there were no hard feelings. Her eyes dazzling as before. Bully for her. Augustus Klept's gang of skinheads glared on. When Hannah arrived, slurringly drunk, spilling nachos on the floor, they were unable to make room for her and she staggered to the back. Sylvia from the COTTEO table watched with real worry in her eyes. She sent Josh to help her. She smiled wanly at me, sad but strong. I really liked her, if you haven't figured that out.

The Abundant Church of God, led by the Reverend Bartalemuw Benson took their usual table but cast suspicious glances at ours. The Messenger had arrived and hunted over our heads for his table, found it, dropped his plate and then went back for more.

Peaches waved at us from the Green Tomorrow table. It was packed and overflowed into all the adjacent ones. More free tickets. Kaisa had bought out the rest of the conference when she heard Augustus was trying to do it. She now handed out bottles of water with her picture on the label as if they were rifles before an assault. Her group cast menacing glances at the BRA boys, but also to all the other groups, sizing them up. Peaches raised her hands questionably when she saw Richard Moensis, the comic from Funny on Fifth sitting by the stage with a sheaf of papers. Standard signaled her he didn't know. He didn't. No one did but me, not all of it anyway.

Donnopher's table had some new faces, a young adult actress starring in a new fantasy series with swords and shotguns on Hulu, and a director who specialized in cars blowing up. His current record, if I recall, was 355 in his last movie. Donnopher pointed me out to him. I smiled. He didn't.

There was a good splash of orange jumpsuits again. It was like old times. Though their leader Adam Tuku had 'translated on' his disciples had been released from custody, and probably having nothing else to do, their day timers alarmingly empty after this week, decided to come to my keynote. They looked so lost, so confused, so disappointed.

"Put a suicide watch on table three," I said, half joking.

"Dumb fucks," said Dara.

"True believers," I said.

"But not the real deal," added Allie. Did I tell you I loved that woman?

Agent Allenby caught my eye from where he sat with Detective Johnson and two plainclothes policemen who might as well have been wearing spinning red-light hats for how discreet they were. They looked like fancy-dressed Michelin men with their flack jackets bulging under their shirts. They didn't dare eat a single bite of their delicious untouched tacos for fear of shooting a button across the room. Detective Johnson had been royally pissed about my plan, demanding to have the spoilers before I started, but I'd held tough, and told him he wasn't invited if he was going to be that way. Allenby, who'd done some research on me, knew my style and convinced him to come.

The last people got through the line and Matt Hanson rejoined Donnopher's table, flexing as inconspicuously as he could when he passed the director's eyeline.

My tacos were gone. My three flans were history. The gang was getting restless. Allie looked at her watch. "If you want to be done by classes," she said. "Time to get started."

"Richard," I called. "Richard Moensis." The comic looked up. "You're on."

He straightened his shirt and took the microphone off the podium.

"Is this thing on? What's with all the rain in Eugene, am I right? This place should be called, 'Don't live here, it's damn depressing' am I right." No laughs. "Maybe I'll start a petition."

Crickets.

He cleared his throat and brought the papers up where he could read them. "Possible trigger warnings; R-rated cursing, monetary disadvantage, mild to mid-level gender differences, death in the background and foreground and side grounds—all around. Murder, suicide, disease with lingering side-effects, car crashes, street violence, violence to groins, endangered small animals, tacos. Reference to religion—lots of that. Drug use, including hallucinogens, marijuana, caffeine, alcohol, sugar and aspirin. Ableism in vocabulary, sense of humor, cultural references, emotional maturity and general literacy. Adult themes such as greed, the environmental crisis, racism, fame, glory, extraterrestrial visitation, the FBI, demonic spirits, sleep depravation, group sex, gay sex, unprotected sex, adulterous sex, religious sects. Rivalries, school lunches, recess trauma, airports, airport food, airport delays, airport security, airport restrooms, airport restaurants, airport escalators, airport shoeshine people and the lack thereof. Politics, cultural differences between city and country, left and right, up and down, between and through. Prejudice against different people, stupid people, shallow people and murdering people, as defined by personal interpretation of the speaker, and there might be mention of kale, and a possible fart joke."

It was a good bit, social satire and callbacks all working together, but it was also prudent. I was about to make a lot of powerful people angry, reveal things not wanting to be revealed, and challenging the beliefs of everyone in the room. Just for added effect, I arranged for a prop to be brought up.

As the eaters finished eating, hard shell tacos exploding like fireworks around the room—lettuce showering like confetti, cheese bursting like tracers—a small card table was brought to the stage by hotel servers.

Curious stares and spilled salsa greeted the happenings, the trigger warning list doubtlessly replaying in everyone's minds. Was this the fart joke?

After a red tablecloth was carefully spread and the table dusted by a waiter in white gloves, they left and I stood up. I winked at my friends and cast a look to Sylvia at her table, who gave me one of The The's uncertain smiles. I returned it before lifting the duffel bag I'd stashed under my table and climbing the stage. Allie woke a new iPad and triggered the projector.

Immediately my face appeared on the wall behind me—my headshot, professionally taken. Watermark in the corner. Then the camera feed and angle shifted to me at the podium in an infinite repeating effect like standing between faced mirrors. It was trippy. I was right at home.

I paused for effect, waiting for everyone's attention to find me.

The room fell quiet.

Looking over the crowd, I saw the exits, recognized my prey, saw that the flan table was being restocked. I lifted the duffel for all to see and then took it to the table and began to unpack it. I took stacks of money bound in bank bands and made nice stacks of these. I then took loose bills and stacked a few of those an inch high, then kind of made a pile of them. I added coins to that, quarters and dimes. Nickels mostly. The largest denomination on the table was a ten, with most being singles. The money was Tessner's and the bank had raised more eyebrows than questions when he picked it up with Allie that morning for me. Three thousand dollars looked like three million. The camera zoomed for effect, then pulled out to show me looking at it.

The crowd grew interested.

"Hello," I said. "I'm Tony Flaner. I'll be your keynote for today's reveal. That's shop talk for me sayin' whodunnit."

"Whoop whoop!" whooped Standard. "The PI is in the house. Bring the noise!"

No one joined him bringing the noise, but I did appreciate it and he had a point. Talking to people after a meal is always difficult. People will listen while they digest, but they won't do much more. A little energy couldn't hurt. Comics feed off audience reaction.

"Let's get that energy up!" I cheered and saw—actually saw—every posture sag, every eye roll, every cliché organ contract at that hackneyed lead-in.

"Can I have a..." I began the call and response, but paused dramatically.

"Wait," I said, pretending to notice the table for the first time. "What's this? Money? Money at the Interfaith Congress of Holistic Enlightened People? This should be a place of enlightenment, not a den of thieves!" I was channeling Ted Neeley from *Jesus Christ Superstar* and actually sang the line 'den of thieves' without meaning to. It had its effect though. Confusion, anticipation, foreshadowing.

I moved behind the table and with one righteous upward swoop, flipped it into the air. Money sprung up kicked like autumn leaves, coins shot out like shrapnel and hit not a few people who were contract bound not to sue me for any injury or damages to property or person or persons in attendance or adjacent, from now to perpetuity, nor reveal the nature or existence of such injury or loss to any persons not similarly bound by written agreement heretofore or hereafter communicated. Gallagher, eat your heart out.

A couple people bolted out and snatched money from the floor as a graphic illustration of my point. Allie was quick to catch it on camera and shame them on the screen.

Waiters appeared and picked up silently and swiftly after they'd been shooed away.

"Shame!" I said. "Shame. This gathering was intended to bring out the best of people, to celebrate those who strive for the spiritual, the meaningful, and the good. What we got was a shit show of greed, lust, and lies. And murders. Multiple murders."

48

I HAD THEIR ATTENTION.

"I was originally hired," I began, "to save a poor old lady from the evil clutches of John Smith and the COTTEO cult. Cult here suggesting the evil sex-oriented suicidal con-game, organized religion and tabloid media often accurately make it out to be. COTTEO however, is not one of those. It is a cult along the lines of cult plus time equals new religion. As they stand now, I think they're the real deal, an organization set up along spiritual lines for the betterment of the whole species. The rest of you, well, yeah..."

I was pleased to see many offended faces. Although I risked a taco barrage, it did show that people were paying attention.

"Let those who were not here for the first day's scrum throw the first nacho," I said. Sylvia tossed a chip on stage. I smiled. "The proof is in the corn chip."

Across the room, I saw a waiter shake his head very disapprovingly. Calling for a food fight would not be appreciated.

"Ted Tessner, shroom grower and drug billionaire, arranged for a peace summit at his place after the first days' riot. Most of you didn't get to go, because reasons. But I got to go, for other reasons. There, two guns were shown, confiscated but later stolen. It's not important whose guns they were, only that some asshat thought it necessary to attend a dinner party at a private home with religious leaders packing heat. I think we can all agree that that was a dick move. What kind of a small-dicked wannabe murderer does that? But, like I said, we don't need to name names. It was Augustus Klept from The Brotherhood of Righteous Action."

"I've got a Second Amendment right—" he began.

"Augustus," I cut him off. "I'm only mentioning it here because both of your guns were later used to kill people. No big deal. Not like it makes you look irresponsible and stupid."

"I don't see—"

"Stay tuned and stop interrupting."

"Oh...okay." He glanced around sheepishly. The other men at his table looked pissed, but he felt the room's liberal eyes upon him.

"The first two killings, with one of Klept's guns, were John Smith and his manager Sangye on the second night of the conference, right before Smith was scheduled to give a keynote address. At first it looked like a murder-suicide but it was clear by looking at the clues, finally—Detective Johnson—that Sangye had been killed before Smith and that his murder was staged to look self-inflicted."

I wondered if the NDAs work against retaliatory police brutality and thought it might under the violence provisions.

"The questions a detective asks are classic and true. Who? How? Why? And why now? Motive, means, and opportunity."

"Who hired you?" the Reverend Barty-B shouting questions from the audience.

"A little ol' lady from Utah."

"Who really hired you?"

"A little ol' lady from Utah."

"Stop calling my mom old!" Hannah, drunk, calling from the back.

"Hush up," came Sylvia's response.

"You heard her, everyone. Hush."

I went on. "This case was an unusual one for me. The problem is usually figuring out who has a motive to kill, but this time, I had an embarrassment of motivated suspects."

I pointed out over the congregation accusingly, dramatically.

"It had to do with Netflix and the zeal of a true believer. The true believer was Sangye. By the way, I never learned if that was his first or last name—and before you tell me Sylvia, it's too late now for the story."

"First name," she said. "Bhujel was his surname."

"I stand corrected."

"No one called him that though. Carry on."

"Okay. I will."

"You never even knew the last name of one of the victims?" called out Detective Johnson. "What kind of detective are you?"

"An effective one." I dropped the mic for effect. The waiter gave me a wide-eyed head shake this time. Dropping thousand-dollar microphones was worse than a Mexican food fight.

I picked it up. "John Smith put together a twelve-part series for Netflix where he talks about religion and faith and spirituality. A very effective and moving series, I'm sure. It's scheduled for this fall. There was, however, a rumor of a thirteenth episode, wherein John Smith would expose religious frauds and fakes. Like me tonight, he'd name names and shame the shame-less. This was the net that zealous Sangye used to snag huge contributions for COTTEO."

"Blackmail?" said Ted, horrified. "Smith was a blackmailer?"

"No. Smith wasn't but I think he was onto Sangye's plan and tried to stop it."

"Seems like you have motive there for Sangye to kill Smith," said Kaisa.

"Yep, except it didn't happen that way. Sangye, the extortionist approached many of the organizations here in this room and made demands for substantial contributions to COTTEO for their new digs in Cottage Grove, just down I-5 from here."

"He never approached me," said The Messenger.

"I know," I said. "I know because I found on Sangye's phone this cryptic message."

Here Allie shone the screen capture of Sangye's phone from my phone, carefully cropped to keep the ick out of the background.

A :-) !
G :-)
B :-) !
Cm ?
P :-(
Cv :-(
H ?
T :-)

"Pretty cryptic, eh? We'll get back to it," I said. "Swimming in motives, knowing we had a blackmailer running around in a room of closeted skele-tons, along with a few flaming wildcards, I had a *why* and, with Sangye no doubt playing the keynote card, the *why now* as Smith was about to publicly make a speech. Sangye surely dropped hints that Smith would drop hints and maybe ruin entire churches in one night. I focused then on opportunity. Who could have killed Smith? We have a pretty good window of when the killings took place through phone call logs and witnesses. Let's go down the list."

I shuffled my papers, found the list, bookmarked it with a five-dollar bill.

"Hannah Rigsdale," I said, "that drunk woman in the back who hired me to save her mother from a benevolent man. She is unaccounted for." Shock from Sylvia. Horror from Josh. Drunk drooling from Hannah. "But she didn't have access to the guns the night they were stolen."

Relief on the aforementioned faces.

"But her new extramarital affair Nazi boyfriend, Augustus Klept, could have retrieved his guns and later given her one."

Gasps. Stares of hatred from the BRA table.

"The Messenger, leader of The Community, did not have access to the gun when it was stolen and he has an alibi for the time of the killing."

The Messenger nodded sagely, wisely, clean of sin and triumphant.

"He was chain-smoking in the stairwell when it happened," I added.

Shocked gasps and sputters from his table.

"Adam Tuku, lord of the orange-clad Homecoming Allegiance, did have access to the guns and was unaccounted for when Smith was killed. He also later appeared, dead, with one of the guns in an apparent suicide. That's what we call a prime suspect."

The few Homecoming members squirmed in their seats when I glared at them.

"Kaisa Woods of Green Tomorrow could have gotten to the guns that night. Right before the murders, she was seen in this very room talking on the phone. Possible suspect. But no proof, unlike Tuku and Klept's gun."

"I must object," said Kaisa.

"Being objectionable in this room isn't much of a stretch," I said.

She shut up.

"Donnopher, representing The Peoplists, have no clear alibi for the time of the killings, but couldn't have snatched the guns the night they were taken. They do however figure prominently because it was when Sangye was employed by them, The Peoplists, that he learned how to dig up nasty garbage on people to extort them to their own nefarious whims."

"You can't say that!" raged Donnopher.

"Actually, I can. You signed the NDA. I watched you.

They had. Trapped in their own trap.

"Besides, it's true," I added.

"That never matters," they said.

"That's also true."

Stopped by the NDA, they relaxed. "Carry on."

"Artstar, face of the Coven, and our Gothic kidnapper and sharer of psilocybin gummies, could have gotten to the guns and has no alibi for the killing time. Another prime suspect."

"Curses," she said.

"The Reverend Bartalemuw Benson of The Abundant Church of God is the only culprit I could scratch off the list early. He has verified alibis for both the time of the gun theft and the killings."

"God be praised," he said.

"At the time of the gun theft, he was propositioning a waiter for gay sex. At the time of the killings he was consummating that deal."

If you've ever seen a fish out of water, flopping on the dock, gasping for air, you know what Barty-B looked like just then.

"Ted Tessner has an alibi for the guns, hot tubbing, and for the time of the killing. So cross him off."

"I was a suspect?" he asked.

"You're on the list." I pointed to the list.

He squinted at the cryptic list trying to see himself.

"The last wildcard was a guy named Vance Derow, a recently pardoned marijuana grower who Ted Tessner helped put behind bars, though he himself was growing grass."

I don't know why Ted thought he'd be free of embarrassment that day. People never think it'll happen to him.

"Vance got his revenge in the newspaper—not by murdering party guests. Support print media."

"And fuck you very much Ted," said Vance from the corner. I'd not seen him come in, but I had invited him. Ted shrunk a bit. Allenby signaled a plainclothesman to watch him.

"Though I do think Mr. Derow shot Beatrice at Ted's ranch," I said.

Gasps.

"Who's Beatrice?" someone asked.

"A mother goat."

"Be nice."

"Really, a goat who'd just had a kid."

"Oh."

"She was shot with a gun. She survived, but some dick shot her."

Vance stared. "Proof?"

"None, thank you very much, just a wild inflammatory true accusation."

"I'll sue—"

"Eh eh eh…" I waved a copy of the NDA.

He sat down.

"So then another killing happened," I said. "Adam Tuku of Homecoming was found shot to death in his room. Suicide, so it appeared."

"It wasn't?" said Perry.

"It was, but I was building suspense."

"Oh. Sorry," he said.

"Clutched in his little murdering hand was not only the gun he'd stolen the night of the party, but also an old phone, just technological enough to trigger a detonator connected to a nerve gas bomb."

"Dammit, Flaner!" Allenby was on his feet.

"It's true, though. I know because I disarmed the faulty bomb right before it was going to go off. It was meant to go off during Barty-B's keynote, but misfired. So, no harm. No foul."

The Homecoming table stared up at me with blank expressions. They really didn't want to be here. Or anywhere. Every new day was a surprise for them.

"What this means is that Adam Tuku was a bat-shit murdering crazy fuck, but he couldn't have murdered Smith."

"How do you know that?" asked Kaisa.

Allie showed the next clip. It was the video of Kaisa talking on the phone and Tuku furtively moving past and into the kitchen.

"This is when Tuku plants the bomb. I think he left the fixings in the employee elevator and then came around this way to plant it. He have the time he did this because Rachael, beloved, murdered, innocent directing Rachael, was called to investigate a guest in the air conditioning space at that moment. Who does that leave?"

"Don't you dare pin this on us," said Artstar, behind dazzling eyes.

"Sangye approached you for extortion, right?" I asked her.

"I told you he did."

"And you didn't pay?"

"No. It couldn't be proved. Note the verb there, Mr. Flaner, 'proved.'"

"You didn't tell me what the secret was he was blackmailing you over, so let me guess."

She stared curses at me. My poison oak began to itch.

"Sacrifice. The Coven makes animal sacrifices," I said.

"Religious freedom," was her retort.

"But not if it were people you were killing. You said the greater the sacrifice the greater the power. What greater than a person, an innocent person. A person who is holy. Someone like John Smith."

"Lies!" she cried.

"Suppositions," I said. "I have no proof you killed Smith, because you didn't, nor that your Coven is moving toward human sacrifice, which you are. The proof I do have shows that you and your cohorts violently kidnapped and tried to murder this adorable little guy!"

Allie showed a picture of Jerry on the screen. The entire room went "Awwwww," as a group, and then started their own curses at Artstar.

"But me and my gang saved him," I said.

Cheers from the Green Tomorrow table.

"The Coven hadn't done anything yet and was too poor to even buy their own goat, so extortion there was a non-starter. The problem to me then became who being blackmailed would kill for the threat and who could have done it. Also, as Artstar pointed out, proof is a thing, and I really needed some. I don't always. But in this case, I found it."

Silence in the room.

"First let us look at the list again."

Up came the list again.

"The letters beginning each row, I reasoned, stood for the groups at ICOTEP. Sangye had to understand his own cryptic code, after all. Why make it too hard? Here we see the list with what I think are the various groups written out."

Allie flashed a new image up on the screen. It was the same list as before but with added names after each.

A :-) ! =ABUNDANT CHURCH OF GOD (ACOG)
G :-) =GREEN TOMORROW (GT)
B :-) ! =BROTHERHOOD OF RIGHTEOUS ACTION (BRA)
Cm ? =THE COMMUNITY
P :-(=THE PEOPLISTS (PEOPLE'S CHURCH OF HIGHER LEARNING
(PCOHL))
Cv :-(=THE COVEN
H ? =HOMECOMING
T :-) =TED TESSNER

"It's pretty clear now, isn't it?" I said.

I really didn't expect anyone to get it from that, but it was a good moment, a little egotistical perhaps to make myself look smart, but it was so obvious and awkward that I felt dumb even before the first person called 'the emperor ain't got no clothes.'

"Explain," said Allenby.

"Sorry, yeah, okay," I said. "I read it like this. A smiley face means that Sangye got something juicy on the cult and has been promised money. The frowny face means that he found something juicy, approached, but they weren't having any of it. The exclamation point means they paid."

"I didn't pay," said Artstar. "We have nothing to hide."

"Then have your picnics in the daytime," I said. "But yes, you'll observe the Coven has a frown face. Swing and a miss. The same is true of The Peoplists, who have more litigious firepower and experience than the Cook County prosecutor's office. Strike two."

"What's the question mark?" asked The Messenger, who'd spent the last fifteen minutes swearing up and down to his table that he's really given up tobacco now.

"It means Sangye couldn't find anything useful for extortion."

"Redeemed," he said too brightly.

"No, I think it means because the cult was too off-the-rails crazy to be blackmailed. An alien god named Oodrakakam from Mlilti 8 in the Ring Nebula-smelling woman you've shagged? Really? How do you shame a group like that? As for Homecoming, they're so apocalyptic and suicidal, a threat of destruction would mean nothing to them."

"I wasn't blackmailed," said Ted.

"No, but he'd put a pinch on you for another million and you agreed. It hasn't funded yet, unlike the money from Barty-B's ACOG and Klept's BRA, who each sent a million dollars into COTTEO coffers this week."

"What would we have to be extorted about?" demanded Klept.

"Did I forget? Sorry. You're a front for Russian propaganda and disinformation, tasked to create disrupting and polarizing opinions while preying on alienated people seeking purpose in a turbulent world, made more turbulent by dicks like you. BRA is a direct line from Moscow, who pays lavishly in oligarch money and imported vodka. Thus, Augustus Klept is, at least, an unregistered foreign agent. Some government agency should really look into that. Agent Allenby, take note."

"Note taken."

"That leaves Green Tomorrow," said Kaisa. "What about me?"

"You did it."

"I beg your pardon?"

"I shook my head. You could have been the real deal, but you're just another crook. Selfish, egotistical, and greedy. You agreed to pay Sangye, got yourself a smiley face, but you thought it cheaper and safer to just kill him, because your secret was a biggie. I don't know how long you planned it, but Klept's gun and the talk at that dinner table about the thirteenth episode offered you cover and a slew of other suspects when you realized you weren't the only one he'd pinched."

"Lies. What would he have to blackmail me over?"

"Green Tomorrow is an astroturfed environmental facade. You get your money from big business, the very people you say you're out to stop."

"We do not!"

"You do. You and your group swoop into environmental hot spots, make a lot of noise and then sadly lose in the end. Sometimes you lose spectacularly, and here's where another aspect of sleuthing comes in, that of temperament. Who'd be likely to kill someone? Who's got it in them? How about someone who's killed before?"

"Who's paying you to say this?"

"You lost two people in São Paulo this year. People who were hiding in a hotel room, but were somehow found by assassins. You knew where they were. You said yourself that you talked to them just before they were killed. And then there's the five missing in the Arctic last year, again people associated with you. Five disappear and then a Finnish petroleum company gets the rights to drill and just coincidentally buys five million dollars worth of Kaisa brand swamp-water money-laundering scheme. Being a church hides your finances, but not theirs."

"You have no proof for any of this," she said.

"Rachael," I said.

"What?"

"You killed Rachael because she had the proof, or would when she went through all the audio and video files to edit it for the conference app."

She stared.

I nodded to Allie.

Up came the film again with Tuku entering the ballroom. There was Kaisa sitting alone at a table talking on her phone. This time, however, we'd matched it up with the sound.

"*Sangye, we can talk about this,*" she said into the phone. "*It would be easier for me to give you twice that much but spread it over four payments. For tax reasons."*

You could hear an olive drop in the room. People glanced around, noting, maybe for the first time, that the room was filled with cameras and microphones.

"You only have rumors," she said. *"Okay. You win. Cheaper for me. I'll be right up with a check. Room 613? On my way."*

"You surprised Sangye," I said, "he didn't foresee violence from you. I think he figured out the astroturfing, but not the betrayals and murders. You wore a good mask. Smith and Rachael were killed from behind, by someone they trusted. And here on the screen and in our minds are your lies and the connection."

The color was gone from her face which was a trick with her tan skin and sharp features.

She found her pride at last, raised her sharp chin, held me with her dark piercing eyes. "I'm just doing what the white men do," she said, "only better than the white men do it."

"Yeah?" was my reply. "That and a bottle of Woods Water will get you dysentery."

49

"AND ON THAT hill we'll put the chapel. It's more than a gathering place but less than a church. We really don't have churches as such."

It was the next day and Sylvia was showing us around the grounds of the COTTEO center. Her kids had left, Josh shepherding Hannah back to Salt Lake and what I knew to be a broken marriage. "Apartments there, dormitories on either side," said Sylvia with excitement. "We expect to be able to house two hundred people, sixty couples, the rest in group living. It's an attack on homelessness. We'll have a fleet of cars they can use too."

"Segregated sleeping spaces?" asked Allie.

"That'll be an option, but not required."

Our flight home was in a couple of hours. We had time to kill, and I wanted to make sure Sylvia was doing alright.

Sylvia had a rental in Creswell on the other side of the freeway from Cottage Grove, where the land for the center had been procured. Cottage Grove is famous for having a covered train bridge. Wow. But also for being the place Buster Keaton totaled a locomotive on another bridge. The town itself actually very nice.

"We'll have work space and fast internet. Travel centers, call centers. Crisis hotlines. A place for single mothers. A place for single fathers. An orphanage."

"Are you going to spend any of the money Sangye brought in?"

"Klept said to keep BORA's contribution."

"It wasn't his money," said Allie.

"No. But he could have asked for it back."

"And the Reverend Benson?"

"No word yet. I'll call him in a week. See what he wants to do. We'll get our first phase up without any of that, provided we don't get cheated by builders. Cost-overruns are ridiculous out here."

"Do not do 'cost plus,'" I said.

"Oh, hell no."

The gang hung on as long as they could. The excitement after my talk was short-lived. Kaisa was arrested on the spot, Augustus Klept was questioned, took the fifth, presented a card with his lawyers' names on it, and was online screaming about oil import tariffs in Europe before the hour was up. Barty-B flew that day to a "hospital" in Florida to deal with stress-related stress. He canceled all appearances. Before he left, Barty-B said one thing to me; "The table prop was excellent," he'd said, "But you missed an opportunity for Judas and the bag of silver."

I knew what he meant.

Allie didn't.

"Judas didn't kill Jesus," I explained. "He took money to let the Romans at him. Kaisa did the same thing to the activists in Alaska and in Brazil. I missed an opportunity for the comparison."

"You can't think of everything."

"But I did," I said. "I just couldn't prove that she'd done that. I'm sure she did, but hadn't the proof then. I concentrated on the COTTEO killings instead."

Later that night, Detective Johnson and Allenby had met with me to go over the cases. Already they'd found a suspicious hammer in Kaisa's luggage. They assured me also that there'd be a chain of evidence linking Green Tomorrow to the Brazilian lumber company and the Finnish oil concern as well as a few other things. Already certain companies were distancing themselves and burning documents.

"It's embarrassing no one looked before," said Allenby.

I could almost feel sorry for him. He thought that the legal apparatus of first-world countries revolved around justice and not money. It was only because I'd publicly shamed Kaisa that someone actually looked at these killings.

Green Tomorrow was done. There was never much there, I found out. They had a big mailing list, but most of it, I was sure, were trolls and echo boxes in some basement. Staff was small and underpaid. Kaisa had a lot of assets, however, houses, yachts, secret holding companies, gold, bags of silver that would be uncovered and used poorly somehow. I was a little sad to see them fold, they looked good on paper, but it was a cancer, actively working against the cause it purported to champion. The worst kind of deceit. I wondered if Kaisa had started out a believer and then fell when the money was offered, or if it was a con from the beginning. I'd like to think it started well and did some good once, but I smelled deep rot and opportunism from the beginning and mourned the chance.

The gang. I was talking about the gang. We had beers and shots at the bar during the afternoon classes—most of which were canceled—and got pretty sloppy.

"How could you discount ACOG and BORA?" asked Perry. "They'd confessed to motive by paying the extortion."

We all took two shots. Whenever someone used an acronym, the rule was to take a shot.

"It's what Standard said," I explained. "When people put out good money, they expect to get their money's worth. They'd paid the ransom. If more came, then things might have gotten interesting, but they'd committed to this much and I didn't see the rush from them."

"There was no ASAP," said Critter, which was mean since he was immune to alcohol. We all took another shot.

"It was ASAP for Rachael, though," I said.

"Et tu, Tony?" Allie wasn't as used to tequila shots as the rest of us.

"She heard Rachael mention the recorded audio and even saw where she'd been sitting during her phone call when Rachael brought up the tape in the AV room."

I waited as the use of the acronym was identified.

"She and Klept planned the protest of his keynote for mutual publicity, but then she used it as cover for the killing. It was a perfect diversion for her newest murder and also as a way to make it look random, again mixing in more suspects. The missing iPad was at once a false lead suggesting theft as a motive, but also she wanted to get it to slow the app development."

Standard took a shot.

"App isn't an acronym, you dolt," slurred Dara.

"Maybe I was just thirsty?" he said and retched a little.

We staggered back to the banquet hall for a plated fish and asparagus meal and Ted Tessner's closing keynote speech. There weren't many conventioneers left. I'd pulled the curtain back and their Ozes would never be the same. The Coven felt they had nothing to be ashamed of so made a knot of wizards at one table in the front. Artstar smiled when she saw my bandages, a new twinkle in her dazzling eyes. I showed her a particularly big sore on my middle finger. The Green Tomorrow folks with free tickets had less regard for the value of their investment and had not bothered to come. COTTEO was there as before and they opened their spaces to the Homecoming people who looked lost and self-conscious in their orange jumpsuits, wishing perhaps they'd brought a change of clothes or a return ticket. The Messenger was shamed away. Barty-B too. Klept caught a private jet to destinations unknown. Donnopher had left without fanfare and taken their fair fans with them. As such, Ted's big talk was to a mostly empty room, though, as promised, the local news media was there.

He spoke of the trials of the weekend, the lessons he'd learned about the world needing leadership. Not sure where he got that, but I knew where he was trying to lead it. At the end, after dedicating his big announcement to his dead manager Rachael, Ted Tessner announced his senate campaign. Knowing the questions would all be about the murders, he left the stage after the announcement and was driven home in a new Rivian by Lewis before the dessert was served.

"I honestly don't know how long we'll be able to carry on without John," Sylvia said as we walked down the gravel road back to her little Honda to go to the airport. "He was..."

"The real deal," I said.

"You hardly knew him, but thanks for saying that."

There'd been one piece of the blackmail the chain of suspicion that I'd carefully left out. That was John Smith himself. The man was a magnet for confession. I'd seen it at the dinner table, I'd experienced it at his ad hoc lobby talk. You just wanted to shed your sins, get absolved and be better in his presence. He facilitated that. Sangye did not need to have the superpowers of the Peoplist's extortion machine to have gathered the information about the other cults. If he'd been in the room with John and one of the leaders, he'd have heard it, or enough of it to put it together. This was a hunch of course, but it made sense. Sangye had used his master's power to try to elevate their cause. Unlike the other greedy cultists I'd met, Sangye was working for good. Like Robin Hood, he was stealing from bad people to give to the good. Their scams could subsidize their truth and so there was a certain pragmatism to it. It was a good idea in its own way.

"Are you going to include psychedelics in your teachings?" I asked.

"There is pushback, but Tessner's was partially based on us using it in certain ways. John thought there was merit, so it'll happen in some way."

"Good."

She looked at me askance then, trying to read something on my face. I thought to tell her about my visions of her dead friend but held back. I didn't want to sound crazy.

"John Smith appeared to me in spiritual form and helped me diffuse the bomb," I said. Of course I did. "When I was tripping, John talked to me, led me, and urged me to find Taku's bomb and save countless lives at the last second."

"That's nice," she said.

"That's nice?" said Allie. "Tony is confessing to seeing a dead saint, and that's all you can say?"

"He was on drugs."

"So?"

"So, it's interesting but hardly proof of anything. It showed his inner processes not an otherworldly visitation."

I didn't argue. You're either on the bus or not. "Yeah, I guess he was on my mind," was all I said.

Waiting at the gate for our plane, Allie pressed me.

"He helped me out of the forest too," I said. "And maybe spoke to me a couple other times."

"Why then?"

"Because I was in real danger of dying to the freaks in black sheets," I said.

Artstar and the Coven denied such murderous intent, but they were madder than those fucking hornets I told you about.

"And he needed me to find the bomb."

I admit I myself wasn't sure about the experiences. Sylvia was right, it could have been my brain putting pieces together, it surely was in fact, but there were still odd details and urgencies that made my cynical soul take note. Allie of course liked to believe such things and took it in stride without half as much worry as it caused me.

"If it was him," I said. "Why didn't he help me solve the case sooner or save Rachael?"

"Who says he didn't?"

"Me. He didn't."

"Well"—and here Allie put her arm around me—"those are small things. Just one life here and life there. Death isn't the end. It's not to be feared. The nerve gas attack, however, that would have had graver consequences. A cultural shock that would have brought untold suffering for a lot of people for a long time."

I thought about that a minute.

"And," added Allie. "He knew you'd solve the case."

"How'd he know that?"

"How could he not?" she said. "You said you're working on it, and you're the real deal."

I looked into her brown eyes and lost myself. Within them, chestnut irises morphed into electric shroom flashbacks laden with feelings, memories, truths I'd seen and had to set aside but now came to be counted. I'm not sure if this trip had done anything for my calm, my inner peace, but it had, at least in one thing, led me to wisdom. I'd found the real deal.

"What's on your mind?" she said and slid her hand to my knee.

"Wanna get married?" I said.

"Sure."

Just like that.

A staticky voice announced boarding for our flight.

We stood up. We held hands. We went home.

IF YOU LIKE THIS, YOU MAY ALSO ENJOY: STOLEN LIVES

A NICK WOLF AND LOLA CALDWELL MYSTERY BY G. WAYNE TILMAN

A hard-hitting detective with a thirst for justice and a Highway Patrol trooper with an obsession for finding the truth team up to take on the case of a lifetime.

Detective Sergeant Nick Wolf is tasked with dissolving a human trafficking ring on one of America's most notorious routes between Tampa Bay and Orlando. When one final victim slips through his fingers, he is forced to pursue, and finds himself facing a dangerous standoff that ends with a career-ending injury.

Forced into early retirement, Wolf is unable to stay away from the action and starts his own private investigation firm, where he crosses paths with Florida Highway Patrol trooper, Lola Caldwell. Instantly drawn to her investigative prowess, bravery, and combat skills, Wolf recognizes her as the perfect partner.

Together, they tackle an array of compelling cases, showcasing their unparalleled expertise, and are led to their most challenging investigation yet—the kidnapping of a prominent judge's young granddaughter.

Will Nick succumb to the shadows of his past, or will he find the courage to let Lola in and find the missing girl before it's too late?

AVAILABLE NOW

ACKNOWLEDGMENTS

Mad appreciation to my readers who really came through this time, Craig Kingsman, Michelle Miller, Audrey Hammer, and Dorothy Diane. Thanks guys! You're the best.

Thanks always to my family, my friends, and the writers who make this journey joyful. Thanks to the light of inspiration, the darkness of contrast, and the greys of understanding. Thanks be to the places I must go—inspiration in every step.

Shout out to my new managing editor, Rachel Del Grosso for helping Tony settle into his new home at Rough Edges Press. Much gratitude.

Last, thank you Oregon for teaching me to appreciate the desert.

ACKNOWLEDGMENTS

ABOUT THE AUTHOR

Johnny Worthen is an award-winning and best-selling author of books and stories. Trained in stand-up comedy, modern literary criticism and cultural studies, he writes upmarket multi-genre fiction, symbolized by his love of tie-dye and good words.

"I wear tie-dye for my friends, but I write what I like to read," he says. "This guarantees me at least one fan and easy dressing in the morning."

Johnny teaches writing at the University of Utah and lives in a house with his wife, sons and assorted cats. There's also a lawn.

www.ingramcontent.com/pod-product-compliance
Lightning Source LLC
Chambersburg PA
CBHW010815250626
47156CB00011B/3086